CLAN NOVEL

BRUJAH

BY MYRANDA KALIS

WHITE WOLF

Myranda Kalis

Dark ages
BRUJAH

AD 1223
Eighth of the Dark Ages Clan Novels

A bsolute darkness descended at once, nearly thick enough to touch. Veronique let out a ragged sigh, closed her eyes, and concentrated on strengthening her other senses. Above her, she could hear Guillaume descending, and so she continued her own climb, listening tensely, feeling her way along completely blind. The sound of rippling water grew gradually louder; her sense of touch told her it was growing considerably damper. As promised, fifteen rungs down, she found the water, sloshing over the top of her boots and coming to midthigh before her foot came to rest on the next rung. She fought down the instinctive, reflexive desire to hold her breath, a tendency she had never managed to shed, and forced herself to release any air she might be holding in her lungs. And then she continued to climb down, the icy water inching its way up her body and finally coming over her head, rushing in to fill her highly sensitized ears with its strange sound-but-no-sound, pouring up her nose and trying to force its way past her clenched teeth. Within her, the Beast stirred slightly in response to her discomfort; she had never learned to swim, never liked being submerged in water over her head, even decades after the fear of drowning had ceased to be a practical concern. She paused for a moment, clinging to the rungs and pressed close against the wall, to discipline herself, and reluctantly, the temperamental little monster subsided. Her joints and muscles complained, for the water was bitterly cold and stiffened her. She did her best to ignore it.

What Has Come Before

It is the year 1223 and France is at war, among the living and the dead. The Fourth Crusade has given way to the Crusade against the Albigensians, pitting French and Toulousain knights and soldiers against one another. Religious ferment and political ambition go hand-in-hand, with each side calling the other heretic and unfaithful.

Among the undead of Paris, the blood runs hot. Only recently, a red-hued comet streaked the sky and caused many to predict the End of Days. Religious battles ensued and vampires said they had seen Caine, first murderer and legendary father of all the undead, on the streets of the Latin Quarter. The prince's main advisor, the Countess Saviarre, was weakened by the mad nights of the comet, and many factions now swarm through the halls of power.

The Queens of Love, the vampiric monarchs who rule much of the French night beyond Paris, have a long-standing grudge against the city's Prince Alexander. Many refugees from the sack of Constantinople twenty years ago have also ended up in Paris, remembering the leadership given to them by the slain Hugh de Clairvaux, the chivalrous grand-childe of Prince Alexander himself.

The diplomat Veronique d'Orleans has done all in her power to ride the wave of chaos gripping the city, interceding on behalf of the Malkavian preacher Anatole and his ward Zoë, and keeping the madness of Caine sightings from spreading. But her efforts may have been for naught. Something is about to give...

Prologue: Chartres, 1213

In the hall below, four thrones sat on a raised dais, and four unbreathing monarchs sat upon them, hearing the case being laid before their august judgment. These three women and one man were among the most powerful Cainites in the whole of France, the Queens of the Courts of Love: Isouda de Blaise, Queen of Blois, elegant in manner and wise in the ways of the Cainite heart and mind; Helene la Juste, Queen of Champagne, afire with passion that often outstripped her wisdom; Etienne de Poitiers, King of Poitou, witty, charming, conniving; and Queen Salianna, the Matriarch of the Courts of Love and the architect of the alliance between the powerful Toreador of France and the Ventrue-ruled Grand Court of Paris. On this night they sat hearing an extraordinary case, a complaint lodged against a fellow monarch.

The galleries above the floor were devoid of their normal contingent of witnesses, heralds and spectators. This was judgment in camera, the queens gathered alone with the advocates. Tonight, the Court of Love tried Prince Alexander of Paris in absentia and in secrecy. The queens and their chamberlains agreed: Ancient though he might be, he deserved no better.

Indeed, the prince now ruled his Grand Court in defiance of the Queens of Love, not in alliance with them as had been the intention. Salianna had sent her own childe, the beautiful Lorraine, to act as his consort. His insistence that she love him, and his foul murder of her and her lover Tristan a century and a half ago, had driven a wedge between the Grand Court and the Courts of Love that no diplomacy, no matter how skillful, had managed to remove, and permanently damaged an alliance that had shown every sign of enduring for ages to come. There was considerable bitterness on all sides of the equation.

On the floor, the advocate assigned to present the case of Prince Alexander of Paris gave his passionate closing oration. He had no chance of winning the night, of course—the entire purpose of this exercise was to find Prince Alexander unequivocally guilty of crimes against Love, crimes in breach of his treaty obligations to the Courts of Love, crimes that would justify his removal from the throne of Paris. But there were forms to maintain, a delicate dance of politics to stage, and the advocate performed that show expertly.

The advocate assigned to speak on behalf of the deceased—the foully murdered lovers, Lorraine and Tristan—took the floor next and presented his own final summation of the case. When he was finished, there was hardly a dry eye to be seen, or else the artistically affected appearance of deep emotion was flawless. Even Queen Isouda managed to look pale and strained on behalf of Lorraine, the childe of her rival, Queen Salianna, lost so many years ago to the deceit and violence of the man granted her hand.

When the advocate was finished, the Court of Love adjourned to consider the arguments thus presented. It was not a long debate: Alexander was guilty of the crimes of which he had been accused. Then there was only the matter of how to bring that judgment to bear. The Queens of Love were not willing to raise arms against Prince Alexander, at least not yet.

No, the Courts of Love decided, the matter must be handled with diplomacy.

Chapter One

Veronique d'Orleans woke quickly, as was her wont, sat up in her narrow cupboard bed, and listened for a moment to the sounds of the world beyond the locked door of her daytime sanctuary in Paris's Latin Quarter. Music filtered down through the floorboards, a rousing Provencal tune that made Veronique's toes itch to touch the floor, partially disguised by a rhythmic thumping that suggested few of the house's patrons were denying the music's call. Laughter—Yvonnet's trilling, distinctive laugh, the answering chuckle of whatever customer she was attending—and their voices, too muffled for Veronique to make out specific words through all the layers of wood and stone and plaster. Water splashing, quite nearby, and two female voices, engaged in a low-voiced but fierce disagreement. Alainne and Girauda.

She reached up and undid the interior locks of the solidly lightproof cabinet door. Someone had come in while she slept to place a fat tallow candle in the sconce and light a brazier in the farthest corner of the chamber from her bed, but the floor was still unpleasantly cold underfoot. It was the middle of January, and so far the winter of 1223 was proving itself especially harsh. A stack of freshly arrived correspondence sat on her writing desk, seals intact; she stood on the very tips of her toes to examine it, her feet refusing to spend more time on the icy stone than they absolutely had to. Several brief notes from her various agents and spies, a handful of invitations to this or that midwinter fete, and a slightly thicker package wrapped in oilskin and tied in ribbons, sealed in black wax and stamped with arms she hadn't seen in more than a decade. She couldn't tell whether

her hands were trembling in excitement or because her blood was about to freeze in her veins. Someone had also moved her shoes and taken away her chemise, and she could just imagine who that was. With an irritated growl, she flung open the door separating the two chambers of her suite and snapped, "Bring them here right now."

The low-voiced argument taking place in the next room abruptly ceased. Then, "Your bath is ready, Vero." Veronique closed her eyes in despair. "Girauda, I'm freezing. At least give me the chemise until I'm finished reading my letters."

"Bath. Then letters. The water won't stay warm forever, you know."

Veronique was forced to concede the logic. She laid the oil-skin package back down with a sigh, squared her shoulders, and went forth to do battle with Girauda and Alainne, both of whom were prepared for her. The wooden bathing trough was steaming gently, lined with towels and scented with herbs—Veronique caught a hint of rose and lavender—and Girauda was standing next to it, a scrub brush and cake of soap in hand. Girauda, her dark hair threaded with iron gray and pulled back in a tight bun, her dark Occitan gaze completely devoid of nonsense, smiled at her as Veronique came into the room on tiptoes. A low fire was burning in the grate and candles cast a golden circle of light around the chair that Alainne had set up, likewise draped in towels, next to a low table containing a vast assortment of vials and bottles, pots and crocks, and more varieties of tiny scissors than Veronique even knew existed. Alainne was fussily adjusting the angle of the mirror she had brought downstairs for the evening's entertainment. Alainne, sunnily fair everywhere that Girauda was dark, youthful and slender as an aspen tree where Girauda was fully rounded and matronly, also turned to smile at her, clearly anticipating the use of a canvas she was rarely permitted to embellish. A fresh, snowy white chemise, discreetly embroidered with fine needlework at neck and hem, her long-sleeved kirtle, and a blue brocade surcoat that she had never seen before hung next to the fire, warming.

"I see you planned this in advance," Veronique muttered and allowed herself to be guided into the bath, which was, she had to admit, quite a bit warmer than the floor. "I'm not attending court, you realize—"

"Of course we realize." Girauda dipped the brush in the bath, soaped it, and applied it vigorously to Veronique's milk-white shoulders, releasing the scent of even more herbs. "Red is for court. Blue is for business meetings."

"Oh, for heaven's sake." She couldn't help but laugh, and lean back into Girauda's scrubbing. "There... right there... ah, good. What's passed today?"

"It's bitter outside," Alainne chose that moment to chime in, coming over to join them and set to work with soft cloths on Veronique's face and limbs.

"No snow, I hope?"

"Oh, no, none. But the wind's keen and they're saying that the river might freeze through if it keeps this cold much longer." Alainne cheerfully dumped a dipper of warm water over Veronique's irregularly cropped hair, then another. "The roads are still clear at any rate, if a little icy."

"Thierry—"

"Thierry is upstairs seeing to the carriage." Girauda passed Alainne the soap and it promptly found its way into Veronique's hair. "We packed your traveling case earlier."

"I'm only going to be gone a night or three. Four, at most." Further commentary was briefly prevented by several dippers of water rinsing her hair.

"And on each of those nights you shall be attired as befits a woman of your quality," Girauda replied, sternly. "We also packed your traveling desk, and anything you might need to correspond. You have but one thing left to do."

"Besides submit to your tender ministrations?" Veronique asked wryly, lifting her dripping bangs out of her eyes.

"Yes. Thierry and Sandrin will accompany you for safety's sake, of course, but you will likely need a lady's maid, as well...."

"Girauda should stay here to oversee the house," Alainne opined, earning herself a glare. "I can more easily accompany you the short distance you travel this time and—"

"Alainne, if I have said it once I have said it a dozen times, you are more needed here. The younger girls require your assistance more often than mine—"

"I am going to be gone four nights at most." Veronique's voice cut across the incipient argument. "And I am more than capable of dressing myself and even applying paint and scent if I have to. You are both staying here." Silence fell as she rose dripping from the bath, stepped out onto the towels set on the floor for her, and allowed Girauda and Alainne to pat her dry. Alainne guided her to the chair, somewhat sullenly, and sat her down. Veronique submitted to a manicure and a hair trim, lavender-scented oil massaged into her shoulders and breasts, and a bit of tasteful embellishment of her natural charms with the paints Alainne was so expert in applying. Even Veronique, who had witnessed the art she was capable of performing on the faces of even the plainest girls, was impressed with the overall effect.

While they were engaged in lacing up her kirtle, she said quietly, "I'm not angry with you for wanting to go. I'm sure it seems better than staying here, some greater adventure, but this is where I need you both to be. You're my eyes and my ears in this place, and my hands." She caught their eyes as they looked up at her. "If I didn't trust you, I wouldn't rely on you, even if I don't take you with me everywhere I go. Do you understand?"

Girauda's expression softened perceptibly. "Ah, Vero. I understand. Forgive an old and stubborn woman her vanity. I wanted to take the measure of this woman you're to meet and work with."

Alainne glanced away, and then back. "I... You know me too well. I wanted the adventure of going on this journey with you... I should have thought."

"Believe me," Veronique replied, as the surcoat went over her head, "when I say that I think you'll both have your wishes before all is said and done. Now, bring me my letters."

The reports were all written in Thierry's careful, Cathedral-school-trained hand, and encompassed a variety of topics, none of which were of any immediate import. Or, rather, none of which were important enough to cause a rearrangement of her plans for the next few nights. The invitations all pertained, as she had expected, to various social gatherings intended to take the edge off the midwinter doldrums. After the excitement of the comet, which had hung ominously over the Parisian sky, sparking the debates between Anatole and St. Lys, and then outright civil unrest, the winter had settled in hard and fierce, with heavy snow and bone-gnawing cold. Voluntarily or otherwise, most of the Cainites in Paris and its outlying regions had found themselves haven-bound since shortly before Christ-Mass; only now were the roads beginning to clear enough to allow for even short-distance travel. Lord Navarre was planning a winter garden party, and Veronique could feel her blood icing over at the mere thought, not only from the concept but the myriad unpleasant possibilities when it came to execution. Navarre was many things, but exceptionally humane was not one of them.

Veronique broke the seals on the oilskin package. Within were three letters, two thick, one thin, each with its own wax and ribbon seal intact. The first was sealed with the arms of Queen Esclarmonde the Black, her sire's longtime friend and confidante, who had, in Veronique's youth, given them both a home in her court at Carcassonne. Veronique was slightly surprised that a response to her own letter had come so quickly from Esclarmonde's court, relocated to mountainous Foix in the wake of the crusade against it, but at least the surprise was a pleasant one. She broke the seal and quickly scanned the first of the four pages, pale eyes tracking across the close-written lines, searching for the pattern of the cipher she had been taught all those years ago. She found it, and smiled as she picked out the first line of Esclarmonde's true message, hidden amidst a sea of courtly pleasantries: Vero, you take a great risk writing to us this way, but I am grateful to hear from you, nonetheless. Then she refolded the heavy parchment and set it aside for greater consideration when she returned, retying the ribbon around it.

The second thick letter was from Aimeric de Cabaret, Esclarmonde's grandchilde, and it took Veronique a moment to discipline herself enough to read his message calmly. She had learned, the summer before, that he had failed to return from a diplomatic mission to Montpellier. Hot on the heels of that, the word had come that he'd been captured by the Prince of Béziers, a northerner installed after the slaughter of the Albigensian Crusade. It had been a subject of considerable gloating and obnoxious satisfaction among no small number of his Parisian clanmates; it had tested all the self-control Veronique possessed not to kill someone and arrange for his ashes never to be found. She had been closest to Aimeric of all of Esclarmonde's kin, childer and grandchilder, during her time in the Languedoc; they were of an age and closer in temperament than most, and she had missed him fiercely when she and Portia finally moved north to the court of Julia Antasia. The slurs slung at him had been difficult to listen to with even feigned indifference, for she knew the man, and considered him more than the equal of any of his northern brethren. A part of her had mourned him as already dead, and refused to nourish false hope that he might survive the fate that had befallen him; Béziers's prince was not noted for his mercy or his tolerance, and if an example of the follies of continued resistance was to be made, Aimeric was a perfect prize in that regard. It had shocked Paris for weeks afterwards when no example was made and, in fact, diplomatic ties were opened between the courts of Foix and Béziers. It drove Saviarre to a public, frothing display of outrage to learn that Eon de l'Etoile, the northern Prince of Béziers, theoretically a vassal directly beholden to Alexander of Paris himself, had concluded a separate peace with Queen Esclarmonde the Black, in blunt defiance of his liege lord's intent that she be dragged from Foix in chains and likely marched through the streets of Paris in disgrace. It drove half the Toreador in Paris insane with rage, when copies of the peace treaty had arrived for the delectation of the Grand Court, that Aimeric de Cabaret had been intimately involved in the negotiation of that treaty. A chill had definitely settled into the air between Paris and Béziers, though no official sanction had yet been levied against its prince, and most believed that sanction was only waiting for the spring to come.

Aimeric's letter was actually somewhat thicker than Esclarmonde's, and likewise encrypted. This one, Veronique sat to read all the way through. Aimeric never could resist the temptation to tell a story, particularly not a story in which he was personally involved, but she supposed she could forgive him that, especially since his version of events was actually entertaining rather than suffused with righteous outrage. And his opinions concerning the character of Eon de l'Étoile were, she suspected, a trifle more accurate than those of anyone currently dwelling in Paris. It helped somewhat that the first line of his coded message was, Don't you wish you were here now?

Oh, my friend. I do wish. Perhaps, when this is all over, we will meet again. She refolded the letter, resisted the urge to slide it into the traveling bag sitting strapped shut at her feet, and opened the third, sealed with unfamiliar arms. And discovered that Aimeric had, even in absentia, served her far better than she knew and probably better than she deserved. The letter was from Eon de l'Étoile, and it was a brief, diplomatically pithy request for her assistance. Apparently it wasn't only the opinion of Paris's Cainites that swift and unpleasant retribution was in the offing for Eon once the spring thaws came. She retied that message, as well, and added it to her mental list of options to consider and review, then locked all three letters in her desk.

Girauda fetched a freshly warmed cloak, and then Veronique hefted her bag to her shoulder in an unladylike display that brought a scowl to her maid's face. Veronique couldn't help smiling at it. "I shall return. If Jean-Battiste turns up sniffing after me, tell him you don't know where I've gone, but that I'll be back shortly. And don't let the little viper in the house if you don't have to."

"Of course not, he stole two girls the last time he was here…."

The cold outside of Veronique's lower-story haven was, as Alainne had warned her, bitter; the wind cut through her clothing and stole any remaining residual warmth before she'd gone two steps. Fortunately, she didn't have far to go. Thierry stood at the end of the alley, lamp in hand, breath escaping him in explosive puffs of frost, huddled inside a hand-me-down wrapping that made him look even smaller than he actually was. Behind him, Sandrin and the driver were making certain that all was in readiness to depart with her cart.

"Thierry, why in the name of God are you standing outside?"

Veronique demanded, shooing him in the direction of the cart's open entrance flap, tied back to allow their entry. "Get in before you catch your death."

Thierry's rapidly chattering teeth nearly amputated the tip of his tongue as he replied, "I didn't want you to fall in a snowdrift and be lost until spring."

"Thank you for the concern," she replied, wryly, "but I'm afraid that, if your fingers freeze off, you're of no further use to me, and I'll have to replace you with someone even younger. Get in. And take this." She exchanged her bag for his shaded lamp, and crossed around to the front of the cart, where the driver and her bodyguard were conversing. The driver was muffled to the eyes in layers of thick wool, clearly none too pleased to be taking to the road on such a raw night, but accustomed to his employer's unpredictable travel needs. Sandrin chimed gently as he moved, indicating that he was hiding a layer of chain underneath his heavy winter clothing. "I trust that everything is in order for our departure?"

"Yes, lady." Sandrin was, unlike most of Veronique's other companions, unfailingly polite. His mother had beaten such good manners into him that not even a decade making his fortune in the mercenary trade could completely break him of them. "I took the liberty of riding out ahead to scout the way earlier. The road is clear."

"Good. Have a care, Sandrin—if it gets too cold to ride, tether your horse and come on the cart." The lamp went to the driver's hands, to be clamped to the front of the cart to illuminate their way, and Sandrin helped her up the steps and inside, lacing the door flap closed behind her.

Thierry had stowed her bag in the long, light-proofed box she used for safe, if not particularly comfortable, daylight travel, and had retreated beneath a pile of lap rugs and embroidered cushions to conserve heat. Veronique smiled down at the top of his head, the only visible part of his body, and squirreled beneath the blankets with him. "Well, Thierry, if you ever wanted the chance to complain about my cold feet, now would be the ideal time...."

Chapter Two

Rosamund d'Islington sat at her desk in the embassy's sole oriel room, her *vade mecum* open before her, a candle burning at the corner behind a shade of painted parchment, ink and pens at the ready. Behind her, a fire burned cheerily and, next to it, her maids Margery and Blanche sat gossiping quietly as they worked together at a bit of sewing. The oriel's unglazed window, situated to the right of her desk, was shuttered firmly and curtained with a thick wool hanging; even so, an occasional breath of stinging cold made it through to stir the relatively warm air in the chamber with a hint of the winter outside. She needed no gifts of the blood to hear the wind whistling shrilly through the house's eaves and roaring through the forest like a bloodthirsty beast on the prowl, thick though the stone walls were. A little shiver, having nothing to do with any response to the cold, traveled through her at the images that her active imagination painted with that thought. Silently, Margery brought a warmed lap robe to lay across her legs. Rosamund smiled her thanks at her maidservant.

She knew that she should be thinking of other things, doing other things, rather than staring blankly at a piece of parchment and indulging in the idle fancies of a dark winter night. She had letters to write: to her sire, Isouda; to Isouda's liege, Queen Salianna, by whose graciousness she was presently housed and employed; to Alexander, Prince of Paris, on whose pleasure and sufferance she was currently obliged to wait. Rosamund picked up her pen, inked it, held it poised to write, and put it back down again. What she really wanted to be doing was pacing from one end of the great hall to the other in an effort to release all the nervous tension that had been accumulating in her for the better part of the last fortnight. That, and chewing her brother Josselin's ear about the Brujah emissary due to visit them sometime in the next night or so.

A fortnight ago, Rosamund had arrived in the near vicinity of Paris with her retinue, armed with letters of introduction, two banners (one bearing the arms of her sire, the Queen of Blois, Isouda de Blaise, the other the traditional Toreador ambassadorial arms to which she was personally entitled), and instructions on whom she was to contact first and how she was to go about it. Before she had departed Chartres, she had received extremely explicit instructions from both her sire and Queen Salianna regarding the customs that prevailed in formal diplomatic relations between the Grand Court of Paris and the Courts of Love. It was, in the currently cool but nominally friendly climate, customary for a Toreador diplomat arriving from the Courts of Love to refrain from entering Paris without explicit permission from Prince Alexander. As a result, several secondary "embassies" had been obtained for the use of the Courts of Love. It was to one of those embassies, a fortified manor house lying just off the road connecting Paris and Chartres, that Rosamund had come.

One of her letters of introduction had gone to the lord and lady of the manor, securing their cooperation and assistance for the duration of her stay. The lord and lady were Queen Salianna's ghouls and had been for nearly as long as Rosamund had been undead; they were unshakably loyal and accustomed to answering nearly every demand made on their resources and abilities with grace and efficiency. They made Rosamund and her sole Cainite companion, her brother-in-blood Sir Josselin, as comfortable as it was possible to be, far from home and in a potentially dangerous position.

The second of her letters of introduction went to the Grand Court itself, to be laid only in the hands of Prince Alexander himself, and the third to another resident of Paris, one Veronique d'Orleans, a Brujah described to Rosamund as another diplomat. Rosamund chose to overlook the contradiction in terms that came of using the words "Brujah" and "diplomat" in the same sentence and took that at face value. Her letter of introduction to Prince Alexander formally requested his permission to enter Paris and take up the currently vacant position of ambassador to the Grand Court. It was signed and sealed by both her sire and Queen Salianna, who provided their personal assurances of her status as both a diplomat and a courier. The letter to the Brujah, Veronique, had been written by Queen Salianna and sealed by her alone; Rosamund had no idea precisely what it contained.

With all three letters sent, Rosamund had settled in to wait for the responses that she knew must come, and to her not inconsiderable surprise, Veronique d'Orleans had replied first. The Brujah's letter had been brief and to the point, acknowledging the receipt of Rosamund's letter of introduction and informing her that they would communicate again soon. And, then, Rosamund had waited. She had waited anxiously for more than a week, expecting Alexander's letter of acceptance of her request to arrive any night. A second letter from Veronique had arrived instead. There was, apparently, some sort of difficulty with regard to Rosamund's entrance into Parisian society; Veronique had not gone into specifics as to what that problem might be, but had expressed her intention to visit Rosamund's temporary embassy to discuss the issue privately. A second, shorter missive had arrived from Veronique a week later, stipulating her intended date of arrival, along with a possible need for accommodations for at least three: herself and two retainers. Rosamund had made the necessary arrangements with her host, and now she waited on tenterhooks for the Brujah to arrive.

With a sudden burst of nervous energy that surprised both her maids, Rosamund came to her feet, draped the lap robe over the back of her chair, and stalked out of the oriel room into the main hall. The hall itself was mostly abandoned save for those few members of her own staff on duty that night, the rest of the household having retired some hours before in order to avoid intruding on their illustrious guest's business. The fire in the main hearth was tamped down and the trestle tables all cleared away, leaving a pleasantly wide and open rush-strewn space in which she could express her frustration and excess energy without stubbing her toes against a wall every four strides. She paused on the dais before the fireplace, took a deep, unnecessary breath and expelled it, trying to force serenity on herself. Raising her hands, she clapped out a rhythm and stepped down into the rushes, executing with flawless grace and inimitable style the opening steps of a dance currently popular in Blois. With something to concentrate on besides the seething frustration clawing away at her breast, she attained a bit of calm, until her servants came out to make the last of the preparations for the ambassador's arrival. Their presence obliged her to stop being silly. She stood to one side as they placed fresh tallow candles in several of the sconces and set up one of the smaller trestle tables, spreading it with fresh linen and setting a fat beeswax candle in a pewter holder in the very center. Rosamund watched these preparations in silence and nodded her approval; as soon as her servants cleared the room, she exploded. "Where the devil is she, it's nearly dawn!"

"The road from Paris is almost as bad as the road from Chartres, ma petite fleur." Rosamund jumped slightly, realizing that she wasn't as alone as she'd thought. Josselin had crept in while her back was turned, and now sat on the small dais before the fireplace, his back to the flaring embers. "And it is still more than a few hours before dawn, in any case. Be patient. I'm sure she's on the way."

Rosamund huffed out the breath she'd taken in an irritated little sigh, and came to join him on the dais. He'd brought an embroidered pillow for her, so she made use of it, tucking her feet underneath her to restrain any further outbursts of motion. She knew they looked a pair, seated together that way, he with his fine blonde hair and laughing blue eyes, dressed in the best of the clothing he'd brought with him to greet the mysterious woman Queen Salianna had placed such trust in, she with hair the color of a new copper obol confined by a fillet and a new cotte of forest green that drew out the color in her own eyes. "I just wish we knew more about her, Josselin. This whole situation is just so... so..."

"Political?" he asked wryly.

"Irregular, is the word I was considering," Rosamund

replied tartly, and rewarded his wit with a poke in the ribs. "Political, I have seen before. Political, I can navigate my way through without the help of some... some..."

"Now, petite, give the lady a chance," Josselin chided her gently. "We know nothing about her, except the fact that Queen Salianna places some faith in her, which, in itself, says much. The queen trusts you in such a way, as well. Pass no judgments until you meet her."

"I'm trying not to." Rosamund realized she was chewing her lower lip, a habit her sire had always deplored, and stopped. "It's... It's silly, I know, but..."

"But?"

"I keep having these horrible visions." Rosamund's voice dropped to the barest whisper. "I keep seeing her walking through that door, dressed as a man, covered in mud and dust to midthigh, with a face like... like... I lack the words to describe it...."

"Petite," Josselin drawled easily, "I think you've been reading too many lais in which the she finds out her he is more than he seems, and vice versa."

"You aren't helping, you know."

"I do my best, petite."

The road to the Toreador ambassador's residence was, in the loosest technical definition of the term, clear. It hadn't snowed in any significant amount in more than a week and, while it was windy, the snow itself was covered in a thick rime of ice, preventing the formation of road-blocking drifts. The road itself was a mess of deep ruts and gullies, but at least it was frozen solid and not a soupy quagmire. They made, in Veronique's opinion, decent enough time until they reached the winding side lane that led to the temporary embassy. There things became slightly more difficult: Progress was hampered by numerous obstacles, not the least of which were frost-covered tree limbs cracking in the high wind and falling across their path, or else discharging their catapult-weighted coverings of ice on the cart's canvas roof, the backs of the horses, and the driver. Sandrin spent much of his time keeping warm by clearing debris from their path. Thierry spent much of that same time making dire predictions concerning their high likelihood of being devoured by wolves, or telling dark stories from his grandmother's day about why one should never set foot outside the city limits in the dead of winter. Veronique, for her part, patiently refrained from reminding her excitable clerk that she was at least as old as his grandmother and knew all those stories as well, but instead suggested that, if they were attacked by wolves, he'd survive, being too skinny to make much of a meal. Strangely enough, that seemed to calm him a bit, and he spent the rest of the trip confining his commentary to complaints about the drafty roof and the jouncing of the cart as it wallowed down the road. Veronique could only agree and hold on.

After a particularly bone-rattling interval of supreme discomfort, Sandrin's somewhat muffled voice sounded, just outside the entrance flap. "I believe we've arrived, milady."

Veronique extracted herself from the mass of coverlets in which she and Thierry were entangled and, miraculously, managed to slide across to the door flap without losing her veil or tearing the hem out of her new surcoat. The lacing was a bit difficult to undo with her cold-stiffened and gloved fingers, but eventually she managed to open enough of a gap that she could peer out at their destination. The temporary embassy had been described to her as a "hunting lodge," a designation that she rather doubted. She lacked the imagination necessary to envision the new Toreador ambassador to the Grand Court voluntarily spending a delay of unknown duration in a glorified wattle-and-daub shack, stinking of smoke and blood and surrounded by skinning yards and trappers' tents. Her first impulse, as it turned out, was correct. The "hunting lodge" loomed out of the gloom, lit by a pair of lamps bracketed next to the main doors and the light of the gibbous moon overhead. The precise dimensions of the "lodge" were difficult to discern, hut to Veronique's eye it was more a fortified manor than anything else, with walls of stone and a shingled roof. Irregular shadows hinted at the presence of outbuildings, and possibly a squat tower as well.

Veronique nodded to Sandrin. "Tell the driver to pull us in.

Then go to the door and knock—there should be someone on duty there—and ask that our presence be announced."

Sandrin's hood nodded, and Veronique pulled her head back through the door flap, tucking the sides together but leaving them otherwise unlaced. Behind her, Thierry put the inside of the cart back in order, roughly folding the lap blankets and stowing them in Veronique's daylight box, then retrieving her courier's case from among the rest of the baggage. The last stretch of the driveway was considerably smoother than the first, and Veronique took the opportunity to pull herself upright, brush out her heavy, ankle-length skirts and straighten her veil, bracing herself on leather straps provided for that purpose. The cart came to a shuddering stop, and over the sound of the horses stomping and blowing and their harness jingling, Veronique heard a door opening and low-voiced conversation. She refrained from doing anything that might damage her reception and waited for Sandrin to come open the door flap and help her down. Thierry scrambled down behind her, carrying the courier's pouch over one shoulder and his mistress's traveling bag in the other.

A sleepy-looking page took the driver and the cart in hand. A young man, possibly a knight in service to Lady Rosamund, was standing close by the door, clearly awaiting her attention. She approached him, and gave him a courtesy. "I am Veronique d'Orleans, Ambassador to the Grand Court of Paris, and I have come to speak to your mistress, whose name is given me as Lady Rosamund d'Islington."

The servant bowed low, and rose to hold the door.

"Lady Rosamund!" Peter came into the great hall at a trot, and barely managed to stop on the fresh rushes. "Lady Rosamund, Raoul commands me to tell you that the ambassador's cart approaches."

Rosamund's heart gave a little lurch and cartwheel of cheer, and Josselin chuckled in her ear. With all the dignity she could muster, Rosamund rose and smoothed her heavy skirts in a single, practiced motion. "Peter, inform Raoul that the ambassador is to be admitted with all haste. Rouse a page and ask him to guide her driver and team to the barns."

Peter bobbed his head in response to these commands, and scurried off to see that they were carried out. Rosamund stood, inhaling calm and serenity and exhaling the desire to rush outside and greet the ambassador—the first official notice she had received from anyone with standing in Paris—on the doorstep. She looked up at the two banners hanging above the table where they would shortly be sitting and tried to extract more confidence than she really felt from them. Her sire's arms and her own, a simple dark green length of silk marked with a single white rose, the traditional symbol borne by all Toreador diplomats.

The sound of the great hall door opening echoed to her ears, and she released the last of her tension with a quiet sigh, letting her hands fall modestly folded before her. Behind her, Josselin rose and stood a pace or two back, and off to one side, a guardian both practical and ceremonial. He wore the sword he was, as a knight, entitled to bear in the presence of all Cainites but princes. Peter returned as well, and took up station opposite Josselin.

Raoul preceded the Brujah ambassador into the hall and announced her with all the ceremony he had in him. "The Lady Veronique d'Orleans, Ambassador to the Grand Court of Paris, craves Milady Rosamund d'Islington's permission to approach and be acknowledged."

Rosamund wet her tongue and replied in a clear and ringing voice, "My permission is granted to Lady Veronique d'Orleans, to approach and be named friend."

Veronique d'Orleans emerged from the short corridor linking the main hall to its doors. Rosamund forcibly restrained a start of surprise. The Brujah ambassador was a very tall woman—she had more than a head on Rosamund herself, and was actually closer in height to Josselin. She was also not, as Rosamund had feared so vividly, dressed as a man. Veronique d'Orleans's hair was modestly covered by a fine white veil bound with a simple circlet, and she was dressed in what Rosamund knew must be the height of current fashion in Paris, in shades of green and blue, a long-sleeved sea-green kirtle and a blue damask surcoat that suited her shape and coloring admirably. There was a faint blush of life about her lips and ivory cheeks. She had done something to make her nicely shaped ice-blue eyes seem even brighter in the candlelight. Very deliberately, the Brujah woman spread her voluminous skirts, lowered her head, and offered an appropriately deep courtesy, which she held. Her servants, who had entered unremarked at her back, offered their own deep bows.

"You may rise, Lady Veronique d'Orleans, as may your companions," Rosamund kept her voice clear and strong, "and approach."

Veronique rose, and stretched a hand out to one of her servants. He was as small and brown as a mouse, with hands that looked quick and deft even in the brief motion he accorded them. He placed a sealed and ribboned document in his mistress's hand; then both he and Veronique's armed protector held their places as she crossed the hall. Rosamund watched her move, careful to avoid becoming entranced by the play of candlelight across fine blue damask or the grace of the taller woman's movements; she was very graceful, and Rosamund knew she would be a fine dancer. Josselin came forward to greet her, and Veronique offered him a second, shallower courtesy, and handed him the letter. He broke its seals and scanned it quickly, his fair eyebrows arching toward his hairline in mild surprise as he reached the seals at the bottom of the document, then handed it to Rosamund.

It was the Brujah ambassador's own letter of accredit, and Rosamund scanned it quickly, as well—and stopped short when she reached the name of Veronique d'Orleans's sponsor. No less a Cainite stood surety for her than Julia Antasia, the Prince of Hamburg, and one of the oldest and most powerful Roman Cainites still awake and ruling her own dominions. That explained much: Julia Antasia shared age and influence and possibly origin with Prince Alexander, and any diplomat who operated under her aegis might very well have an easier time obtaining his indulgence, or at least his tolerance. Rosamund glanced up at the patiently waiting Brujah, who smiled kindly at her.

"Lady Rosamund," Veronique said, "I believe that we have much to discuss."

Veronique permitted Sandrin and Thierry to accompany Rosamund's servant to the kitchens to warm themselves and take a bit of hot soup and mulled cider. She waited until the last echo of their footsteps faded before she spoke again. "I fear, Lady Rosamund, that I do not bear any good tidings tonight. I had hoped to have better news for you, but events have conspired against me in that regard."

If the Toreador girl—not a girl, Veronique was forced to remind herself, not a girl any longer, no matter how young she was when Embraced—was disappointed by this, she did not permit much of that disappointment to show on her face. "I admit that I suspected as much, Lady Veronique. Please, let us sit and talk." She gestured to the table, clearly set solely for their use. "May I offer you refreshment, as well?"

"I am well for the moment."

Sir Josselin drew the chairs out for both women, and then settled to a position a few feet away, on guard at Rosamund's back. Once they were both sitting, Veronique asked, "I assume that you are familiar with the situation in Paris as it currently exists?"

"I have been kept abreast of events, yes," Rosamund replied guardedly. "There is little—fact or rumor—that originates in Paris that does not eventually reach the Courts of Love, as you may well guess."

"I had assumed as much. The difficulty that arises here is primarily the result of recent years' excitement." Veronique undid the straps on her courier's case laying on the table before her and extracted a handful of wax-sealed reports, depositions taken by Thierry from her various eyes and ears about the city, carefully shorn of any incriminating details of identity, and passed them across the table to Rosamund. "The Countess Saviarre, I fear, is feeling a trifle insecure this season. She has been tightening her grip on the city, and strictly limiting the amount of diplomatic and social congress that takes place under the prince's aegis—not that there has been much in the way of it this winter. She has, it appears, been turning back emissaries since late last autumn. Had my opinion been solicited, I would have advised that you wait until spring to come to Paris."

Rosamund's shoulders stiffened slightly, and she looked up from the papers. "I am certain that my Lady Isouda and my Lady Salianna had their reasons for pursuing this course at this time."

"That was no slur, Lady Rosamund," Veronique said evenly, "merely an observation. As it is, we must deal with the situation as it presently unfolds. I do not think your letter of introduction, and any requests you sent with it, actually reached Prince Alexander. If it did, he has been convinced or compelled not to act on it. We must find some means of dissipating that interference."

"Can you not accomplish that task?" Rosamund's coppery brow rose in a delicate, questioning arch. "You are far better established than any other assistance I might call upon at the Grand Court."

Veronique shook her head slightly. "Not yet. My position at court is not precisely tenuous, but it is also not as strong as it could be—not strong enough to successfully maneuver around Saviarre on the issue of your embassy, at any rate. I do, however, enjoy a good working relationship with Lord Valerian, the prince's most capable diplomatic envoy. We may be able to enlist his assistance in this matter. He is one of the few Cainites in Paris who can approach Alexander directly, without Saviarre's interference."

"What will you need me to do?" Rosamund leaned forward slightly.

"Do you have another copy of your letters of accreditation from Queen Salianna and Queen Isouda?"

"Three, actually, and another copy of the letter of introduction."

"I will need one copy of each of those documents, as well."

"That can be done. What else?"

"I will need you to be patient, and to lend me your trust. We are engaged in the same enterprise, you and I. The risks we take are the same, the dangers we face are the same, and the rewards we reap will be the same. But we cannot gain anything by acting hastily or working at cross-purposes. Are we agreed?" Veronique, very deliberately, met Rosamund's eyes. And she did have lovely eyes, a bewitching green-hazel that Veronique could easily imagine men willing to kill and die for.

Rosamund, after a moment of silent consideration, finally murmured, "Yes," and dropped her eyes modestly. "Patience, I think you will find, is my cardinal virtue."

The night waned, and the three Cainites retired to their day-time chambers, slightly rearranged to accommodate the presence of the Brujah ambassador. Rosamund politely yielded her room to Veronique. Josselin's bed became Rosamund's and he moved, with his squire Fabien, to a pallet in that same chamber. A wooden screen had been set up to partition the room and give them both a bit more privacy as they disrobed and slept, but it did not impede their conversation as they prepared for their rest.

Rosamund's serving women were well trained and accustomed to their mistress's quirks. They assisted her in disrobing, Blanche brushing out the cotte and hanging it up to air, Margery fetching warmed water to bathe Rosamund's face and neck, both assisting in brushing out and braiding her long hair for the day. On the other side of the partition, they could hear Josselin's servant aiding him in much the same way. "What did you think, Josselin?"

"I think it's a little too early to be making any real judgments, petite," Josselin said.

Rosamund resisted the urge to throw a comb over the top of the screen in a (probably vain) effort to hit him. "I'm not asking you to pass judgment, Josselin—what did you think of her?"

He was silent for a long moment. "She... seems forthright enough. I do not think she was trying to deceive or mislead you; she was too direct for that. Whatever else she might believe, she genuinely holds that Countess Saviarre is set against you and must be worked around—but, since our Lady Isouda and Lady Salianna believed that already, it merely confirms suspicions. That may be why Lady Salianna recommended that you work together."

"Evading Saviarre, you mean?"

"Yes. I think—and this is only groundless supposition based on wild speculation, mind you—that there may be something more than simple politics to her interest in aiding you against Saviarre." Another pause, somewhat longer, punctuated by a few low-voiced commands to Fabien. "I was watching her colors. There was nothing I could name solidly, but there was a hint about her that suggested that her interest is less than completely neutral. She comes from Orleans—I could harass Oderic to see if he knows her and inform you of my results. There may be some sort of history between our lady ambassador and Countess Saviarre, though it begs the question that, if there is, why was she accepted in Paris no matter who spoke for her?"

"That would be excellent. And, yes, there are more questions lacking answers now than there were before." Rosamund rose, and let her maids remove her chemise. "But at least we can be relatively certain that, on the issue of Saviarre, Lady Veronique and I are not, in fact, working at cross-purposes. The countess's influence on Prince Alexander must be broken if I am to have even the smallest chance of repairing the rift between the Grand Court and the Courts of Love."

"The question then becomes," Josselin said, "what precisely does Lady Veronique stand to gain from aiding in that mission—the effort to heal the wounds of the past, and bring the two courts into closer alliance again? Or, rather, what does her patron stand to gain? From what I've heard of her, Julia Antasia rarely meddles in the affairs of other domains, though I suppose she might he moved to take action if the need, or the reward for doing so, were great enough."

"Now, that would be wild speculation based on nothing but our own best guesses," Rosamund said. Blanche turned down the covers on the bed, and both of Rosamund's maids set about preparing themselves for rest, one to sleep on the pallet at the foot of her bed, and the other to share the sheets with their mistress, to keep her warm through the chilly winter day. Rosamund herself slipped beneath the embroidered, fur-lined coverlet and linen sheet, attempting to make herself comfortable, even as her thoughts raced speedily enough to banish the beginning tug of daylight fatigue. "Yes... I think you should speak to Oderic... and I will keep you apprised of events in Paris... when we actually get to Paris...."

"As you wish, petite. Sleep now. We'll have more than enough to do when we rise this evening...."

"Yes... we will. A good rest to you, Josselin."

"And to you, *petite*. Sleep well."

The room that Veronique was escorted to showed signs of a recent, thorough cleaning: The floor had been swept, the mattress on the bed turned and fluffed, the linen and coverings all smelled of fresh closet herbs. Even the pallet set at its foot was freshly made up. Sandrin pronounced the door stout as well as lockable from the inside, and the room itself, constructed in the space beneath the upstairs solar, was without windows and completely sealed against light. A chest had been provided for storage, along with the usual assortment of pegs for hanging garments. Rosamund's man Raoul helped Thierry fetch a basin of water and a cloth for Veronique to wash the paint off her face. Sandrin stood guard outside.

As Veronique awaited their return, she went about the soothing evening rituals of her own toilette, and considered the exchange she had just had with the Grand Court's newest would-be diplomat. The brevity of that conversation allowed her little ground on which to base a reasonable opinion, but in that time, Rosamund had nevertheless demonstrated an admirable degree of intelligence and a willingness to act where action appeared to be necessary. Salianna had apparently not been lying when she wrote Veronique and informed her that Rosamund had been sent to Paris deliberately ignorant of all her elders' objectives, of their motives in choosing this time, and her person, as ideal for attempting diplomatic rapprochement with the Grand Court. Veronique chewed that thought over with considerable distaste, then laid it aside for the day. There was nothing she could do about it now, at any rate, and there was always the possibility that Rosamund was a much more skillful dissembler than she seemed. One did not necessarily earn the white rose through the expression of supreme moral rectitude and personal probity, after all, though in the case of Rosamund, Veronique was inclined to grant the benefit of the doubt.

News of one of Rosamund's exploits had come to Veronique some years before, in a letter from her sire Portia, dwelling at the court of Julia Antasia in Hamburg. Portia had not mentioned Rosamund by name—referring to her only as "one of Salianna's pets"—hut had described the events as best she knew them: a near-disastrous embassy to the court of Jurgen of Magdeburg, a tangled web of intrigue and treachery, in which the Toreador ambassador came out smelling the best of all the participants, after Jurgen himself. Rumor circulating among the Cainites of Paris had provided Rosamund's name, and more detail: treachery in the ranks of the Toreador embassy, though not apparently at the order or with the knowledge of the ambassador herself, aided and abetted by parties interested in thwarting more congenial relations between the Black Cross Fiefs (the domains of Jurgen's sire and liege, Lord Hardestadt) and the Courts of Love. Rosamund had apparently handled the situation with considerable tact and skill, salvaging what could have been a total disaster, making assurances to Jurgen and his sire that the Toreador malefactor's treason would be punished, and generally rising to the challenge. Veronique rather hoped she would be able to manage a repeat performance in Paris, where both the pressure and the stakes would be higher.

Thierry returned, bearing a wooden pitcher of warmed water, a towel and a facecloth over one arm, all of which Veronique made use of, thinking all the while. It had been in her mind when she departed Paris to make two stops this trip, one to visit Rosamund and enlist her active participation in the effort to bring her into the society of the Grand Court, and one to pay a visit to her old colleagues Anatole and Zoë, to inquire if there was anything they needed of her, or required at their new haven. They and their followers—mostly Cainite "refugees" from the east, along with a handful of local converts to Anatole's particular brand of worship—continued to dwell outside the city, only barely acknowledged and actively unwanted, a constant irritant to Saviarre and no small number of Cainite Heretics with whom they had clashed off and on for years.

Anatole had permission to enter the city walls and haven there, but not with his flock. They were, for the most part, capable of taking care of themselves when it came down to it, but Veronique nourished a concern for them, anyway. Anatole wasn't the most mentally focused man ever to find himself leading a religious crusade and his chief disciple and adopted daughter, Zoë, was herself little more than a child. Veronique looked after them as best she could, and had, in the process, benefited from their endeavors over the years. Now, however, it seemed somewhat more urgent to return to Paris as quickly as possible and recruit Lord Valerian's efforts on Rosamund's behalf. The kernel of an idea was forming in the back of her mind, vague in its precise details as yet, but sure in one thing—she would need all the skill she could muster to bring her thought to pass.

Jean-Battiste de Montrond did a very good impression of being beside himself with frustration. "What do you *mean* she's not here?"

Alainne looked up from the face of the girl she was expertly rouging, and gave him a narrow-eyed look. "Lady Veronique is not in Paris at the moment. She will return shortly. And what are you doing in here?!"

That last was fired past his shoulder, at the young woman standing in the doorframe, looking halfway between silently lust-struck and mortally embarrassed at her inability to do her duty. She did not answer, and only took a tentative step away, more seeking the shelter of the doorframe than actually leaving Alainne and Jean-Battiste's presence.

"Go on!" Alainne ordered. "I'm sure there's a student upstairs with your name on his lips." The girl scurried out, chemise fluttering, and Alainne turned the full force of her considerable personality back upon her mistress's guest.

"My dear Lady Alainne," he began.

"Don't you 'my dear' or 'my lady' me." Alainne stood and wiped her hands on a damp towel. "You heard me. Lady Veronique isn't here right now. If you've a message for her, you may leave it with me. Otherwise, you are—"

Jean-Battiste slid an arm around Alainne's waist and pulled

her close, offering her his most heartfelt smile, along with a dosage of the sincere blue eyes that had won him passage beneath girls' skirts from Brittany to Sicily. "Alainne, you aren't still angry with me over those two little chits, are you? Truly, you cannot possibly be—those girls were flighty! Untrustworthy! They would have run off with the first drover to whisper sweet nothings in their ears and you would have had to replace them anyway…."

Alainne, unfortunately for him, didn't lift her skirts for any man who didn't pay up front in deniers de provins. "Yes, I am still angry with you about that, so you can scrub the honey off your tongue, take your hand off my bottom, and give me the message if you have one. If not, I'll scream for Philippe and we'll see how high you bounce when you hit the cobbles."

"You're a hard, hard, uncompassionate woman, Alainne." Jean-Battiste sighed, reached into his tunic, and withdrew a note, compactly folded and sealed in wax. "But I'll forgive you. One night, you'll be happy to see me…."

Alainne snatched the note and spun out of his loosened grip, giving him a bump with one nicely curved hip in passing. "Yes, and that night will be shortly after the Last Trump. Don't you have a business of your own to tend to?"

"Is it my fault all the best-looking girls want to work for you, and so I must seek outside my own establishment when I desire to drown myself in feminine charms?"

"You're so full of dung your ears stink."

"They do not. I washed them just tonight."

Alainne couldn't help but laugh as she went about straightening up her worktable, carefully packing away her store of cosmetic ointments and perfumes. "Oh… all right. I'm fairly certain that Veronique doesn't want you corrupting the girls, but since I'm already corrupt, you can sit and drown in my feminine charms."

Jean-Battiste captured her hand and deposited a kiss on her knuckles with a courtly flourish. "You are, indeed, a goddess, and I shall worship forever at the altar of your kindness."

"Oh, stop." She snatched back her hand and swatted him with a damp towel.

Jean-Battiste smiled easily and settled himself on one of the cushioned benches scattered about the room. Alainne fed up the nearest brazier a bit, fetched her basket of dried herbs, and sat down to her idle evening work of making bath sachets. In truth, they'd passed many a night this way in the last several years, since Veronique and Jean-Battiste had made their little "arrangement," exchanging gossip and rumor, idly flirting back and forth, and simply enjoying one another's company. Alainne didn't trust him as far as Philippe or Veronique could throw him, but he was better company than any of the debauched students that made up the majority of their clientele, and had a better ear for gossip than most men could claim. "Has the furor finally died down?"

Jean-Battiste's lips quirked slightly. "That depends entirely upon how you define 'died down.' If you mean, are people over on the isle still frothing at the mouth and proclaiming the imminent second coming, the answer is 'no.' If you mean, has everyone completely forgotten about it… well, the answer is also 'no.' For myself, I'm rather sorry the pitch has died down—the whole affair was good for business, to be honest."

"You noticed that, too? Nothing apparently induces honest tradesmen to drop their coin on wine and whores like the conviction that the world might end tomorrow." Alainne snorted with amusement. "If it'd kept up another five months, I might have been tempted to ask Veronique for my share and retire to some hospitable convent somewhere."

"Alainne, you know such thoughts strike me to the soul— you would be utterly wasted on the cloister. Except mine. Mine would have you in a moment." He offered another winning smile, which she ignored. "Hard-hearted. You know, part of this game involves you granting me at least the illusion of hope…"

Alainne shook the pestle she was using to grind bath herbs at him. "If I give you an inch, you'll take a foot. And part of this game involves you paying for the pleasure of my companionship, which you've not yet done. You have no idea how boring it's been here lately—if I wanted to listen to poetry in a language I don't even speak, I'd move to Narbonne, not spend my time rousting out unruly Latin scholars."

"Ah, my lady craves news. Well, I think you'll find that everyone else is finding this winter to be less than satisfactory on the lurid innuendo front, as well—and you've no doubt heard the results of St. Lys's little follies from Veronique already."

"Losing his head, you mean? Yes, I'd heard. Pity, that. He wasn't a bad sort as far as serpent-tongued heretics go—at least he wasn't the sort of heretic who thinks everyone should be dead from the waist down, or else your only possible destination is Hell." Alainne snorted and shook her head. "I know Veronique tends to favor that Anatole creature, but I can't imagine why—the last time he was here he took the opportunity to remonstrate with the girls about the evils of the flesh and exhorted them to marry for the sake of their souls. Or take up a profession of faith, even if they didn't go into the cloister! Can you imagine Nicolette as a beguine? Neither can I."

"Anatole," Jean-Battiste replied, not without irony, "has a more useful stink of piety about him."

"Perhaps, perhaps not. I just wish Veronique would let us accidentally push him into a vat of hot, soapy water every now and again. I'm sure Zoë would thank us. Have you heard from her lately?"

"Zoë? No. They're squirreled away out there in the woods, keeping their heads down, the last I heard. What was left of St. Lys' men and those red friars were both hunting them before the snows started—" He held up a hand to forestall her worried question. "If they'd been caught, we'd have heard something by now, I assure you."

"Ah, good. I'd be lying if I said I didn't fear for that girl, sometimes. I had hoped Veronique could convince Anatole to let her winter here in the city with us—a filthy little refugee camp in the woods is no place for a girl her age!"

"You think a whorehouse is a better place for a girl her age?" Jean-Battiste asked, honestly amused on numerous levels by that statement.

"Mind your tongue, snake—this is a whorehouse where she could bathe regularly and learn how to read and write doggerel in Latin."

Further banter was interrupted by the sound of wooden

wheels rattling on the cobbles outside. Alainne half-rose in surprise. "That has to be Veronique's cart—she's home early."

"And I fear that must be my signal to climb down a drain and escape before her wrath finds me here," Jean-Battiste rose, and captured Alainne's hand for another kiss. "Can you tell her one thing for me, my heartless beauty?"

"Oh, I suppose… what might that be?"

"The good Bishop de Navarre's party. She'll want to attend it, no matter how personally distasteful she may find the man." A quick smile. "If for no other reason than because I'm providing the party favors."

"I'll let her know. Go, now."

He went.

Veronique spent the next several nights engaging in the lifeblood of her profession, namely, writing letters. She decided, after much interior agonizing, to accept the invitation to Bishop de Navarre's winter fete. She had, she felt, kept her head down quite long enough. A good part of the responsibility for instigating the religious debates of a few years past—and the ensuing civil unrest—could be legitimately laid at her door; she would have to face any socially unpleasant accusations arising therefrom sooner or later. On the whole, she preferred sooner. Ideally, before she began executing any further noticeable political moves. If nothing else, de Navarre's party would offer an opportunity for anyone cherishing a grudge to make that bias known, as well as granting her the opportunity to read the relative social climate of the court. All things being equal, she doubted the winter doldrums had permitted much tension to dissipate yet. To de Navarre, she sent a politely worded note.

To Lord Valerian, she wrote an even more politely worded letter, in which she briefly outlined the situation surrounding Lady Rosamund's embassy and cordially requested a meeting to discuss some means of resolving that situation. Valerian, she knew, was the truest elder statesman of the Grand Court, an experienced and canny politician, the instigator and survivor of countless intrigues and diplomacies. He had, until the last handful of years, been in service to the Grand Court primarily as Prince Alexander's chief envoy, plying his trade as far east as Byzantium and as far north as Scotland. His face and his manner were well known throughout most of the more civilized Cainite courts in Christendom. When he'd returned from his last visit to Constantinople, instead of dispatching him back to the field, either Alexander or Saviarre had elected to keep him close to home. Veronique rather suspected that wise decision to have been Alexander's; she had observed, as best she could, the public interactions between Valerian and Saviarre, and was inclined to characterize their relationship as coolly professional. They seemed to be allies of necessity, more so even than convenience. She doubted there was much personal loyalty involved in any of the political bonds between them. Veronique had no illusions regarding her ability to deceive or manipulate Valerian. With him, she thought it much safer altogether to err on the side of honest political self-interest.

Dame Mnemach was another little-seen elder power of the Grand Court, and another potential ally whom Veronique acknowledged would have to be handled quite delicately. The Nosferatu warren of Paris enjoyed little palpable power in the Ventrue- and Toreador-dominated Grand Court, where the high-blooded Cainites showered their derision on the "pretensions" of their "lesser kin." Nonetheless, the Nosferatu wielded a subtle influence Veronique had learned to respect. Posture though they might, there were few among the high-blooded who had never found a use for the talents of the Nosferatu, and some favors were not paid for in coin alone. Dame Mnemach, the matriarch of the Nosferatu, was rumored to be older than the city itself, to have dwelt on Ile de la Cité from before the time of the Romans and to have a stronger claim by law and custom to territory there than any Cainite but the prince himself. Those claims were naturally less than respected by the more arrogant members of the Grand Court. There had been, over the years, nearly open bloodshed between Mnemach's kin and Bishop de Navarre over conflicts arising from his violation of her domain. Alexander had made the minimum gestures necessary to smooth the matter over, neither explicitly reprimanding the Lasombra for his actions nor reaffirming Mnemach's sovereign claim of domain, and left it to simmer quietly, flaring up every now and then as new provocations occurred. Veronique had watched the situation with interest, and kept her ear to the ground in an attempt to determine how deeply Countess Saviarre was involved in fueling or perpetuating the conflict. It seemed very much to fit with the countess's past history of playing opponents against each other, then sweeping in to clean up the mess and collect the credit for doing so. Veronique had thus far obtained no hard evidence of any such maneuvering on Saviarre's part, though that hardly proved anything.

A lack of evidence regarding Saviarre's specific malice had also hardly prevented Dame Mnemach from taking an instantaneous dislike to the countess—or, more likely, Mnemach had sources of intelligence that Veronique could only guess at and had all the evidence she needed. The Nosferatu matriarch was not known for her unannounced appearances at court, but when she did bother to attend functions or respond to her prince's requests for her counsel, her withering disdain for the prince's chief advisor could hardly be overlooked. She apparently did not believe that subtlety was the best weapon in all cases, though, to be just, Saviarre returned the contempt with interest, and didn't overly trouble to hide it, either. Veronique had been attempting to make direct contact with Mnemach for more than a year, in between various other activities, and her efforts had, in the form of the note delivered by Jean-Battiste, finally borne fruit. Mnemach was willing to meet with her, face-to-face, to discuss the possibilities of an alliance of mutual benefit. Veronique wrote her a short note indicating her understanding of, and agreement to the terms required, which she left precisely where she was instructed to, no more and no less.

Chapter Three

Lord Valerian, like most of the high-blooded Cainites in Paris, dwelt on the island on the Seine that was the historical heart of the city, the Ile de la Cité. His was a compact house that was neither ostentatious nor extravagant, and which doubled, on occasion, as a diplomatic mission for Ventrue beholden of foreign lords but in good standing with the Parisian court. Veronique had never been within its walls, but she had heard, from those who had, that it was laid out in a manner similar to those Roman villas familiar to Valerian from his breathing days, or as close as he could come to it in the colder, wetter north. Several nights after writing him, she received an invitation to visit that place and discuss politics in a much more civilized fashion. She replied, plans were made, and two nights after that, her cart pulled up outside the well-lighted entrance to Lord Valerian's home.

Veronique was met at the gate and helped down by the first of a succession of well-groomed, well-dressed, and exceptionally well-mannered young men and women who served Valerian's household needs. There was one to help her out of her cart and guide her up the walk to the house, one to take her cloak and gloves at the door, one to guide her to the solar to await Valerian's arrival, and one who offered her sustenance, which she declined. She had made up her mind before leaving home not to let herself become too impressed by surroundings that could only be described as "impressive." She found herself failing in that resolution as she waited, as patiently as she could, for her host to present himself.

The house really was laid out almost exactly like a Roman

villa—it reminded her, sharply, of Julia Antasia's private haven in Hamburg: Many of the modifications, the architectural concessions to the harsher climates of the north, were very much the same. Valerian's solar had more in common with the Roman atrium than anything else, with a full-blown impluvium in the center, around which a collection of chairs and strangely constructed, cushioned benches were gathered. The roof was solid; Veronique supposed the water filling the impluvium was drawn from below somehow, or replaced regularly, as it didn't smell or appear stagnant.

Most of the furnishings were, in fact, of simultaneously familiar but unusual form: backless chairs, sculptured benches, even a pile of oversized embroidered cushions. There was no fireplace: the room was heated by braziers scattered at regular intervals, and the lamps were lavishly decorated metal burning what smelled to Veronique like olive oil. Mosaic tiles glittered underfoot as she rose and paced the confines of the room, examining the exquisite furnishings and indulging in a minor pang of something close to, but not quite, homesickness. A quiet pining. As much as she had missed Orleans and Carcassonne while in Hamburg, she missed Hamburg occasionally now that she was in Paris. A bad habit in a traveling diplomat, but there it was. A small smile touched the corners of her mouth as she came into the corner of the atrium farthest from the door, and found Valerian's lararium with its tiny ivory images of the household gods, arranged in their miniature shrine around a fresh honey cake and a wooden cup of wine. Some things never changed. Lady Antasia had such a shrine also and tended it assiduously, and Portia carried her little ivory lares with her everywhere she went.

Veronique glanced about, surreptitiously, and found herself all but alone: A maidservant tended the braziers at the far end of the room. Veronique reached through the slit in her surcoat, drew a silver penny from her purse, and laid it on the shrine next to the plate containing the honey cake. It had taken her a long time to become accustomed to such gestures. In the beginning, Portia had had reason to be thoroughly exasperated with her stubborn childe's good Catholic abhorrence of even such gentle vestiges of the pagan past. Veronique no longer considered herself a good Catholic and had learned, under the tutelage of her sire and her mentor, to regard the past and the ways of the past with the respect they deserved. And, every now and then, to lay an offering on others' altars.

"Ah, here you are. Forgive my tardiness, milady—there was a bit of household business that commanded my attention."

Veronique turned quite deliberately and offered Lord Valerian a courtesy, refusing to show any trace of surprise, though he'd come up on her quietly. "A good evening to you, Milord Valerian. And no apologies are necessary."

"Come, milady—rise." He waved her up and caught her hand in his own, depositing a kiss on her knuckles. If he noticed her addition to his altar, he made no sign of it, and Veronique permitted him to draw her away from the corner, out into the well-lit center of the room next to the impluvium. Valerian dressed, as always, as befit his station, in clothing of fine quality without a stitch of excess ornamentation or embellishment, his sternly handsome face clean-shaven, his iron gray hair barbered and combed. "It's been quite some time since I last entertained an envoy from my good friend Lady Antasia, and before we speak of anything else, you must tell me how she fares."

"She was yet well when last we corresponded—enmeshed in the affairs of state, as usual, but good in spirit, at least. She asked, should I have the opportunity to speak with you personally, that I remind you of the summer villas outside Rome and the debates that you enjoyed across the garden wall." Veronique felt a bit bold relaying that as Lady Antasia had written it and was actually relieved when Valerian's face creased in a smile so impish with pleased recollection that it was nearly a grin. She was quietly astounded. She had never seen the man smile so openly at court and hadn't been certain that he could.

"Iulia does, indeed, delight in reminding me of such things whenever the opportunity presents itself, rare though those opportunities may be these nights." They continued their perambulation around the impluvium. "And I believe, milady, that you have just given me the excuse I needed to renew my correspondence with her. I thank you."

"It was my pleasure, Lord Valerian, to give you that cause."
Veronique replied, modestly, and earned herself a somewhat
more sedate smile.

"Spoken like a true Antasian diplomat. Come into the office.
I promise you a discourse on more substantive topics than the
congenial past."

Valerian's office, much like Lady Antasia's, was a very proper
Roman tablinum, only slightly modified. It was longer than it
was wide, with no true doors, only sliding wooden screens at
each end to close it off from the rest of the house; the furniture
consisted of a heavy desk, a scattering of chairs and benches,
and the chests and shelves that contained the books of the
house and other such documents of Valerian's trade. Veronique
made herself comfortable on one of the benches. Valerian seated
himself as well, after removing her letter from a locked correspondence chest sitting on his desk. "I admit that it was almost
more curiosity than anything else that induced me to respond
to your request, milady."

His change in tone alerted her: The moment for pleasant
reminiscence was past. She folded her hands neatly in her lap
and smoothed her expression. When he turned to face her, his
diplomat's mask was firmly in place, the calm nonexpression
of a professional listener. She responded in kind. "Curiosity,
milord?"

"Indeed." He opened her letter and made a point of scanning it briefly once more. "I confess myself curious as to why an
agent from the court of the Prince of Hamburg would involve
herself in the affairs between Paris and the Courts of Love. It
seems a touch outside your patron's interest."

"Lady Antasia's interests are wide-ranging, much like her
agents," Veronique replied evenly. "In this case, her interest lies
in promoting a rapprochement between the Grand Court and
the Courts of Love—the better to facilitate a diplomatic resolution to events in the Languedoc."

Valerian's steel-gray eyebrow flicked up. "Interesting. Say
on."

"As you are no doubt aware," Veronique continued in
the same cool and even tone, "the situation south of the Tarn

remains... unsettled. And the violence being bred there has begun, in ways great and small, to spill over into the lands of the Black Cross—including milady's. She feels that, were a strong and united alliance between the Grand Court and the Courts of Love to take shape and face that crisis, it could be defused diplomatically and to the ultimate benefit of all."

"I fear that the situation in the Languedoc passed the point of diplomatic resolution quite some time ago—but the proof of that is yet in the future," Valerian replied. "I take it, then, that your mission is to execute Lady Antasia's will in the matter of assisting the reunification of the two Courts."

"Yes."

"This is no small task you have taken on, Lady Veronique."

Veronique resisted the urge to reply, 'You have no idea'. "I am not unaware of that, Milord Valerian, but the cause is just, and the task must be done. I am but a humble servant of my prince, and if I cannot serve her interests well in this matter, I cannot serve them at all. Hence my interest in acquiring your assistance."

Valerian was silent for a long moment, regarding her steadily. Then he rose and paced the few steps it took to reach the doors at the far end of the tablinum, cracked them open, and murmured instructions to the servant waiting there, in a voice too low for Veronique to make out individual words. He returned, and his face had transcended the blandly courteous, becoming actively opaque. "I assume that you have been in some contact with Queen Salianna."

Veronique considered for a moment before answering that, uncertain how much she wished to give away at this point in the proceedings. Finally, she replied, "Yes. We have been in correspondence."

"How do you assess her commitment to this endeavor? She has, in the past, been of decidedly lukewarm temperament with regards to relations between the courts, you must admit." He seated himself and set her letter aside.

"In the past, she has been in a position where the relative temperature of her support for the Grand Court has had little ultimate consequence," Veronique pointed out. "Within her own sphere of influence, her position has been unassailable, but that is no longer entirely the case. The longer the war with Esclarmonde the Black drags on, the more unstable the basis for her own safety becomes. Inasmuch as she perceives strengthened relations with the Grand Court as beneficial to her personally, I believe her to be committed to achieving that goal."

"That," Valerian said, "is a very unsparing assessment, Lady Veronique."

"I do not serve Queen Salianna, Lord Valerian. I cannot afford to regard her interest in this matter through the lens of idealism. If there were nothing for her to gain from initiating this diplomatic effort, she would not have attempted it in the first place." Veronique met his eyes squarely, for the first time. "I do not trust her more than I must—but I do trust her not to place her interests at unnecessary hazard. I think she is in earnest both in engaging with Lady Antasia to serve mutual goals and in the effort to repair relations between the courts. I believe that she sent Lady Rosamund d'Islington to serve as her ambassador, rather than coming personally, because she does not wish the enmity between herself and Countess Saviarre to poison the atmosphere at court, and weaken the diplomatic effort."

He glanced away. "Queen Salianna is wise, then. I suspect the Countess Saviarre will not greet the prospect of normalized relations with the Courts of Love with any particular pleasure."

"That is why I approached you, Lord Valerian, and not the countess for assistance in this matter. I have reason to suspect that Countess Saviarre has already intercepted one attempt by Lady Rosamund to communicate with the prince or his agents, and likely stands ready to continue stonewalling her until Hell freezes over solidly."

Valerian's gaze snapped back to her. "Do you, now?"

Lady Rosamund dispatched her formal request to approach Paris more than a month ago, Lord Valerian, craving to be acknowledged as Ambassador of the Rose for the Courts of Love and take up residence at the Toreador embassy on Ile de la Cité. She has received no reply. I am forced to assume that Prince Alexander never received her request, nor any of the other documents detailing her credentials."

Valerian's lips compressed into a thin, tight line. She caught a flicker in his eyes that might very well have been anger. He mastered himself quickly. "I suspect that you may be correct in that, Lady Veronique. Countess Saviarre has been—" a muscle twitched in his cheek; if he were a lesser man, he might have grimaced—"exerting herself quite strenuously of late to protect the prince from those aspects of governance that might unsettle him."

"Countess Saviarre," Veronique replied bluntly, "has been vastly overstepping her bounds as advisor for quite some time now, Lord Valerian. The instability of the Courts of Love, and the recent activity of the Heretics has only encouraged this tendency in her—to the detriment of the Grand Court, I have begun to fear."

"You are not," Valerian assured her, in a tone so dry it should have sucked all the moisture from the air, "entirely incorrect in that observation. And you were also wise to come to me with this request. Do you know if Lady Rosamund is prepared to make another attempt at approaching the Grand Court?"

"I believe that she is. In fact, she dispatched another copy of her letters of introduction and her credentials with me when I requested them of her."

"Good. I will require those documents, Lady Veronique, and any such assurances that you yourself would choose to provide, before the feast of St. Theodorus."

"You will have them. And I thank you for your help, Lord Valerian."

"Do not thank me just yet.

Chapter Four

Veronique rose as early as she could, forcing her lead-weighted limbs into motion and her sluggish mind to think while the last light of the day was still brightening the sky. She had no desire to be late for her meeting with the Nosferatu envoy who was to act as her guide, if for no other reason than to avoid inadvertently giving offense. Alainne met her at the door to her suite with warm water and towels, of which she made grateful use, then turned to dressing herself for what she suspected would be a rather active night. Some time before, she'd had cause to dress herself as a man for purposes of both disguise and ease of movement—heavy skirts appropriate for court or the city streets didn't lend themselves as well to the practical difficulties of traveling cross-country in the foulest weather imaginable, and she doubted they'd do much better trying to navigate the Nosferatu warren. She had a pair of men's wool hose for such occasions, along with a short chemise of the sort worn by men and a longer over-tunic, and a pair of sturdy boots. As she tied off the last of the laces, Nicolette presented herself and Veronique took the girl into her arms, drank lightly and quickly, then sent her off to bed. Girauda handed Veronique her cloak as she slipped out the door.

Veronique carried no torch or lamp with her, nor did she go out with any of her usual assortment of protectors or companions. She had explicitly warned Jean-Battiste not to try to follow her the night previously, and she hoped the little serpent had the sense enough to heed her. He knew the value of his own hide and protected it assiduously, but she doubted not at all that curiosity, and the desire to gain an edge, could sometimes get the better of him. Fortunately, she saw no sign of him during her quick walk to the designated meeting place, even though she pushed her sight to its limits just to make her way through the city's dark streets. It took her some time, and a few missteps, to reach the meeting place—in the shadow of a small church where the red monks who so inflamed Anatole sometimes lectured—and she hunkered down at once to wait, and to hope that no one but the envoy noticed her.

She didn't wait long. She was huddled in the lee of the building, her cloak wrapped tightly around her to keep out the odd errant thread of breeze, when a small figure came into view, heavily wrapped against the cold. It was hobbling painfully, bent as though its back had never known how to straighten, leaning on the staff it carried in one hand and lighting the way with a lamp held in the other. She stayed where she was, watching closely, waiting for a sign that this was her contact. Instead of approaching her, it turned down the street in front of the church, ignoring her entirely, its walking stick tapping rhythmically on the cobbles. The regular tapping ceased before it could have gone more than a half-dozen paces past the alley in which Veronique waited; she placed her back against the wall of the church and scanned the vicinity to see from which direction it would come back. A flicker out of the corner of her eye showed her that the small, shrouded figure was circling through the churchyard, lamp shuttered, walking stick abandoned or perhaps some trick of the blood employed to render it more indistinct, to come up on her left. She turned to face it.

It came to a halt an arm's length or two away. She couldn't see enough of its face to tell if it was nonplussed or not. The voice that emerged from behind the scarf concealing its expression was gravelly, abrupt, and assuredly male. "Veronique d'Orleans, is it?"

"I am she," Veronique replied, calmly.

"Guillaume. Follow me."

Guillaume led the way, taking Veronique down streets that even she had rarely traveled during her years dwelling in the Latin Quarter, narrow and twisted alleys strewn with garbage and damp with not-quite-frozen effluvium. Since they weren't speaking, Veronique was actually grateful for the chance not to breathe; she could nearly feel the stink clinging to her, and she had no desire whatsoever to taste it. She also suspected that her guide wasn't by any means taking her by the most direct route to their destination, though she could hardly blame him for that. The Nosferatu had little reason to trust any high-blooded Cainite, herself included. She hoped for the chance to earn that trust but didn't expect it to be extended without thought. Were she in Guillaume's position, she wouldn't make it easy, either. Despite her best efforts to keep herself oriented, Veronique was fairly certain that she'd never be able to retrace their steps without a guide or a trail of breadcrumbs to assist the endeavor.

Guillaume's lamp, the only part of him clearly visible within his wrapping of ragged cloak and woolen scarves, bobbed to a halt. "Here. Hold the lamp. Stand back."

Veronique did as he said, glancing around as she did so. They were, in essence, in a cul-de-sac. There were breezeways between the buildings clustered all around them, but those gaps were far too narrow for a full-grown adult or even most children to pass through safely. The alley they had come down was, itself, barely wide enough to admit her; she'd brushed one shoulder or the other against a wall the entire way down, though Guillaume had had no such difficulties. A glance over her shoulder, straining her vision to the utmost, showed her a tangled cat's cradle of narrow alleys, empty but for themselves, a cold wind whistling among them.

Guillaume stripped off his ragged cloak and many scarves, balling them up and shoving them into a malodorous pile of debris leaning against a wall. He had permitted the illusion masking his appearance to fade as they walked: Now his true form was revealed completely. In the dim yellow light of the lamp, his skin had the translucence of old parchment, stretched taut over misshapen bones, his lips pulled back in a snarling rictus that exposed a mouth full of jagged, discolored teeth. Veronique did her best not to stare, forced herself to express no horror or morbid fascination or pity, glancing quickly down to follow the motion of his long-fingered hands. He was feeling along the seams in the cobbled alley, clearly searching for something…

He found it, pulling a loose stone out of the alley and, reaching down to grasp the thick iron ring concealed beneath. With a grunt of effort and a heave of his deceptively slender shoulders, he lifted an entire chunk out of the alley, cobblestones cleverly mortared together and jointed in some way that Veronique couldn't see, to produce a kind of trapdoor. Veronique stepped closer and looked down. A dank odor emanated from below, along with the rippling echo of flowing water. A shaft of some kind.

"Lamp," Guillaume said. Veronique handed it back to him, and he crouched down, pushing it into a niche at the top of the shaft, illuminating narrow, mortar-sealed bricks punctuated at intervals by iron rungs and handholds. "You first."

Veronique took a breath and wet her lips. "Master Guillaume…"

"What?" He looked up. The deformation of his face erased any expression he might have made, but his tone was sharp.

"Master Guillaume, I must ask you—does this way go by water?"

"Ah. Yes." He gestured downward. "The shaft sinks down— at fifteen rungs, or ten if it runs damp, you will find water. Ten more, and the downward shaft ends, and the side shaft begins— you will have to pull yourself through it, there are handholds on the bottom."

Veronique's shoulders relaxed slightly. "So… no swimming, then?"

"Some. At the end." He gestured for her to go, a bit more emphatically.

Veronique bit her lip. "Master Guillaume, I never learned how to swim."

Guillaume let out a bark of what she assumed was laughter and shook his hairless head. "You still go first. I'll pull you with me at the end."

She opened her mouth to argue, then closed it again and nodded tightly. She removed her own cloak, folded it as neatly as she could, and tucked it atop Guillaume's in the pile of refuse. He stepped back to let her into the shaft. She sat on the edge and felt about with her feet until she encountered the first of the rungs she could stand on: They were a woman's height apart, and she had to climb carefully, for the shaft was narrow. Her back brushed against the rear wall with every motion, and one of her shoulders grazed the side wall, as well. The walls were damp with condensation, and the surface of the iron rungs slick and crumbling with rust. She descended three or four rungs, and Guillaume slithered down after her, heaving the cobblestone cap of the shaft closed above them—and blowing out the lamp.

Absolute darkness descended at once, nearly thick enough to touch. Veronique let out a ragged sigh, closed her eyes, and concentrated on strengthening her other senses. Above her, she could hear Guillaume descending, and so she continued her own climb, listening tensely, feeling her way along completely blind. The sound of rippling water grew gradually louder; her sense of touch told her it was growing considerably damper. As promised, fifteen rungs down, she found the water, sloshing over the top of her boots and coming to midthigh before her foot came to rest on the next rung. She fought down the instinctive, reflexive desire to hold her breath, a tendency she had never managed to shed, and forced herself to release any air she might be holding in her lungs. And then she continued to climb down, the icy water inching its way up her body and finally coming over her head, rushing in to fill her highly sensitized ears with its strange sound-but-no-sound, pouring up her nose and trying to force its way past her clenched teeth. Within her, the Beast stirred slightly in response to her discomfort; she had never learned to swim, never liked being submerged in water over her head, even decades after the fear of drowning had ceased to be a practical concern. She paused for a moment, clinging to the rungs and pressed close against the wall, to discipline herself, and reluctantly, the temperamental little monster subsided. Her joints and muscles complained, for the water was bitterly cold and stiffened her. She did her best to ignore it.

She counted rungs in her mind and, at twenty-five, she found the bottom of the downward shaft and felt around for a second opening. She found it, even narrower than the first, its ceiling low and its bottom thickly ridged with hand- and footholds. She gripped as best she could, and pulled with all her strength, propelling herself along, keeping the momentum going with her feet. Something slimy squeezed out from underneath her questing fingers; she jumped, startled, sucked in an involuntary lungful of water, and slammed the back of her head into the top of the shaft, hard. Stars danced inside her skull, and the Beast woke, growling, as she sought for another handhold and pulled herself farther forward, wishing she dared to open her eyes. Her limbs were trembling with the need to lash out at something. She ground her knuckles into the bottom of the shaft and focused on the pain, forcing herself back from the edge of fear-driven frenzy. She reached the end of the shaft with surprising suddenness and tumbled down the sharp drop-off, thrashing for a moment in a desperate search for the rough-cut stone of the edge. She had no idea how deep or wide the pool of water at the end of the shaft really was, but with arms and legs stretched at full extension she encountered only slippery stone that slid from beneath her questing fingers, and nothing else.

A strong, long-fingered hand caught her wrist as she scrabbled for a handhold and a ropy, muscular arm caught her across the shoulders, orienting her in the right direction. She stopped struggling, not wanting to hinder Guillaume's efforts. He kicked off hard and dragged her up with him, water rushing past her face as they rose rapidly. They broke the surface within moments. Veronique reached up, rubbed hard at her eyes to clear them, and spat out a mouthful of water.

They had come up in a flooded section of the old quarries that underlay much of the city, and whose stone had built its oldest structures—a low, hollowed-out dome of grayish-white stone and a rough-carved crescent ledge, surrounded by a subterranean lake of cold, dark water. And there was light: A dozen candles illuminated the chamber from niches carved into the rock face above the ledge. From her position in the water, Veronique could see no sign of an exit, but she didn't suppose that actually meant anything; surprises seemed to be the order of the night. Guillaume towed her to the edge of the ledge , and helped boost her out, waterlogged and stiff. Fortunately, the ledge was also roughly carved and abundantly supplied with handholds. A glance around showed her the exit—a second, square-mouthed shaft bored through the stone, vanishing into darkness beyond the light of the candles. There was no one waiting for them, though there was a low wooden trough along one side and a chest near the exit.

"Take off your clothes," Guillaume said. Veronique glanced a question at him and he gestured at the trough. "Your clothes. Leave them there." He was already disrobing.

Veronique could feel herself trying to blush. She scrambled to her feet and quickly turned her back, fingers fumbling with the laces of her boots, hose, and tunic.

It took her a moment to get everything undone and set aside, wondering if this was specifically for her benefit, or if Dame Mnemach preferred to meet all her visitors in the skin that God and Caine had given them.

"Here." Veronique darted a look over her shoulder. Guillaume was holding a garment out to her, which she gratefully accepted; it was a sort of rough-spun tunic, knee-length, cut low at the neck, sewn together at the shoulders and waist, but otherwise open. Veronique supposed it was better than absolute nudity, but not by very much, particularly given the way it clung to her still-damp body. It comforted her only slightly to note that Guillaume was clad similarly and, despite the expressionless mask of his face, apparently liked it as little as she.

He took a candle from among the dozen burning on the ledge, and took the lead again, down the long, dark tunnel into the heart of the Nosferatu dominions. "Come—she waits."

They walked for what felt like hours to the wet and chilled Veronique, traversing what seemed to be miles of narrow corridors bored through the rocky heart of Paris, only a few of them navigable by a woman of her height. She spent a great deal of time crouched to avoid cracking her head on low-hanging ceilings, and on no less than three occasions, they went through passages on their hands and knees. Veronique rapidly gave up trying to keep track of their route, as they seemed to turn completely around at least once, and the path was obviously designed to confound any sense of direction she might possess this far underground. *Remember, Vero, you need this woman's help—you need her good will—if (his will yield you (hose things, it will all be worth it. It will all be worth it, and you can froth at the mouth about it when you get home....*

"Almost there."

Veronique chose to interpret that remark as encouragement. From somewhere up ahead, she could hear the sound of voices; she concentrated a bit, and the unintelligible babble of echoes resolved itself somewhat. A single female voice, speaking—no, not speaking so much as incanting—a rhythmic chant in a language that seemed at once familiar and indefinably alien. At the end of her invocation, a chorus of voices responded with a chant of their own, a ritual reply. It sounded, to Veronique's ear, almost like a mass.

They reached the end of the tunnel with startling suddenness, the transition from dark, barely lit passageway to dark, barely lit and cavernous chamber difficult to perceive even with vision more than naturally acute. Veronique found herself standing at the edge of a chamber whose precise dimensions were impossible to discern but which gave the disturbing impression of vast size. It fell away overhead into darkness so complete that Veronique was half-surprised it contained no stars; the extremities were similarly bounded in unrelieved shadow. It was obviously a part of the old Roman quarries as well; the wall she stood closest to still bore perceptible marks of chisel and wedge in the grayish-white stone, and the scattered puddles of lamp and candlelight revealed walls stratified into layers of ledges. And those ledges were occupied: She caught a glimpse of huddled figures, some carrying lights, some sitting comfortably in the darkness, some muffled in layers of clothing meant to disguise the contortions of their forms, some naked or all but naked, some little more than a flicker of unnaturally brilliant eyes in the shadows or the vague suggestion of a blurred shape. There was no way to tell how many there were, but they were gathered in a loose semicircle around a single figure, illuminated by a widely spaced circle of candles. Guillaume reached back and grasped her wrist, and she throttled the instinctive desire to pull away and follow him on her own. His palm had the texture of dry-rotted leather and, despite herself, her skin crawled at his touch. He led her around the outside of the circle, hanging close to the wall, and blew out their own candle as soon as they came within range of other lights. Veronique placed her feet carefully. The floor was uneven stone covered in sand, and she could just see herself stubbing a toe or skidding on a loose bit of flooring and making a fool of herself in front of all the Nosferatu in Paris. Guillaume didn't appear to begrudge her the caution and was, himself, making his way as slowly and carefully as possible, keeping one hand pressed against the wall as he led the way. Eventually they found what he'd been seeking, an unoccupied ledge, on the lowest tier above the floor; he helped her up and silently bade her to sit, which she did. He rested a hand on her knee to make certain that he had her attention, then held his finger to his lips and gestured toward the center of the room. She nodded her understanding, and he removed his hand, settling in at her side to wait.

Dame Mnemach stood before her people, haranguing them in a language of which Veronique understood no single word. Every few moments she would stop, a chorus of voices would answer her, and she would speak again. After a while, Veronique began to recognize a pattern as certain words were used and repeated. She watched, equally disturbed and fascinated, and physically had to resist the urge to whisper questions at Guillaume. If the entire evening thus far had been a test, the willingness to wait patiently to satisfy her curiosity was no doubt a part of it. And she had come too far now to throw away this chance on a curiosity that could be dealt with later.

A part of her had always known that Dame Mnemach was, even among Nosferatu, an unsettling individual, and an equally unsettling sight. When the Nosferatu elder came to court, she always came masked—physically masked, rather than relying on any occult means to conceal her appearance. She generally wore enveloping dark robes and a long cloak and gloves of some kind; she occasionally wore ornaments that some said were carved from the polished bones of Christian children. Veronique put little stock in that particular slur, since it was so typical of much high-blooded snobbery, though Mnemach's ornaments were, from what she could determine, actually made of bone, as was her mask—bone ornately inlaid with panels of colored stone in strange spiral patterns. Thus attired, Mnemach would occasionally come to court, speaking to no one but the prince or his attendants, and then vanish again, leaving behind another storm of whispers.

Here, in her own domain, among her own people, Dame Mnemach did not trouble with such affectations. The matriarch of the Nosferatu stood all but naked before her assembled subjects, bathed in the light of a dozen candles, adorned in ornaments of bone, her skin marked with the raised ridges of old scarifications and glistening still with freshly painted markings. Unlike many of her kind, Mnemach had not been crippled by the blood of her sire—her limbs and spine were not twisted; she had no trouble standing or gesturing; her voice was not a guttural croak emerging from a misshapen mouth. She was hairless, yes, but otherwise tall and straight, her limbs strong, her form smoothly rounded, and her flesh as translucent as water. Blood pulsed through a thousand visible veins, the action of her muscles and tendons clear to the naked eye, her bones dark smudges wrapped in layers of semi-opaque tissue. Her dark voice caused the lineaments of her throat to pulse like a songbird's.

Veronique was quietly astonished. Mnemach exuded a profoundly disturbing, sensual aura—it poured from her with a passion that few could match, seeping into the air from her very pores. Had she not been Nosferatu, Mnemach would have been uncomplicatedly beautiful and frankly sensual for eternity. Since she was Nosferatu, her beauty was edged in horror, her sensuality in menace. Veronique was struck by her intensity and could hardly tear her eyes away, and she was not alone. The force of Mnemach's personality held her people in thrall, invoked their sensuality in response to her own. Veronique realized that the little puddles of light and shadow on the ledges above her own were beginning to meld together as their occupants joined one another, casting aside their garments and their modesty. For the second time that night, Veronique could feel her embarrassment trying to become palpably obvious; she

locked her eyes on Mnemach and tried to ignore the passionate cries of the matriarch's followers as they coupled with each
other and pleasured themselves.

Dame Mnemach was not much help to Veronique in that
regard. She watched with a soft smile on her face, the tips of her
fangs just barely visible and her eyes hot with desire, a desire
her followers were quite willing to assuage. They came to her
in ones or twos, painted with marks to match her own, and
rubbed themselves against her flesh, begging for her attention,
the slightest caress or touch, and she indulged them. But she
did not permit them to drink of her, nor did she drink of them.
Eventually the numbers coming to her tapered off; above, on
the ledges, the gathering began to melt away, withdrawing to
continue their devotions elsewhere.

Veronique dared a glance at Guillaume and found him
regarding the rest of the room with an attempt at stony indifference, his hands tightly clenching the fabric of his tunic.
She looked away before he could notice her attention, but it
was a bit of a comfort to know that she wasn't the only one
simultaneously disturbed and affected. Across the room, a bit
of wall detached itself and shuffled across the sand-covered
floor towards Mnemach, a dark length of cloth draped over its
emaciated arms. Veronique blinked, deliberately, unsettled for
the thousandth time. That tiny figure, no larger than a child,
blended perfectly into its background, its skin grayish-white, its
eyes black pits, and Veronique felt all the hair on the back of
her neck trying to rise. It handed Mnemach a dark tunic and
set about darkening all but one of the candles. The matriarch
of the Nosferatu slipped her tunic over her head, gestured care-
lessly in their direction, and turned away to stride toward the
far, shadowed side of the chamber, her servant trotting ahead of
her, candle in hand. Guillaume hopped down off the ledge and
Veronique followed him closely.

Dame Mnemach and her servant beat them to the far side
of the room, of course; Guillaume was deliberately regulating
their pace to keep a respectful distance behind her, without
completely losing sight of the light her servant carried. That
was fortunate; the far wall of the chamber was punctured with

literally a dozen apertures of different sizes and heights, all at slightly different levels. Mnemach could have taken any one of those, but she selected one close to the floor, high-ceilinged and wide enough for Veronique to walk comfortably. The route also involved fewer twists and turns, and all of the corridors were smooth-floored and even. Veronique wished she'd had the sense to start counting paces from their starting point. Ahead, the clear light they were following vanished behind a curtain that diffused its radiance somewhat. The development did not appear to disturb Guillaume, and Veronique decided not to let it bother her either. They came to the curtain a moment later, and Guillaume held it aside for her, gesturing for her to precede him. She nodded cordially to him as she passed, a gesture that he returned, though he spoke not a word. Neither did he follow.

The room she stepped into was obviously Dame Mnemach's private quarters, or near enough to it that the difference hardly mattered. It was roughly circular, its domed ceiling plastered over and supported by arches and vaulting, and roughly divided into two halves. One half contained the source of its warmth, a fire pit sunk into the floor and surrounded with a high guard of mortared stone, a wooden hood in place to guide the smoke from the cheerfully burning fire up and out. The floor around the fire pit was completely devoid of flammables, bare stone scattered with sand. The other half of the room was also dominated by a pit—a bed pit, also sunk into the floor, and filled with a mass of cushions and coverlets and heavy furs. There were no chairs or benches or even chests for storage, only more cushions, wide and nearly flat, embroidered in strange designs, and even more furs. Veronique stood at the edge of the room, her back to the curtain-door, uncertain of what to do next.

Dame Mnemach made no immediate move to rectify that uncertainty, but stripped off her tunic and tossed it into a corner. Her twisted little servant emerged from the opposite side of the fire, carrying a bucket of water and a cloth, which she used to sponge away the markings she could reach. She then permitted her servant to cleanse her back and buttocks. Veronique put her hands together behind her back and studiously attended the effort of keeping her temper and her nerves under control.

Eventually, her patience was rewarded. The servant was dismissed. Mnemach sent a long glance over her shoulder that gathered Veronique up and drew her across the room, her feet sinking ankle-deep into furs and cushions as she went.

"You intrigue me, Brujah." Mnemach's voice, even without the amplification of a large chamber, was low and deep, a velvety contralto that made every word she spoke a knowing caress. "And you surprise me. The one is a pleasant diversion, and the other something I am no longer accustomed to."

I've been hearing a lot of that lately. Veronique bit down on that reply and murmured instead, "I hope that it is my offer that has intrigued you more than anything else, milady."

The corners of Mnemach's mouth curved slightly, and she sank down into the mass of comforts that constituted her bed, gesturing for Veronique to follow. After a fractional hesitation she did so, settling herself onto a cushion and doing her best to tuck her feet underneath her.

"Your... offer." Mnemach reached back and unbound the ties of her necklace, removing it and setting it aside on the edge of the bed pit, then began on her bracelets and anklets. "You are the second person in thirty years to come to me, petitioning for an alliance."

Veronique didn't quite know how to respond to that. Mnemach was clearly determined not to make a single thing easy, or direct. She supposed she should have expected that much. "And did that request please you?"

The matriarch leaned back into her pillows and regarded Veronique steadily, unblinkingly, for such a long moment that the Brujah woman could barely restrain her discomfort. Finally, Mnemach replied, "I do not think you truly know what it is that you propose. Saviarre is not an opponent matched to an infant such as yourself. What you ask is for me and mine to take a risk whose benefits, if it succeeds, will hardly redound to our credit, and whose consequences, if it fails, will likely fall on us with all force."

"Not so, Dame Mnemach." Veronique kept her tone even and steady. "I will not ask you or your people to take any risk that I myself am not willing to face—that the rest of my allies—"

"The Courts of Love are not your allies, girl. Salianna"—the name came off Mnemach's lips with undisguised contempt—"is not your ally. She will use you until there is no further advantage to be gained from you, and then she will cast you aside, as she has with so many young Cainites before you."

"I know that they aren't my truest allies—there is no friendship between us. But our arrangement is one of mutual benefit... and I have my own safeguards against treachery from Queen Salianna." Veronique leaned closer. "I do not trust her—but I need her assistance. I know that you cannot possibly trust her—but do you distrust her less than Countess Saviarre, or more?"

"Point," Mnemach allowed, dipping her head slowly, once. "Salianna and I have no love for each other, and we never shall. But Saviarre and I have long been at war, and there can be no peace between us that will not end in blood."

"I suspected that much was true." Veronique blinked and deliberately looked away to break the sudden tug of attraction Mnemach's quiet passion gave her. "I do not ask this lightly, Dame Mnemach. I will be honest and say that I do not believe that any effort I mount against Saviarre will succeed without your aid. Saviarre is too well entrenched at Prince Alexander's side. Her will and his are too inseparable as far as this city is concerned."

"Do you know what power it is that she holds over him?"

Veronique looked up quickly. Mnemach's expression was even more opaque than Valerian's best diplomatic mask. She replied warily, "No, I do not. It is... not a secret I have been able to uncover." Then, more reluctantly, "Queen Salianna suspects that Saviarre obtained possession of the Rose of Lorraine, and is somehow using it to weaken him, to bend him to her will."

"I take it that you do not share that belief." It was not a question.

Veronique answered anyway, almost in spite of herself. "No. It seems... unlikely that Alexander would succumb to such a crude attempt at manipulation. Whatever his faults were before Saviarre came to Paris, he was not a fool, nor was he a weakling."

"No, he was not that." Something in Mnemach's tone caught

Veronique's ear. She sounded almost regretful. "Alexander is no longer the man he once was—I do not know that he will ever be that man again. But you are correct in your assessment that Saviarre lies at the root of his decline and if anything but further misfortune is to come to Paris, to my city, she must be removed, and be made to pay for the crimes she has committed against my people."

"I ask only for your help in bringing her to that justice, Dame Mnemach."

Mnemach chuckled, low in her throat. "You will ask for more than that before all is said and done, Brujah, but I will permit you your illusions for now. Very well. You shall have your alliance and my assistance in bringing low our mutual enemy, Countess Saviarre. We shall define the specifics of our arrangement at a later time...."

Veronique felt a tension that she hadn't been aware of easing out of her shoulders.

"But, for now, I require a symbol of your commitment to this effort." Mnemach showed her fangs in a smile that entirely failed to reassure Veronique. "In the warrens, we seal our pacts in blood."

"You wish me to drink of you?" Veronique was very grateful that that came out steadily.

"I do not ask you to do anything that I am not willing to do," Mnemach replied serenely—and tore open her own wrist in a single swift motion. The sharp, salty-sweet scent of her blood filled the air, rich and heady. Dark droplets, black in the dim light of the fire, rolled down her wrist and hand and spattered across her thigh.

Veronique watched it fall, unable to speak either to acquiesce or deny, her fangs straining in her jaw involuntarily. Her mind, for an instant, was totally blank of conscious thought or objection, mesmerized. A small voice remarked, in the back of her mind, that what Mnemach desired of her—a single drink, to seal the pact—was not unreasonable. The danger was high, and the Nosferatu had no reason to trust in her or her good intentions. She reached out and took Mnemach's hand in her own, dark blood flowing over their fingers, and lifted the bloody wound to her lips, touched her tongue to its sweetness, and drank, sinking her own fangs into the matriarch's flesh. Dimly, around the vast pleasure drinking of Mnemach gave to her, Veronique felt the Nosferatu taking her free hand, drawing it to her own lips. Mnemach's fangs pierced her and the pleasure rose even higher, filling her until it washed away anything but the pulsing, throbbing awareness of her own ecstasy. It seemed to go on forever.

It didn't last long enough. When she came back to herself, Veronique was lying curled next to Mnemach, pillowed in cushions and naked but for a linen-lined bed fur, the Nosferatu matriarch stretched out languidly at her side, smiling like a cat with cream dripping off its whiskers. Mnemach reached out, and caressed the loose tendrils of pale hair from Veronique's brow.

"Rest, Brujah. We'll continue our negotiations later."

Chapter Five

To Brother Anatole of Paris, shepherd of the flock of Biere, greetings.

I apologize for the length of time between this letter and my last correspondence. Events have been moving quickly here in Paris and I have been much engaged in the activities of my trade. I write you this night to request a meeting, as soon as you are able. We have much to discuss.

By my hand,

—Veronique d'Orleans

To Lady Rosamund d'Islington, Ambassador of the Rose, greetings and felicitations.

I pen these words to you with the greatest possible satisfaction, and with the best possible news for you and for our endeavor. As per our meeting, I sought assistance regarding your embassy from Lord Valerian, who graciously accepted my request to intercede on your behalf directly with Prince Alexander. That intercession occurred last night, and Lord Valerian reported to me its success—Prince Alexander has accepted the assurances of your patron, Queen Salianna, your sire Queen Isouda, Lord Valerian, and myself that your mission is of wholly diplomatic nature intended to foster renewed relations between the Grand Court and the Courts of Love.

You shall, I expect, be receiving official notice from Lord Valerian as representative of the Grand Court in the next few nights. Do not ask how Lord Valerian accomplished this, for I do not possess detailed knowledge of the particulars. My sources suggest that Lord Valerian *and the prince met behind closed doors for several hours, and that Countess Saviarre was not present at the proceedings, being entirely involved in an issue of some domestic importance that Lord Valerian kindly brought to her attention. We must remember to thank him accordingly.*

By my own hand,

—*Veronique d'Orleans*

Snow was falling the night Anatole arrived to answer Veronique's request for a meeting personally, bringing with him his adopted daughter Zoë, to the delight of the rest of the female residents of the house, along with several ghoul attendants to carry out various shopping errands while they were in the city. The servants of the house set up two extra pallets in Veronique's light-proofed bedchamber for Anatole and Zoë and made the men comfortable with hot spiced wine and good soup and the promise of a warm place of their own to sleep when they wished it. Girauda and Alainne quickly took in Zoë, whom they wanted to measure for a new dalmatic and to find a spare pair of shoes, perhaps one that one of the other girls was willing to give up. The little Ravnos girl kept shooting Veronique desperate looks from where she was held prisoner on the opposite side of the sitting room, sitting on a bench in nothing but her chemise while Girauda examined how her threadbare garment was sewn together and Alainne made the arrangements for a hot bath. Occasional bits of argument floated to Veronique and Anatole where they sat together, on the far side of the room, conversing quietly.

"…I don't have to go upstairs for the bath, do I…?"

"Oh no, dear. We'll have the tub and water brought down here; that's what we do with Veronique…."

"Good." There was depthless relief in Zoë's voice.

"She thrives," Veronique observed, with a little smile, turning back from the glance she cast across the room. Zoë was a tiny thing, but she had a temper that doubled her size and capacity for generating havoc, and it was sometimes quite easily set off. Tonight, she was displaying vast patience. "She is much more at peace with herself than she was when first I met her."

"She has found her peace in the hand of the Lord," Anatole replied, a smile of his own lurking at the corners of his mouth. "Though, as with everyone, she does suffer her little lapses. It was good of you to accommodate us on such short notice, Veronique."

"It's no trouble at all—I'm glad you came so quickly in this wretched weather. And it's no hardship on my household to shelter you, so put it from your mind." She drew a sheaf of parchments from the lockbox at her feet. "I'm afraid that I have little good news to impart."

He accepted the papers and glanced at them cursorily. "Saviarre?"

"Saviarre. The countess appears to be setting her pieces in motion on several fronts. I do not doubt that she'll be moving against you as soon as she practically can." Veronique leaned closer. "I'm half-surprised she hasn't acted already."

"I suspect that she has." Veronique looked up at the cool deliberation in Anatole's voice. "St. Lys's rabble gave up hunting us quickly enough. Brother Gerasimos thinks that they may have headed south, into Toulouse." He paused. "But the defenders of the camp have reported seeing spies lurking on the fringes and suspect that someone has been tracking the movements of our foragers all winter."

Veronique let her sight expand. Her physical vision went gray and indistinct, human forms rendered into flat, dimensionless shapes limned in a flickering nimbus of color. Anatole's was scarred, threaded through with fresh black stains that bracketed the steady, translucent colors of his aura like the framing in a stained-glass window. He was extraordinarily focused tonight. The flame-like rippling that usually characterized his aura, a sign of the unbridled passions and ineffable visions that ran through Malkavian blood, was much muted. She released her sight before he realized what her momentary silence actually meant. "Then it's likely that she knows where you are."

"Yes." Tranquilly.

"Do you agree," she asked carefully, "that something must

be done? It was no minor pawn of hers that you removed from the board when you brought down St. Lys—it was, quite literally, one of her bishops. She'll not overlook that. You've proven yourself too dangerous, too capable of dealing with threats, both Cainite and mortal."

"Do you know what I've always hated most about politics among our kind, Veronique?"

The question caught her by surprise. "What?

"Chess metaphors," he replied, succinctly. "You should try to meet Lucita of Aragon one night—I think you'd get along almost abnormally well. And, yes, I do understand what you mean. You think it's becoming too dangerous for us to remain this close to Paris, do you not?"

Veronique opened her mouth, and closed it without saying anything. Finally, after a moment of considering whether or not to laugh, she decided to stay on topic. "Yes, as a matter of fact, I do believe that. Believe me when I say that I don't want to see any harm come to you or to Zoë or to your flock. I think you should seriously consider abandoning your efforts here for the time being and seek safer climes, at least until Saviarre's outrage spends itself a bit."

"That may or may not happen any time in the next thousand years or so."

"That's true. But I suspect if you sit still and leave yourself a target for her outrage, it won't wait much past the spring thaw to present itself in its fullest flower."

Now it was his turn to fall silent as he considered. He paged through the reports that she had handed him, scanning their contents slowly, his expression thoughtful. Evidently, something had caught his eye. "Do you consider the author of these reports a reliable source?"

They had come, in fact, from Aimeric de Cabaret. "Yes. He has lived in the south, all his life and unlife—when it comes to the situation there, he knows precisely of what he speaks." She raised a hand to forestall the question she saw forming. "He is not a follower of the Shining Blood himself, nor is he particularly sympathetic to their cause. He is a diplomat in service to Queen Esclarmonde the Black and, while Queen Esclarmonde has always been sympathetic to the bonhommes, she has no love in her heart for the Heretics who hide behind them."

"Thus one of the bases for her alliance with the Prince of Béziers, if I recall aright."

Veronique was surprised again. Anatole rarely paid much overt attention to the politics that went on around him and didn't appear overly interested in the details at any time. "Yes, that's true. Queen Esclarmonde and Prince Eon de l'Étoile made peace over their mutual contempt for the Heresy, among other things, I don't doubt."

"Then you believe this report is truthful when it says that the survivors of St. Lys's little court have been sighted in the south, and that they may be... congealing around a new leader?" Anatole looked up from the papers, intensely bright eyes narrowed at the thought.

"I think it's more than possible. The south has always been a breeding ground for the Heresy—even now, it still is, despite the crusade and the wars. It has too many adherents among the Cainite lords, is too well rooted to completely extirpate in one blow. And the Heretics are much more faithfully supported in the south than were St. Lys and his followers here in Paris." She reached over and tapped the page Anatole was reading. "I'm certain that at least a few of the higher-ranking leaders of the Heresy managed to avoid losing their heads, and any one of those could become the center of a revived Heretical Church, if permitted to do so. Queen Esclarmonde and the Prince of Béziers do not intend to allow that, but they will need more experienced assistance, more force, than they can currently bring to bear on the situation. At least while simultaneously attempting to defend their domains from other threats."

"You're suggesting that I go south to help them," Anatole observed.

"I'm suggesting that you go south to help them, and help yourself, as well. I have been in diplomatic contact with Queen Esclarmonde and Prince Eon de l'Étoile already. They stand ready to offer you and yours sanctuary in the south, in their domains, in return for your assistance in rooting out the Heretics from their lands." Veronique paused and let him consider that for a moment, then continued. "Even as unsettled as the south is just now, you'll be safer there, under the direct protection of a prince rather than existing at the sufferance of one."

"Dare I ask what you expect to gain from this?"

That question didn't surprise her at all. Anatole could be nearly as brutally direct as she herself when he wanted to be.

"Advantage against Saviarre."

"Mmm."

"Well, you asked."

"That I did. I don't suppose I can blame you for being a political animal." The corners of his mouth turned back in a wry smile. "I cannot answer you on this proposal tonight—I must consult with Zoë, and the rest of my people, before any decision can be made. Is that sufficient for now?"

"Yes. I didn't expect you to answer at once, anyway." Across the room, a wooden screen was being erected to preserve Zoë's modesty at her bath. Veronique raised her voice slightly. "Is the water hot enough, Zoë?"

"Oh, yes." The girl sounded as though she were simply melting with the pleasure of being both warm and clean simultaneously.

"Good. Is there anything else you desire while you're here?"

Zoë's response was prompt. "Can Anatole have a bath, too? And a haircut?"

Veronique turned back to him just in time to catch him blinking, an expression of completely Anatole-like befuddlement on his face. She couldn't hold in a smile. "I think that can be arranged…."

Despite the prevailing foul weather, messages flowed southwards to Foix and Béziers, carried by messengers unconcerned by physical privation. Dame Mnemach was entirely correct in her belief that Veronique would ask for more than just an alliance before all was said and done. Nosferatu messenger-beasts, bred for intelligence and endurance, made their way south via wing and waterway, carrying diplomatic correspondence between far-flung warrens, invoking the assistance of kin to kin. Nosferatu couriers followed close behind, bearing more detailed messages destined for hands in the mountain fortress of Queen Esclarmonde and the reconstituted city of Prince Eon de l'Etoile.

They took even greater pains than usual not to be noticed, since the spies employed by Countess Saviarre to watch even the most innocuous movements of her presumed enemies were out in force, ferreting away in the effort to keep their demanding mistress happy. The activities of Veronique d'Orleans had dominated their efforts of late, but it could never be safely presumed that no attention was directed towards Mnemach and her kin—they had, after all, been enemies of the countess much longer. Saviarre's irritation with Veronique was fresher, though, and more recently aggravated by her diplomatic assignations with Valerian and the Courts of Love, and by Veronique's continued support of the lunatic prophet Anatole and his band of malcontents. Veronique seemed quite content to let Saviarre's baleful eye fall on her, and let the witch try to puzzle out exactly what she was up to at any given time. There was no way to avoid it, and so Veronique tried to make it work to her advantage, drawing Saviarre's various eyes with a flurry of minor projects, long-delayed correspondence dispatched to Hamburg, preparations for the Bishop de Navarre's midwinter gathering, and other activities that mostly kept her close to home.

All the important correspondence—letters to Lord Valerian and Lady Rosamund, communications with Dame Mnemach, and the messages to Queen Esclarmonde and Prince Eon—went out through stringently secured means. In less than a month the first courier arrived in Foix, bearing tidings that he would yield only to the queen herself. Less than a week after that, the second courier made his way into Béziers.

Aimeric de Cabaret was, for a change, alone in his private suite of rooms, and enjoying the opportunity to be both alone and private for the first time in months. Béziers was a beehive, constantly busy, and Eon de l'Etoile, damn his eyes, enjoyed being in the middle of it the way pigs enjoyed wallowing in mud. Only in the midst of profound, barely contained disorder was the Prince of Béziers truly happy; only when there was some problem to solve or some crisis to manage was he actually close to being at peace. Aimeric, who had witnessed and participated in significant amounts of disorder prior to his arrival in Béziers, found Prince Eon's boundless enthusiasm for trouble almost exhausting, and looked forward to the peace and quiet that the deepest parts of winter would bring, even in the more clement south.

Tonight, there was a fire crackling in Aimeric's hearth to drive away the chill and damp, and nothing at all pressing to tend to. Prince Eon was locked in his office with his seneschal, going over the state of the exchequer, making certain that finances were flowing as expected and projects were proceeding at an acceptable pace. Crepin, the sheriff, was in the field with his men, hunting someone he could destroy with impunity, his tolerance for diplomatic solutions having spent itself some months earlier. The Mouse was keeping much to herself of late, tracking developments both in Béziers and among the city's neighbors through the reports of her spies. She expected something to break loose before winter was fully past, some move on the part of the Tremere of Narbonne to oust Eon and gain the favor of Prince Alexander of Paris for schooling his errantly independent vassal. Aimeric didn't doubt that possibility one bit, but was also willing to acknowledge his limitations. A sorcerer he wasn't, and he didn't know any who could claim the title; Foix had no official diplomatic relationship with the Tremere warlocks, desired none, and thwarted their efforts whenever possible. Béziers was as secure as their efforts could reasonably make it. If sorcery took the field against them, they would have to adapt to that eventuality, as well.

Aimeric's harp rested against his shoulder, and he caressed an idle, formless melody from its strings, trying his best to think of nothing but the music, the flow of note into note, the action of sword-callused fingertips on taut strings. It had been a long time, an unpleasantly long time, since he last managed to shake away the distractions of the world completely, the demands of politics and his position, and lose himself in a pleasure so simple and so fundamental to all his inner peace. A pretty, clever melody. A well-trained voice singing counterpoint. His eyes drifted closed as the song began to take shape.

Someone scratched at his chamber door.

He laid his hand across the strings to still them, mastered the surge of irritation that crept up his spine, and called in his most pleasantly even tone, "Enter."

It was one of the Mouse's young pages, a quiet, levelheaded boy. He bobbed a quick bow as he entered. "My apologies, Ambassador, and my Lady Mouse's respects. She asks that you join her in the rookery as soon as you can."

"The rookery? Has a message come in?" Aimeric rose and laid his harp in its place of honor, on its own cushioned bench next to his chair.

"I'm sorry, Ambassador, but I don't know. She sent me off to fetch you straightaway after she checked the birds, though."

"Then I suppose I shouldn't keep her waiting any longer."

The Mouse's rookery lay on the uppermost floor of the haven's single, squat defensive tower, in the corner that offered the fewest advantages when it came to observation or attack. At her request, the house ghouls had constructed a modest wooden hutch in that corner, sufficient for one or two full-grown adults to stand out of the wind and weather, and filled with innumerable perches and ledges to accommodate her collection of avian spies and messengers. The Mouse was, her name notwithstanding, extremely fond of birds: Her rookery contained crows and owls, and she kept doves and songbirds caged in her private rooms. She kept tidbits in her pockets to feed them and regularly called mice and rats to their doom, not only to reward her own pets, but also to deprive prying eyes of their rodent agents. When Aimeric reached the top of the tower, lit by a pitch-fed brazier sputtering in the light, misty rain, she had one of her favorites balanced on her wrist, the giant crow picking breadcrumbs off her palm. It looked up as he approached, let out a raucous squawk, and fluttered away to perch out of the wind.

The Mouse turned to face him, wrapped in her usual layers of fine brown wool, hut with her mask, rather than a scarf, in place. Tonight she chose to look like a wizened old granddame, deep-set dark eyes drooping at the corners, prim little mouth lined with wrinkles that showed her no stranger to smiles.

Aimeric did not believe she had ever shown him even the slightest reflection of her true face. "I apologize for my peremptory summons, Ambassador, but I thought you would like to see this without a dozen eyes watching."

She extended her hand, turned it palm upward, and opened her fingers. A tiny metal message capsule lay there, leather ties still attached, cap stamped with an unusual marking.

Aimeric frowned. "I thank you for your summons, Milady Mouse, but is this not unusual? That is not the mark you showed me, which represents Béziers." He spoke Latin, a language that they shared with each other but few others in the city.

The Mouse replied in that same tongue. "It is not. This is the sigil that represents Paris. It came in tied to my pet," she gestured slightly at the giant crow, who managed to look pleased with himself, "and he was gone from the rookery for less than a day."

Aimeric reached out and accepted the message capsule. "You think he was summoned to carry a message for someone close by?"

"I think it possible," the Mouse replied neutrally. "Read it, and tell me what you think."

He removed the top of the capsule and let the tightly rolled slip of parchment inside fall out onto his palm, stepping more fully inside the rookery to get out of the worst of the wind and the mist, and to take advantage of the candle the Mouse had lit. It was four lines of closely written text, the strokes so fine that it looked as if they were inked in place with the tip of a pin. The corner of his mouth twitched slightly as he read, and realized from whom the note must have come.

"Oh, yes... This did, indeed, come from Paris," he murmured, hoping the depth of his amusement didn't show in his voice.

"What does it mean?" She demanded, sounding puzzled. "When I read it, it sounded like poetry—and bad poetry, at that."

Aimeric snickered. The Mouse looked at him, hard, questioningly. That was too much. The snicker turned into a chuckle, and from there into a full-blown laugh. Béziers's mistress of spies rolled her eyes heavenward, and waited patiently for him to calm himself, and regain his powers of speech.

"Ah—I'm sorry, milady." Aimeric blinked a tear of mirth off his lashes. "It is bad poetry. Horrifically bad poetry. And the only person who would have cause to remind me of it currently dwells in Paris." He held the strip of paper up so that it fell open, lengthwise. "It is also a request for a meeting. I suspect there's a Parisian messenger somewhere in the city, waiting for a response."

"Are you certain?" The Mouse frowned, and took the scrap from his fingers, scrutinizing it carefully. "It might be a trick—a trap of some kind. Crepin's hunting the Brothers of the Black Mountain, but even he can't account for all of them. There might be another assassin still in the city, trying to lure you out."

"That is not beyond the realm of possibility, I admit. However, what makes me think this message is genuine is this: My idiot brother does not know this joke, or why these words would mean anything to me beyond acute personal humiliation, but my friend in Paris does." That, and the pattern of letters in the hidden cipher, which read, *Send reply*. But he didn't tell her that; there were, after all, limits to his trust. "May I borrow one of your birds, milady?"

Aimeric was much more direct in his correspondence than Veronique had been in hers. The message he sent out, tied in a protective capsule to the leg of the same crow, was short: *Name the place & time*. The reply arrived the next evening. *The beggars' court, tomorrow night. Come alone.*

Eon de l'Etoile was not entirely pleased with Aimeric's determination to follow through on the invitation. "This isn't very wise, you know," said the Prince of Béziers.

Aimeric laced his hands together behind his head and raised his arms, letting his page get at the laces of his gambeson, fine-linked chain chiming gently as he moved. "I realize that, milord. But it's not the first unwise thing I've ever done, and I seriously doubt that it will be the last."

"It will be if someone takes this gilt-edged opportunity to remove your reckless head from your shoulders, Aimeric! At least let one of the men follow you—if nothing else, he can raise an alarm if you're attacked." Eon thought Aimeric was taking the entire situation far too lightly; it hadn't helped that he'd gone around with an impish twinkle in his eyes for two whole nights after receiving the message. Aimeric de Cabaret in a wicked good humor was a dangerous thing, indeed. "How can you be certain that this letter is from the Antasian ambassador? Wouldn't she use a more regular means of contacting us than this?"

Variations of that question had been on the lips of every member of Eon de l'Etoile's inner circle since the arrival of the initial communication. Aimeric had answered them all in variations of the same way. "Milord, there's no way I can explain this to you in terms that you'd accept as reasonable. Veronique d'Orleans knows me well—better, it seems, than my own brother does. She knew that I'd know what she meant by that verse; it's an old jest between us." He paused as he slipped his surcoat over his head, dark blue with the white rose of a Toreador diplomat in the center of his chest. "And, as for regular means, it would very much depend on her situation. If she thought a regular courier stood a good chance of being intercepted or suborned, she might very well engage in less traditional ways of making sure her message reached us intact. The woman is no fool, and if half of what we've heard about the situation in Paris is true, she may be in some danger herself."

"You trust her." It was not a question.

"At least as much as I trust you, milord." On went the sword-belt, cinched tight, the weapon itself lying against his thigh; the message had not, after all, said to come unarmed. And while some might call him reckless, he was rarely called a fool by anyone but family. "Possibly more."

Eon closed his eyes and sighed. "Very well. I won't forbid you to do this, nor will I interfere in it. Have a care."

"Of course." Aimeric turned and bowed with a flourish to his prince and theoretical captor. "May I have a brotherly kiss for good luck?"

To his mild surprise, Eon actually did lean in and kiss him on each cheek. "For good luck. Come and go safely."

Aimeric smiled puckishly. "Wait up. I'll be home soon."

In the north, it snowed. In the higher elevations of the Pyrenees, it snowed—Foix was an icebound boring hell most of the winter. In the southern lowlands, it rained. Béziers and the surrounding Bitterois region, located close to both the River Orb and the coast of the sea, enjoyed relatively mild weather, year-round. Tonight, the sky was not so much raining as breathing out a heavy, cool mist. The air was thick with a fog that drank light. Aimeric carried with him a well-shuttered lamp and the capacity for amazingly good night-vision, both of which he made use of during his stroll down the dark city streets. His reassurances to Eon de l'Etoile notwithstanding, he was not entirely free of doubt or trepidation.

Not a month before, a particularly skillful and bloody-minded assassin had managed to penetrate the security around the prince's haven, and it was only with the golden counte-nance of Fortuna smiling down that he'd been caught before anyone's head had rolled. The killer had been an agent of the Brothers of the Black Mountain, a band of dedicated malcon-tents and staunch supporters of Queen Esclarmonde, who had taken the sudden peace breaking out between Foix and Béziers as a personal affront. They were also, to Aimeric's vast annoy-ance, led by his own brother-in-blood Lozois, who seemed to take Aimeric's part in bringing about that little miracle of diplo-macy as an even greater personal affront. Aimeric had been the specific target of the assassin, though the stubborn idiot was also instructed, if the chance fell into his hands, to murder the Prince of Béziers or any other member of the prince's inner cir-cle. Sheriff Crepin was beside himself with outrage, and a rather unpleasant example was made of the would-be assassin quite promptly. As it stood, even the Mouse had no clear idea of how many other such partisans might be lurking in or near the city, or when they might be planning to strike, or what targets they might attack when and if they did make a move. She continued to search out that information, and had mobilized a small army of spies, informants and agents to comb the city and bring her any significant drop of news.

And yet a foreign messenger managed to hide in the city,

and contact them through their own beast-spies. It was, without a doubt, a worrisome proposition. Aimeric permitted a certain corner of his mind to be concerned about the unpleasant possibilities and to prepare to deal with them if the situation fell out that way, but a more optimistic part of him was inclined to doubt that this was an elaborate trap. For one thing, whatever sense of humor Lozois possessed had clearly died a horrible, screaming death years before, along with his sense of perspective and any grasp he might have once possessed on the nature of politics. For another, his brother couldn't tell good poetry from wretched immature doggerel, and wouldn't know the specific verse that the message contained, in any case. Aimeric had personally made certain all the copies of that particular embarrassment had gone into a festival fire, except the one that Veronique d'Orleans had insisted on keeping. Its invocation, here and now, led him to believe that she was, indeed, at the root of the message.

The beggars' court lay behind Béziers's newly rebuilt and reconsecrated cathedral, dedicated to the city's patron saint, Mary Magdalene. Not as grand as the building it replaced, it nonetheless expressed the same values of Christian charity that its predecessor had. The rear courtyard was a place for the city's destitute to come and beg for a scrap of bread or a bowl of soup, and to come for shelter from the worst of the winter weather, when that weather tended foul. By night, it was nonetheless mostly abandoned by all but the truly poverty-stricken. Widows told dark tales concerning the ghosts of the unhallowed dead of Béziers, those struck down by violence within the walls of their own church, returning to the place where it used to stand to cry out for vengeance against their killers. Aimeric could almost see their faces, twisted in howls of grief and lamentation, etched in the interplay of mist and dim lamplight.

He crept into the courtyard, slipping around the corner, clinging close to the church wall, and darkening his lamp. Without that minimal light, and with the moon hidden behind the clouds, it was nearly pitch black. He stood still for a moment, letting his vision sharpen until he could make out the dim suggestion of shapes, lighter shades of darkness, and he had a sense of the court's dimensions. Even so, he couldn't tell if any of those shapes were another man-shaped being. He stepped away from the wall and moved into the approximate center of the open court, stepping as quietly as possible, the gentle ringing of his mail muffled by surcoat and cloak. He took a breath and whistled, a simple tune, to which he'd once set some fairly wretched poetry.

There was something moving in front of him. He set the lamp down and, beneath his cloak, gripped the hilt of his sword a bit more firmly, prepared to move quickly if the situation seemed to warrant it. A figure limped out of the enveloping fog, wrapped in the distinctive clothing of a leper and leaning heavily on a staff. Aimeric could hear joints crackling uncomfortably with every labored, hitching motion, and he felt a momentary stab of pity for any wretch immortal so afflicted.

When the figure spoke, its voice was, despite the rheumatically twisted body it was attached to, low and clear and young. "Aimeric lo Chansonneur de Cabaret, Knight-Ambassador of the Rose?"

"I am he," Aimeric replied, faintly amused at the use of his full name as a recognition code.

"I bear tidings from the north, for yourself and for your prince." Aimeric tensed slightly as the messenger reached among his clothing and extracted from somewhere inside those enveloping robes a packet wrapped in oilskin and bound in rough twine ties. The package changed hands without ceremony.

"Is a reply expected?" Aimeric asked quietly, once he'd stashed the package inside his own surcoat.

"I have been instructed to wait for one, if you request it." The courier's voice barely rose above a whisper, hardly enough to stir the air between them.

"Stay. The prince knows you are here—I will request that he waive formal presentation, to preserve your anonymity. This area is—"

"Ground free from violence. Yes, I know. I will not feed here, nor will I kill when I do so elsewhere."

"Do you know where the prince's haven is located?" The courier murmured assent. "Haunt the neighborhood near there.

I will request that you be permitted to hunt and shelter there until our business is complete, and it will be easier to contact you."

"I thank you for your consideration."

"I thank you for your service. Go carefully."

"And you, Ambassador."

To His Highness, Eon de l'Etoile, Prince of Béziers,

Eon's eyes automatically skipped the four lines of honorific flattery that customarily opened any piece of official diplomatic correspondence aimed at him.

I give you greetings from Paris and write to you in response to your request for my assistance and in the hope that I may offer it to you. It was wise for you to refrain from sending a personal envoy to plead your case with His Highness, Prince Alexander, as I fear such an envoy would either be turned away or suffer immediate arrest and be held as a hostage against your good and obedient future behavior. The civil unrest and associated religious hysteria of recent years has led the prince's advisor, the Countess Saviarre, to take a more active hand in the governance of the city, and I fear that she bears you no love at all, and has possibly poisoned the prince's mind against you.

Eon read aloud to Aimeric and the Mouse, having already perused the document twice himself, and looked up with a decidedly wry expression. "Well, we knew that was coming."

"Saviarre's malice is no small obstacle to overcome, my Prince," the Mouse whispered. "Even before the unrest, she ruled Paris in all hut name, if my kin in the warren there are to be believed."

Aimeric responded dryly to that, "Believe it, Milady Mouse. The woman is subtle, but not that subtle—I visited Paris twice, before the war, and even then she was spinning her webs. I was personally surprised that she only sent Valerian out of the country instead of finding some excuse to have him killed. He was the only person I met there who did not hold his official position in the court because he had, in some way, acquiesced to her will."

Eon nodded in acknowledgement of both those points and read on.

All is not lost, however. Lord Ambassador Valerian's return to the city has kept certain avenues of diplomacy open to us, and he has shown me that he is more than capable of evading Countess Saviarre's prejudice when the situation seems to warrant. I do not doubt that he will be of invaluable assistance when it comes to normalizing relations between Paris and Béziers. He remains dedicated to the service of the city and his prince, and tends, to my eye, to believe that both are best served by promoting peaceful resolutions to conflicts rather than persecuting war. At your request, I will inquire with him on your behalf.

My personal advice in this situation is that you must, in some way, ease the sting of your apparent "treachery" (Countess Saviarre's term for your decision to pursue peace with Queen Esclarmonde, not my own) by making a gesture of continued solidarity and good will toward Paris. As you may be aware, Paris spent much of the last few years convulsed in religious upheaval, at the center of which lay the Bishop Antoine de St. Lys, a powerful and well-placed proponent of the Heresy of the Shining Blood, and Brother Anatole de Paris, an ashen priest of significantly less heretical nature and leanings. The debates between the two, along with sundry other happenings of an apparently occult nature, spawned considerable strife that only began die down when the Bishop St. Lys was destroyed. Brother Anatole and his followers remain encamped outside of Paris, where they remain the focus of Countess Saviarre's malice, as well. I cannot directly prove a material link between Countess Saviarre and the late Bishop St. Lys, but it is my personal suspicion that he was, in some way, the countess's agent.

I do not believe that she herself subscribes to the doctrine of the Heretics, but they were certainly useful as a political and social lever, a tool that is no longer available to her. My sources suggest to me that the remainder of St. Lys's particular "congregation" fled south into the

*Languedoc and may very well be seeking a new bishop or other eccle-
siastical authority within their faith to attach themselves to in service.
Brother Anatole and his band would very much like to pursue these
malcontents, but they would prefer not to come south unless they can
be assured of a civilized welcome in a domain that does not resent their
presence, and where the rulers are of a mind to support their goals.*

*It is my understanding, Prince Eon, that you yourself have dili-
gently pursued the destruction of the Cainite Heresy within the lands
you claim as your own.*

Eon looked up and speared Aimeric with a probing look.

Aimeric inclined his eyebrows slightly in response. "Don't
look at me like that, milord—it's not as though you've been
unclear about your dislike of the Heresy, you know."

The Mouse chuckled softly.

*It is therefore my suggestion that Your Highness permit the repu-
tation that your past actions have garnered to work for you in this
case, as well. Brother Anatole's band is, from the perspective of Paris,
little better than a pack of brigands squatting in the royal territories;
they are barely acknowledged or tolerated, even after their decisive
action against the Heresy in the city. Prince Alexander has refused
them legitimacy time and time again, arid yet they refuse to go away so
long as they feel their mission in Paris is incomplete. My suggestion is
this: You may help resolve a situation that Prince Alexander considers
unacceptable, but which he is unable or unwilling to resolve himself, by
inviting Brother Anatole's band to take up arms and spread the word
against the Heresy in your dominions. Brother Anatole's band is relatively compact in size, with a good number who are not Cainites at all
but ghoul and mortal hangers-on who provide for the band's needs. By
this action, Your Highness shows himself to still be a friend to Paris,
willing to assist a fellow sovereign in need, and that there is no personal hostility toward Paris in your diplomatic attempts to secure the
borders of your own domain. It also gamers Your Highness the manpower and skills of a group of dedicated enemies of the Cainite Heresy,*

who have accumulated a great deal of practical experience in hunting the Heretics, as well as diagnosing and diffusing their sometimes subtle influence.

I have dispatched this communication south with a courier who has been instructed to wait for Your Highness's reply, if that is your wish. I stand ready to continue acting on Your Highness's behalf in Paris even if this proposal does not meet with your approval. I request only that Your Highness bear in mind that the winter wanes quickly, and if a proposal for a peaceful resolution to the tension between Paris and Béziers is not on the table before the spring thaw arrives in the north, a peaceful resolution may by that time be impossible.

By my own hand,

—Lady Veronique d'Orleans

"I have instructed the messenger to bide here in Béziers," Aimeric remarked into the silence that fell once Eon de l'Etoile finished reading aloud.

"Thank you, Ambassador." Eon laid the letter on the table between them for the others to peruse as they wished. They were in the inner circle's meeting chamber, a room long enough for him to pace unobstructed while thinking matters through. He began pacing at once. "Well, that was a message none of us wanted to hear, but by which we shouldn't be surprised.... Your thoughts?"

The Mouse and Aimeric glanced at one another, and Aimeric let her take the lead. The little Nosferatu woman picked up the letter, and quickread its pages. Straining a little, she managed to raise her voice above a whisper, a step she only took when she wished her words to have more impact. "I think this woman has a better grasp on matters in Paris than any of us could possibly claim. Even myself. The probability is very high that Countess Saviarre will make a summer project of destroying either this Brother Anatole and his followers or us, and possibly both. There is also the possibility that she will invest her effort in destroying Brother Anatole and leave us alone for the time being—but I doubt she will permit any diplomatic gestures we make towards Paris to succeed while she is engaged on another front." She coughed, roughly, and her voice dropped back to its accustomed level. "There is some degree of danger, no matter what choice we make, my Prince. There is no way to avoid it. It is a risk we chose to take when we opened diplomatic relations with Queen Esclarmonde."

"I think," Aimeric added calmly, "that the proposal is not without merit. There are risks, but there are also significant gains—this ashen priest," he pronounced the words with only trace amounts of distaste, "has apparently made himself loathsome to the Heresy by virtue of both word and action. No doubt many of his followers also possess useful skills and knowledge in that regard. Coupled with the knowledge of local dangers possessed by the men Queen Esclarmonde and yourself can provide to that enterprise, the force that we could bring to bear against the Heretics would be considerable."

Eon turned and paced back from the door. "And the diplomatic angle with Paris? Do you consider the reasoning there sound, as well?"

Aimeric shrugged slightly. "Honestly, milord? It is literally impossible to tell how Alexander of Paris will react to any overture. I think, however, that offering to remove an irritant that's been galling him for the better part of a decade cannot possibly aggravate him more. As for Countess Saviarre, it is in her best interest that diplomacy fail. We will have to rely on the efforts of our friends in Paris to make certain that it doesn't."

Eon sighed. "It is as you say. We've put ourselves in harm's way, and now we have to hope that others can help us avoid a fatal blow. Not," he smiled wryly, "that I regret that decision at all. I would like to contact this Brother Anatole directly and speak to the man himself before I commit to any course of action. I would also like to contact Lady Veronique and Lord Valerian for more detailed information on how they would present our case for us at the Grand Court. And I suppose we should call Crepin in and ask him what he thinks, as well...."

"Do we have to?" Aimeric and the Mouse demanded, almost simultaneously, then glanced at each other in surprise.

The Prince of Béziers chuckled softly. "Yes, I think we must.

You know how he gets when he thinks politics and diplomacy might end up trumping his chance to break heads." And, so saying, he raised his voice to call for his secretary.

Chapter Six

Veronique already regretted her decision to attend the Bishop de Navarre's garden party a good week before the event was scheduled to take place. Her women were taking the opportunity to harass her about it almost constantly. They'd already remade one of her older kirtles into a somewhat newer style and applied tiny embroidered embellishments to every portion of it that had any chance of being seen. She would be wearing red, it had already been decided, with a matching surcoat whose decoration drew, in the opinion of Girauda and Alainne, flattering attention to her swanlike neck and statuesque figure. It made Veronique wish nightly that she'd chosen to keep her private staff entirely male, since she could count on Sandrin, Philippe and Thierry not to care what she wore, nor try to dress her if they did.

Unfortunately, the women also knew one important fact—Veronique had to bring one of them with her. As an acknowledged ambassador, she enjoyed a certain status within the Grand Court and there were times when she occasionally needed to bow to the proprieties of that status. One of those times was, of course, at a public gathering, such as the bishop's party. As an ambassador, she was entitled to have present one guard and one servant; every ambassador present would come with one guard and one servant. If she didn't, there would likely be gossip, and she rather wanted gossip there to be about anything but her unconventional ways. After consulting with Girauda, to make certain that the older of her two maids would not be offended by her decision, Veronique announced that Alainne would be accompanying her to the bishop's residence, to her very evident delight. Alainne spent the rest of the week making certain that her own best chemise and surcoat were fit for public consumption, and questioning Veronique closely about what her duties would entail once they were there.

Veronique answered those questions as best she could, but kept other, specific aspects of the Bishop de Navarre's previous gatherings to herself.

The entrance to Bishop de Navarre's house was lit with torches and manned by servants, who guided guests to the garden and took their horses to the stable. Perhaps it was simple fortune, or exceptionally good planning on de Navarre's part, but the night was the warmest of the late winter thus far, the air still and above freezing, even next to the river. Even so, the garden was a strange and wonderful sight. Veronique heard Alainne, hanging close at her shoulder, breathe in sharply in surprise as they stepped through the arch that marked the garden gate.

Veronique could practically see how it must look to Alainne's eye: a wide courtyard bordered in jardinières of flowering plants sculpted from ice both clear and colored, dwarf fruit trees hung with ornaments of blown glass lit from within by tiny beeswax candles, metal lamps sculpted in the shapes of legendary beasts burning fragrant oils, a triangle of trestle tables containing polished howls from which liveried servants served chilled viands. And, drifting among it all, tall and beautiful men and women, exquisitely clad in silk and fur in a thousand colors, their hands aglitter with jewels, their eyes bright with predatory interest. Had Veronique not known them all, had she not known the monstrosity so many of her own kind hid behind their wonderful clothing and discriminating tastes, she would have thought them superbly romantic, as well. Alainne let out a sigh of pure delight.

"Lady Veronique d'Orleans, Ambassador to the Grand Court!"

Veronique and her companions, Alainne and Sandrin, entered the garden once they were announced, and she began circulating immediately. Most of the guests were still loitering outside in the garden itself, socializing and sampling the winter fare, despite the open doors to the house in the rear portico. The faces were all familiar, high-blooded locals and diplomats from various neighboring courts who had managed to present themselves and have their credentials accepted before Saviarre began turning envoys away. The primary topic of conversation was, of course, the impending arrival of Lady Rosamund d'Islington, ambassador of the Courts of Love, and the situation surrounding her sudden embassy to Paris. Speculation was naturally running utterly rampant, with the rumors tending toward the wildly inaccurate but entertaining. Veronique, whose involvement in the whole enterprise of getting Rosamund's embassy accepted was known by only a very few, didn't waste the opportunity to drop a few tidbits of her own into the stew, just to watch the information circulate and reshape the way the others considered the situation.

"Alainne, fetch me a bowl." Alainne glanced at her at the peremptory tone she used, but bobbed an obedient curtsey and went to do her mistress's bidding. Veronique caught Sandrin's eye and sent him off after her with a nod.

Veronique kept her back to the trestle tables and concentrated on conversing with the charming young ambassador from Lebach, who was both intelligent and witty. "Milady Veronique," he said, "I think your servant is unwell...."

Alainne returned, white as a sheet, the small ceramic bowl of drink held carefully in both hands, Sandrin's hand on her elbow steadying her. Veronique took some pity, then, and accepted the bowl. "Sandrin, please take Alainne inside to the servants' room so she can warm herself. Thank you."

The servants' room would be another eye-opener for Alainne, who had never attended a gathering of this type before, and if it didn't cure her of any romantic delusions that she might be entertaining about the realities of Cainite existence, nothing would. She let Sandrin lead her off without resistance; Veronique knew she could trust Sandrin to keep his own mouth shut and his eyes open, and to monitor closely the sort of gossip Alainne engaged in once she recovered from the initial shock.

Veronique took a sip of the drink that Alainne had brought her—semi-frozen blood, dark and sweetened with honey and spiced with cloves—and circulated a bit more outside. In one corner, her host held court amid a cluster of the locals, and she drifted in that direction to pay her respects. Bishop de Navarre was in an almost offensively good humor, greeting his guests by their Christian names and commending to them the viands outside and, inside, the musicians and dancing. When she presented herself, he captured her hand and raised it to his lips. "My dear Veronique, it is a pleasure to see you—I was beginning to fear you'd never again grace our society with your shining presence."

"You flatter me, Your Grace." Veronique found him retaining possession of her hand, and tucking it into the crook of his arm as he walked, allowing her no easy escape. She briefly toyed with the notion of ripping his arm off and beating him with it in retaliation.

"Not at all, not at all. Your fair countenance brightens any gathering you choose to favor." His hangers-on all found things to do elsewhere as the two of them strolled along the length of a jardinière filled with flowers whose stems were charcoal black and whose flowers were red as arterial blood; Veronique suspected a clever use of water and Lasombra shadow-weaving. "I admit that I was somewhat amazed when you chose to favor mine, as there has, in the past, been little love lost between us."

Veronique covered her twinge of annoyance by taking a long, deliberate sip from her bowl. "I bear you no ill will, Your Grace, and I will admit, after spending a number of months engaged in nothing but going over my own accounts, a bit of diversion suited my desires. Your invitation fulfilled that need admirably."

He chuckled, his dark eyes glinting with humor. "Now you do flatter me."

"Not at all." She reached out and brushed one cold fingertip over an icy carmine flower petal. "Dare I ask how you achieved this effect?"

"Are you become a Toreador now, milady?"

Veronique recognized the danger in that question and responded accordingly. "Does one need to be a Toreador to appreciate a thing of beauty, milord?"

One dark eyebrow inclined. The Bishop de Navarre, unassisted by any trace of Toreador blood, could not be accused of lacking a taste for the beautiful. Rumor suggested that he preferred beautiful girls and boys for his bedmates and servants; his house and garden were filled with rare and exquisite ornaments of all types; and in his clothing he preferred rich fabrics in expensive colors and heavy jewelry set with stones that caught the light whenever he gestured. "Touché. There have been rumors, my dear, that your services have been engaged on behalf of the Courts of Love, in support of their own ambassador."

Veronique smiled tightly. "Have there? You know how rumors travel, Your Grace—give it long enough, and the Virgin herself will be interceding with Prince Alexander on behalf of the Toreador."

"So you're saying that rumor is untrue?" He watched her, his expression amiably closed beneath his well-trimmed beard and heavy brows, an expressive mask.

Veronique returned the favor, keeping her own expression pleasant as she finished her bowl. "The Toreador have made diplomacy another art they cultivate as diligently as you do your blossoms, milord. What use could they possibly have for me? You'll recall that the Courts of Love chose to honor Hardestadt with their favor a decade ago, not my Lady Antasia. Until they do, there is no reason for my patron's interests and theirs to coincide in any hut the most oblique of fashions."

The bishop's eyes narrowed slightly, then his expression relaxed in a smile as false as his general amiability. "A wise tack to take, milady."

She offered him a suitably deep courtesy. "I have always believed so, milord. With your leave, I believe I will go inside and warm myself. You serve an excellent beverage, as always, but chilling."

"Of course, my dear." He caught her hand and kissed it again, and permitted her to excuse herself.

She disposed of her bowl at the trestle tables, and felt his eyes on her back all the way up the portico stairs, and into the house. A wave of warmth and music greeted her as she entered the lower floor of de Navarre's haven, a small hall cleared of tables, with padded benches and cushioned chairs set against the walls, filled with a handful of Cainites and a double handful of house servants. A fire crackled in the well-tended fireplace, screened to prevent a random spark from leaping out to ignite the fresh rushes and bunches of herbs strewn across the floor, and a group of musicians played behind a wooden screen in the second-floor gallery. Despite the melody the musicians were providing, no one was dancing. All of the Cainites inside were local members of the Grand Court with no particular interest in overflattering their host or somehow currying his favor. One of them was Prince Alexander's younger childe, Sir Olivier, flanked by two bodyguards and one of his favorite ghouls, conversing quietly with whomever addressed him. Veronique moved in that direction.

Sir Olivier had, unlike the eternally boyish Alexander, been Embraced in the full flush of his mature beauty, more than twenty years of age and graced with dark curls and blue eyes prone to laughter. He had the sort of polished courtly graces that eased all of his interactions with the Toreador members of the Grand Court, could dance and play an instrument and ride, could compose a passable attempt at poetry, and could converse wittily and on a broad number of topics. He was, in Veronique's opinion, the most consistently underestimated man in Paris, due primarily to the use that his sire put him to—acting as Prince Alexander's voice and hands in dealing with Cainites and mortals who might balk at taking instruction from a man of Alexander's evident physical youth. Most Cainites of the Grand Court viewed Olivier as a spineless pawn of his Methuselah sire, without an opinion or thought of his own in his pretty, empty head, a prejudice that Veronique did not entirely share. Olivier permitted others to take him too lightly, and even encouraged that tendency when he could, but betrayed his intelligence and awareness of the ins and outs of politics and diplomacy to those he chose to favor. He had, in the past, favored Veronique, perhaps because she never treated him with contempt or condescension, nor made any comparisons between himself and his older brother-in-blood, the long-absent Sir Geoffrey. Veronique had never met Geoffrey, who had departed for the Holy Land on crusade before she herself returned to Paris, but he continued to cast a long shadow even in absentia, particularly over his younger brother. The sibling rivalry there wasn't as poisonous as she'd seen it become in some domains, but it wasn't entirely absent, either.

"Lady Veronique," Olivier greeted her politely, with a smile and an abbreviated bow. "I had wondered if you would turn up tonight."

"It seemed a good enough excuse to drag myself across the river, Sir Olivier." She dropped him a curtsey of her own. "How has the winter found you? Well, I hope?"

"As well as can be expected," he assured her, somewhat more wryly than was his usual wont. She marked it, and inquired with a questioning eyebrow.

"As far as winter doldrums go," he continued, "it hasn't been very dull from where I sit. I fear that Milady Countess Saviarre did not take the loss of Bishop St. Lys in the debates of 1220 with any particular equanimity."

"Ah." Veronique offered a wry expression of her own. "I can only imagine. I trust no difficulties arose for you as a result of that particular incident?"

"Other than having to listen to renewed vituperations about Malkavian religious zealots and eastern freeloaders? Not at all." Olivier waved the handful of hangers-on away, leaving them standing with only a ghoul bodyguard in ready attendance. "I fear that you were the subject of considerable invective, as well, milady. Will you take a word of advice, if I trouble to give it?"

This was unusual, as well. "If you have advice to offer me, Sir Olivier, I will of course accept and consider it."

His voice lowered slightly. She sensed, at a level beneath conscious awareness, that he was doing something, perhaps to protect their conversation from casual eavesdropping. Olivier then said, "Milady Countess Saviarre stopped just short of begging the prince to withdraw his recognition of your diplomatic credentials and have you declared Furore and outlaw. I believe the only reason she stopped is because she's not quite ready to pick that large a fight with your patron. I doubt, however, that her restraint will survive another serious challenge—Hamburg is far enough away that an outraged letter is more likely than any more vigorous response to you being hounded out of Paris by the sheriff." He paused. "My advice is that you back away from your support of the Malkavian and find some diplomatic way of soothing the countess's ruffled feathers. You do your cause no good by making that woman your enemy."

Veronique swallowed the hot retort that leapt to her lips—Perhaps Saviarre should look to the defense of her own rights—and nodded slightly in response, hiding her balled fist in the fullness of her skirts. "Sound advice, milord, and I thank you for it."

His expression went from faintly concerned to faintly distressed as he read her reaction correctly. "Milady, I meant no offense to your friend, and no insult to you. I hope you realize this and understand that I believe the Grand Court would be poorer for your absence."

Veronique forced the tension—the combat tension, the need to release the sudden lash of the Beast's temper in some violent way—out of the line of her shoulders and spine. After a moment, she even felt comfortable offering him a genuine smile, and a verbal response. "Truly, milord, I am not angry with you, or with your advice. You have given me good counsel in the past, when I first arrived in Paris, and I have no reason to doubt your wisdom now. I may not want to hear it," she shrugged expressively, "but then, what diplomat does enjoy learning that her efforts are failing? I can only thank you for your honest concern."

Sir Olivier's face relaxed in a smile of his own, a genuine and unaffected expression, before he allowed his face to settle back into the lines of his good-humored social mask. "I look forward to seeing you more often on the isle once spring comes, then?"

"You certainly shall. I personally cannot wait for next week."

"The presentation of the new ambassador, you mean? God's teeth, it's going to be a spectacle for the ages. Every Toreador who ever harbored the vaguest ambition of currying favor with Isouda de Blaise is going to be there—Lord Richard is half-mad trying to coordinate security, and the herald claims he's had blazons not seen since Charlemagne was in diapers submitted for accounting in the standing arrangements." Olivier shook his head in dismay, with no trace of mockery anywhere in it.

Veronique couldn't help it; she chuckled, and let him take her arm, leading her back into the swirl of the gathering.

"You laugh—but, then, you're not going to have to be standing on the dais in some cloth-of-gold confection specially constructed by trained professionals who never take into account the discomfort of their victims before embarking on a new sartorial adventure." He sounded authentically aggrieved as he steered them through a mass of human servants, most of whom were dressed briefly and suggestively enough to draw predatory eyes to every one of their natural charms. Veronique caught sight of a familiar face, bracketed by two Cainites vigorously discussing who would he the first to sample her, and glanced away.

"You'll be down in the audience making witty remarks about other peoples' hair." His gaze followed the direction of hers, took note of where it had tended, and then came back to her own, their eyes briefly touching. He lowered his own first, along with his voice. "I'll never understand how de Navarre keeps servants if he treats them like..." He gestured in the direction of the young woman done up in straps of well-treated leather, hobbled and only semi-clad, who had once found shelter in Veronique's house before being seduced away by Jean Battiste's silver tongue.

"No, milord, I don't think I'll ever understand it either," Veronique replied, dryly. "You'd think he would eventually grow weary of it. And speaking of weariness.

"You can't be weary—it's hardly midnight, much less dawn. And you still owe me a dance from the last party you escaped from early."

"I fear that I'll have to deny you the pleasure again, milord. My maidservant was feeling unwell, earlier, and unlike our host I—" She bit off what she was about to say, and tried, unsuccessfully, to transform it into a demure rejoinder, "I feel that I should take her home and pour soup into her until she's better."

"At the revel after the ambassador's presentation, then."

Olivier pressed a kiss to her fingertips in parting. "As you wish, milord."

"I require your promise, milady."

She laughed again. This time, it attracted the attention—and ugly looks—from a number of Cainite women whose company Sir Olivier had rejected in favor of her own. "Very well, you have my promise—I will dance with you at the presentation, so I do swear on my honor as a diplomat."

"Excellent. I can hardly wait."

Veronique found her host and made her farewells to him in the midst of another bout of courtly behavior. De Navarre, however, didn't extract a promise to dance. Then she collected Alainne and Sandrin from the servants' quarters and, together, they made their way back across the Seine towards home. On the way, Alainne rode close to her side, clearly deep in thought. Veronique decided not to give it a chance to fester.

"You have something on your mind, Alainne. Speak."

Alainne nodded slightly at that but didn't immediately respond. Finally, after a long moment of contemplating her horse's ears, she asked, "They're not all like you, are they? Your kind?"

"No, they're not, and, yes, that is why I brought you with me tonight." Alainne shot her a look from red-rimmed eyes. "I can only say it so much—I know you, Alainne. You'll only believe a thing when you see it, and tonight you've seen only a fraction of what I've witnessed in my years. No, they aren't all like me. In fact, most of them aren't like me. They may be charming, they may be handsome and witty and civilized, but those things are only on the surface."

"Jean-Battiste—"

"Jean-Battiste is no different. I only trust him as far as I must and no further for a reason, Alainne. Like many of the ones you saw tonight, he's a monster at the core—you saw Marguerite in there. Never forget that, if you'd been foolish enough to succumb to him, it might have been you." Veronique forced herself to lower her voice, and gentled its edge. "You're no fool, and I won't treat you like one. But I hope this night taught you that this isn't a splendid courtly game or some wonderful adventure, and the people with whom I must deal aren't the immortal knights and ladies of fairy tales."

Alainne looked away.

Chapter Seven

L ady Rosamund d'Islington was humming softly to herself, a tune that none of the other assorted Cainites or mortals sharing the antechamber truly recognized, and which she herself did not realize she had chosen. It was not a song usually heard in *Ile-de-France*, or among the Courts of Love; it did not come from the Languedoc, and no troubadour had ever sung its words. The last time Rosamund herself had heard it was the last night she had spent in her parents' modest home, the last night before she was sent away to fosterage at the court of the beautiful and wise Lady Isouda de Blaise, who had taken one look at the girl Rosamund had been then and perceived at once the woman she could grow into, if life permitted. It had been sung to her, by a grandfather now decades dead and buried, to soothe her childish fears, to ease the grief of leaving home. Though she didn't realize it, Rosamund always hummed it when she was nervous or frightened and needed to calm herself.

She was trying very hard to keep herself as utterly calm and collected on the inside as she appeared to be on the out. There, she was without flaw. Mindful of the need to make an immediate and powerful impression, she had prepared for the occasion months in advance. Her dress was of cream-white silk imported from the east, and while the cut was in no way inappropriate or excessively forward, the way the fabric clung to her body's slender lines showed them off to excellent advantage. Only the gilt embroidery embellishing the neckline permitted observers to determine where the creamy fabric of the garment left off and the pale silk of her own skin began. The embroidery continued over her breast, forming an exquisitely rendered rose of golden petals, leaves and thorns. She had bathed in rosewater and dabbed oil of roses behind her ears, on each breast and behind her knees. She walked in a cloud of sweet, subtle perfume. For tonight, at least, her hair was completely uncontained by braid or veil, hanging loose down her back, brushed to a high sheen, a thousand shades of copper, fire and gold, ornamented by a simple golden circlet. On her right hand, she wore a ring, its signet worked in the shape of a rose, given to her by her sire after the completion of her first foray into Cainite diplomacy.

Josselin had been struck silent by the sight of her, when she emerged from the guest room at Lord Valerian's villa, where she had spent the last nights prior to her formal presentation. At first, she didn't quite realize that the rapture had taken him until his squire, Fabien, tugged at his sleeve to bring him out of it. Then a warm surge of pleasure and surprise washed through her that she could even affect her brother so, who had known her since she was twelve years old and gawky, with freckles and skinned knees. Just recalling that moment gave her courage now, when she needed it most, standing on the threshold of the largest diplomatic endeavor she had ever undertaken, an enterprise even more important than the gesture of good will offered to the Black Cross. Having Josselin firmly at her shoulder didn't hurt either, dressed almost as splendidly as she in mail polished to a high shine and a sky-blue surcoat that both bore his arms and brought out his eyes—her silver-gold swan knight, champion, protector, sibling and best friend, all at once. She caught his gloved hand, squeezed it tightly, and succeeded in not pacing.

They were in an antechamber in Prince Alexander's haven awaiting the return of Lord Valerian, who would escort them to the main receiving hall, where they would both be formally presented, she as the Ambassador of the Rose for the Courts of Love and Josselin as her champion and guest. Intellectually, Rosamund knew that Lord Valerian had likely not been gone for more than a few moments since their arrival on the premises, and that it was only her own nerves making it seem like hours, like forever. That knowledge, unfortunately, didn't help conquer the nervousness in any way, shape or form. She was being given far too much time to overthink and second-guess her every decision—perhaps she should have worn the green...

There was a perfunctory knock on the chamber door, and it opened before Rosamund could even gather breath for a reply. Lord Valerian stepped inside, flanked by Lord Richard. Both men bowed fully to her, acknowledging her rank, and she replied in kind, offering them a deep curtsey, which she held. "Milords?"

"My Lady Rosamund d'Islington, Ambassador of the Rose and envoy of the Courts of Love, His Highness Alexander, Prince of Paris, craves the honor of your presence." Lord Valerian's well-trained baritone caressed each word of the formal announcement. "He sends his servants Gnacus Eligius Scaevola Valerian and Lord Richard to escort and defend you. Will you answer His Highness's request, and accept the gift of his protection?"

"My Lord Gnaeus Eligius Scaevola Valerian and Lord Richard, I do accede to His Highness's wish, and accept the gift of his protection, for both myself and my brother, Sir Josselin." That was a minor breach of protocol, but not unheard of. Most ambassadors did, after all, travel with their own protectors and require their presence even in entirely civilized circumstances.

Lord Valerian offered his hand, which she accepted, allowing him to draw her to her full height. "Then rise, Lady Rosamund, and come into the presence of he who welcomes and defends you."

The distance between the antechamber in which they had waited and the reception hall in which they would be received was short. Rosamund walked it with her hand and arm resting properly atop Valerian's, an entirely decorous separation between their bodies. Josselin, bearing her ambassadorial standard, flanked her on the right, and Sheriff Richard flanked Valerian to his left. As they walked, her nervousness fell away completely and, without conscious prompting, her entire carriage changed, the line of her shoulders and spine losing its tense stiffness and relaxing into an expression of pure confidence as she came completely into her element. A liveried herald opened the heavy oak door to the receiving chamber as they approached and announced, as they paused before it, "Lord Ambassador Gnaeus Eligius Scaevola Valerian, of the Grand Court of Paris! Lady Ambassador Rosamund d'Islington, of the Court of Love of Chartres! His Excellency, Lord Sheriff Richard, of Paris! Sir Josselin de Poitiers, of the Court of Love of Chartres!"

Lord Valerian guided her through the doors and, at the threshold, stopped and formally yielded her hand with a kiss. Rosamund curtseyed to him, then turned to face the Cainites gathered at the head of the room, and approached with a firm and measured step, her bearing flawless, exuding what she hoped was the proper combination of dignity, humility and poise. Though she could not appropriately look either right or left without breaching the Grand Court's formal protocol of presentation, she was peripherally aware that the receiving chamber was both smaller than she had imagined it and much fuller than she had ever thought it would be. Pike-bearing guards in the prince's distinctive livery stood on each side between her and what felt like an extremely substantial crowd, their weapons crossed between them, a living barrier.

She couldn't afford to let it concern or distract her. She kept her head held high at a self-assured but not arrogant angle, progressed forward ten paces, adjusting her stride to allow for the distance to the dais at the front of the room, and dropped a deep presentation curtsey, which she held for the appropriate interval. Rising, she progressed forward another five paces, which brought her to the midpoint of the room, and she curtseyed again. When she rose this time, she couldn't help but notice more details about the trio of Cainites gathered on the dais before her, though she was deliberately trying to avoid becoming entranced in their glittering appearance. Such missteps had sunk more than one Toreador diplomat's chances of making a good first impression, and she was fiercely intent on not repeating that error. The only one seated—it had to be Prince Alexander, from his evident physical youth and rich costuming—was rising to greet her, a breach of protocol in itself, but one that, as prince, he was entitled to make if it suited him to do so. She progressed another five paces, and when she went into her presentation curtsey, this time she stayed down, and addressed the dais in a clear, ringing voice. "My Lord Prince, I, Lady Rosamund d'Islington, Ambassador of the Courts of Love, come before you this night to offer my service and my counsel as my sires have before me, and to reaffirm before the witnesses here gathered the bonds of friendship and loyalty between the Grand Court and the Courts of Love."

Rosamund kept her eyes fixed firmly on the floor, waiting for her words to be acknowledged by the man standing on the dais. To her surprise, there was, rather than a verbal permission, a rustle of embroidery-stiffened fabric and the sound of quiet footfalls on the floor in front of her, and then a cool hand took possession of her own. She permitted that hand's owner to draw her to her feet, and in an instant, she was standing face to face with Prince Alexander himself.

Rosamund caught her breath. She was told, before she left for Paris, that Prince Alexander had been Embraced young, and that he was extremely well favored. She hadn't expected him to appear a shade younger even than herself, a beautiful beardless youth, his classically sculpted face framed in dark ringlets, his lovely eyes outrageously long-lashed, dark brown flecked with hints of amber. She found herself caught in his gaze before she could remind herself not to look into his eyes. Without glancing down, he raised her hand to his lips, and pressed a kiss to her knuckles with such reverence that she felt herself quite shockingly flattered. When he glanced away from her, out into the crowd, she felt the separation almost physically. Then he raised his own voice and spoke, his mellow tenor reaching every corner of the room without effort: "I, Prince Alexander of Paris, do accept the service and counsel of this, our ambassador, Lady Rosamund d'Islington, in whose person the friendship and loyalty of the Courts of Love has found its fairest setting. Let her be made welcome in our city and among our people."

A low murmur of affirmation ran through the assembled court and, at Prince Alexander's delicate prompting, Rosamund turned with him and offered a courtesy to them, as well. Now that she was turned toward them, she could glance about for familiar faces without breaking the gravity of the moment. She found Veronique d'Orleans toward the far end of the room, closer to the doors than the dais, clad in green velvet, her veiled head a good bit higher than any other woman's. Rosamund wondered if she ever exposed her hair in public. A number of Toreador cousins were scattered at various places about the room, distant relations seeking their fortunes among the intrigues of the Grand Court rather than the Courts of Love. An unusual figure standing close to the dais caught her eye—tall, draped in voluminous dark robes that covered every inch and allowed no hint of gender, hooded and gloved, wearing a mask the color of old ivory, its cheeks marked with red streaks that reminded Rosamund of bloody tears. Proximity to the dais suggested someone of extremely high rank within the body of the Grand Court, but she couldn't recall a mention from any of her briefings on the subject regarding a Cainite who affected such a peculiar public appearance.

"I would add my greetings, also, Lady Rosamund, and my hopes for the success of your mission." Rosamund permitted Alexander to guide her around to meet the owner of that sentiment, who was approaching from across the dais, her hand resting comfortably on the arm of her liege's childe, Sir Olivier.

The Countess Saviarre. Rosamund offered her a curtsey, though not so deep as the one she had given Prince Alexander, nor did she hold it, rising to gaze serenely at the woman Veronique d'Orleans assured her was their most venomous foe.

Countess Saviarre had a reputation, even among the Courts of Love, for her beauty and she was, in truth, quite lovely—but her beauty was in no way welcoming. Rosamund felt there was something severe about her, something almost too tightly, rigidly controlled, and it stole the pleasure her countenance could have held. There was nothing soft or gentle in her, though she was entirely, gracefully feminine in her bearing, and modest as well. Her clothing, though of fine, expensive fabric and excellent make, was of conservative cut and color. Like Valerian, she indulged in no excessive ornamentation nor any public displays of ostentation and made no attempt to outshine her ruler. Her strikingly handsome face was outlined in a linen wimple; her hair was entirely covered by her veil. She wasn't even wearing any jewelry, except for the chain of office binding her mantle, and a small signet ring on her right hand, likely also a symbol of her office as the prince's first advisor.

"Milady Saviarre," Prince Alexander murmured quietly to them both, "is most diligent in the performance of her duties. It is my hope that you shall come to work closely together during the course of this embassy, and that good results will blossom of that effort."

"Milord Prince, I shall certainly make every endeavor to serve both you and Milady Queen Salianna," Rosamund replied serenely, glancing up at Saviarre and focusing on a point just beyond her right shoulder. "And it is also my hope that the Countess Saviarre and I shall work closely together on such issues of diplomacy as will ease the tension between the courts."

"Well spoken, Lady Rosamund." The very corners of Countess Saviarre's mouth turned back in the faintest and slightest of smiles that in no way reached her eyes. "And I promise you that we shall, indeed, work closely together in the coming nights. Shall we adjourn the hall, Milord Prince, that we may all seek a more comfortable setting for conversation?"

"Yes, I believe we shall." Never relinquishing Rosamund's hand, Alexander gestured toward the herald manning the door, whose stentorian voice promptly announced the dismissal of the formal court and the beginning of the reception. "Come, Milady Rosamund. The Grand Court awaits the chance to meet you, at long last."

Veronique was, despite her less-than-exalted place in the hierarchy of the Grand Court, in an exceptionally good humor. That less-than-exalted place offered her an excellent vantage point for observing virtually the entire room and everyone in it. There were, at times, compensations to being at least half a head taller than most of the rest of the court. As a consequence, Veronique got a good look at the reactions of Prince Alexander, Countess Saviarre and Sir Olivier when Rosamund entered the room.

Poor Olivier looked, at that instant, completely stunned. His eyes went wide, and probably without his conscious awareness, he moved fractionally forward on the dais, though not so far that his sire noticed the motion. Olivier, as always, stood to Alexander's left and slightly behind the highchair on which the Prince of Paris customarily held court. Veronique did not suppose she could blame him for that reaction—Rosamund truly was stunning, and Veronique was unashamed to admit that a reaction stirred in her own veins at the sight of the Toreador diplomat. She had come dressed as a bride, and carried herself as a queen. The force of her presence penetrated three ranks into the assembled courtiers and dragged almost every eye with her as she crossed the room.

Saviarre's initial reaction was less extreme than Olivier's but no less telling. Her serene and untroubled expression slipped, and for just an instant, coldly predatory fury bloomed on her face for all the world to see. Or not, as the case might be— Rosamund was a fairly substantial distraction. But Veronique saw and, out of the corner of her eye, she caught the Bishop de Navarre marking the reaction as well. And Veronique had no doubt that Mnemach, standing on the opposite side of the dais from Saviarre, hadn't missed the slip either. Saviarre mastered herself quickly enough, sliding her blandly welcoming high-court official's mask back on before too many unfriendly eyes could notice the lapse, and particularly before her prince could see it.

Alexander's reaction—to rise, his expression that of a man waking from a long night of unrestful sleep and terrible dreams, pure wonder in his gaze—shocked more than just Veronique, and a quiet susurrus of whispered commentary had passed through the witnesses on either side of her. She had not been resident in Paris during the time euphemistically referred to as "Prince Alexander's infirmity," but many of the more senior hangers-on at the Grand Court had, and, properly motivated, their tongues wagged freely. Even during the worst of his grief-stricken madness following the destruction of his first consort, the unfortunate Toreador girl Lorraine, in public Alexander had never showed a trace of human weakness. Ruthless despotism and lack of tolerance for courtly gossip, yes; the suggestion that he was emotionally undone or suffering from the results of his own follies, no. To see him rise to his feet and breach his own

laboriously detailed protocol when greeting the new ambassador from the Courts of Love set the rumor mill in motion before
the court was even dismissed.

Veronique was enormously satisfied with that result, so
much so that she even recessed graciously down the corridor to
the reception hall, where servants were offering viands, a group
of musicians were playing and clots of courtiers were gathering
to exchange innuendo. Her second diplomatic soiree in less than
a week, and for a change she was enjoying herself immensely,
just trailing through the room, listening to reactions, taking the
pulse of the court. The initial impulse seemed to be that, by
sending Rosamund d'Islington as their ambassador, the Courts
of Love were finally in earnest in their efforts to repair the relationship that had been so badly damaged so many years before.
The most common question was, why now' The most common
suppositions on that score revolved around the ongoing strife
with Queen Esclarmonde the Black, whose stubborn refusal to
lie down and die had seriously inconvenienced Queen Salianna,
and that if certain new princes in the South kept getting ideas
about dealing diplomatically with her, the situation for the
Courts of Love could only grow more dire. Wilder speculations
involving roving bands of Furores and feral Heretics spiced the
mix, and Veronique picked up a few useful tidbits of innuendo
to add to her own espionage efforts. Rosamund's companion,
Sir Josselin, kept finding himself cornered by Parisian Cainites
desirous of picking his brain for details about his sister-in-blood.

The Countess Saviarre, being soundly ignored by her liege
lord in favor of the charms of Rosamund d'Islington, found
an excuse to remove herself fairly early on, claiming a matter
of minor but unignorable domestic importance required her
immediate attention. No one, Veronique noticed, was particularly heart-stricken to see her depart, including her ruler, her
ruler's childe, the newest ambassador, and most of her own circle of semi-loyal cronies. Countess Saviarre had a way of stifling
festivities by her very presence. After she left, Rosamund actually managed to coax Prince Alexander onto the dance floor.
Veronique found herself backed into a corner by Sir Olivier,
who ruthlessly extracted the dance she had promised him and

a few more besides, in retaliation for keeping him waiting so long in the first place.

Toward the end of the night, Veronique found the excuse to approach Rosamund and Prince Alexander and offer her public greetings to Rosamund for the first time. To her credit, Rosamund accepted those greetings gravely and without a hint in her voice or bearing to suggest that they had met before. Shortly thereafter, Veronique excused herself, collected the long-suffering and exceptionally patient Sandrin from the servants' quarters, where the sheer population density in the prince's haven that night had required him to wait, and repaired to the cart for the ride home.

To Veronique's surprise, there was something waiting for her when she climbed inside: a small wooden box that she hadn't brought with her, sitting on one of the seats. From its grain, it looked as though it had been carved from one solid piece of wood, and rather than having a lock or visible hinges, it was tied shut with a piece of scarlet ribbon wound through a charm carved of yellowed bone. That told her who it came from—Dame Mnemach—but not why. She held the box tightly on her lap all the way home and opened it as soon as the door to her private chamber was closed. Inside was a brief note sealed with an unmarked blot of wax, and three fat, cylindrical candles, the wax incised with characters from an alphabet that Veronique did not recognize. She cracked the seal on the note and read.

The servant of Night uses his shadows for more than the construction of pretty trifles in his garden. He possesses eyes and ears in the darkness that not even I can claim. When you wish the shadows to see and hear nothing of what you do or say, make certain to have a strong enough light by your side.

Chapter Eight

Veronique woke the next night to news that put her in an even better mood. Thierry was waiting in the sitting room with a handful of depositions from agents who reported in regularly, and a number of pieces of correspondence. One of them bore the arms of the Prince of Béziers, and it was all she could do not to snatch the letter out of Thierry's hand.

She slit the seal open, skipped the paragraph of honorific blather at the top, and scanned the first several lines. A slow smile grew over her face.

"Good news, I take it?" Thierry asked around a mouthful of bread. Girauda had taken one look at him and immediately began stuffing food into him, providing a bowl of soup and a portion of roasted meat to go with his bread and cheese and warmed wine.

"Don't talk with your mouth full," Veronique replied automatically. "And, yes, it is excellent news. The Court of Béziers is willing to take in Anatole and his followers."

Thierry frowned, hut swallowed before saying anything else. "Isn't that a little dangerous for Z—I mean, for them?"

"It would be a good deal more dangerous for them to stay here." Veronique refolded Eon de l'Étoile's letter, murmuring under her breath, "I think I would like it better in Béziers.... When you're finished eating, Thierry, I'll need you to take some dictation for me."

"Of course, milady." Veronique watched him shovel soup and bread into his mouth for several minutes, then reached out and caught his wrist in between bites. Naturally, he tried to pull away; naturally, against her strength he was unable to do so. She pulled back the rough sleeve of his scholar's robe and examined his hand and wrist, its slenderness and extreme pallor. She glanced up and saw clearly that his face was even thinner than usual.

"Thierry, you do realize that you're only pretending to be a starving student? You can come here for a hot meal and a warm bed whenever you need one. You are one of my people." She released his wrist.

"I know," Thierry replied, in his tiniest, meekest mouse-voice, nibbling at a piece of meat. "I just..."

Veronique waited patiently for him to continue, watching his face as he considered and discarded phrasing in his thoughts. Finally, he said, "I feel wretched, coming here and sponging, even if I've nothing to report. I feel as though I'm not doing enough to earn my keep. You write your own letters most of the time and I—"

She reached over again and rested her hand on his, stilling their agitated motion. He looked up, his pale brown eyes shining in the candlelight. "Thierry, your worth to me is greater than you can imagine. Half the people I rely on as my eyes and ears in this city cannot even write their own names. You're their voice to me—and the news you bring to me is always vital to my plans. Just because I can write for myself doesn't mean I don't need you."

Thierry reached up with his free hand and brushed hastily at his eyes. "Lady—"

"None of that from you. Come here." Veronique scooted down the bench slightly and padded the cushion at her side. Obediently, he joined her, looking mildly chagrined. She slit her wrist with her thumbnail and offered it to him; he accepted, and drank slowly, gingerly, as though he expected her to heave him into the street anyway. Instead, she wrapped her free arm around his thin shoulders and rested her cheek against his hair. When he was finished, and she licked the wound clean, she asked, "You've been ill, haven't you?"

"A bit of a cough, last month. It wasn't serious—it went away by itself in a few days." He was, naturally, not very willing to leave her side at the moment and Veronique herself wasn't in much of a hurry to move; his warmth felt pleasant against her.

"Nonetheless, if you sicken again, I want you to come to me immediately. You're all skin and bones this season." Veronique gave herself a little shake. "Finish that soup or Girauda will beat us both with a willow switch. Then get your lapboard. We've some writing to do tonight."

For the first two weeks following Rosamund's presentation, her social calendar was completely filled, according to her seneschal Peter. Veronique was not inclined to doubt that statement completely, despite Thierry's assessment of Peter as a weaselly little functionary overwhelmed by his own sense of importance. Rosamund's busy schedule gave Veronique the opportunity to get all of her own ducks in a row with regards to the information she needed to present.

She wrote again to Anatole to inform him of the results of her correspondence with Eon de l'Etoile, only to discover that the Prince of Béziers had beaten her to the punch. Anatole had also received word from him, along with a request for certain assurances from Anatole regarding the behavior of his followers, a request the Malkavian had not considered particularly onerous. Veronique was prepared to deem that mildly miraculous, given Anatole's vigorous faith and general dislike of strings attached, at least until she got to the admission that the cleric and the prince had many things in common, deep personal piety being only one of them. She felt a momentary stab of pity for anyone living in Béziers—particularly Aimeric—who was going to have to deal with those two at their first face-to-face meeting. Arrangements were being made to house Anatole and his followers in a fortified manor near Béziers proper, and an advance party led by the exceptionally even-tempered Brother Gerasimos was preparing to take to the road as soon as the way south was clear enough to travel conventionally.

A week after receiving this happy news, Rosamund finally found the time to respond to Veronique's request for a face-to-face meeting, which was set for a few nights later. This time she brought Thierry and Philippe with her, and promised herself that once things settled down a bit she'd spend more time simply socializing with all of her people. None of them should feel useless or unworthy, and soothing their fears cost her nothing, in the end.

The official embassy of the Courts of Love shared the same neighborhood on Ile de la Cité as Lord Valerian's home: The driver had no difficulty locating it, even in the dark. Rosamund's new house was also much more conventional in its layout, the city home of a noble family in service to her patron who spent most of the year in the country. Veronique and her retinue were shown in promptly by the seneschal Peter, who was on much better behavior when Veronique herself was present, and left to wait in the solar, a pleasant room equipped with a fireplace, cushioned benches and chairs, and several shuttered windows. A request to the servant left to attend their needs brought a pitcher of wine for Thierry and Philippe, and a ceramic candle dish for herself, which she set out on the small trestle table that occupied the center of the room in the lack of a real bed for the absent lord and lady. On this she placed one of the candles that Mnemach had given her and lit it. Something tingled at the edges of her awareness, tickling her ears like a sound just at the edge of hearing, then subsided; the candle burned with an abnormally clear, bright light. She couldn't help but notice that even the shadows dancing before the light of the fireplace seemed nearly frozen in place.

Rosamund joined them before the candle had burned down a quarter-mark. Veronique rose to greet her, dropping a polite curtsey, and both Thierry and Philippe offered their best bows; Rosamund waved them up from the doorway and approached, a harried look about her. "You might have warned me, Lady Veronique."

"Warned you?" Veronique asked, trying not to sound as amused as she felt; the Toreador woman looked as though she'd just escaped from her toilette, and possibly from the attentions of another would-be caller.

"They're relentless. Worse than the Courts of Love at their worst! I've never seen more idiotic reasons to make a social call in the whole of my life—excuses that I'd be ashamed to use!" Rosamund seated herself in an agitated flurry of skirts. "You'd think that none of them had ever met a woman diplomat before. Honestly, I'm beginning to feel like the main attraction at some... some menagerie!"

"You're new and unexpectedly intriguing." Veronique seated herself, as well, and offered Rosamund a wry smile. "And given the impression you made at your presentation, a feeding frenzy was likely unavoidable. Your one saving grace is that the Grand Court tends to be jaded and easily bored—they'll keep at you until the new wears off, and then you'll get some peace from all hut the most serious ones."

"*I suppose you enjoyed just the same treatment when you first came to court." Rosamund smoothed her damask skirts over her knees.*

"More or less." The corner of Veronique's mouth twitched back, uncontrollably.

"Then you could have warned me," Rosamund retaliated, aggrieved.

Veronique covered her mouth before the chuckle lurking her throat could escape. After a moment of imposing discipline on herself, she replied, "Yes, I could have. I confess that I wanted to see how you would react to all the attention. I will admit that I contemplated murder more than once before my first week was out, and chased most of the more irritating ones away before the end of the second. You're much more patient than I, Lady Rosamund."

"It is," Rosamund muttered, "my cardinal virtue. And, tonight, neither here nor there. What has brought you to my door this evening, Lady Veronique?"

"I wished to keep you apprised of my activities here in Paris, and I did not dare share those details with you in any other way. Countess Saviarre's agents have been extremely interested in me of late—I fear that any correspondence between us is in serious danger of interception." Veronique gestured to the candle casting its circle of radiance over their conversation. "Moreover, even meetings of this kind may not be entirely secure. It is my strong suspicion that Bishop de Navarre may be in collusion with Countess Saviarre—if he is, even the shadows hiding in the corners of this room may be our enemy."

Rosamund sat up even straighter in alarm. "But that means—"

Veronique gestured again. The candle's flame visibly danced, and the shadows lying on the table visibly held still. "This candle is the gift of an ally whom I trust entirely, and who has no reason to love either Saviarre or Bishop de Navarre. It prevents the good bishop's shadows from spying upon us—we may speak freely while we sit in its light, though I suspect we must use this gift wisely. I do not know the process that goes into their manufacture, or if more than a few are available to us, and we should guard our words when they are not in use."

"Sorcery." Rosamund crossed herself, reflexively. "I did not know you were allied with the Tremere ambassador—"

"I am not. This candle did not come from the Tremere." Or, if it did, Veronique had no idea, and wasn't sure that she wanted to know, in any case. "It came from a party interested in our success in breaking Saviarre's hold on power."

"Which is, I suppose, another task on which you've been working while I've been entertaining half the curious layabouts in Paris. Forgive me, Lady Veronique, I—"

Veronique waved the apology aside. "You've only just arrived. And, even so, you've achieved more in two weeks than I have in all the time I've been here—I doubt that Prince Alexander knows I exist from night to night, but I understand that you have managed to capture his attention."

"Yes. I have." There was a certain pensiveness in Rosamund's tone and her gaze, when she fixed it on Veronique, was troubled. "Lady Veronique, I hardly dared ask anyone who's called on me for… for prurient gossip, but…"

"You've noticed it, then." Veronique replied, bluntly. "The miasma that surrounds Prince Alexander from time to time."

Rosamund looked vastly relieved to have her thoughts spoken so openly. "Yes. I had feared I was just imagining it. Miasma is a… good word to describe it—it's… almost as though… Do you remember the sun?"

"I'm not so old as all that. Yes, I remember the sun."

"It's as though he were the sun, and a cloud suddenly passes in front of him." Rosamund, Veronique noticed, tended towards expressive gestures when she was speaking of something she felt strongly about. "Sometimes it's a thin little wisp and it passes quickly—sometimes it's a thunderhead, and there's a storm pouring down just beneath the surface of him. He seems... very troubled, in those times."

Veronique was silent for a moment, considering. "Prince Alexander," she finally replied carefully, "has never fully recovered from the loss of his first consort, I have been told by those in a better position to notice such things. He is no longer maddened by his grief, but neither is he wholly the man, or the ruler, he once was. His reliance on the counsel of Countess Saviarre has weakened him in the eyes of some—and others believe that Countess Saviarre is somehow manipulating his spells of miasma for her own benefit."

"How could she accomplish such a thing?" Rosamund wondered aloud. "Prince Alexander is—well, you've been in his presence, Lady Veronique! The man is..."

"Overwhelming in close quarters, yes. But he is no longer as strong in mind as he used to be, and this is a fact that we must keep in consideration, no matter how powerful he may seem at any given time." Veronique caught Rosamund's eye. "Countess Saviarre certainly knows it, and that truth is at the core of her power."

Rosamund nodded her understanding, and Veronique continued.

"I have been here long enough to observe Countess Saviarre's methods of operation. She is, whatever else she might be, an extremely skilled politician and a canny manipulator." Veronique gestured Thierry forward, and he presented her with a sheaf of parchments, the latest depositions from their own surveillance efforts; these she handed to Rosamund. "In the past, she has made strategic use of various crises first to obtain and then solidify her hold on power—in truth, from what I've managed to determine, at least a few of those challenges to the stability of the Grand Court, she personally staged in order to obtain the credit for successfully defusing them."

Rosamund looked up from the documents, visibly appalled.

"Yes, I know. It's a dangerous game, hut one which has yielded dividends for her in the long run. She rules Paris in all but name, despite Prince Alexander's personal power."

"Bold. She obviously doesn't lack… courage is, I suppose, the best word." Rosamund chewed briefly on her lower lip.

"No, she doesn't. She does, however, have her own failings—which we are going to exploit." Veronique laced her fingers together to control any nervous gestures. "There are two chinks in Countess Saviarre's armor, two weaknesses in her control of the situation in Paris that we can make use of. The first is Bishop de Navarre's ongoing feud with the Nosferatu warren." Veronique paused briefly at the expression that crossed Rosamund's face but made no comment on it. "The matriarch of the Nosferatu, Dame Mnemach, who attended your presentation, is one of the oldest Cainites in this city—in fact, she laired on Ile de la Cité before Prince Alexander came to rule here."

"The one in the mask!"

"Exactly. Countess Saviarre is either at the root of that feud, as Bishop de Navarre's patron, or else is attempting to manipulate its outcome for her own ends. She may even have her own separate, private feud with Dame Mnemach. In either case, the situation has failed to go entirely as she might have hoped, I suspect." She shook her head slightly and cast a glance at the candle; it was burning down quite slowly. "Prince Alexander has not favored Bishop de Navarre's claim in the matter—I suspect because, as a Ventrue, Prince Alexander cherishes some innate distrust when it comes to the probity of a Lasombra—but neither has he offered very much open support for Dame Mnemach, who is, after all, of low enough blood despite her age to have some prejudice held against her, as well. As it sits, Bishop de Navarre and Dame Mnemach are at stalemate. She cannot strike at him directly without inflaming the feud and forcing Prince Alexander to take an active hand in its settlement, which may not redound to her favor; and he cannot strike at her, as his efforts to introduce agents of his own into the Nosferatu warren have all failed rather bloodily."

"I take it that you personally do not favor Bishop de Navarre's position in this squalid little epic." Rosamund murmured questioningly.

"No. Bishop de Navarre is, if you permit the observation, an oily little weasel who hopes to aggrandize himself on the carcass of the Grand Court. He is utterly loathsome, and he precipitated a fight that he can't finish in the name of rousting out a woman whose claim of domain is, in every way, superior to his own." Veronique heard the heat coming into her own voice and paused to let it drain away again, knowing that at least part of that passion was Mnemach's blood speaking through her. "In any case, I seriously doubt that he would consider an alliance with a faction dedicated to unseating his own patron. On the other hand, Dame Mnemach has been most receptive in that regard."

Rosamund blinked. "You've made an alliance with the Nosferatu?"

"After a fashion, yes. Dame Mnemach is deeply and personally interested in breaking Saviarre's grip on Prince Alexander. He was, after all, her ally at one time, if not her friend. The Nosferatu will assist us in such ways as they can." Veronique fixed Rosamund with a somber look. "They would also like you to formally receive their ambassador, Monsieur Guillaume, as a gesture of trust and solidarity, if for no other reason."

Rosamund was far too well bred to actually gape in surprise. Instead, she simply looked at Veronique in mute shock and horror. Veronique shrugged slightly. "To be brutally honest, Lady Rosamund, after what I went through in order to obtain their assistance, I have to say that entertaining a formal visit from a Nosferatu diplomat should he something less than completely traumatic. And an ideal gesture of camaraderie."

"Do I even want to know what you did to obtain their help?"

"No."

Rosamund closed her eyes and massaged their lids briefly, expelling her breath in an exasperated sigh. "Very well. I take it your communications with them are reliable enough to arrange this little encounter?"

"Indeed they are. Have you any preference in that regard?"

"As soon as possible." Rosamund, it was clear, believed in swallowing bitter doses quickly.

Veronique nodded. "Saviarre's second failing is even more significant: her failure to deal successfully with the Byzantine refugees—who have been here long enough that they hardly qualify as 'refugees' any longer, to be perfectly frank. Not to mention the various problems that have arisen from that failure."

"Yes, I understand that that situation has given birth to considerable furor over the years." Rosamund gave Veronique a hard look of her own. "I also understand that you've fanned a bit of that from time to time, as well."

"I have. I first met the current leader of the refugees, Anatole de Paris, when he was passing through Orleans in the company of his adopted childe, Zoë. Our paths have crossed with startling regularity since then. Anatole and his band of zealots actually lie at the core of my current plans. A hypothetical question for you, Lady Rosamund: If you were personally attempting to unseat Countess Saviarre, what lever would you use to crack her grip on power?"

The look Rosamund gave her was not precisely friendly. "I would, of course, use those resources that somehow existed outside of her control—or which had actively resisted it in the past. Such as this Anatole and his colorful band of malcontents?"

"You'll get used to dealing with colorful malcontents before this is all said and done, I'm sure." Veronique smiled slightly. "Anatole is a threat that exists outside of Saviarre's control, that much is true. She attempted, last summer, to sweep him off the field using her less-than-capable pawn, the unlamented Bishop St. Lys, and failed. That failure "rattled her control, somewhat, and unsettled her to the point that she has been pushing the edges of Prince Alexander's tolerance for her open meddling. It has also shown him that she is not as capable of dealing with every threat that presents itself as he might have previously believed. This is our lever: Saviarre's failure—which will become our success."

"Success?" Rosamund frowned. "To succeed there, you'd have to find some means of… of dealing with the refugees, and this Anatole creature." A pause. "You said that he is your… That you've crossed paths in the past."

"We have. And I do not doubt that we'll cross paths in the future, also." Veronique let her own smile come out in response to Rosamund's look. "I have found a means of dealing with the refugees, and with Anatole, and it's even a means of which he personally approves. Soon, Anatole and his followers will be moving south to Béziers, where they have been offered sanctuary and welcome by Prince Eon de l'Etoile, who makes this gesture in the hopes of repairing his own relationship with the Grand Court, which seems to consider him in something of a foul odor. There, Anatole and his followers will hunt the Cainite Heretics responsible for so much of last summer's unrest and bloodshed in the company of Prince Eon, who shares a considerable passion for persecuting the Heresy wherever he finds it."

Rosamund's expression was, for a moment, completely blank. Then she murmured, "Holy Mary, you're utterly mad."

"I have already obtained Prince Eon's and Anatole's enthusiastic cooperation, I assure you." Veronique leaned forward slightly. "This is our lever. Saviarre could never have managed this in a thousand years of trying—her pride would not permit her to negotiate with low-blooded guttersnipes, she would never lower herself to deal diplomatically with a man she has publicly derided as a weakling coward and a traitor. She has cut her own throat and handed us the blade."

"But—the risk! If this somehow fails at the last hour—"

"Saviarre herself has shown us that, in Paris, advantage only accrues to those willing to take personal risks, Lady Rosamund."

Rosamund was silent for a long moment, chewing her lip again. Then her shoulders straightened, and her expression became resolute. "What do you need me to do to enable this mad scheme of yours to succeed?"

"I need you to do precisely what you have already been doing—continue your efforts to gain the confidence of Prince Alexander. And he prepared to speak in support of me if the situation seems to warrant it." Veronique caught Rosamund's eye again. "We will succeed. I promise you this, Lady Rosamund."

"I wish I had your confidence," Rosamund admitted, wryly.

"Before the end, you will."

Deep beneath the streets of Lutetia, called *Paris* by those who did not remember the nights before the coming of Rome and its legions, Dame Mnemach was feeling extraordinarily pleased with herself and her endeavors of late. She held a letter, written by the hand of a Brujah diplomat, a faithful and accurate report of that diplomat's activities, the sort of letter one might send to a trusted friend rather than an ally of convenience. Mnemach supposed that was a hint.

It was, at the moment, a hint she was seriously considering.

It had been a long time since any Cainite, young or old, had succeeded in surprising Mnemach in any way. She was ancient and crafty in her wickedness; she had watched empires rise and fall, she had survived and constructed countless intrigues and acts of violence. As a child, she had watched the city of her people abandoned and burned to the ground to deny its use to the Roman legions advancing to crush the rebellion of Vercingetorix and his allies. As an adult, she had struggled to make her place within the society of her people against a vicious and implacable rival, and had eventually achieved her victory, taking the robe and mask of witch-priestess, speaker-for-the-gods. As a Cainite, she had outlived, outlasted, and out-schemed all comers, and made the undercity of Lutetia her own, ruled it as queen and goddess as Alexander ruled the city above the skin of the earth. Nothing in the circus of Cainite or human behavior had actually caused so much as a momentary twinge of astonishment in decades, at least.

This Brujah had surprised her. It wasn't necessarily an unpleasant sensation.

Clever Veronique had kept her eyes open and her ear to the ground. She had discerned Saviarre's weak point and was preparing to strike at it. Not a killing blow—Saviarre was too thoroughly entrenched at Alexander's side for one strike alone to remove her from power—but a telling one. Successfully executed, it would weaken her, expose her to further retaliation by those who had begun to chafe under her rule, who longed for a return to the nights when the Grand Court was a thing of glory, the premier Cainite gathering place in all of the Western Empire, not a declining and irrelevant anachronism rapidly being overshadowed by the waxing influence of the Courts of Love.

Mnemach knew that the Grand Court's glory was irretrievably gone. It would never again be what it once was, and that was neither a bad thing nor a good one. It would change, as all things changed or else stagnated and died, and what rose from that transformation would be a new challenge to navigate, a new reality to make her own. Another, larger part of her looked forward to what the future would bring; for good or for ill, the role of her people in the life of the city would be one of those things that assuredly changed, if but slowly.

Soon, those changes would begin. Perhaps, one night, she would even tell clever young Veronique why she and Saviarre were such bitter enemies, and let her judge for herself if the price demanded for Mnemach's aid was too high. Or perhaps not. Time alone would tell the tale.

Until then, Mnemach was content to bide her time, and let the Brujah spin her schemes. If there was one thing the matriarch of the Nosferatu possessed in abundance, it was patience.

Chapter Nine

The winter waned. Slowly, the weather warmed, rain replacing snow; the ground began to thaw, and the roads began their transition from ice-coated hut passable to the usual soupy spring quagmire which could only be navigated by ducks. And, apparently, Nosferatu couriers. Veronique managed to get another letter to Béziers and its reply hack before the late-March rains began in earnest. The wording of the statement she would read to Prince Alexander at the Annunciation Court was critically important, and she very much wanted the Bitterois and Anatole to approve it beforehand. The Prince of Béziers sent his own remarks as well as those of Aimeric de Cabaret, who was constitutionally incapable of refraining from literary critique. Anatole came to visit her in person, and approved, with an adjustment or two of his own.

Veronique wrote the final draft of the statement based on their input, shamelessly filching diplomatic flourishes from Aimeric's suggestions, as he no doubt had intended. Then she sent a note to Prince Alexander's seneschal, formally requesting an audience during the Annunciation Court proceedings. The Grand Court sat in full, formal session four times a year, and everyone—local officials and foreign diplomats alike—was expected to attend those gatherings and offer counsel if asked. Smaller sessions, devoted to local business alone, met every other month, and attendance at those functions was voluntary. Annunciation Court was a formal high court session, the first of the year, and Veronique ardently desired the opportunity to present her petition before every Cainite of consequence in Paris. Otherwise, she would be forced to wait until the smaller session in May.

The reply came back promptly: Though the Annunciation Court schedule of audiences was extremely full, her request had been granted, and she would be permitted to speak toward the closing of proceedings. Veronique gave the seneschal her thanks and spent the rest of the week in a state of barely controlled nerves, planning all the other aspects of her presentation. She had no hope of matching the impact Rosamund had managed during her arrival; she didn't have the budget, nor, she admitted to herself in a moment of brutal honesty, the personal beauty or flair for style. Girauda and Alainne worked to soothe her and applied their own talents to the enterprise. The night of the Annunciation Court, she rose early and submitted to their attentions without argument, muttering her speech to herself under her breath, practicing lines with varying inflections and letting her maids ruthlessly bully her into doing exactly what they liked. They bathed her in lavender water, perfumed her with lavender oil, and dressed her in the red kirtle that, at some point, they had found the time to embroider with gold and black thread around the neck, sleeves and hem. Alainne exerted all her art, and the result was a fine roseate flush around lips and cheeks that almost precisely mimicked life. Veronique's deep red mantle, lined in dark marten fur and clasped with the heavy golden chain that Prince Julia Antasia had given her when she took up the office of ambassador, went over her shoulders. Her hair was trimmed into a fine, pale blonde arch around her face and caught in a new net set with tiny seed pearls beneath her circlet.

"You look like a queen," Girauda said approvingly, as she and Alainne surveyed the full effect. "If you don't slouch that is, Vero."

Veronique reflexively stood up a bit straighter, adjusting her posture, rolling her shoulders to force out the tension and shaking out her spine. She reached up to touch her hair, exposed beneath the open weave of the net. "Are you certain this is all right? It's so... short."

"Everyone can't have copper hair down to their bottom, Veronique," Alainne replied, amused. "It suits your face—it draws attention to your eyes that way."

Veronique wasn't entirely convinced but didn't want to tell Alainne her business. She smoothed her hands down over her breasts and belly, outlined in fine red fabric. "Thank you… it's beautiful. Not too showy?"

She received a chorus of disgusted looks in reply.

"You're right, you're right," Veronique admitted. "I'm sure it's fine." She took a deep breath to banish the last of her nervousness and gave them both her most brilliant smile. "Well. I'll give you all the details when I get home."

Veronique was one of the first members of the Grand Court to arrive and be placed in the reception chamber, and therefore had the opportunity to watch everyone else coming in as well. Rosamund and Lord Valerian arrived early, too, and the three of them stood chatting, as did the various other early comers, until the room grew too full to allow it and they had to retire to their set places. Annunciation would be almost as well attended as Rosamund's own presentation; Veronique knew that, if she were still living, her palms would be clammy, and her heart would be fluttering. She wondered, vaguely, if Rosamund had been this nervous just before she walked through those doors to face Prince Alexander for the first time. And this wasn't even Veronique's first time, though it was the most important audience she had ever requested, with the highest risks and the greatest consequences. She deliberately took several deep breaths, closed her eyes, and let the words she intended to speak crawl through her thoughts, a soothing internal litany.

Prince Alexander, Sir Olivier, and Countess Saviarre entered. He gave his ritual greeting to the assembled Grand Court and they gave its ritual reply, and the business of the court began. As the seneschal had told her, the schedule was quite full, mostly with minor business that everyone wanted to present while Prince Alexander was in a demonstrably good humor. Seventeen petitions in all were presented before Veronique was called to step forward and approach the prince's throne.

Veronique could perform the ritual approach with its measured steps and deep courtesies in her sleep, having practiced it until the motions became engrained in her muscles, as natural as breathing had once been. Tonight, she executed them with all the gravity she could muster; at the final curtsey, she addressed the Cainites seated on the dais and recited the formal petitioner's formula in her clearest, calmest voice: "My Lord Prince, Alexander of Paris, your servant and counselor Lady Veronique d'Orleans, Ambassador to the Grand Court, craves Your Highness's permission to rise and present a proposal for Your Highness's consideration."

"You may rise, Lady Veronique d'Orleans, ambassador of our sister, Prince Julia Antasia, and present your petition." Alexander's response was also formula, slightly modified. There were nights when Veronique seriously wondered if he meant a bit of the sentiment when he declared Lady Antasia his sister. It was possible; they were both Ventrue.

Veronique rose to her full height, standing perfectly straight. Out of the corner of her eye, she caught sight of the masked and robed Mnemach, called to formal court twice in less than two months, and felt herself weirdly calmed, silently supported. She began speaking in her most coolly modulated diplomat's voice. "Your Highness, I come to you this night with tidings of great significance and a proposal to enhance the security of your throne and your demesne. If I may?"

Prince Alexander's dark eyes had narrowed a fraction at her opening statement, though his youthful face remained serenely neutral, impossible to read. He nodded his acquiescence, and Veronique drew a sealed parchment document from the pouch sewn inside her full skirt. Alexander motioned Sir Olivier forward to accept the document, which he did, flashing Veronique a puzzled look while his back was fully to his sire. He placed the parchment in Prince Alexander's hand once he had verified that the seals were, indeed, intact. Alexander inclined a dark eyebrow at the sight that met him as he examined those seals, a single, deliberate interrogatory gesture that commanded Veronique to continue.

"As you see, the document in your hands is sealed in the arms of both Prince Eon de l'Etoile, Prince of Béziers—" The mention of that name sent an audible reaction through the room, a hissing chorus of whispers—"and my own lady, Prince Julia Antasia of Hamburg." And that name silenced the whispers entirely.

"As you know, I came to the Grand Court some time ago as Milady Prince Antasia's diplomatic envoy, to attend her interests, and to advance those interests to the best of my abilities. One of milady prince's most profound interests is, and always has been, the security of her own dominions, which have been repeatedly threatened by unrest spilling over the border from the Languedoc into the Fiefs of the Black Cross. Proponents of the Cainite Heresy and Furore malefactors, rousted from the lands of the south by crusade and political unrest, have moved north into her domain—a fact which milady prince has never considered particularly acceptable, but which she could not contain at the source, the conflict between the Courts of Love and the Grand Court."

A second flurry of whispers passed through the crowd at this pronouncement; Prince Alexander's face became, if possible, even more blandly unreadable than it had been before. Veronique gestured at the parchment in his hands and continued. "In crisis, however, opportunity often hides, awaiting recognition. Such an opportunity rests in Your Highness's hands, even now. At the behest of Milady Prince Antasia, I opened diplomatic relations with Prince Eon de l'Etoile of Béziers in the hopes of bringing about a peaceful resolution to the quarrel between his city and the lords of the Grand Court. Milord Prince Eon craves Your Highness's friendship yet, for he served Your Highness's vassals loyally for many years, and he would not cast aside the love he bears for you. Milord Prince Eon also begs that Your Highness understand that, as all princes do, he must secure the borders of his domain from those that would despoil it, and in that regard, diplomacy often fares more successfully than the sword."

The whispers became a low rumble of open conversation, rising to such a peak that the herald was forced to call for silence before Veronique could continue speaking. "Milady Prince Antasia and Milord Prince Eon therefore jointly offer the following proposal: For many years, the stability of Your Highness's domain has been threatened by the presence of both eastern refugees fleeing the destruction of Constantinople and the brazen activities of the Heretics of the Shining Blood.

Recently, those Heretics who aligned themselves with the late Bishop St. Lys have traveled south into the lands claimed by Prince Eon de l'Etoile and have made themselves odious to him. The eastern refugees, those adherents of Your Highness's late grandchilde, Sir Hugh de Clairvaux, under the leadership of the ashen priest Anatole de Paris, are greatly desirous of the opportunity to travel south to continue their crusade against the Heretics.

"As of this night, Prince Eon de l'Etoile stands ready to offer permanent sanctuary to Brother Anatole de Paris and his followers in his domain, in exchange for their assistance in crushing the Cainite Heresy in the lands administered by himself and his allies. Further, Milord Prince Eon stands ready to protect Your Highness's domains from further incursion by these loathsome fanatics, and to pursue such diplomacies in the south as Your Highness deems needful. It is the ardent hope of Milord Prince Eon to assist in bringing about a peaceful, diplomatic resolution of the conflicts in the south, between the Grand Court and the Courts of Love, and to continue for many years in friendship with Your Highness and Your Highness's vassals."

Veronique dropped a final, deep presentation curtsey when she finished speaking, and held that gesture. The room was utterly, dreadfully silent, and it took all of her nerve and her self-control not to rise unbidden just to see how the rest of the court was reacting.

Then, "You may rise, Lady Veronique d'Orleans."

She did so, grateful that her heavy skirts concealed how unsteady her legs were feeling beneath her at the moment. Prince Alexander's expression was as opaque as before, but Saviarre was visibly struggling to contain her reaction, and Sir Olivier was staring at her as though she'd just pulled a maul from beneath her kirtle and struck him between the eyes with it.

"This is a proposal of considerable merit," Prince Alexander said finally, after a moment of silent consideration, a response that set off another tide of whispers, "from a vassal whose loyalty and friendship we once considered entirely and irreconcilably alienated from us. A princely gesture of peace and service, and one worthy of the line that produced him." Alexander fell silent for another moment, his thumb idly caressing the upraised Etoile seal on the parchment he held. "We cannot, of course, answer Prince Eon de l'Etoile's most generous and unexpected proposal at once, for we must consult our counselors and consider our response carefully. Lady Veronique, will you communicate this information to Prince Eon, as well as our appreciation of his efforts on our behalf?"

"Your Highness, it would be my pleasure to do so." Veronique replied, in precisely the same coolly measured tone.

"Very well. Herald. Court is adjourned. We will see any remaining petitioners at the small court on May Day." Alexander rose, and the entire court hurriedly dropped curtseys and offered bows in response to his sudden movement. "The privy council will convene in one quarter hour to discuss this proposal. Clear the court."

Veronique rose from her final curtsey of the evening, just as Prince Alexander turned his back and departed the room, cracking the seals on the parchment he held as he went. To her right, she thought she caught the hint of a maliciously pleased chuckle, but when she looked in that direction, Dame Mnemach was already gone. To her left, she caught a flicker of pale green skirts as Rosamund recessed along with the rest of the court. Veronique did not yet dare to catch her eye before so many others. And, before her, Saviarre's dark skirts swept across the dais as she moved to follow her prince—and the look she bestowed on Veronique was cool with depthless malice. Veronique replied with the faintest hint of a smile and an entirely proper courtesy, before turning to depart.

Chapter Ten

To Milord Prince Eon de l'Etoile of Béziers,

We offer our deepest and sincerest greetings and felicitations to you, our kinsman, and do pray that our missive finds you well despite the tribulations in which you are embroiled.

We write to you in response to your communication, received by us at the Annunciation Court from the hand of your agent, Lady Ambassador Veronique d'Orleans, in service to our sister Prince Julia Antasia. Having verified the authenticity of the seals appended and reviewed the contents of your proposal, we find that we are sufficiently intrigued to enter into the following agreement, pending approval of the following enumerated points.

Primus, your gracious offer of permanent sanctuary for our long-time guests from the east and for our loyal, if troubled, subject, Brother Anatole de Paris. After due consideration, we have decided to accept this offer in the spirit in which it was intended. We have corresponded with Brother Anatole and have determined that he harbors no reservations with regards to this enterprise. We stand ready to assist you in whatever way you require to expedite the journey of Brother Anatole and his followers.

Secundus, we approve the actions taken by Brother Anatole and Eon de l'Etoile, Lord Prince of Béziers, against the blight known as the Cainite Heresy and offer all of our support to the suppression and destruction of these vile fanatics.

Tertius, the proposed independence of the domain of Béziers from obligations of honor to Paris. This is a matter that will require significantly more discussion, as it is an issue of no small importance, and we do not choose to either concede or refuse this point, at this time. We request that, in the interest of maintaining diplomatic ties and continuing negotiations on this point, that you dispatch an ambassador at the soonest possible opportunity.

By my hand,

—Alexander, Princeps Lutetius

"It was my understanding that you were having her watched."

When the Countess Saviarre was angry, she spoke in her coolest, calmest voice. A lesser Cainite might raise her voice, or pepper her speech with an invective, or lapse into the accents of her native language, but not Saviarre. No, when Saviarre was truly angry, angry enough to kill, she completely lost any trace of persistent linguistic tics, became chill and flat and inflectionless as she pulled her control close around her and denied herself the release of a frothingly emotional first response. She preferred, on the whole, to make her decisions in cold blood, or at least the illusion of cold blood, and permitted no outward manifestation of wrath to give a lie to the appearance she wished to project.

Bishop de Navarre had only seen her publicly lose her temper once in all the years of their association, and that was when the news had arrived in Paris concerning the alliance between Eon de l'Etoile and Esclarmonde the Black. He knew the entire court had missed a second display by the skin of her immense inner well of self-control when Veronique d'Orleans had come before Alexander to present a petition on behalf of the Prince of Béziers. And he knew, also, that he was missing a private, personal show of rage solely on the basis of his continuing personal value.

"Milady, I have had the woman under constant surveillance since last summer." The good bishop chose his words carefully. "Her every movement has been monitored as closely as possible, given the resources at my command, and how thinly those resources are currently spread."

Saviarre's eyes, a shade of blue so dark as to seem black in the light of the single candle they shared, visibly hardened, and her voice cooled still further. "It is a poor craftsman who blames his tools, de Navarre."

De Navarre forcibly restrained a sharp retort—I could say the same to you, milady—holding it firmly behind his teeth until the desire to spit it out faded. Instead he gestured outward into the darkness surrounding their island of light, the circumference of a single candle's radiance. No breath disturbed its flame and yet the shadows lying against the windowless walls danced and flickered. "I have human eyes and ears in plenty, lady, but they can only see and hear so much. Yes, Veronique d'Orleans dwells and works her mischief among the refuse of this city—but she's bought their loyalty with a coin we cannot easily devalue. She actually cares about their poxy wives and snot-nosed whelps, and she exerts herself to their help when she's not harassing us. And I have only so many shadows at my command, most of which are dedicated to other tasks."

Saviarre stared through him for a moment, her expression completely opaque, before nodding once, shallowly, in acknowledgement of the point. "How did she do it, de Navarre?"

"Evade us? I can only guess."

"Then do so."

De Navarre ground his teeth, and silently acknowledged to himself that Saviarre wanted him to put her own fear into words. "I suspect," he replied, again, quite carefully, "that she may very well have made common cause with the Nosferatu. It is not beyond the bounds of possibility. Their methods of communication have never been within our sphere of observation and only barely at the edge of our attempts at control."

Saviarre exhaled slowly through her teeth, a drawn-out sound of pure, cold menace. When she spoke, her voice was completely blank of expression, and de Navarre could hear the howls of all-consuming hatred behind every word. "Mnemach. I will see that misbegotten whore burn for this, and her puppet beside her." She stood, abruptly, her skirts swirling around her ankles, the darkness eddying around her like black smoke. "What resources would the task of summoning more shadows require," she asked in that same empty, inflectionless voice, "and how soon would you be able to do so?"

De Navarre took a breath, and released it, without speaking. Her eyes bored into him, unblinking. After a moment of silent consideration, he replied, just as coolly as she, attempting to plane the excitement from his voice and body language. "It depends on what sort of shadows milady desires. Sacrifices of sufficient quantity and quality, in any case—the smaller shadows will come for—"

"I seem to recall hearing once of shadows capable of more than simple acts of espionage."

"Such things do exist, yes."

"Then we shall require them. I think that it is time, Your Grace, that we begin reminding the vultures of this court precisely who it is that rules here."

De Navarre was gone. The servants, dismissed by their mistress, had long since retired to their beds. Silence reigned.

The Countess Saviarre sat staring into the heart of a candle, watching it burn down with a fixed intensity that would have deeply disturbed any observer. Her face was devoid of expression, and she sat with the unnatural stillness that only a Cainite elder could possess. Her eyes were alive with a hate and fury that bordered on madness, reflecting the candle flame in points of hot crimson.

I have permitted myself to become too... distracted of late, the thought finally articulated itself within her, after a titanic struggle to put the concept into words she was willing to accept. That lunatic ashen priest...St. Lys... the broom star... all of the last few damned years... Distraction. All of it.

The Countess Saviarre was no longer accustomed to having her weaknesses manipulated by anyone but herself. It had been a long time since anyone had dared the attempt, and even longer since someone had succeeded at it. She had founded her personal power not only in Alexander's weakness, but in the personal venality of Paris's courtiers, their desire for a ruler who would turn a blind eye on their attempts to aggrandize themselves so long as they avoided challenging her, and their collective fear of her. She had made a few quietly illustrative examples in the early nights of her rule, and those examples had served to warn the court not to trifle with her. Those who might have been inclined to do so became the objects of even more examples, or else had slunk out of Paris to seek their fortunes elsewhere. Lord Valerian, had he been present to witness it, would have been appalled.

He would have the opportunity to be appalled now. She had known, for some time, that de Navarre was beginning to chafe at the restrictions she had placed on his little experiments, the limits under which she insisted that he labor. She knew it had taken him vast personal control not to exceed the scope of his instructions last summer when the opportunity to wreak untold havoc had reared its head, and she thought that permitting him a bit of slack in his leash now would be a proper reward for his discretion. And a proper means of retaliating against Mnemach and her poorly considered little insurrection.

Saviarre admitted to herself, with some difficulty, that she should have foreseen that Mnemach would try to take advantage of any weakness she might display. Should have but had not. She ground her fangs in frustration. Distractions. Well, soon there would be one less distraction, and she would be free to concentrate on the real problems. Mnemach. Veronique d'Orleans. And Brother Anatole and Eon de l'Etoile would be in one place, to be crushed at leisure. Perhaps, if he succeeded at his current set of tasks, she would permit de Navarre to have what he wanted, after all, and the dark corridors of Mnemach's little warren, a place where no light ever came, would indeed become a kingdom of shadows.

She would think on it.

"Out."

Queen Salianna's ladies-in-waiting, each and every one a well-bred girl, leapt to obey their lady's abrupt, low-voiced command, dropping curtseys, murmuring polite nothings, gathering up their sewing and their instruments. The last one out, sensibly, shut the door of the solar behind her and fled, placing discretion over the better part of gossip. For a long moment after her flock of brilliantly plumed and accomplished young women had gone, Salianna, Queen of the Courts of Love, sat in her chair next to the fire, struggling silently with herself, the parchments she had just been delivered clenched in one small, white hand:

A true lady did not speak in a peremptory or curt fashion even to household servants, much less to promising young women whom she was instructing in the feminine arts. A true lady was sweet-voiced and pleasing in tone and word at all times. True ladies also did not throw delicate objects forcefully at the walls, but Salianna felt the uncontrollable compulsion toward that behavior, as well. Anything to reduce the pressure inside her ribs, the sudden wash of fury reddening her vision, the need to twist someone's head off just to put her own temper back in order. Her throw reduced a fragile ceramic vase, currently empty of flowers, to powder against the far wall of the solar; amazingly enough, watching it disintegrate actually made her feel somewhat better. It allowed her to reopen the letters she had received and consider their contents in a slightly more objective frame of mind.

Veronique d'Orleans had, perhaps predictably, exceeded the scope of her mission. Yes, Rosamund d'Islington was successfully installed in the Grand Court, and was already cutting the swath that Isouda de Blaise had all but promised. Yes, the damnable Countess Saviarre was struck a blow, perhaps even a crippling one, and for the first time in two centuries, her eminence in Paris was seriously challenged. Yes, Veronique was positioning herself to continue that campaign, settling in to lay siege to Saviarre's station with the intent of isolating and destroying her. And, yes, the queen had even begun to believe that the little Brujah witch could actually do it. It was clearly not the only thing she intended to do, however.

Salianna's hand balled into a fist and it took all her self-control not to find something else to throw. Peace between Béziers and Paris. The reopening of formal diplomatic relations in an association that had been almost fatally strained. An at least tacit acknowledgement of the legitimacy of diplomatic ties between Béziers and Foix. A peaceful resolution being sought to "events" in the Languedoc. The very last thing Queen Salianna herself had wanted, no matter how well it advanced the effort to permit Rosamund d'Islington to work more freely or to weaken and dispose of Saviarre. Esclarmonde the Black could not be permitted to regain Alexander's favor, could not be permitted another legitimate chance to clear her name. The only thing left for Esclarmonde the Black to do was yield, and die, quickly or slowly.

Oh, yes. Veronique d'Orleans had *vastly* exceeded the scope of her instructions, and Salianna had to wonder if that had been her plan all along. Mastering herself, Salianna rose, and summoned a servant to fetch her secretary.

"Tell me, Ambassador," Eon de l'Etoile remarked, dryly, "did you think, last year at this time, that any of this might occur? Even once?"

Aimeric de Cabaret, who was wearing what Eon thought to be an extremely self-satisfied smile, laid the letter, freshly arrived from Paris, down in the middle of the table and admitted frankly, "No."

"Oh, good. I'm glad I'm not the only one deficient in imagination."

Aimeric was still chuckling helplessly when the Mouse and Crepin entered the council chamber. They took in the sight of their ruler and most favored hostage sharing a fit of hysterical giggles and exchanged a glance of their own.

"Good news, I take it?" the Mouse whispered, somewhat doubtfully, and reached for the letter.

"Oh, yes. Oh, yes, indeed, milady. Read it." Eon put his chin in his hand, his grin growing gradually wider as he watched her read, and the expression that grew on her own face. Wordlessly she handed it to Crepin and sat down, looking thoroughly astounded.

"I can't believe he actually agreed to it," she murmured, shaking her head a bit to clear it, as Crepin snorted in disgust and tossed the letter down on the table again.

"He didn't agree to *all* of it." Aimeric finally recovered from his fit of mirth long enough to respond intelligently. "I expect convincing Paris to recognize the independence of Béziers will be an uphill climb of unpleasant duration."

"But he asked for an ambassador, at least, which is something." Eon picked up the letter, folded it, and placed it in his correspondence chest. "Opinions?"

"Perhaps we should send Isarn back to your grandsire and ask *them* to send us someone with the brains God gave a post?" Mouse suggested.

"He's too useful for hitting people. Ambassador?" Eon glanced at Aimeric.

He smiled wryly. "Are you asking for my opinion, or if I suddenly crave a trip to Paris?"

"Both."

Aimeric was silent for a long moment, his expression sobering completely. "Truth, milord? Send no one. The situation is too unsettled. Queen Esclarmonde sends no ambassadors to Paris lest her envoys become hostages, and weapons to be used against her. You would be wise to do the same—there is no formal peace between Béziers and Paris yet."

"And if we fail to send an ambassador there will not be a peace," the Mouse pointed out in a fierce whisper.

"We already have an agent in the court of Paris who has done us good service unasked," Aimeric countered, looking to the Prince of Béziers. "Veronique d'Orleans did not have to exert herself on our behalf and yet she did so. It is true that she is already the ambassador of Lady Julia Antasia, but she may be willing to act as your agent as well, milord. And, more to the point, her diplomatic credentials, and the power of her first patron, immunize her far more completely than any Bitterois ambassador you might send."

"Crepin?" Eon deliberately turned to his sheriff.

"Little as I like to admit it," Crepin muttered, and flicked a look at Aimeric, "the singer has a point. We cannot assure the security of any ambassador we send, not along the road and certainly not once in Paris. Better to put our trust in someone already there, who can likely care for herself."

Eon blinked. "A lesser sign of the—no, that's not entirely true. You've agreed on things in the past."

"We have?" Aimeric asked, with wide-eyed innocence.

"You must have," Eon replied, firmly. "Very well. I will consider the advice you've given me in this matter. Thank you all... and hopefully this situation will continue to resolve itself in our favor."

Chapter Eleven

Rosamund d'Islington found the scent of rain soothing—she always had, and suspected the fondness derived from memories of her childhood, growing up in wet and misty England. Moreover, the winter was fading rapidly, and even after dark the weather now tended toward unseasonable warmth: The earliest of the spring flowers were already in bud in the embassy's well-tended garden. Consequently, when Lord Valerian accepted her invitation to visit, she ordered the windows in the solar opened to chase out the mustiness of the winter months, and the entire room cleaned. By the night of Lord Valerian's visit, the solar smelt gently of lemon oil and beeswax, the walls were newly white-washed and the floor freshly scrubbed, and most of the older cushions and hangings replaced. A dozen candles brightened the room (including one, its inscriptions hidden by a blue blown-glass shield, sitting on the mantle over the fireplace and holding the shadows in place), and the windows were still partly open, admitting the scent and sound of a soft, early spring rain.

Rosamund was not at all nervous about meeting with Lord Valerian. In truth, he was one of the few members of the Grand Court whose honor she felt she could trust completely, which put him head and shoulders above the majority of the Parisian Cainites she'd met thus far. He was truly a gentleman from another era and carried himself accordingly, with dignity and nobility, his probity beyond question. Rosamund appreciated fully why Veronique believed his support vital to the success of their mission. Veronique, however, was deeply engaged in making certain Brother Anatole and his followers had everything they needed to ensure the success of *their* mission, as well as keeping a weather eye on Countess Saviarre. That gave Rosamund an opportunity that she had desired—the chance to build her own contacts within Paris's diplomatic community.

Lord Valerian arrived precisely at the hour stipulated, having walked the short distance between his home and the Toreador embassy, his fine woolen cloak beaded with moisture. Rosamund hurried to make him comfortable, and he waved aside her efforts with a genial smile. "My dear, the pleasure of seeing you again is more than comfort enough. How have you been?"

"Milord Valerian, you flatter me." Rosamund led him to the most comfortable chair in the solar. "I have, as you've probably guessed, been quite busy."

"I don't doubt it at all, my dear. All I ask is that you tolerate it as best you can." He patted her hand and seated himself. "It was good for you to make the time to see me, Lady Rosamund, for in truth I desired to see you, as well. Have you seen Lady Veronique d'Orleans recently?"

Rosamund hesitated slightly. "We have corresponded, but we haven't met personally. She is also quite busy with her current activities. May I ask why...?"

"Lady Veronique suggested to me that her patron, my old friend Lady Julia Antasia, and yours, Queen Salianna, have made common cause on certain aspects of politics and diplomacy, when she requested my assistance with regards to your embassy," Valerian answered her semi-articulated question. "It seemed possible to me. Lady Prince Antasia cannot appreciate heavily armed bands of malefactors from the Languedoc marauding in her territory. I cannot, however, credit the idea that Queen Salianna would approve of any diplomatic scheme that might redound favorably to the position of Queen Esclarmonde of Foix."

Rosamund, thinking of the letter she had received from Queen Salianna the night previously, responded frankly, as well. "Truthfully, Lord Valerian? She did not. In fact, I have reason to suspect that she is rather displeased with Lady Veronique's political strategy in that regard."

"Lady Veronique is not, I think, of dishonest temperament."

Lord Valerian caught her eye and held it. "But I do not think her actions are entirely devoid of deceit, and I suspect that she has her own agenda here in Paris, separate and distinct from any service she owes to the Courts of Love."

"Who among our kind does not have some sort of private agenda, Lord Valerian? In this, Lady Veronique is no different from anyone else." Rosamund demurely lowered her eyes. "I suspect that her interest in aiding the courts of Queen Esclarmonde and Prince Eon de l'Etoile is personal. My sources suggest that she spent many years of her youth in the south, and she may yet have colleagues there who begged her assistance, as well."

"Possible. I suspect that her interest in thwarting Countess Saviarre may be of more than dispassionate political origin, as well." Rosamund looked sharply at him. "I can prove nothing of that point, milady, it is merely an instinctual inclination on my part. And I will tell you, whatever her motivations might be, it pleases me to see Lady Veronique taking such actions against the good countess. Saviarre is no friend to you, or to the Courts of Love—nor to anyone who might exercise some limiting effect on the power she wields here in Paris."

"I've noticed that about her, yes," Rosamund replied dryly. "I doubt, however, that she would choose to oppose the will of Prince Alexander actively—surely she isn't *that* overconfident in her power."

"She is not—but I fear that you cannot yet rely on Prince Alexander's support against her, either." Lord Valerian reached into the front of his surcoat and extracted a slender letter, which he pushed across the table to her. "You may rely upon mine. And, for what it's worth, I believe you may rely upon Lady Veronique. And there is one other who may yet be of assistance to you."

The letter was sealed with a purple ribbon embroidered in gold at the edge and a blot of golden wax stamped with familiar arms, little seen of late in Île-de-France. Rosamund's eyes widened. "Milord Valerian, this is… most unexpected."

"I am not unaware of that. I only just received word of it, myself—though if he chose to write, I suspect that he is quite close to home, and confident that his messengers will not be intercepted." Valerian smiled with a certain grim pleasure. "He will, I assure you, be our ally. He has never been Saviarre's friend, nor has he suffered her efforts to control his actions, and he knows how to defend himself against her machinations. I ask that you exercise caution in your endeavors until he is in Paris."

Rosamund tore her eyes away from the letter and nodded quickly. "Of course, milord. We cannot proceed rashly, in any case. I thank you for bringing me this excellent news."

"It was my pleasure." Valerian caught her hand, and raised it to her lips. "I ask, milady, that you excuse the shortness of this visit—I fear I have many other errands to run before my night is over."

"Of course, milord!" Rosamund rose, and motioned the servants sitting attendance next to the fire to fetch Lord Valerian's cloak. "I hope that we will have cause to meet again soon."

Valerian smiled that grim, pleased smile again. "Milady Rosamund, I am quite certain that we will."

"Josselin."

Josselin de Poitiers looked up from the task at which he was laboring to find his sister standing in the door of his chamber, a harried look on her lovely face and a letter in one hand. He laid his sword and whetstone aside and rose to greet her. "What is it, *petite fleur*? Not bad news, I hope."

Rosamund flashed him the briefest of reassuring smiles. "No—not bad news. I have a task for you... I need you to ride south for me."

A little thrill of anticipation ran up Josselin s spine. "How far south, dare I ask?"

"Chartres. I need you to deliver a letter to Queen Isouda." She paused, and handed him the letter; it was so recently sealed that the wax was still warm. "And then I need you to continue south down the Rhone road. You probably will not have to ride as far as Arles. You're likely to find what you're looking for long before then."

Something about her tone warned him, and he looked up,

scrutinizing her closely. "What, precisely, am I looking for, *petite*?"

"You'll know when you see it. I don't dare speak of it, Josselin, lest an unfriendly ear overhear. I ask that you trust me in this. Can you do that?"

He shook his head. "What kind of question is that? Of course I trust you." He captured her hand and kissed it. "When do I leave?"

"Tonight. Make use of the manor house if the road is bad—but I need you to make Chartres as quickly as possible."

"Of course, petite. Let me wake Fabien, and I will be on my way."

"Go with God, Josselin—and please, whatever you do, be careful."

"Always, *petite*."

"You know, ever since you came here, the entire city has been in an ungodly uproar, and just when things seem as if they're about to settle down, you stir them right back up again." Sir Olivier gave Veronique a mock-stern look across the table they sat at, in the middle of his garden beneath a canvas canopy, watching the rain bruise the first spring greenery.

Veronique inclined an eyebrow. "Am I to interpret that as a request to desist, milord?"

"Would you consider it if it were?"

"No. You'd be bored senseless a month after I ceased stirring things up, and so would I."

Sir Olivier let out a startled laugh and shook his head. "You're probably right but, God's teeth, woman, couldn't you have warned me, at least? So I could have done more than stand there gawking, you understand."

"I understand. And I'm sorry." Veronique offered an apologetic smile. "I would have warned you if I could have, but the negotiations themselves were undertaken in the utmost—"

"Secrecy?"

"Security," she continued smoothly, "and I didn't feel it wise to break that security before I had the situation entirely in hand. You understand the risks, Sir Olivier."

"Unfortunately, I do," he said ruefully. "I don't know how you can do it night by night, Lady Veronique—as much as I love my existence, and my work, I do not think I'll ever be quite as wholly immersed in it as you seem to be."

"It's not so terrible as all that, milord. You might be surprised one night to discover how rewarding the field of diplomacy can be." She felt the smile tugging at the corners of her mouth again, and let it come back to stay. "If I may be so bold, milord, I think you would make a superior agent for His Highness abroad, perhaps even the ruler of your own domain."

"Lady Veronique, you must tell me what I've done to make you wish such a godforsaken fate on me, and I'll make amends at once." Olivier shuddered theatrically.

The candle burning between them was not a shadow-freezing gift. Veronique arched a questioning eyebrow. "Surely, milord, you desire your own dominion, some night? A court of your own, to arrange as best pleases you, a consort and courtiers to see to your every whim…"

Olivier snorted, a most unregal gesture. "If being prince is anything like being the prince's first errand-boy—and I've considerable reason to believe that it's even worse—the answer to that question is *no*. There's a reason I was never tempted to go south and carve out a domain of my own, you know, and it's because being prince is much like being the roast goose at a feast. The ones that aren't carving you up are waiting for the chance to chew on you. Look at your friend de l'Etoile—prince of a burntout wreck of a city that he had to rebuild from scratch with his own blood, surrounded on all sides by bottom-feeders waiting for the chance to take it from him." He shook his head. "If that's the pleasure I'm to derive from rulership, I'll take service any night. And I notice that you're not precisely falling all over yourself trying to claim a piece of that goose, either, milady."

Veronique chose not to correct his designation of Eon de l'Étoile's friendship, and watched the shadows flickering out of the corner of her eyes. "I'm temperamentally unsuited to it, I fear. Someone would say something foolish to me in council and I'd have to tear his head off and plant flowers in his empty skull."

"Has anyone ever told you that you have an unsettling command of imagery, Lady Veronique?"

"Often."

"Well, I'm glad you know. And you do realize that, if you were prince, you'd be *allowed* to rip empty heads off and no one would be able to gainsay you?"

"Yes, and while that would certainly soothe my temper, it wouldn't do my soul much good, now would it?"

Olivier laughed and shook his head again. "I'd suggest you could go to Brother Anatole for confession but that would likely entail quite a lot of travel to accomplish. Incidentally, when I suggested that you distance yourself from him, I didn't think you'd take that quite so literally."

Veronique chuckled herself. "That was, milord, simply a case of reality and metaphor coming together in a most unusual way." She sobered. "As congenial as I'm finding the company, milord, I fear I do have other errands to run before the sun rises. If I may be so bold... the invitation tonight was yours."

"Indeed, it was." Olivier straightened up slightly, the change in his body language subtle but telling as he shrugged away the affected posture of an empty-headed courtier. "It wouldn't be much of a guess to assume that you have fairly reliable communications in the south."

"That is true," Veronique admitted, somewhat warily.

"Have you received any news from your resources of late?" He raised a hand to stave off her immediate response. "I don't want to know who they are or where they might be placed. I just want to know... Have you received any unusual gossip? Rumor? Innuendo?"

He seemed genuinely agitated about something. "Nothing untoward, I will admit. But the roads arc slow, too. Even rumor can only travel so quickly through a foot of mud. Dare I ask why?"

"I don't suppose you'd take 'no reason' as an answer, would you?" She gave him a look, and he sighed in surrender. "No, I didn't think so." His voice lowered to barely a breath, nearly inaudible against the background murmur of the rain. "There's a vicious rumor circulating that my beloved elder brother

Geoffrey may be on the way home, unheralded and unannounced, having landed in Marseilles some nights ago. If it's
true, he's most likely coming up the Rhone road and traveling
in the utmost secrecy."

Veronique's eyebrows arched. "I admit that I hadn't heard
that rumor from any source, milord."

"Damn. I'd been hoping you might have been able to con-
firm or deny it for me—God's teeth, I hope it's not so." He offered
another theatrical gesture of dismay.

"I take it you're not eager to renew your acquaintance with
your brother-in-blood." Veronique could not, in fact, remember if Olivier had even been Embraced before Geoffrey had left
Ile-de-France.

"We've never met. And I will admit that I'm not looking forward to the first meeting—I'd rather hoped he'd stay in
Outremer and carve himself a domain out of the Latin Empire.
I have it on good authority," Olivier's tone dried considerably,
"that Geoffrey and our sire do not entirely get along like peas in
a pod. Nor did he find Countess Saviarre's company particularly
convivial—but, then, I can hardly hold that against him. Would
a boring summer this year be too much to ask of heaven?"

"Evidently, milord." Veronique rose in a rustle of skirts.
"But, since you asked so nicely, I'll see what I can do to intercede
on your behalf."

Olivier's laughter followed her down the garden path.

Chapter Twelve

Jean-Battiste de Montrond genuinely couldn't get enough of the isle and its society. He did, after all, make all his best money there among the high-blooded elite of both Cainite and kine, pandering to the vices of the thoroughly depraved among each species. His clientele tended to be a perversely inventive lot and the sheer *imagination* they were willing to pour into the process of satisfying their basest lusts never failed to entertain as well as enrich him. The previous summer had, indeed, been a windfall in that regard, and he wasn't bored once while providing the jaded and the innocent alike with the tools necessary to gratify their hysteria-driven urges. Winter had, as always, brought a certain abeyance to his activities and a slowing of his business, but now that winter was over, he could count on the explosion of spring madness to refill his coffers and provide him with all the amusement he could possibly desire.

It was therefore with considerable personal satisfaction that he received the first of what he knew would be an increasing flood of correspondence from his regular clients. Bishop de Navarre craved his presence on Ile de la Cité to discuss a matter of some importance—which meant, Jean-Battiste knew, that the good bishop required his procuring services yet again, and less than three months after his last such request. The man certainly did use up his playthings quickly. An exchange of notes set the time and place—two nights hence at the bishop's residence—and gave Jean-Battiste the opportunity to take a quick inventory of the merchandise he had in stock and consult his records regarding de Navarre's past purchases. The man had a marked predilection for youth.

Jean-Battiste arrived precisely one-quarter hour before the stipulated meeting time and was shown in immediately. He expected, nonetheless, to wait for a considerable interval beyond that time. De Navarre invariably let him sit for a while—it was, Jean-Battiste supposed, a way for the Lasombra to remind him where the power really lay in their relationship, no matter how often de Navarre called on his services. Jean-Battiste found that more than a little amusing.

Much to his surprise, he wasn't guided into the customary antechamber where he would while away an hour or so mentally undressing the women of the house. Instead, he was taken directly to de Navarre's office, a long, windowless room completely devoid of anything resembling human cheer, where the bishop preferred to do all his business. De Navarre was already there.

And he wasn't alone.

Jean-Battiste stopped dead in the doorway, and only continued forward because there was a large, unfriendly young man with a sword at his back and no obvious way to get past him. The door slammed behind him and he heard, distinctly, the sound of a bar being set in place outside.

The Countess Saviarre, seated in what had to be the most comfortable chair in de Navarre's house, smiled genteelly at him, and gestured him forward. "Jean-Battiste de Montrond, I presume?"

Jean-Battiste darted a glance at de Navarre, standing behind the countess's chair, and received no help; the man was as transparent as a statue. Jean-Battiste offered Prince Alexander's first advisor the deepest and most courtly bow in his repertoire. "I am, indeed, that man, Milady Countess—Jean-Battiste de Montrond, procurer of many fine and exotic things to tempt and please the tastes of Caine's children. How may I be of service to Your Excellency?"

"You may cease your sniveling and attend me closely."

Jean-Battiste grimaced at the floor and straightened up. It was true: Give a woman, any woman, a little power and she completely lost any appreciation she might once have possessed for finely honed flattery. "Of course, Your—"

"I know who and what you are, serpent." Countess Saviarre's voice cut across his before he could even attempt to establish the atmosphere of businesslike cordiality that he tended to favor. "You are a slaver and a whoremonger, an importer of exotic substances, only some of which may be used recreationally, and a confidence artist of the highest possible caliber." Jean-Battiste felt obscurely flattered by that; it didn't last long. "You are also an information peddler who maintains no lasting or fixed loyalty to anyone but himself, and *that* is the part I wish to do business with—not the part that thinks himself charming. Am I making myself clear?"

"Crystalline, milady," Jean-Battiste replied dryly. He gestured at the empty chair across from hers at the table. "If I may...?" She nodded her permission, and he sat. "What sort of information does milady require? I'll warn you, the gossip's been a little stale this winter...."

"I wish to know," Saviarre replied coldly, supported by de Navarre's most penetrating dark-eyed stare, "everything that Veronique d'Orleans does. I want to know where she goes. I want to know to whom she speaks. I want to know who comes to see her, and whose letters she returns the most quickly. I want to know how many grains of lavender she uses in her bathwater. *Everything.* I also desire to know who her principal agents are in both the Latin Quarter and the Ile de la Cité. The mortals."

"Ah." Jean-Battiste's heart performed a gymnastic exercise which involved attempting to leap all the way up his throat only to plunge, twisting and writhing, into his stomach.

"You will, of course, be compensated for your efforts in this matter," Saviarre continued graciously.

I most assuredly will. "Milady's request is intriguing, I will admit. And possibly highly remunerative."

"And yet I perceive a certain lack of enthusiasm on your part."

Jean-Battiste considered how to phrase his concern. "Milady is clearly well informed—it therefore surprises me a bit that you seem unaware of Veronique d'Orleans's knack for identifying and neutralizing," he paused, considered, soldiered on, "spies, provocateurs, and other such individuals of low character."

"She tolerates *your* existence in her territory', serpent, so her character judgment cannot be flawless." Saviarre, it was clear, didn't see any need to resort to ego-stroking flattery when a skewer worked just as well.

"Veronique and I do not share territory," Jean-Battiste replied, after a moment of easing the stiffness out of his neck. "She has hers and I have mine and we don't poach each other's herds. Well, *she* doesn't, anyway. And she defends what's hers... vigorously."

"As do I." A cool smile touched the corners of Saviarre's mouth. "I did not summon you here to permit you to refuse me, serpent."

"I knew you were going to say that." He sighed. "Very well. Compensation. I desire formal acknowledgment of my claim to domain in the Latin Quarter—my sole and sovereign claim, excepting no others. If I'm going to jump naked into the lioness's den for you, the Quarter will be mine after all is said and done."

The countess's eyebrow inclined fractionally. "You certainly don't lack for arrogance, do you?"

"Call it what you like. I tend to consider it restricting competition in the fields of information brokerage and vice mongering." He offered her a toothy smile of his own. "Also—"

"*Also?*" Incredulously.

"Also," Jean-Battiste continued doggedly, "once all is said and done, I want first pickings of Veronique d'Orleans's properties and chattels. She has several lovely possessions that would look better in my house than in hers. I intend to have them with or without your cooperation, so you might as well let me take them without a fight."

"Your arrogance," Saviarre's tone was frosty, "is rapidly becoming unamusing, serpent."

"As I said, you may call it what you like—but you're also asking me to actively betray a woman who can twist my head off without breaking a sweat and," Jean-Battiste added sweetly, "who has obviously defeated your other attempts to monitor her activities, or else you wouldn't be coming to me. Am I wrong?"

He cast a glance at the Bishop de Navarre and caught him

looking peevish, which answered that question to Jean-Battiste's satisfaction. Saviarre's look was stony. She did not, however, admit to anything. "You may also surmise what you like. Very well. Your demands, however insufferable in their arrogance, are not without merit, nor are they excessive considering the risks involved in the task at hand. I take it that you accept."

"I do accept, and I thank milady for her gracious patronage." Jean-Battiste managed, just barely, to keep that from coming out mocking. "I can tell you one thing right now that might make matters a bit clearer—little Veronique has evidently made common cause with the Nosferatu, who, I'm sure milady knows, harbor you no particular good will. I don't know the full extent of their involvement or what the particulars are, but I suspect she's been passing communications through the warren."

Saviarre literally hissed. It was easily the least pleasant sound Jean-Battiste had ever heard coming out of a delicately feminine mouth.

"As to who her agents are… well, that will take a bit more work. There is, however, one that I can name for you right now."

All the roads leading south were just as bad as Josselin had feared they would be, but he rode them as hard as he dared, anyway. It hadn't ceased raining for more than a few hours at a stretch since he'd left Paris, he was absolutely certain of it. He was soaked to the bone and covered in the mud in which he'd slept more often than not, buried and covered with canvas tenting, but at least he didn't have to worry about taking ill. Poor Fabien was in even worse condition, sniffling more or less constantly, but he had stoutly refused to be left behind in Chartres, and Josselin had finally relented to the logic that he'd need assistance from someone familiar with his needs. They had paused in Chartres only long enough for Queen Isouda to read the letter Rosamund had sent, and for that lady to add her own urgent command for Josselin to continue his mission.

They were now fifteen miles outside Chartres, having ridden until the gray and rainy day had forced them to stop, seeking shelter in a way-stop along the road, rising and riding again. Josselin now felt he knew precisely for whom he was searching, from the sheer urgency in Queen Isouda's orders to him, but he had no idea if he would actually succeed. Unless his quarry had some effective means of traveling by day—a light-proofed cart or other conveyance, a vehicle that would find the mud-bogged roads virtually impossible to navigate at any time, day or night—theoretically Josselin would be able simply to ride his quarry down. Even moving quickly, there was only so much speed a party could possibly make, particularly allowing for the weaknesses of Cainite travelers, especially if they couldn't travel by day.

That theory, however, was not thus far bearing itself out. The road south of Chartres was almost completely empty of travelers, or signs that any travelers had passed down it going either direction recently. No one who did not *have* to travel was on the road. He reflected, somewhat dolefully, that it had taken them almost two full nights to travel fifteen miles; he didn't expect that they would make Arles in less than a month if the weather continued to be uncooperative.

Almost as though reading his mind, the rain, which had faded down to a gentle drizzle, hardened again and the wind began to rise. Fabien, riding next to him with their lamp on a pole, head down inside his oiled cloak, sneezed and shuddered. Josselin made a decision. "The first waypoint we come to, we stop. We both need a roof over our heads and a fire, I think."

"You'll get no argument from me," Fabien muttered, as soaked and miserable as Josselin himself.

They hadn't gone another mile before they found the horse. Fabien, to his credit, spotted it among the foliage off the road as they passed by. He claimed he heard it blowing, and it was even possible: Fabien's love of horses was rivaled only by his love of Josselin. He was out of his saddle and approaching the beast before Josselin could utter a warning, taking its bridle and mur-muring sweet nothings to it. The horse, fortunately, appeared to be too weary to bite, kick, or do any of the other things it might have done to ruin Fabien's night further.

Josselin smelled the blood before he'd gotten two paces, clear and distinct over the earthy scent of the mud and the clean scent of the rain. Fabien was stroking the beast's nose as

Josselin approached, carrying their lamp, and even in the dim light he could see that its nostrils were distended, its jaws dripping bloody foam. His squire looked up at him, and shook his head sorrowfully, cheeks streaked with tears. Josselin nodded his understanding, and set the lamp on a nearby stone. "Hold him still until I check his saddle…."

The horse was, indeed, still saddled and panniered, all slick with human and equine blood. Josselin undid the straps on the panniers, careful not to spook the beast, and began removing items—an oilskin sack containing provisions, a smaller oilskin pouch containing documents sealed in wax and ribbon, and at the very bottom, a length of silken cloth. Had Josselin's stomach still been capable of sinking, it would have, as he drew that item forth and held it up to examine by the dim light of the lamp. In the near-dark, the hue of the cloth was black, bordered in metallic golden thread, and the arms were a horse, rearing between two *fleurs-de-lis*, embroidered in silver.

Geoffrey's arms. Josselin swore with feeling.

"I'll… I'll take care of him." Fabien's voice shook slightly, not from the cold. "Go… hurry… he couldn't have come far."

"I'll leave the lamp."

Josselin rode slowly, following the faint but pungent scent of mingled human and equine blood back to its source. His eyes were virtually useless in the dark and the rain, and to see where he was going, he had to rely on the well-trained senses of Sorel, his ghoul from colthood, the finest mount his sire had ever given him. Sorel was almost miraculously surefooted even in near-total darkness, so when he whickered and sidled to avoid something in his path, and the scent of blood abruptly sharpened, Josselin was relatively certain they'd found something. He dismounted, swallowed his pride, and got down on his hands and knees in the mud, feeling about carefully. He encountered the body a few moments later and, despite its coldness, it groaned aloud as he laid hands on it.

"Easy," Josselin murmured soothingly, crawling about to get a better sense of how his prize was positioned, and discovered him lying sprawled half on his side and half on his face.

The scent of blood was strong and Josselin found his fangs lengthening involuntarily in his jaw as he rolled the man over. His clothing was soaked through with rainwater and mud, and he was chilled nearly to the same temperature as his undead masters, but this man was alive, breathing raggedly, his heart beating unsteadily. Josselin doubted he would live long enough to find shelter.

"...My..." A raspy, breathless croak. "...Milord... Geoffrey..."

"Yes!" Josselin nearly shouted it. "Where is he, man? I'm from the court of Chartres—I'll see him safe if it's in my power."

A wet, wracking cough rattled the body, and Josselin smelled a renewed scent of blood. "...Tell him... tell him... it was... as he said...."

"I will, I swear it—*but where is he?*"

"Rou—" He choked, coughed. The blood-scent became over-whelming, and the breath rattled to an end in his chest.

For the second time that night, Josselin swore with a deep passion.

"Is the water warm enough for you, milord?"

"Yes, my dear. Quite."

Geoffrey le Croisé, childe of Alexander, was profoundly bemused. He had had, before coming to the barely tolerated Tremere chantry in Rouen, a fairly fixed mental image of what the abode of a godless vampire wizard would look like. It had included many things—torture chambers ringing with the cries of tormented innocents, murky glass jars containing things too horrible to contemplate pickled in brine, possibly strange markings that didn't bear close examination scrawled on the walls. His imaginings had not included a full-sized bathhouse staffed by comely young specimens of both genders, all of whom were apparently very eager to please. Nor had he expected his host, whom he had never met before this night, to be astonishingly handsome and well-made himself, in direct contradiction of every imagining that insisted a wizard ought to be a desiccated old stick of a vampire with a beard down to his knees.

Goratrix had, thus far, been quite full of surprises. Geoffrey reclined a bit further into the bath—a large, Roman-style bath, sunk into the floor and ringed in mosaics of nymphs and satyrs at play, lined in fine linen cloth from Cambrai and scented with lavender. Overhead, rain drummed with increasing violence against the roof, and Geoffrey closed his eyes, inhaling the warmth and grateful to be inside.

"We have been having absolutely repulsive weather for most of the year thus far, milord." Goratrix's smoothly modulated voice slid itself into Geoffrey's silent contemplations. "It pleases me greatly that you made such good time from the coast, and arrived safely, as well."

Goratrix spoke the Northern French langue d'oïl with the faintest hint of an eastern accent and enunciated every word with the clarity and precision of a professor of rhetoric, even when he was lounging in a hot bath having his back washed by a boy young enough to be his son. He was watching Geoffrey with the heavy-lidded expression of a man who was enjoying himself immensely and looked forward to much more enjoyment in the immediate future.

"Your hospitality has been excellent thus far, Maestro—you have my thanks for taking myself and my companions into your house on such short notice." Geoffrey nodded to the semiclad girl hovering to one side and permitted her to lave his chest with warm water. Excepting only the servants attending them, they were alone, this part of the bathhouse reserved for the use of the regent and his guests and walled off from the rest of the structure. "I trust you have had the opportunity to review and consider my proposal."

"Indeed I have, and I find chat proposal most intriguing." Goratrix waved his attendant away and leaned back against the linen-draped edge of the bath. "I do, however, have some questions."

"Questions?" Geoffrey echoed, inclining an eyebrow.

"Yes. If I recall correctly, milord, you indicated to me that your sire is a sorcerer." There was no particular question in his tone.

Geoffrey chose to respond as though there had been one anyway. "I did, in fact, indicate that to you, Maestro. Is that a problem?"

"Not so much a problem as an issue of intellectual curiosity. I have witnessed many strange and wonderful sights over the years," the regent's tone was decidedly wry, "but I have never before heard of a Ventrue who could accurately claim, much less wear, the title 'sorcerer.' Dare I ask how your illustrious sire came by that exalted designation?"

"You have not been dwelling here in the west for very long, Maestro, and so I will forgive your lack of direct knowledge in this matter." Geoffrey scoured his voice clean of the faintest trace of amusement. "My sire is a sorcerer. Admittedly, I have never personally witnessed the practice of his art but it has been my understanding that most sorcerers are secretive about such things, and in that he is no exception. Nor does he publicly flaunt the depths of whatever arcane knowledge he might possess." He paused for a moment. "Except in one instance, of course—the sorcerously contrived execution of his unfaithful consort, the Lady Lorraine, whose destruction, as you can well imagine, was intended to be... educational for all observers."

The Tremere's eyes narrowed a contemplative fraction. "I do not suppose, milord, that you are in your sire's confidence with regards to where he received his sorcerous education, or from whom?"

"You may suppose that," Geoffrey assured him, mildly.

"It is a curiosity. I do believe there is *a* sorcerer in Paris—but I am not entirely convinced that that sorcerer is the illustrious Prince Alexander himself." Those words had the sound of musing done aloud. "I do not doubt your word, milord, that your sire gives the appearance of possessing some form of arcane knowledge...."

"Meaning?"

"Meaning that I am both curious and intrigued. I visited Paris briefly, some years ago, and was permitted audience with your sire precisely twice—once at my presentation, and once when he invited me to leave his city and not return unless I wished to enjoy the accommodations available to those who had chosen to defy him." A second, thoughtful pause, of shorter duration. "He is powerful, and I have seen and felt his power for myself, at close range. His charisma and will radiate strongly enough to overpower the sense of any Cainite of lesser age—or personal strength. But I did not see anything about him, none of the telling marks, that would indicate deep arcane knowledge. Is it possible, milord, that it is not your sire who is the sorcerer, but one of his advisors?"

"That is… not beyond possibility. Lorraine's execution was not public, only the results of it," Geoffrey admitted. "I would not put it beyond him to claim personal credit for the deeds of another."

"I am not at all unfamiliar with that sort of behavior." The regent's tone was decidedly arid. "The situation in Paris is liable to be quite unpredictable. And, of course, quite dangerous, with or without unknown sorcerous variables added into the state of affairs."

"That it is." Geoffrey waved his attendant back as she moved in to wash his limbs. "I make no secret of it, Maestro—but if there is danger, it is a danger that I and all of my allies will face together. I will not hide behind anyone's skirts, nor expect others to take risks that I myself am not willing to face."

"Admirable sentiments. And I do find the compensations that milord kindly offered to be quite satisfying." The corners of Goratrix's mouth quirked back slightly. "However, given the unpredictable nature of the situation, before I accept milord's kind offer I must request a few alterations of terms."

The girl laved water over Geoffrey's tensing back. "Such as?"

"If the sorcerer in Paris truly is your sire, milord, then there is no apprentice or even journeyman magus in my chantry who is capable of standing against him. Since we cannot make that determination from a distance, I propose to accompany you when you return to Paris." Goratrix held up a hand to still any immediate protest—which, in fact, Geoffrey was not inclined to make. "I am aware that there are dangers in this—but, as you say, the benefits may very well outweigh the risks. In your company, I will be able to act directly to your benefit, diagnose the arcane forces involved in Paris, and counter them accordingly."

"A most generous offer, Maestro."

"I have observed that generosity and self-interest often walk

hand-in-hand among our kind, milord. In return for my generosity, I would like, once all is said and done, sole personal possession of any arcane or sorcerous tools and materials that we
may discover during the course of this commission—in addition to your kind offer of a Parisian chantry, and for aid against
our enemies in the Pyrenees."

Geoffrey shook his head slightly, the gesture half-apprecia-
tive, half-annoyed. "I was warned, Maestro, that you do not lack
for boldness, and I see that your detractors were correct in that
assessment."

"My detractors tend toward a certain pallor of spirit themselves, milord. If you wish to master the fire, you must risk
being burned. And if you wish to gain anything—there are
times when you must simply ask for what you want." The man
had a damnably easy, open smile when he wanted. "In this case,
I wish to know where and how your sire came by his education,
if, indeed, he possesses such an education. And the only way to
accomplish that task is to examine his tools and his books, since
I doubt His Highness will be available for consultation on that
matter."

"You have a point, Maestro, one which I will concede as just
and commensurate with the personal risks you choose to take."
Geoffrey leaned back and submitted to the bath-girl's attentions.

"Excellent. I shall have my scribe draw up the appropriate
documentation for us to review tomorrow." Goratrix's smile
went lazily pleased. "But tonight, milord, I insist that you take
your leisure in peace and safety, beneath my roof—for I doubt
we will see much of either before all is said and done."

Chapter Thirteen

"I swear, if I live to be a thousand, I never want to arrange for two dozen frothing Cainite religious fanatics to move farther than two feet *ever again*." Veronique scattered drying sand across her most recent piece of correspondence and flopped back in her chair.

Girauda, seated next to the fire with a basket of sewing, chuckled.

Veronique turned a doleful look on her. "I'm glad you find this amusing, old woman. You know, I could send you back to Toulouse with them…."

"No, you couldn't." Girauda bit off a piece of thread and smiled benignly. "Because if you did, you would have to sew for yourself. And for everyone else here. And before the month was out, you would all be going naked."

"I'm not *that* incompetent with a needle." Then, with massive reluctance, "So long as I'm sewing up someone's gut, and that's mostly the same thing, you know."

"If you say so, Vero." Sweet, motherly condescension dripped from every word.

"Men, why didn't I just go with *all* men!" Veronique muttered, folding the note and dripping wax on the edge, which she sealed with her thumbprint, and added to the stack of outgoing notes. "Have you seen Thierry lately, Girauda?"

The old Languedocien woman looked up from the pair of hose she was darning. "Not in the last day or two. He seemed a bit harried when he was here last, though. *That* boy," she added firmly, "needs a wife."

"He's married to his copybook," Veronique replied wryly.

"Well. If he turns up tomorrow morning, have him deliver these letters. If not, have Philippe do it. They're mostly arrangements for merchants to supply Anatole and his band with provisions and transport."

"I shall. Have you any other instructions?"

"Tell Thierry to be here when I rise tomorrow evening—if he turns up. I need to speak with him." Veronique rose and shrugged her cloak over her shoulders. "I think I'm going to go for a walk. I need to feel the wind on my face."

Girauda knew her habits well enough not to argue, and didn't even bother to suggest that she take Philippe or Sandrin with her. Veronique's restless spells were unpredictable in their timing and duration but never indicated a desire for company of any sort. She stepped out into the alley and set out with no particular destination in mind, no lamp and no obvious weapons, driven by the need to be up and moving. It was, she supposed, her personal manifestation of the spring madness that led some to the doors of Jean-Battiste's establishment, and some to the doors of her own. It made her want to prowl the streets in search of something. She did not know what that something was, and never had. In one instance, as a mortal woman, she had found the wounded servant of the Cainite who would eventually become her sire, had taken him home and tended his injuries. On another, after she had been dead for nearly a hundred years, it had led her to Alainne, lying bleeding and beaten in an alleyway very much like the one they lived on.

Tonight, her restlessness led her down by the river, which was running high and gray with rain and snow-melt, its voice a low rushing rumble in the dark. She walked for a long time, fixedly thinking of nothing, letting herself go as the spirit moved her. Eventually she stopped, staring across the expanse of the river, glistening with the reflected glow of lights still burning in the houses and gardens on Ile de la Cité. From across the distance came the faint hint of music—not, she thought, a dance tune, but something slower and more somber, out of place with the warming, shortening nights of spring, a song borrowed from winter.

Abruptly, Veronique became aware that she was being

watched. The hairs on the back of her neck twitched and all of her senses refined themselves in response, heightening her awareness of herself and her surroundings. She forced herself not to tense, letting her hand fall naturally to her side and grasping the long dagger she wore hanging from her girdle through the slit in her surcoat, drawing it with the minimum necessary motion. Mortal men had the annoying tendency to regard a woman walking alone the way wolves regarded a sheep strayed from the flock. Cainite men were almost as bad, and had much less excuse. She had, in her time, broken a few arms, a few more legs, and, when a fool was *really* insistent, slit a throat or two.

She caught a flicker of motion out of the corner of her eye, a mistily indistinct figure approaching, heavily muffled and leaning on a staff that, once he was sure she'd seen him, he proceeded to thump around with great verisimilitude. Veronique couldn't help shake her head, and grin a little.

"Alms," Guillaume rasped, sounding convincingly pathetic. "Alms, lady, sweet Christian charity for the poor and crippled, I beg of you."

"Of course, grandfather. Here," she switched the dagger to her offhand, reached into her purse, and extracted a silver penny, "buy yourself a warm meal and a spot of floor to sleep on."

He pocketed the money with alacrity and a glimpse of his true face, grinning toothily. "The blessings of Our Lord and His Gracious Mother on you, good lady. Forgive an old man his curiosity, but what might a godly woman such as yourself be seeking here in the dark and the fog on such a cruelly damp night?"

Veronique slipped the note he'd pressed into her palm down into the bottom of her purse and switched the dagger back to her good hand. "Memories, grandfather, of my husband lost these many years in an accident on this very river, and me without even his child to comfort me."

"A woeful story, and you widowed so young and beautiful, good lady. Take the advice of an old, old man, who has outlived all but one of his children—seek you another husband and other children to be your comfort." He didn't waste the opportunity to pat her companionably on the shoulder in passing as he hobbled off into the fog beyond them, moaning dolefully for alms.

Veronique watched him go, waited to make certain that he wasn't going to double back, then slipped her dagger back in its sheath and went back the way she had come.

Had Veronique chosen to linger a quarter-hour longer along the bank of the Seine, she would have been treated to an unusual sight. The mist was already thickening into a soupy fog that efficiently limited visibility along both banks of the river; even the mild spring breeze wasn't really sufficient to thin it, though it did swirl and eddy quite naturally. That, by itself, wasn't unusual for the season. The particularly dense fogbank moving swiftly downriver against the prevailing wind at a constant rate of speed might very well have excited comment, had anyone been able to see it.

Geoffrey le Croisé's barge made its way towards Ile de la Cité under the cover of a sorcerous mist that not only concealed them from easy observation, but deadened the sound of the oarsmen, as well. It contained Geoffrey; his entire retinue of twelve men-at-arms and six knights (three ghouls, three Cainites); the Tremere delegation in the form of the magus Goratrix and four mortal attendants; and a good deal of baggage, the Tremere portion of which no one wanted to examine too closely. Geoffrey was being forced to admit, not entirely reluctantly, that Goratrix was thus far earning his keep. The fog was entirely his project in concept and execution and, thus far, it had apparently worked. The Tremere stood at the prow of the barge, surrounded by his four attendants, working the weather as he had done each night since their departure from Rouen.

Goratrix had an actor's flair for the dramatic, and played to the prejudices of his audience quite expertly, Geoffrey thought, manipulating the fears of the men to his own benefit. And the men had, from the start, feared him; before two nights were out, they were grudgingly respecting him as well. From a dread sorcerer they seemed to expect certain things—inscrutable comings and goings, peremptory summons, strange demands that didn't bear close examination—and he'd given them all those things, with interest. He swept about the barge looking grim and unapproachable, surrounded at all times by the fawning deference of his assistants, who appeared willing to submit to any indignity if it would aid their master's endeavors. He had also delivered on his promise to protect them from unfriendly eyes, and done so in a manner that kept the men buzzing, complete with circles drawn in chalk and salt and steady, rhythmic incanting in a language that no one recognized, and the occasional localized rumble of thunder just to underscore the unnaturalness of it all.

To Geoffrey, the magus showed another face entirely: intelligent, wittily conversant on a number of topics, as willing to listen as he was to offer semi-solicited advice. Geoffrey could practically feel him projecting the image of the immensely knowledgeable court sorcerer, whose feet were nonetheless firmly on the ground, with all his might. It was not an entirely unsuccessful *effort*. This Tremere, at least, could be cultivated.

They were almost home. The advance party, consisting entirely of his most trusted mortal servants, had been in Paris for at least two weeks, carrying out his orders. In theory, they had made his haven, long vacant and looked after by a series of mortal caretakers, livable again and cleaned out any spies who might be lurking among the staff. In theory, they had also made contact with those Cainites who would tend toward sympathy for his cause, via the letters he had sent along with them. If things had gone as planned, there would be a party waiting at his private dock to assist with unloading and to brief him on the situation.

The dark bulk of the isle loomed out of the fog on the left, and the barge's crew made ready to tie up; up ahead, Geoffrey could see the faint glow of lanterns diffused through the mist. The barge drifted into its slip with hardly a bump to jostle its passengers, lines were tossed ashore and caught, and soon the hardy little craft was tied up and being unloaded. Geoffrey paused only long enough to nod his thanks to the sorcerer, who had ceased his weather-working in favor of overseeing the unshipping of his baggage, and went ashore, to find his seneschal waiting for him.

"Milord." The man bowed deeply, voice thick with obvious personal relief. "Thank God you've arrived safely."

"Nicolas." Geoffrey clasped his servant's shoulder. "The journey itself could have been better, but I'll not complain about that now. What's passed?"

"The house is prepared for your arrival, master, and that of your guests—sufficient chambers have been prepared for all, though I fear some of the men may have to bed together." Nicolas spoke rapidly, as was his wont, as they climbed the stairs leading up from the dock toward the house. "The house itself was in much better condition than I had feared—evidently Lord Valerian exerted himself in your absence to make certain it remained livable, and to reinforce the orders you sent."

Geoffrey smiled with genuine pleasure. "How good of his lordship to think of me. And how is the excellent Lord Valerian faring these nights?"

"He seems quite well, milord, and was greatly pleased to receive your letter." Nicolas's voice sank slightly. "He was also glad to extend your correspondence to the new lady ambassador from Chartres."

"Even better." They had reached the rear courtyard, which was rapidly filling with baggage and men, all being quietly dispersed in various directions by the household staff, only a few of whom Geoffrey recognized. "Is the staff sufficient for your needs?"

"Oh, yes, milord. We had to let a few go when we arrived." That statement, delivered in the blandest voice and expression Nicolas was capable of meant that a few bodies had floated downriver with the spring flood. "But, in general, they have worked out marvelously. Again, thanks very greatly to Lord Valerian's kind assistance."

"I see I'm going to have to do something quite extraordinary to thank Lord Valerian," Geoffrey murmured as they went inside to his study, which had the distinct look and scent about it of having been cleaned from floor to ceiling. Unless he was seriously mistaken, most of the furniture had been replaced, as well. "Close the door."

Nicolas did so without argument. As he did, the cringing

servility went out of his bearing, and he stood straight, becoming the man who had fought at Geoffrey's side across the Holy Land. Wordlessly, Geoffrey drew the knife hanging at his hip, slit his own wrist and, as Nicolas went to one knee at his side, gave it to the most faithful and trusted of all his servants to renew his strength. There was a hint of silver beginning to show in Nicolas's dark hair, and Geoffrey ran his fingers over it with a trace of regret. "I'm sorry to have asked so much of you, old friend, but you have done well, and served me better than I deserve."

Nicolas leaned back on his heels and rose, drawing a cloth out of his belt and dabbing neatly at his bloodstained lips. "If not me, then who, milord? You lead, and I follow. You command, and I obey. It is the way of things. And things here, with one exception, proceed well."

"The exception?" Geoffrey licked the wound closed and cleaned his knife, sliding it away.

"Renaud's party was ambushed on the road south of Chartres and killed to the last man—butchered, by a force that outnumbered them at least two to one."

Geoffrey closed his eyes, clenching his hands against his thighs until the spasm of emotions that flared inside him went away enough to speak clearly. "Were they tended to?"

"I have had news that the Lady Isouda's men made certain they received Christian burial. One of her own *chevaliers* found the only survivor, who perished before help could be sought." Nicolas, as he always did when thinking of men lost in the field, reached up to stroke a knuckle over the long scar marring one cheek. "It does tell us that your enemies here in Paris fell for the ruse—and that their spies were who and where we thought they were."

"And that they were willing to kill in order to prevent me from coming home," Geoffrey added, a smile of grim satisfaction touching his lips. "Very well. Let it be war. Can you see to the men?" The look Nicolas gave him answered that question more fully than words. "You're right, that was a foolish question. Send my secretary in."

Veronique found several surprises waiting for her by the time she reached home, not the least of which was Jean-Battiste in her downstairs sitting room, flirting with Alainne. Neither of them had the grace to look at all ashamed as she entered, cloak still dripping. "What the devil are *you* doing here?"

Jean-Battiste tore himself away from whatever idiotic thing he was about to say in his continued effort to get under Alainne's skirt and offered the sort of loftily superior look that always induced the urge to murder him. "Good evening, Veronique. Out tending the sick and feeding the hungry again?"

"No." Veronique hung her cloak next to the fire to dry and turned her back to the fire, more chilled than she'd thought by her evening walk. "I reiterate, *what are you doing here?* I seem to recall leaving standing orders that you're out of my favor unto perpetuity."

"I shouldn't be, right now—I applied the profit I turned from those airy little twits I liberated from your motherly clutches to the outstanding balance you owe me. Quite a substantial reduction, by the by." The little snake caught Alainne's hand and deposited a kiss on her knuckles. "Run along and be a bad girl, my dear. I need to talk to your esteemed employer alone."

Alainne shook her head, rose, and cast Veronique a look. "Don't forgive him just yet—he's holding back on something; I just know it."

"I'll keep that in mind," Veronique assured her as she exited, closing the door behind her. "Well? What is it?"

"You could be just a little nicer to me, you know. It wouldn't kill you." Jean-Battiste didn't even artistically pout at her, though she could tell it was a near thing. "Have you been to the isle lately?"

Veronique's eyes narrowed a fraction. "Not in the last few nights. I've been busy helping with the arrangements for Anatole's little trip south."

"Pity. You've been missing some wonderful gossip." He raised a hand, preparatory to ticking off points. "I really ought to make you pay for this, you know."

"You can add it to my tab," Veronique replied, sweetly, "and I'll give you a finder's bonus if any of it turns out to be true."

"You cut me to the quick. Point the first," Jean-Battiste turned down his index finger, "rumor has it that several letters bearing quite unusual arms have been circulating amongst various diplomats—including the inestimable Lord Valerian and the radiant Lady Rosamund d'Islington, among sundry others." He turned down a second finger. "Point the second, the arms on those letters match those of that long-absent luminary of the Grand Court, Geoffrey le Croisé, the eldest childe of our esteemed prince." Another finger. "Point the third, there seems to be someone busily going about reopening Lord Geoffrey's house and hiring several new mortal servants to help staff it." His smallest finger. "Point the fourth, rumor also has it that a large body of armed men attacked and slaughtered another body of armed men on the road south of Chartres last week, and the men who died were either knights or mercenaries in service to Lord Geoffrey—rumor is rather specific about the point that they appeared to be carrying his banner." Jean-Battiste waggled his thumb in an extremely aggravating manner. "Care to give me a point the fifth to torture everyone with? Any messages from little Lord Geoffrey turn up?"

"No." Veronique replied tersely. "This has all happened recently?"

"Yes. I suppose this is what you get for letting yourself be distracted by the minutiae—" Jean-Battiste's mouth snapped shut as she stepped away from the fire in his direction.

Veronique throttled the desire to yank the snake's forked tongue out at the roots, checked her move in midstride and crossed instead to the door, which she flung open. It didn't improve her temper in any way to find three of her girls clustered in the hall outside, clearly hoping either to overhear something juicy or to ambush Jean-Battiste on his way out. *"Don't you have something you should be doing?"*

They fled. She turned to face Jean-Battiste. "Out. I have work to do."

His eyebrows quirked upwards but he made no argument, rising and strolling past her with nonchalance that wasn't entirely feigned. "Does this mean I'm not going to get a finder's fee for this?"

"It depends on what's true and what's not." Veronique smiled grimly and raised her voice. "Philippe! Please show Jean-Battiste to the door."

The snake winced. "That wasn't very nice. Or necessary."

"I know. But I enjoyed it anyway." She slammed the door in his face.

Veronique waited until the sound of his footsteps had faded to dig the note she'd received out of her purse. It was terse and, unfortunately, did not entirely illuminate the situation: *Bide. Believe nothing you hear. Do nothing rash.* Veronique swore in each of the four languages she spoke, unlocked the door to her bed-chamber, and stalked inside. There, sitting on her desk, was a letter.

It gave her pause.

It was bound in a purple ribbon bordered in gold, its sealed turned upward—a rearing horse, between two *fleur-de-lis.* Geoffrey le Croisé's arms.

A little smile tugged at the corner of Veronique's mouth.

Thierry did not appear the next day, nor on the day after that. Veronique drafted most of her staff into service running errands, carrying messages, and attempting to contact various pieces of her far-flung network of informants. On the first night, Thierry's absence vexed her, but she made certain a firmly worded message was left at each of his several regular haunts regarding her desire to see him at once. On the second night, concern replaced vexation, but the night was too full of work to do anything to assuage that concern.

On the third night, Veronique took to the streets in the company of a fully-armed Sandrin and of Philippe, who took the task of carrying her physicker's basket. She was beginning to suspect that Thierry had seriously understated how ill he'd been over the winter—it was typical of him, and once he sickened, he often took longer than usual to get well again, even with her blood helping him. The sharpness of his mind made it too easy to overlook his physical frailty, and she soundly cursed herself for not looking after him sooner.

Thierry was easily the most cautious of all her servants—he

didn't, after all, shelter under her roof but circulated through-out the Latin Quarter in the guise of an impecunious univer-sity student at perpetual odds with fortune. He changed his place of residence every few months, in the knowledge that any place he returned to habitually could become a trap as well as a haven. It took them some time trolling among taverns and stew-houses, a few low-voiced remarks of an unsubtle nature from Sandrin, and a bit of silver judiciously spread around to finally convince someone to yield Thierry's current address. That turned out to be the sort of dockside tenement that could charitably be described as a flophouse, and a brief conversation with the landlady-cum-laundress-cum-harlot who ran it ascer-tained that Thierry rented an attic room. The fact that he stub-bornly refused to share it with anyone was evidently a matter of considerable grievance with her, despite the extra he paid to ensure his privacy.

Veronique gritted her teeth, paid handsomely for the infor-mation, and let Sandrin, carrying a lamp, proceed her up the rickety stairs, which groaned alarmingly under their weight. Behind her, Philippe muttered steadily under his breath about dragging Thierry back to the bathhouse by the scruff of his scrawny neck, provided the house didn't collapse around them. Up ahead, Sandrin went in complete silence, lamp in one hand and a drawn knife in the other, clearly on edge. Veronique felt it, as well—a frisson of unease that raised the hair on the back of her neck and made her palms itch for the haft of a weapon. There was something very, very wrong about this place, but she couldn't put her finger on precisely what.

Thierry's room was little more than a garret beneath the house's poorly shingled roof, but it had a solid door and a lock that Sandrin had to pick. Veronique held the lamp while he worked and appallingly found that her hands trembled, the light flickering unsteadily. After a moment, she whispered to Philippe, "Is it… a bit too cold in here?"

Philippe's teeth were chattering too hard to answer imme-diately; she took that as a yes.

The lock sprang open, and Sandrin pushed the door open. A wave of cold rolled out over them, making the lamp flame dance wildly for a moment and cutting through their clothing like the crudest breath of winter. It actually drove Sandrin back a step or two, and frosted over the damp floorboards beneath their feet.

Veronique found that her mouth and eyes were extremely dry, almost parched, and it took her a moment to work up sufficient moisture to speak. "Take the lamp." Sandrin did as he was told, without argument, though his knife remained drawn. "Follow me closely."

And, so saying, she stepped across the threshold into Thierry's room. It took her a moment for her eyes to adjust to the dim light coming in from behind her and, initially, she thought they had picked the wrong lock, for the room bore little resemblance to a living space. There was wreckage scattered in every corner, broken chairs, a table missing three of its legs lying against the far wall, a black splotch of dampness staining the irregular bulge of a chimney flue. It took her a moment to realize that she was looking at the remains of Thierry's possessions, tossed about and smashed as though by a strong wind. His bedding lay entirely crumpled and stuffed into one corner.

Veronique's heart lurched out of its place behind her ribs and tried to run away when she took in the shape crushed beneath the shredded blankets. She took an involuntary step in that direction.

"Lady," Sandrin's voice was low and tense, and echoed by Philippe, an instant later, "Veronique, don't—"

She leaned down and peeled away a layer of threadbare cloth. The body beneath it was wearing Thierry's clothing; that was the only reason she recognized it. A part of her was distantly surprised that there was no stench of decay or other signs that his body had been invaded by carrion-eaters; it was clear that he'd been dead for quite some time. Nor could she tell from looking precisely what it was that *had* killed him. His body looked… shriveled. The skin was a translucent, jaundiced yellow, shrunken across his bones, mouth frozen open in a soundless wail, eyes sunken into the skull beneath withered lids. Veronique swallowed hard, reached out and stroked a finger down his cheek; the skin was dry and taut as parchment paper rather than damp as most corpses tended to be. It was as though whatever had killed him had sucked all the juice out of him, all the blood and every humor, leaving behind only a desiccated shell.

Sandrin caught her shoulder and pulled her away, speaking low and quickly, "Lady, we must get out of here. Whatever killed him may still be nearby."

Veronique nodded mechanically and let him guide her out ahead of him. Philippe preceded her down the stairs, silent this time, keeping one hand against the wall to maintain his balance; Veronique kept one hand knotted in the back of his tunic, and Sandrin followed at two paces remove, walking nearly backwards in his effort to watch for an attack from behind. No attack came. They reached the street much more quickly than they'd reached the attic and at Veronique's low-voiced command walked briskly away, in the direction of home.

An icy rage was coiling itself inside her breast, a cousin to the fury washing her vision red and beating within her skull; she knew, if any bystander saw her just now, there would be no mistaking her for anything but what she was. She retained just enough sense, and control, to take one of the roundabout routes home, in case they were being followed, and to give her temper time to cool. It didn't help. Her rage refused to be abated by walking, or trying to speak calmly to herself, or by the silence of her guardians, who knew better than to talk to her when she was in such a state. It took all of her strength not to run away, mad and furious, and kill the first thing to cross her path, howling like an animal as she did it. As they came nearer to home, she slowed her walk, and her companions slowed as well.

She took a long, deep breath, and released it, without speaking. A second breath, and the words finally emerged. "You saw. You saw what she did to him, to strike at us—to strike at me. And you're my witnesses to this, as well—*I will tear that Ventrue whore's heart out with my own hands.*" A third, more ragged breath, as grief began to overpower rage. "Come. We have to tell Girauda and the others, and make certain his body is decently cared for, at least. Tomorrow night is soon enough to think about everything else."

Chapter Fourteen

Lights burned day and night in the house of Geoffrey le Croisé, and no particular effort was being made to hide the fact of his return any longer. His arms were raised on a banner-pole above the door, which was guarded at all times by unsmiling men clad in mail and boiled leather, armed with sword and polearm, who turned away all visitors. Lord Geoffrey was returned, but he was not yet receiving guests, it seemed, though his doorkeepers accepted and faithfully delivered correspondence. His pages and errand-runners were abroad at all hours, delivering messages, patronizing merchants, taking deliveries, engaging in business of considerable import. It seemed as though Geoffrey's entire staff was clad in purple, and rumor suggested that he'd liberated every bolt of silk and linen in Tyre to accomplish that feat. The arrogance of it was marked, and remarked on, extensively, along with every other bit of news he'd brought with him: the attack against his men on the road south of Chartres; his own stealthy arrival in the city by means he apparently cared not to explain; the letters he sent only to select diplomats attached to the Grand Court. He was in the city two full nights before he deigned to communicate with his sire, Prince Alexander, who was in a black fury at the presumption—but not so black that he denied Geoffrey's request for a formal audience.

Geoffrey, Veronique d'Orleans couldn't help but note, was making himself a wonderful distraction, and it wasn't a tactical opening she was inclined to waste. Thierry's death forced a rapid reorganization of her own intelligence-gathering apparatus, with a special focus on consolidating and protecting the sources she had left. She took another loan from Jean-Battiste and paid for the families of two of her more vulnerable agents to leave the city entirely, to take up residence with kin dwelling in the country around Orleans. Sandrin and Philippe spent more time acting in defense of spies than of the women of Veronique's own house—who insisted they could take care of themselves with or without the assistance of the bathhouse's clientele, who would be loathe to lose their favorite girls. Veronique personally took to the streets, taking reports, issuing orders, and collecting information, which she passed on to Dame Mnemach. Within seven days, they identified five of Saviarre's most prolific mortal agents in the Latin Quarter and on Ile de la Cité. Mnemach continued to counsel patience, advice that Veronique found harder and harder to cleave to as the nights passed. She sensed something in the air, the scent of imminent danger, and she itched to respond to it in some active way.

Rosamund d'Islington was even more aware of the scent of imminent peril than Veronique d'Orleans, as she was much closer to the easily perceived source.

The Grand Court was afire with rumors. Gossip a good century or two old was dusted off and brought out for the edification and amusement of those who hadn't been in the city to hear it when it was fresh the first time. The fact that Prince Alexander and Lord Geoffrey had never quite gotten along as well as they possibly could was chewed over at length, their differences in personality and temperament discussed until every possible nuance of meaning was extracted from the analysis. Geoffrey had never been exactly *disloyal* to Alexander, everyone was quick to point out, God forbid it. Geoffrey held his honor far too dear to sully it with treasonous talk or behavior. He did not, however, trouble to construct an illusion of excessive warmth—or of any warmth at all, no few people pointed out. Clearly, he chose to prove that he could grant his sire all honor and service without the pretense of personal affection. It was a stark contrast to the evident filial devotion Sir Olivier, Alexander's younger childe, held for his sire, and that became a point of gossip, as well. Everyone wanted to see for himself how the sparks would fly when Geoffrey and Olivier met for the first time.

Rosamund found it all extremely educational as well as enormously beneficent to her own efforts. Geoffrey was an almost perfect distraction—his presence in the city drew the attention and the efforts of everyone who would otherwise be attempting to curry favor with Prince Alexander.

It left the political field to her, and she took to it with all the weapons at her disposal.

"I thank you for receiving me on such short notice, Your Highness." Rosamund addressed the floor at Alexander's feet, from the depths of a presentation curtsey that put her knee almost to the floor.

As before, rather than acknowledge the gesture verbally, Prince Alexander took her by the hand and drew her to her feet, raising her hand to his lips. For an instant, as before, she was completely struck by him: his youthful and beautiful form, his compelling aura of strength, his great and troubled mind. She lowered her eyes before she could become completely caught in it.

"My rose, no request from you could ever be called peremptory. Come, let me show you my hospitality." He tucked her hand into the crook of his arm and guided her into his sitting room.

They were in Prince Alexander's private chambers, a part of his haven that only a select few had ever entered. Rosamund was immensely honored, and also somewhat surprised, for her request had been of a diplomatic nature and she'd more than half-expected Countess Saviarre to invite herself to the meeting. The prince's first advisor was not present in the room he led her to, and that room was not decorated in a fashion that rumor had led Rosamund to expect. Prince Alexander was said to have the tastes of a Spartan, spare and unadorned, appreciative of the functionality of pomp and ostentation but unattracted to splendor for its own sake. This room was, quite simply, dazzling, its floor half-covered in carpets imported from the east and half in glittering Roman mosaic, its walls plastered and painted with a garden mural and its ceiling with the sun and moon and stars, its tall, thin windows glazed. The furniture was Lebanese cedar cushioned in pillows of crimson silk shot through with gold, and Prince Alexander led her to the finest chair, next to the warmly crackling fireplace, and sat himself in its twin once she had settled herself.

Rosamund found that she couldn't fail to comment on the gloriousness of their surroundings. "Milord Prince, you do me too much honor—this is a setting fit for a queen, and I am but a servant of milady."

"You do yourself a disservice, Milady Rosamund." Prince Alexander's smile caught her and momentarily erased the social pleasantry forming itself in her thoughts. "For you are no mere servant, but a queen-in-waiting." Had she been mortal, she would have blushed at the pleasure of it, and she felt herself warming, even so. "You flatter me, Your Highness, and I do believe make fun at the same time."

"Oh? How so?" *Was* he teasing her? His smile was warm and his tone was bantering.

Rosamund made a teasing *moue* of her own. "For to win the crown you see me wearing, my sire must seek me a husband— and I fear that she prefers me a maiden perpetual, wise and virtuously unwed, like Athena."

"What a cruel sire you have, milady." Prince Alexander leaned back into the cushions of his chair, lacing his fingers together before his chest. "Shall I intercede on your behalf? Make one of the conditions of the renewed amity between your court and mine a royal wedding to seal the bargain? My childe Olivier is quite profoundly smitten with you, I must admit."

Rosamund laughed. "Milord, now I know that you tease me. Sir Olivier has hardly spoken two words to me since I came to Ile de la Cité." She sobered. "I thank you for your generosity in this matter, though I think, were a royal wedding to be arranged, there are others, more highly ranked, who should receive that honor first."

"Does the illustrious Queen Salianna expect a matrimonial stamp on the diplomatic formalities, then, milady?" Prince Alexander's eyebrow inclined a questioning fraction.

"I do not think such an option is beyond consideration, Milord Prince, though milady has not mentioned it specifically." Rosamund drew her own dignity back around her, straightening her spine and folding her hands demurely in her lap. "Before an alliance marriage is discussed, Prince Alexander, I suspect that milady will wish to renegotiate the boundaries of power between the Grand Court and the Courts of Love in light of events in Anjou and the Languedoc, where the situation remains considerably unsettled."

"I doubt that not at all," Prince Alexander replied dryly. "Queen Salianna seems quite intent on preventing any possibility that diplomacy may break out between Paris and Foix."

"The rebel Esclarmonde the Black and her resistance remains an issue of considerable import to milady queen, yes." Rosamund replied, carefully. "Though she welcomes the return of Prince Eon de l'Etoile to the fold of Your Highness's favor, she questions his wisdom in engaging in diplomacy with a traitor and rebel against Your Highness and the rule of the Courts of Love."

"Lady Rosamund, you know as well as I that the internal politics of the Courts of Love may have had more to do with the accusations against Queen Esclarmonde than any treason of hers, real or imaginary." The prince's dark eyes glittered. "It pleases me that she remains contained in Foix, where she can do little real harm, and I will leave the lessoning of her in the capable hands of Queen Salianna. Any other points of discussion concerning the dispensation of the Languedocien territories under her control will have to wait until such time as those territories are available—which would be when Queen Esclarmonde's head is presented to me on a pike."

Rosamund felt a prickle of unease run up her spine, the change in him was so extreme; one moment amiable, even flirtatious, the next icily cruel. "Prince Eon may exert himself to—"

"Prince Eon may exert himself all he likes—he is a bastard upstart mistake from the line of my old friend Valerian's youngest childe. That, coupled with the fact that he's willing to take that Malkavian fanatic away from Paris, is the only reason his head is still attached to his shoulders. Should he overstep himself again, not even that will save him." Alexander's tone was coolly flat, without inflection or consideration. "I have little tolerance for the follies of youth, Lady Rosamund, particularly when they impinge upon my rights as sovereign, lord and liege. And your lady should bear in mind that she hasn't the excuse of youth to explain any folly in which she might engage."

"I will keep that in mind when communicating with her, Milord Prince," Rosamund replied so meekly that it evoked a response.

"Now, this is what I feared. The harsh words these unsettled nights have forced me to speak have disturbed and alarmed you—and I did not intend to dismay you in any way, my rose." He turned that startlingly warm and bright smile on her again. "You are here, exerting yourself to my benefit, and you have nothing to fear from me, sweet lady."

Rosamund felt, for an instant, as though that were completely and utterly true, and returned that smile with the sweetest and most sincere response she had ever found within herself. He reached out and took her hand in his own, raising it to his lips again. "Now come. I think we have had enough dry and dolorous conversation for one night. There are musicians visiting from Toulouse that I wish you to hear."

"How lovely," Rosamund murmured, finding herself caught, again, in the darkness of the prince's eyes. "My brother-in-blood, Sir Josselin, is a singer of some skill—he had a friend in Toulouse who wrote songs just for him, at one time." She let him draw her to her feet. "Are they here for... for the celebration of Lord Geoffrey's return?" She knew at once that she had put her foot wrong with the mention of Geoffrey's name. Alexander's grip tightened on her hand, the pressure edging close to pain, and his entire expression froze, turning his face into a mask hiding some cold and wrathful emotion. It burned clearly in his eyes for a moment, and then it was gone—his posture relaxed, the grip on her hand eased, and his expression softened somewhat. "No, my rose—they are not here for Geoffrey's enjoyment."

Prince Alexander's formal reception hall was more densely

packed than Veronique had ever before seen it—even Rosamund's presentation, crowded though it was despite the season, had been less frilly attended than the official return of Lord Geoffrey le Croisé. There was not a member of the Grand Court, no matter how minor, no matter how far from the city itself their personal domain might lie, who had failed to make the journey, who wanted to miss the chance to collect God alone knew what capital in the shifting political and social environment of Paris. Barely landed ashen knights less than a decade undead rubbed shoulders with Cainites who had owned their domains since the time of Charlemagne; Roman-era relics exchanged social pleasantry with low-blooded gutter-scum. They were crammed together elbow-to-elbow, patricians and plebes, diplomats and politicians, mortal servants and Cainite lickspittles, five ranks deep on each side of the central aisle, which was delineated by a rope of braided purple and cloth-of-gold. The polearm-bearing honor-guards stationed at regular intervals along that route were, Veronique noticed, not Prince Alexander's men—they wore Geoffrey's arms on their purple tabards, over mail that, while polished, had seen some use in the field.

A low murmur of conversation ran around the room, rising and falling as particular bits of rumor and innuendo found a new home in ears that hadn't heard them yet. Tongues wagged incessantly. Veronique did her best to block the majority of it out; there was little idle courtly rumor could tell her now. She did keep an ear open to see if anyone else had any stories to tell of strange deaths among their servants, or unearthly happenings of any type, but heard nothing of interest where she stood; the gossip tonight was all quite banal—politics and catty social backbiting—and it tried her temper more than she wanted to admit.

There was a shift among the courtiers gathered toward the front of the room, a pall of silence falling that gradually quieted even the most persistent whisperers. Prince Alexander's somberly clad herald had emerged onto the dais on which the prince's throne sat, and cleared his throat several times. Once he was certain he had the undivided attention of the court, he signaled the fanfare and announced in his stentorian voice, "Alexander, *Princeps Lutetius.*"

Prince Alexander emerged from the recessed entryway to the rear of his throne and strode forward to accept the homage of his court; for an instant, the hall was filled with the sound of almost a hundred Cainites and mortals struggling to find sufficient room to bow or curtsey appropriately. In a display of truly princely generosity, he held them in those singularly uncomfortable positions for the minimum possible time, waving the court up and seating himself in a single graceful gesture. He was, Veronique noticed, dressed much more flamboyantly than was his usual wont, in a nearly toga-length tunic in the richest shade of Tyrian purple thickly bordered in gilt embroidery, rings flashing on his elegant hands and a heavy jeweled collar holding a mantle of cloth-of-gold lined in ermine over his shoulders. He gestured, and the herald's voice rang out again.

"Sir Olivier de Normandy." Olivier, like his sire, favored a minimalist approach to titles and, also like his sire, looked as if he'd been attacked by a tailor imported from the Holy Land. There was a bit more gold and a bit less purple in his costume, and he wore no rings or other accouterments that might interfere with his ability to draw the sword he wore at his side—which, despite the jewel-encrusted hilt, was probably functional. That brought Veronique's eyebrow up slightly. Even Olivier did not usually come armed, no matter how modestly, into the presence of his sire, unless the prince requested it.

The herald spoke a third time. "Lady Countess Saviarre d'Auvergne."

Saviarre did not adorn herself in the purple, that would have been too bold for even Alexander to overlook, but she did the next best thing. She wore a dress of dark blue damask silk embellished in silver and, for a change, wore her dark hair bound in a net of silver thread set with tiny, brilliant stones, the first sign of feminine vanity Veronique had ever noticed. The rest of the court noticed, as well, and buzzed a bit about it until a second brazen fanfare sounded and, from outside, came the rhythmic tread of more than one set of feet on the flagstone floor. The doors swung open, and the herald announced, over a renewed murmur, "Lord Geoffrey le Croisé, childe of Alexander, Princeps Lutetius."

It was not Geoffrey who stepped through the door, but Geoffrey's standard-bearer, a compact, older man with a rather distinctively scarred cheek and an air of grim purpose about him. As he passed, the honor guard lining the aisle snapped even straighter in their posture; when he reached the front of the room, he set the pole on which he bore his lord's arms and went smartly to one knee, bowing his head to the ruler of Paris. Alexander's expression perceptibly darkened, despite the flawless execution of that gesture. Before he could speak, however, the standard-bearer's lord made his entrance.

Geoffrey le Croisé swept through the doors of his sire's audience chamber in full armor—a heavy hauberk of combat-worthy chain and guard-plates on his legs, polished to a mirror finish, his sword belted to his side. That weapon was no gilt and jeweled piece of courtly ornamentation but a thing that had seen battle, its leather-wrapped grip darkened with age and worn with use. His tunic was of precisely the same shade of purple as his sire's, marked both with his own arms and, on the shoulder, the cross of a knight sworn to crusade. Otherwise, he wore no decoration, no circlet, no rings, no heavy chains of office or rank. His dark brown hair was cut short and he was clean-shaven, and his only scent was good leather and the oil he used on his steel.

Geoffrey's figure impressed the crowd even more than Rosamund's had. Every eye in the hall followed him as he strode down the aisle, disdaining the elaborate courtesies of the approach protocol, his youthful, handsome face grim, lilac blue eyes coolly appraising of the man sitting before him. The court was too shocked even to whisper and Veronique wished, for a moment, that she'd come armed herself. Alexander's attention flowed out to meet his errant eldest childe and it was clear that the Prince of Paris was nor pleased. Geoffrey's stride did not check, despite it, and he only came to a stop once he reached his standard-bearer's shoulder. There, he bowed, from the waist, a simple and wholly correct gesture that was nonetheless the least of the appropriate courtesies he could have offered.

Once again, the entire room was too stunned to respond immediately. Sir Olivier was visibly shocked, as well. Saviarre's mouth tightened into a thin line. When it became obvious that Geoffrey had no intention whatsoever of bowing a single fraction more, Alexander, his face a mask of cool cordiality, finally spoke. "You may rise, Lord Geoffrey, our childe and loyal liegeman, to whom we give our fondest welcome and greetings."

Geoffrey rose smoothly and stood silent for a moment, the entire room waiting for him to speak. "I give you greetings, Milord Prince and sire, and come before you this night, your most loyal and devoted servant, to beg your aid in a matter of the highest justice."

That provoked a response from the court, a vigorous flurry of whispers that fell silent when Prince Alexander rose from his throne. "We shall, of course, hear the matter you our childe choose to bring before us. We shall adjourn and—"

Geoffrey did not choose to let his sire finish that statement. "Milord, I ask also that this matter be laid before the open court, that its nature and resolution be known to all, along with milord's wisdom."

The silence was almost physically oppressive. For a moment, no one dared move, much less make a sound. Alexander's fury at his eldest's presumption was a battering ram, clear as a shout ringing off the walls, and even the strongest, oldest members of the court nearly cowered before it. Except Geoffrey: He, somehow, stood against it, almost insouciantly, his face still, his back unbowed. It was his right to make that request, but none had dared to publicly and directly gainsay Alexander's express will in the living memory of the Grand Court.

"Very well," Prince Alexander's voice was low and cool and held the promise of severe retribution in the near future. He settled back into his chair. "Speak, that all may know the nature of your grievance."

"That is a very apt choice of words, milord, for I am deeply grieved." Geoffrey half-turned and gestured at the doorkeeper, who in his turn motioned to someone further down the hall. Several someones, as it turned out, a half-dozen unarmed pages clad in Geoffrey's livery and hearing four leather-bound wooden chests between them. These they set on the reception hall floor with a series of solid thumps, bowed smartly to their liege, and retreated from the hall at his gesture.

Geoffrey turned to face the throne in which his sire sat impassively. "Milord Prince, my childe Sir Hugh de Clairvaux is dead—destroyed by the treachery of an Assamite whore, of whose perfidy you have already no doubt heard. There is, however, more than one side to the tale of my childe's destruction." The grief and outrage were perfectly audible in Geoffrey's voice, even to the rear of the room, and the force of presence he exuded underscored those emotions, causing a sympathetic murmur to run through the audience—even from those who had never sired, much less lost, a promising young childe. "I admit the part of my own responsibility in the ills that befell my childe in the Holy Land—I was not there to assist or advise him, having been detained in my own journey east. Had I not been, I suspect that events would have unfolded somewhat differently."

He paused, not for effect, but to extract a thick sheaf of parchment from the smallest of the four chests, a casket of the sort in which confidential correspondence might be kept. "Sir Hugh was murdered while I was still in transit but, when I arrived in Byzantium, I made a thorough inquest into his death, and the events surrounding it. I sent a copy of the notes and findings relating to that sad event to Paris but, as I received no reply to my letter and my messenger did not return, I am forced to assume that some ill befell that correspondence on the road." Veronique was impressed; she had never heard a veiled accusation delivered in such an utterly neutral tone before. Saviarre s back went subtly straighter where she stood next to Alexander's throne. "I do, however, have another copy to present to Your Highness tonight."

He held out the stack of parchments, bound in a ribbon and sealed with a thick wax medallion, and Sir Olivier came forward to receive it at Prince Alexander's gesture. If any words passed between Geoffrey and his younger sibling, they were so low only those closest to the dais stood any chance of hearing them. Sir Olivier examined the parchments briefly, ascertained that the seal was intact, and presented them to the prince—who handed them immediately to Saviarre without looking at them.

"In summary," Geoffrey continued smoothly, no overt reaction showing in either tone or posture, "my childe Hugh was, indeed, murdered by an Assamite. He had, however, begun to behave in an erratic and, some might say, irrational fashion some time before the actual instance of his destruction. Questioning his men in regard to this, I determined that he had been behaving oddly since the sack of Constantinople—specifically, since he received the request to... retrieve certain relics and antiquities from the Greeks' own Church of the Holy Apostles." He paused, and extracted another packet from the correspondence chest, a number of thick letters, tied together with a ribbon. "When I questioned my childe's men more closely, they admitted that Sir Hugh informed them that he had received instruction from Paris to loot the Church of the Holy Apostles, a claim I initially found to be quite ridiculous." He untied the ribbon binding the letters. "Until I found these pieces of correspondence among Sir Hugh's personal effects." He unfolded one, and held it up for the prince to see. "This is not your handwriting, Milord Prince—but it is your seal, and it does contain an order to retrieve certain artifacts, described by name, from the Holy Apostles and to send these artifacts to Paris as soon as possession of them was secured."

The silence in the room was so tense no one dared whisper or even move, lest unfriendly attention fall on them. Prince Alexander sat utterly still and calm, unmoved and unmoving; Sir Olivier looked naked, unabashedly appalled as the implications stole over him. Saviarre might have been dyed alabaster statue for all the reaction she displayed.

Geoffrey let the letter fall to the floor at his feet. When he spoke again, his voice was thick with outrage. "Grave robbery, Milord Prince. My childe, Sir Hugh, was ordered to *rob* the graves of the emperors of Byzantium, to violate their tombs and steal the goods they were buried with, the relics of their reigns. And some ill befell him while he was at that ungodly task—a task ordered by someone here in Paris, acting quite fearlessly under your aegis and using your personal seal to add legitimacy to their perfidy—an ill that drove him mad and, ultimately, to his destruction. Yes, Milord Prince, my sire, I am most thoroughly aggrieved."

"Such dramatics ill suit you, Lord Geoffrey." Saviarre spoke and Veronique privately wondered how she dared, stepping forward and gesturing with the documents she held. "*This* is the substance of your grievance? The slanderous ramblings of your mad childe's followers and a handful of letters whose veracity cannot even be determined? For this you—"

"Hold. Your. Tongue." Geoffrey bit each word off with savage precision and Veronique felt the compulsion weighing each word the length of the room away. "My grievance is addressed to my Prince and my sire—and you will be silent in the presence of your betters."

The pure fury that suffused Saviarre's face was a marvel to behold and even more marvelous was the fact that she fell back to Alexander's side, visibly unable to speak. Geoffrey turned the full force of his attention back on his sire. "Is it true, Milord Prince? Does this woman speak with your voice in all things, now? Am I to take her arrogance and her folly as your own? Are her orders your own?" His voice rose and he spun back to the chests, yanking open their lids and spilling their contents across the flagstone floor, a king's ransom in gilt and jeweled reliquaries. "Am I to take it that you believe, Milord Prince, that these gaudy baubles are worth more to you than the survival of *one of your own?*"

"*Enough.*" Alexander's voice rang off the walls with a force that had more than half the court cowering before the fury in it. "Be silent."

Geoffrey had as little choice in that matter as Saviarre. Alexander rose from his throne, the invisible force of his rage battering at the whole of the room, driving the entire court to its knees—except Geoffrey, who kept to his feet grimly, swaying as though he were standing against the fiercest wind that ever blew, and Dame Mnemach, who held her ground without visible effort. Finally, after a moment that stretched on forever, Geoffrey yielded, and fell heavily to one knee, bowing his head in submission, if not respect. Veronique saw all this from her place cowering quite involuntarily against the back of the Milanese ambassador.

"We shall review the information that you have brought to us, Lord Geoffrey." There were likely places in the frozen lands of the Norsemen colder than Alexander's tone, but not by much. "And consider it fully in the light of your behavior here this night. You are dismissed." His dark eyes swept the room. "You are all dismissed."

And, so saying, he swept from the room, his rage still rippling behind him like the echoes of a scream.

Two nights later, Veronique crept out of the Latin Quarter to meet with Geoffrey, taking the greatest possible precautions to avoid being seen or, if seen, recognized. Geoffrey was, fortuitously, contracting with both the landless, prospect-free younger childer of the Grand Court and copious numbers of human and Cainite mercenaries, to fill out the ranks of his own court and forces, both severely depleted by the demands of the Crusades. Veronique, to Alainne and Girauda's horror, simply hacked the rest of her hair off with a sharp knife, bound her breasts down as tightly as possible, and wore men's clothing loose enough to disguise the unmistakably feminine curves of her hips and legs. Fortune aided her further by making the night foully damp and allowing for a heavy cloak to complete the disguise. With one of Sandrin's swords belted at her hip and that worthy accompanying her, they became two Flemish mercenaries seeking employment at the house of Lord Geoffrey le Croisé, complete with a plausible history that she devoutly hoped they wouldn't have to use. Inside her tunic, Veronique carried a carefully worded invitation sealed with Lord Geoffrey's arms, which at no point mentioned her name hut indicated that the bearer was to be admitted to the house without delay.

There was no delay at the door of Geoffrey's house. His men were both exceptionally well-trained and obedient to their lord's commands. Veronique and Sandrin were shown into an antechamber, liberated of their dripping cloaks, and much to Sandrin's disgust, their weapons. The guards provided hot wine for Sandrin and the offer of sustenance for Veronique (which she declined) and asked both guests to wait. They did not, in fact, wait for very long before a freshly scrubbed purple-clad page arrived to summon them into Lord Geoffrey's presence. Veronique was privately pleased by the expediency and the sense Geoffrey displayed. The halls of his house were empty of idle loiterers who might see her face and remember it at some unfortunate later time; there were guards, and the page guiding them, hut other than that, no one. A superior grade of discipline appeared to be in effect among the men under Geoffrey's command, as well: there was no chatter, no dicing, and no public displays of drunkenness among the guards they passed. Sandrin made approving noises about the quality of their arms and armor, a point on which Veronique was inclined to accept the superiority of his professional opinion.

Geoffrey's office was in the rear of the second floor of the house, a long, windowless room almost completely devoid of decoration or comforts. Its walls had been freshly whitewashed, the cushions on the backless benches appeared to be new, and there were fresh rushes on the floor. Otherwise, it was very much the room of a man who preferred to spend the majority of his time in the field, with his men and horses, and that coincided perfectly with the image Veronique had of him from rumor and the reports of her agents.

The room was not empty, though Geoffrey was not present. A low fire burned in the grate at the far end of the chamber, before which was sitting a small round table and three chairs, one of which was occupied. That occupant glanced up from the small book he held in one slender, long-fingered hand as they entered. "Lady Veronique d'Orleans, I assume?"

Veronique stopped at the door and glanced a question at the page who had guided them. He shrugged slightly and murmured, "Another guest of milord, Lord—ah—Lady. Milord Geoffrey should be with you both shortly." And, so saying, he bowed, and closed the door at their backs.

She turned to face the reader, who had taken the opportunity to rise. On his feet, he was a hair taller than Veronique herself, blade-slender in fancifully embroidered clothing of expensive make, and exceptionally well-favored, with a set to his posture and his smile of greeting that suggested he knew exactly how comely he was. Veronique wanted to smack the look off his face but heroically refrained, motioning for Sandrin to follow as she approached him. She spoke no word until she removed the last of her candles from the courier's satchel Sandrin carried, set it in its holder, and lit it.

"Yes, I am Veronique d'Orleans, and I am an ambassador to the Grand Court of Paris." She looked up, blue eyes spitting sparks. "And you are obviously an idiot of the highest order to be bandying my name about openly when I am clearly in disguise. Who the devil are you?"

He tore his eyes away from the candle and the effect it was having on the shadows dancing on the floor before the fire, and somehow managed to look simultaneously wildly intrigued and deeply insulted. "Woman, you had best keep a civil tongue in your head. I am—"

There was a token knock on the door, and it swept open again, admitting Geoffrey and his scarred standard-bearer. Veronique turned at once, began dropping a curtsey, remembered her lack of a skirt, and turned the gesture into a bow; out of the corner of her eye, she saw the pretty idiot offering a stiff-backed bow of his own, as though he were unaccustomed to offering gestures of homage.

Geoffrey waved them up after only the most perfunctory of pauses. "I give you greetings, milord, milady, and beg you to forgive my tardiness—household business. I'm certain you both understand."

"Of course, milord," Veronique murmured, rising, echoed closely by the idiot. Who was apparently a lord, also. Veronique felt a certain pain forming behind her eyes.

Sandrin pulled out a chair for her unbidden, and she sat, checking the urge to smooth the nonexistent skirts over her knees. The idiot seated himself directly across from her, and Lord Geoffrey placed himself at the apex of their little triangle, with his servant stepping around to tend the fire. Geoffrey, to her surprise, regarded the candle with almost as much interest as the pretty fool had displayed. "Ah—this must be the gift I've heard so much about."

"Gift?" The idiot asked, slightly irritated, clearly having not heard much at all.

Lord Geoffrey smiled a slightly impish smile. "A gift of light—"

"From a friend who dwells in darkness," Veronique completed for him. "Yes, it's one of those candles, milord. I'm glad you've been informed."

The idiot gave them both the sort of long-suffering look masters usually bestow on apprentices who think they're too clever by half. "Milord...?"

"Ah, I'm sorry, milord." Geoffrey gestured to Veronique. "This inestimable visitor is Lady Veronique d'Orleans, the diplomatic envoy from the court of Prince Julia Antasia of Hamburg, and the agent of a good number of people besides, it appears. Lady Veronique, this fine gentleman is Lord Goratrix, regent of the Tremere chantry in Rouen, and an envoy of his clan, as well." He pointed at the candle. "And this is a gift from a silent partner."

Veronique's eyes widened involuntarily, and it fell off her tongue before she could think of a reason not to say it. "You *cannot* be serious."

Lord Geoffrey's smile vanished. "I assure you, Lady Veronique, I am not. Lord Goratrix is as fully committed to this endeavor as you and I, or else he would not he here tonight."

Veronique flicked a look across the table and felt a renewed surge of irritation; the idiot *Tremere regent* had the most unlovable smirk imaginable lurking at the corners of his mouth. She laced her hands together on top of the table, lest one of them find their way across it, and forbore to expound on how much this revelation was making her doubt Geoffrey's sanity. "As you say, Milord Geoffrey. The regent," she managed to issue that title without sounding like it needed to be spit out, "has, indeed, chosen a dangerous course."

Geoffrey chose to ignore any possible double meanings in that statement. "Thank you, Lady Veronique. I'm aware that you must consider this entire situation extremely irregular. We must also, I fear, keep this evening's meeting fairly brief. I must depart soon to oversee certain activities at my country house, and I have much yet to accomplish here before I can leave. Lady Veronique, what is the current state of your operation?"

"My operation is in a hit of disarray, milord," Veronique replied coolly, "One of my most trusted agents was murdered earlier this month and his death has required a bit of reorganization within my household."

"Your intelligence gathering is impeded?"

"Slightly. Not enough to prevent me from acting."

"Good. It is my understanding that you managed to identify several important pieces of Saviarre's own spy network." Geoffrey's gaze was intent.

"Yes." Veronique did not elaborate, and she shot a glance at the Tremere, who looked irritated at being left out of the conversation.

"Excellent. I will need you to move against them as soon as you possibly can."

Veronique deliberately blinked. "Milord?"

"Eliminate them by whatever means you choose, Lady Veronique," Geoffrey clarified, helpfully.

"Milord, this seems a hit precipitate." Veronique said, carefully. "Is there some reason for this sudden spate of action of which I should be aware?"

"No." Geoffrey also did not elaborate.

"No, there isn't a reason, or, no, you aren't going to tell me?" Veronique realized that her interlaced fingers were slowly starting to ball into fists, and ordered them to stop.

"If I may…?" The Tremere chose that moment to interject. "Milord, I also admit that I am somewhat at a loss—as I will be remaining here in the city, as well."

"You will both be engaging in the same task," Geoffrey replied calmly. "Isolating Saviarre and disposing of her agents. You may accomplish this by whatever means you choose, provided that you do not bring about open warfare in the streets. Even my sire wouldn't be able to overlook that for very long, I fear. To that end, I suggest you share the information that you've both managed to acquire and coordinate your efforts accordingly. I have already received assurances that our silent partner stands ready to assist and support your endeavors, having been significantly irritated recently by the activities of Saviarre's partisans."

"You're right, milord, this *is* rather irregular," Veronique didn't trouble to hide the distrust when she glanced at the Tremere again.

Nor did he particularly conceal his distaste. "Milord Geoffrey, I seriously doubt that—"

"Lord Goratrix, Lady Veronique." Geoffrey cut them both off. "This is not a topic subject to debate. You will work together. I will require results. If you cannot trust one another, trust this— we are all in the lion's den together, and we will all be ripped to pieces together if our efforts fail. Am I making myself clear?"

"Yes, milord," Veronique murmured, the Tremere echoing her an instant later. The look they exchanged was not precisely pregnant with hope and goodwill.

"Excellent." Geoffrey smiled, faintly, at them both. "Lady Veronique, as a sign of good faith, why don't you tell Lord Goratrix about the origin and uses of this admirable candle? And, then, Milord Goratrix, you can tell Lady Veronique that interesting fact you discovered about the sorcerous defenses active here on the isle."

That same night, a messenger rode into Paris, coming from Chartres and hearing a message he would surrender only to Lady Rosamund d'Islington. The satchel he carried contained two letters, one for Lady Rosamund and one for Prince Alexander of Paris. Lady Rosamund's letter contained instructions that she was deeply loath to carry out. The letter to Prince Alexander contained something even worse.

Chapter Fifteen

To His Highness Alexander, Princeps Lutetius,

My fondest greetings and wishes for the continued wellbeing of Your Highness and Your Highness's dominions.

We received with pleasure the word of our emissary, the Lady Rosamund d'Islington, regarding Your Highness's great interest in restoring the amity that existed between the Grand Court and the Courts of Love, which has been sorely strained these many years. We are entirely willing to discuss the specifics of shared governance, as well as those aspects of governance which shall remain separate and inviolate, and other such mechanisms to preserve the dignity of both our domains. It pleases us to embrace Your High' ness as brother and fellow monarch, and to hail the dawn of a new era of peace arid friendship between your subjects and our own.

Our emissary also suggested to me that Your Highness would not be adverse, once our negotiations have been completed to the satisfaction of all, to an appropriate gesture to seal the final peace between us. An alliance marriage would, naturally, suit as the most appropriate of such gestures. We are certain that Your Highness's childe Sir Olivier will make an excellent husband to the Lady of the Courts of Love who is awarded the honor of his wedding oath. There is, however, an issue of some importance in which must be resolved before any other negotiations may occur, and most assuredly before Sir Olivier is granted the hand of one of our finest roses.

The matter I refer to is, of course, the issue of Your Highness's late consort, the Lady Lorraine la Belle. As I am certain Your Highness knows, the events surrounding Lady Lorraine's demise have never been formally addressed in accord with the agreements that existed between the Grand Court and the Courts of Love at the time of her destruction, nor was the issue of her fidelity, or lack thereof, addressed according to the laws of the Court of Love itself. This event has cast the darkest of the shadows that have lain between Paris and the Courts of Love and we feel most ardently that this matter must be formally resolved before any other discussions continue, lest it continue to fester and poison the relations between our courts.

We therefore propose and request the following course of action: the convention of a formal Court of Love, in Paris, to try the issue of Lorraine's infidelity against Your Highness according to the laws adhered to regarding such matters of the heart. We would personally sit as Queen of Love, to hear all evidence presented and adjudicated accordingly, and to pronounce formally the verdict of the Court of Love. We make this request in the hope of setting this matter to rest once and for all, to the satisfaction of all involved parties including Your Highness and the bereaved kin of Lady Lorraine. Our emissary stands ready in Paris to accommodate Your Highness in all ways with regards to education in the laws and customs of the Courts of Love, and to bear word of Your Highness's decision.

We remain your sister and friend,

Salianna, Queen of Love

"**H**ow dare she!"

It was strangely satisfying, Countess Saviarre thought on the night Queen Salianna's letter arrived, to see Alexander of Paris actually lose his temper for once. The prince was a being of melancholic, rather than choleric, temperament. Normally, when he was angry, he withdrew into himself and brooded obsessively on the source of his rancor, the origin of the slight that galled him, and told no one, even his most trusted advisors, the substance of his thought, or his complaint. It made him damnably difficult to read, and even more difficult to soothe, once he fell into that inner cycle of slowly building rage and inevitable retribution.

"The *bitch*! The arrogance of that overreaching little whore! How *dare* she attempt to lord it over me?! By all the gods that ever were, I'll see her bleed for that!"

Unfortunately, Prince Alexander in a full-blown frothing temper had the irritating tendency to sound like a ten-year-old boy whose fourteen-year-old sister had just administered him a sound thrashing. It took all of Saviarre's immense inner well of self-control not to rise from her place, kneeling next to his chair in the solar that had once belonged to the ill-fated Lady Lorraine, and slap him hard enough to restore him to some semblance of sense. The semblance of sense didn't really serve her goals, and she doubted that it would do well to remind him of her personal femininity at the moment.

She knelt still, and let him rage, and reminded herself that his anger weakened him far more than it inconvenienced her. She watched, out of the corner of her eyes, while he paced the length of the room, the pages of the Salianna's letter clenched in one white-knuckled hand. Saviarre made no sound, and drew no attention to herself, but neither did her eyes ever leave him. Eventually, the heat of his wrath faded. It was very much like watching a poorly tended fire collapsing in on itself, falling from flame to flaring embers to cold ashes. He came, and sat himself in his chair, and she embraced his knees comfortingly.

"It wasn't my fault, Saviarre," Alexander whispered, after a moment of silent consolation on her part. "It was not my fault. I loved her. I loved her with all my heart and soul, as I have never loved any woman before her or since. I loved her and she betrayed me. For what should I feel remorse? For what should I be judged by any law? She pledged herself to me and gave herself to her own *brother-in-blood*! The filthy harlot—" His voice broke, and Saviarre reached up to brush away the roseate tears staining his cheeks.

"My Prince, milord, do not let them do this to you," Saviarre crooned, gently. "They have no right to judge you, and no right to demand it as a price for a peace they need and desire more than you."

"No. No, they do not." Alexander took a ragged breath and released it without speaking.

"Milord, my sweet and gentle lord, the right of refusal is yours. Refuse them! Do not let them make a spectacle of you, or of your grief. You have suffered enough. You have judged your-self more harshly than ever they could—and it is your pain that this demand of theirs mocks." She caught his hand and kissed it fervently. "Milord, I beg you, for your own sake, do not let this go any further!"

Alexander's hand cupped her chin gently, and tilted her face up to his. "Your loyalty sweetens your wisdom, my Saviarre. So long as you never turn from me, I will have the strength to face whatever comes."

"There is nothing in this world that would turn me from you, Milord Prince. I shall always be by your side." She offered him a tremulous smile, as though she were on the verge of tears at the sight of his anguish, and received a smile in return.

"I shall hold you to that. Come. The night wanes, and there is much to do before either of us may rest."

He rose and helped her to her feet.

Saviarre was in a fine mood for the rest of the evening, and that unusually good humor filtered down in displays of gen-eral munificence to whomever was fortunate enough to cross her path. Fortunately, no one crossed her path whose contin-ued existence would have strained that benevolence. She even spared Sir Olivier, whom she was inclined to regard as a spine-less lickspittle without a brain to trouble the whistling void between his ears, the sharp edge of her tongue when he ques-tioned the wisdom of rejecting Queen Salianna's request out of hand. Instead, she bestowed upon him the accumulated fruits of her experience in dealing with politicians of Salianna's ilk, which he accepted graciously by ceasing his annoying prattle about potential consequences.

She left the inner-council chamber as Alexander's secretary was arriving to take the dictation of what she devoutly hoped was a truly scathing piece of diplomatic correspondence. There had, over the last few months, been an unfortunate number of people who had gotten above themselves, rising out of their proper, humble station and demanding more than they were due. It wouldn't do to let those fools be further encouraged by the nearly treasonous behavior of Lord Geoffrey le Croisé, or the unexpected diplomacies of the Prince of Béziers. Queen Salianna was, of course, the first fool in line to be slapped back down and to whom the terms of engagement between the Grand Court and the Courts of Love would be dictated, not the other way around.

For the first time in years—since that damnable broom-star first appeared in the skies in the spring of 1220, in fact—Saviarre did not feel herself even slightly distracted by events or one bit bored. It was, in her opinion, quite a glorious sensation to be clear-minded and totally focused again.

Her good mood lasted until she reached her inner chambers, which were, as always, devoid of servants, though immaculately attended. There a note waited for her on her writing desk, neatly folded and sealed in unstamped black wax. Its message consisted of one unsigned line:

I have lost contact with all of my agents in the Latin Quarter.

Suddenly, Saviarre's mood wasn't quite so golden.

Veronique closed and locked the study door behind her. "Is it done?"

The Tremere looked up from the arcane design carved into the face of the table he was sitting at, and lifted his shoulders out of their weary slump in an effort to assume some of his customary supreme confidence. He didn't quite succeed. "Yes. Or, at the very least, as done as I can make it."

Veronique hesitated slightly. "This house, of course..."

"Of course." He gave her a decidedly irritable look. "Neither of us are actually fools, Lady Veronique, and it would please me if you'd stop treating me like one."

She made a noise in the back of her throat that was neither agreement nor disagreement and crossed the room, Geoffrey's study, which had become their regular meeting-place over the last two weeks. "Very well, you're not a fool."

"I hear something unspoken there." He roused himself enough to manage a wan attempt at a smile and, despite herself, Veronique felt a twinge of concern.

"Are you well?" She sat, careful not to touch the surface of the table, inscribed with what Goratrix had described as a "geomantically precise" map of the city and its environs. "You seem not yourself tonight. I've been here a whole five minutes and you haven't been obnoxious once."

Goratrix hesitated slightly before answering. "Some acts of sorcery are more draining than others—I'm certain you've noticed such weaknesses in yourself." Veronique nodded slightly. "In this case, laying a web to repel the shadows from this place and from your abode without the need for candles was quite a vigorous exertion."

"I can only imagine. You look like you've been dragged around the isle by your hair." Veronique reached into her courier's satchel and withdrew four tall, thick candles, wrapped in parchment and tied together in a bundle. "These are the ones you asked if I could obtain. Our silent partner, by the way, suggests that you're insane for even thinking of this scheme."

"Our silent partner wishes she had thought of it first." Goratrix accepted the bundle, a wry smile tugging at one corner of his mouth. "Believe me, the intrinsic madness factor has crossed my mind a time or two in the last few nights. But if it succeeds, we'll have pulled the fangs of our enemy's most pernicious weapon."

"If." Noncommittally. "Is there anything else you need me to procure.?"

"No. I've everything I need." The corners of his mouth twitched. "Though I'll expect free baths forever when all's said and done."

"If we all survive to see all said and done, you can have free baths nightly and a Toulousain virgin to keep you company," Veronique replied, tartly.

"I'll hold you to that." He set the candles aside. "How does your part of this little conspiracy fare?"

"Almost abnormally well. I keep waiting for the other boot to drop." She leaned back in her chair. "We sent the last of Saviarre's rats down the river two nights ago, with the help of some of Geoffrey's men in plain tunics."

"Have you heard from his lordship of late?" Goratrix ran

a finger along one of the whorls carved into the surface of the table, marked in carmine paint.

"Not in the last week, no." The most recent letter had come from Geoffrey's country estate, whence he had repaired with the majority of his men and contained with it a general letter of credit that permitted her to draw on his manpower and resources as she required. It rankled her somewhat that she did, in fact, require it, though the ability to strike decisively at Saviarre's lackeys eased most of the sting from that. "And you?"

"No. His lordship is paying out information very scantily, though I can hardly blame him. I do, however, feel that our time may be growing short, and our options constricting." He glanced up from the design he was tracing. "Rumors? Gossip? Innuendo? You have no idea how much I hate being sequestered here with no one to talk to but apprentices and guardsmen."

"You may be correct with regards to the constriction of our options." Veronique admitted. "There have been rumors that Alexander received a letter he didn't like very much at all from Queen Salianna, but he hasn't yet decided what to do about it. If so, Salianna may have just committed to a course of action, whether the rest of us are willing to embark on it or not."

The Tremere hissed between his teeth. "Do you think it's likely that she'd do such a thing without consulting us first?"

"I believe that Salianna will ever and always do what is best for Salianna." Veronique replied, bluntly. "And, to be perfectly honest, I doubt the idea of consulting us ever crossed her mind. She is, after all, a matriarch and queen among the Courts of Love, and we are merely the means to achieving her ends. It's the same with Geoffrey—he just makes a better show of pretending we're all equal partners in this enterprise."

"You're very young to be so cynical, Lady Veronique." Goratrix's eyebrow twitched slightly, and he smoothed it down with the tip of one finger.

"I'm not cynical. I'm brutally honest." She rose. "If there's nothing more, Maestro, I must be going."

He rose as well, to show her out. "Have a care, Lady Veronique. The protections I worked will prevent shadow-spies from hiding in the corners of your haven, but I can't be certain

if they will guard you against other forms of intrusion. I've
not made a deep study of the shadow-magics, but the little I do
know suggests the art is a versatile one."

Veronique nodded. "Warding against the shadow-spies
was a great boon, and you have my thanks for it. Shall we meet
again in five nights' time, to discuss our next moves?"

"Unless something urgent arises before then, yes."

"As you wish. Go with God, Maestro."

"And you, Lady Veronique."

Lady Rosamund was forcibly resisting the urge to pace around
the antechamber in which she and Lord Valerian stood awaiting Prince Alexander's pleasure. It did not help her state of mind
that they'd been waiting for that pleasure for the better part of
two hours on a short, early summer night. Sir Josselin, standing
by the door, had a dark look about him at the insult and indifference. Lord Valerian was attempting diplomatic mildness, but
there were visible signs of concern leaking around the edges of
his mask.

For herself, Lady Rosamund was far too apprehensive to
be insulted. Having spoken privately with Prince Alexander
on more than one occasion, and knowing the contents of the
letter that Queen Salianna had sent him, she knew also that
there was little possibility he would accept the matriarch's suggestion placidly. In fact, she couldn't imagine what might have
prompted Queen Salianna to send such a demand in the first
place, so close on the heels of Lord Geoffrey's return and his
accusations before the assembled Grand Court. It was almost
as though she had suddenly decided to alter her strategy completely—not to defuse a conflict but provoke one—without so
much as a consultation with her allies. Rosamund knew that
Veronique must be in a perfect froth about it, as well.

Josselin cocked his head slightly, listening. "Someone's coming down the corridor, milady."

He came away from the door and stood at her back, ever
the loyal knight-protector. She offered him a smile full of grati-
tude, which he accepted, and Lord Valerian nodded his thanks,
as well. That worthy gentleman rose, and placed herself on

her other side, just as a brisk knock sounded on the door and the door swung open to admit Prince Alexander's seneschal. "Milord Prince Alexander will see you now, Lord Valerian, Lady Rosamund."

Prince Alexander awaited them in his private receiving chamber, a room less than half the size of the reception hall, windowless, elegant in its decor but not particularly welcoming for all that. Most of its space was taken up by a long trestle table around which backless, padded benches were arranged, with one real chair at its head, which the prince occupied. He did not rise to greet them, merely inclined his head in a gesture of regal arrogance that stiffened even Lord Valerian's spine. Lady Rosamund's heart sank when she saw that he was accompanied by the Countess Saviarre, standing at his elbow and regarding them all down the length of her nose.

"Please, be seated and comfortable." Prince Alexander's tone was low and mellow, even welcoming, and for some reason it failed to soothe Rosamund at all. "Would you care for refreshments? Valerian, my old friend? My rose? Sir... Josselin, I believe?"

Rosamund dropped a deep curtsey in response to this largesse. "No, milord, but I thank you for the consideration." Behind her, Lord Valerian and Josselin also murmured their polite refusals. Josselin took her hand and aided her in seating herself on the cushioned, backless bench and took his place at her back; Lord Valerian chose to seat himself on the opposite side of the table, so they were nearly flanking Prince Alexander's high seat.

"I know why you've come to me tonight," Prince Alexander continued in that same mellow, pleasant tone. "Milord Valerian, you've heard disturbing rumors about certain communications I have recently received from the Matriarch of the Courts of Love. You are also deeply concerned about the actions of my errant childe Geoffrey, and how those actions may have damaged the relations that exist between us. Milady Rosamund"— he turned his dark-eyed gaze on her and she felt, as he did so, that he was not so much looking at her as *through* her—"you knew the truth of those disturbing rumors and have come in the hope of soothing my wrath and salvaging the mission you were sent here to accomplish, now rendered to quite an impressive ruin by the actions of your own patron."

Lady Rosamund and Lord Valerian glanced across the table at each other. Lord Valerian, being the most senior diplomat of the Grand Court, took the lead. "Milord Prince, no one is more aware than myself of the burdens and troubles under which you labor—"

"With all due respect, Milord Valerian," Countess Saviarre's voice cut across his, shocking Rosamund to the soles of her feet, "that is not the case. You have only dwelt in Paris for a short time since your return, and in the last century you have spent more time apart from the Grand Court than as a personal observer of its life and vicissitudes. I do not doubt your loyalty to milord prince,"—she glanced down at Alexander, who returned the gesture with a minute trace of visible affection—"but I fear that your regard for Lord Geoffrey may blind you to his faults."

"Milady Countess," Valerian said, the ice in his tone lowering the temperature in the room by a considerable amount, "I can assure you that I am in no way blind to Lord Geoffrey's faults. He is pigheadedly certain of the rightness of his cause and possesses, in full measure, the follies of youth inasmuch as he tends to disdain measured discussion unless one is telling him something he wants to hear. He does, in fact, remind me of another member of his lineage whom I once knew well."

Prince Alexander shook his head, with a wry smile. "I'd forgotten the edges you could have on your tongue, Valerian."

"I save them for special occasions now, Milord Prince." Lord Valerian's tone didn't quite warm. "And, yes, I do fear that Geoffrey's intemperance has damaged your regard for him. He is not, in truth, rebellious, Milord Prince, only relatively young and immoderate in his passions. I ask, milord, that you not harden your heart against him until he does something genuinely unforgivable."

"Such as accusing me of complicity in the murder of his idiot childe, before my own court?" Prince Alexander's tone was flat.

Lord Valerian was silent. Rosamund, greatly daring, leaned forward in her seat and laid her hand over Prince Alexander's, where it rested on the arm of his chair. He glanced at her in surprise. "Milord Prince, I feel that I must speak on Lord Valerian's behalf. I also feel that Lord Geoffrey is not genuinely rebellious against Your Highness or your rule. He is grieving, and that grief has made him angry and thoughtless. How would you respond, Your Highness, were Sir Olivier taken from you by violence which you could not prevent? Might you not also lash out, even against those who had no part in the wrong?"

Prince Alexander's expression softened fractionally, and he kept possession of her hand, wrapping his fingers around hers gently. "My rose, my hotheaded childe does not deserve such advocates as you and my old friend, but since you both insist on championing him, I shall give him another chance. If he comes and craves my pardon meekly for his transgressions against my person and the dignity of my office, he shall have that pardon." He glanced at Lord Valerian. "Is my word on that sufficient, Milord Valerian, or do you think the intemperate little whelp requires it in writing?"

"I think, Milord Prince, that the intemperate little whelp still values your word enough to take it at face value," Lord Valerian replied blandly. "I shall make certain he receives word of your graciousness."

"I thank you, Valerian." Prince Alexander turned his attention back to Rosamund and she felt the full force of it settling on her like a freshly warmed ermine cloak on a cold winter night. "And you, my rose? Is there another for whom you would speak tonight?"

It took Rosamund a moment to organize her thoughts. "Milord Prince, I am entirely aware that you received a letter from Milady Queen Salianna, one which contained a bit of provocation itself."

"One could say that." Prince Alexander did not relinquish her hand, but most of the warmth bled from his expression. "Queen Salianna, I fear, has always tended to reach for more than she could grasp, and this is no exception."

"Your Highness, I do not believe that Queen Salianna deliberately set out to offend or displease you," Rosamund continued, carefully. "To do so would make no sense, for I believe she is firmly committed to restoring to its full glory the alliance between the Grand Court and the Courts of Love."

"I fear that you give Queen Salianna far too much credit, my rose. She is a great deal more mercenary in her inclinations and alliances than you may suspect." Alexander flicked a glance at Lord Valerian, who parried it with an entirely neutral diplomatic mask. "For example, I do not doubt that she would back any serious rebellion raised against me by my idiot childe Geoffrey and attempt to ride his successes into realms of power she has never managed previously to attain. Do you know, my rose, if she has had any contact with Geoffrey?"

Rosamund blinked, and an honest answer came from her lips before she could think of a way to couch it diplomatically. "If Queen Salianna has had contact with Lord Geoffrey, those communications have not passed through my hands, or the embassy in Paris, Your Highness. Of that, you may be certain. I do not personally believe that Queen Salianna would favor Lord Geoffrey's cause in a quarrel—he is, as Your Highness has noted, immoderate and disinclined to listen to reason."

"Salianna does not deserve *your* advocacy, either, my rose." Prince Alexander favored her with a genuine smile. "Milady Saviarre, please read Queen Salianna's letter for the edification and amusement of Milady Rosamund and Milord Valerian."

Countess Saviarre produced, from somewhere inside her voluminous skirts, a parchment still weighted with ribbons and wax seals, from which she read in a clear, neutral tone. When she was done, Lord Valerian lifted a hand to massage his eyes, and Rosamund felt a certain unpleasant sensation rather like being thrown out of doors only to find bloodthirsty vandals encamped on the doorstep.

"I believe, Milady Rosamund, that you were sent here to negotiate in the pretense of good faith." Prince Alexander drew her eyes back to him. "I also believe that Queen Salianna intended all along to use that pretense as long as it was convenient to her personally, then cast you undefended to the wolves of the Grand Court. That part of her scheme, at least, has failed, for I do not consider you personally answerable for her arrogance." He squeezed her fingers comfortingly. "You will remain here in Paris as the only acknowledged ambassador of the Courts of Love, even should she attempt to recall you. I will not permit her to remove you from my side. I will also not permit her to attempt to dictate terms to me, for a restored alliance that adds more to her position than it does to mine."

Countess Saviarre stepped forward, and laid a folded letter on the table between them, seals up. Prince Alexander placed it in Rosamund's hand.

"I charge you, Lady Ambassador, with delivering my formal response to the hand of your queen and I tell you now: There shall be no Court of Love, no judgments passed within my domain by any but myself." He pressed her hand gently to take the sting from his words. "We shall continue negotiating in the assumption of good faith, but Queen Salianna shall have no spectacle of me."

"I see that your heart is hardened against this option, Milord Prince, and so I shall not press you to change your mind." Rosamund lowered her eyes modestly. "I shall make certain that milady queen receives your message promptly."

"Excellent well." Prince Alexander rose, and both Lord Valerian and Rosamund followed him, offering appropriate courtesies. "Come—we are none of us enemies here. Let us retire to the garden, and discuss more pleasant things. If naught else, Geoffrey did bring me several pleasant additions to the decor."

Chapter Sixteen

On the second week of June, just as the weather was beginning to show genuine signs of soon-to-be insufferable summer heat, Veronique and Sandrin left Paris for the refugee camp occupied for so long by Anatole de Paris and his doughty band of would-be crusaders. They would be leaving soon; the preparations for their departure were complete at both ends, and Veronique wanted to see them off. The camp, when they arrived in it, was in a state of previously unimagined organization, with baggage-carts and dwelling-carts neatly arranged and being just as neatly loaded, and no apparent confusion or unwillingness to participate in manual labor gumming up the works. Veronique supposed that even immortal ennui over living in a shack in the forest could only last so long when you were moving to the civilized south and the promise of a fortified dwelling.

Anatole was, naturally, in the center of it all, overseeing and directing with the somewhat harried look of a man who was only just realizing the size of the bite he'd taken. Veronique knew the feeling and dismounted, taking the package Girauda had sent along with her from the pannier as she did so. He smiled as she and Sandrin approached.

"Lady Veronique," he said, "have you come to see us off?"

"How did you guess?" Veronique asked, and handed him the bulky package, tied in leather twine. "Another vision?"

"Not this time." He chuckled softly, and hefted the bundle. "Dare I ask?"

"It's mostly clothing for Zoë—a new dalmatic and a chemise or two. And an extra pair of shoes. Girauda and Alainne swore they wouldn't let you leave without making sure that girl is properly attired for the south." Veronique's lips twitched at the look on his face. "And a packet of hath herbs and a large chunk of that lemon soap she liked so much."

"Good God." Anatole shook his head, flagged down a ghoul with nothing in his hands, and instructed that the package be delivered to his daughter and for his correspondence chest to be fetched from his wagon. "The *enfante* is turning out to have a remarkable talent for marshalling troops when she puts her mind to it. She's no doubt off organizing anyone she thinks doesn't have enough to do."

Veronique made a point of glancing around at all the highly organized and vigorous activity going on around them. "And that would be all of three people, yes?"

A chuckle. "Something like that. Come, sit by the fire for a moment."

A closely watched blaze burned in the camp's central fire pit, tended low, over which a cauldron of soup was bubbling and several rabbits roasting. Sandrin had a bowl of soup and a cup of wine pressed on him before he could argue, and Veronique and Anatole settled a short distance from him.

"I trust you have everything you need? Nothing last minute that I may be able to provide?" Veronique asked, settling her courier's satchel on her knees.

"If there is, I cannot imagine what, and so it cannot be very vital." Anatole glanced pointedly at the satchel. "Is there anything I might do for you?"

She undid the straps of the satchel and extracted a bundle of letters, tied together but individually sealed. "If it wouldn't inconvenience you, Brother, I would appreciate it if you could deliver these for me. You need only make certain that they reach Sir Aimeric de Cabaret."

He accepted the bundle without complaint. "Sir Aimeric is, evidently, a man of much business." The ghoul returned, carrying Anatole's correspondence chest; the packet went inside, and another letter came out. "A missive for you arrived with the last diplomatic correspondence package from Béziers—I hadn't yet found the time to deliver it to you."

Anatole handed the letter over. The seal was Aimeric's own and Veronique looked up from it to ask, "If you don't mind, Brother? I may have another letter to add if it's a matter of grave import."

"Not at all."

Veronique broke the seal and rose, walking closer to the fire to get better reading light. The readily visible content was Aimeric at his chatty, gossipy best, and the coded secondary message was terse. Queen Esclarmonde wished to know if Veronique had any advance knowledge of Lord Geoffrey's return, or of any relations Lord Geoffrey might have with Queen Salianna. Veronique closed her eyes and winced slightly. She had hoped to delay this night a bit longer, but now there was nothing further that could be done to help it; she would either have to speak the truth, and lay out the entirety of her plan, or else lie to a woman she respected soundly. Neither option seemed particularly palatable at the moment. Veronique opened her eyes, and read the last of the missive. The final line was a personal request from Aimeric: *If you should chance to see him, give Sir Josselin de Poitiers my fondest greetings and my hopes that we will meet again in Toulouse some night soon.* There was no code attached to those words that Veronique could discover, and it surprised her slightly to realize that Aimeric and Sir Josselin, Lady Rosamund's brother-in-blood, knew each other.

Veronique refolded the letter and rejoined Anatole, who waited patiently for her a safe distance from the fire. She tucked the message into her courier's satchel. "Nothing more to add tonight, Brother, but thank you for that message, and thank you for carrying my correspondence for me. I appreciate the service."

"You are entirely welcome, Lady Veronique. And it is the least I can do to repay the services you have rendered me." He smiled. "Can I induce you to stay the day? The night wanes, and I doubt that you will reach Paris before the dawn finds you."

"If it would not be an imposition, Brother. I have other errands to run, as well, and will not be returning to the city immediately in any case. We've a tent..."

"Nonsense. We've beds to spare with the advance party

already in Béziers. Come." He rose. "We'll make you at home, one last time before this part of our journey together comes to a close."

A pang went through her then, and she realized exactly how much she was going to miss him. She accepted his hand up and spontaneously hugged him tightly around the neck. He seemed, for an instant, extremely surprised, and uncertain of what to do with his hands, then relaxed into the embrace, and returned it. "Now, don't weep or mourn. We'll meet again, I'm sure. After all, I still have to introduce you to Lucita of Aragon."

When Veronique rose the next night, most of Anatole's camp was already broken down and abandoned, with only a handful of its previous inhabitants remaining, two Greek Cainites and their retainers. She paused in her errand-running long enough to speak with them, briefly, and ascertain that they were the only remaining members of the band that had resisted the call of faith. They were, both of them, embittered to the soul by their lot in existence; Veronique felt great pity for them, realized they'd likely be a good deal more trouble than they were worth, and promised to do what she could to ease their entry into the Grand Court, if Prince Alexander could be induced to receive them. Then she left, riding hard for Lord Geoffrey's country estate, closer to the edge of Biere Forest than the refugee camp and further to the north.

Geoffrey's country estate was an armed camp masquerading as a vineyard. The estate, La Forêt, produced precisely two things: an extremely fine variety of wine that it exported all over Christendom, and exceptional numbers of well-trained, well-equipped young knights, who also found their way across the world. Sir Hugh de Clairvaux had, as a child, been fostered to the Lord of La Forêt for training in arms and thereby came to the attention of his Cainite sire. It was a deceptively small place, a fortified manse rather than a castle, nestled on the side of the single forested hill that hadn't been cleared for cultivation. Its safety precautions were, however, stringent, and Veronique and Sandrin passed through three layers of security before they were permitted to enter the house proper, and even there they were kept under guard until Geoffrey consented to see them.

Veronique did her best not to feel irked by this, but couldn't quite help it, and so she was in a decidedly foul temper by the time she and a thoroughly disarmed Sandrin were escorted to Geoffrey's study. This room, much like the one back in Paris, was strictly functional, minimally furnished, but had windows overlooking an interior courtyard in which butts had been set up for archery practice. Geoffrey was giving dictation at a long writing desk, attended by two secretaries, a half-dozen pages, and two armed (but unarmored) knights. He looked up as his guests entered, nodded sharply once, finished his sentence, and murmured, "Gentlemen, Lady Veronique and I must consult alone. Please leave us."

Geoffrey's companions departed with a number of suspicious looks in the newcomers' direction, but closed the door behind them and even suffered Sandrin to secure it from the inside. Veronique crossed the room in three quick strides, set her satchel down on it, and extracted the letters she was carrying for Geoffrey. "Our mutual friend sends her greetings and felicitations."

"You may speak freely, Lady Veronique." Geoffrey flicked a glance at the candle burning on his desk. Its carvings marked it as the product of Mnemach's sorceries.

"Very well. The situation in Paris has tensed. Rumor—rather than hard facts available to me through my usual channels—suggests that Queen Salianna may have made a move without consulting us." Her eyes narrowed slightly as that announcement failed to elicit a noticeable response. "Or, rather, she may have made one without consulting me or her own envoy, Lady Rosamund."

"There is some truth in that rumor." Geoffrey admitted, neutrally.

Veronique slapped the letters she carried down on the table. "Lord Geoffrey," she began, struggling to keep the immense irritation she felt out of her tone, "if you know the truth of this matter, I would appreciate knowing it as well. I cannot operate effectively if my left hand is prevented from knowing what my right hand is doing."

Geoffrey accepted the letters and examined the seals before

choosing to respond. "Queen Salianna, at my request, issued a politely worded ultimatum to my sire. She gave him a choice: Submit to the judgment of the Courts of Love with regards to the death of his former consort, the Lady Lorraine; or else any further negotiations between the Grand Courts and the Courts of Love were in serious jeopardy, if not entirely over."

Veronique stared at him, stunned beyond speech for a moment as the audacity of that statement sank in. "Are you insane? Good God, milord, it's not been a month since you all but accused the man of collaborating by proxy in the murder of your childe—are you trying to bring down his wrath on anyone who's ever thought poorly of his rule? Do you realize how severely this compromises Lady Rosamund's position, and how badly it could reflect on anyone who has ever defended you to him?"

"No, milady, I am not insane." Geoffrey's voice cooled and hardened, and his anger chilled the room where Veronique's had begun heating it. "But I will not hide behind a woman's skirts to protect myself, nor will I permit the struggle to secure my patrimony lie solely in the hands of—"

"Of the women who have been doing all the work to secure your patrimony thus far, milord?" Veronique snapped, her temper flaring. "Not hide behind a woman's skirts? Milord Geoffrey, I submit that you've done little else for nearly two decades—and now you seek to rearrange a delicate political situation to suit your need to be personally involved, no matter how much damage you may do to the stratagems of those attempting to aid you. Saviarre will not be dislodged from her position in the Grand Court by violence alone, milord, and it was my understanding that I would be given the time necessary to contrive her undoing."

"You have been given time, Lady Veronique. You have yet to produce measurable results." Geoffrey glanced away, and reached for the knife he used to open his correspondence.

It took every ounce of self-control Veronique possessed not to snatch the blade up first and start removing Geoffrey's fingers until she was certain she had his undivided attention. "I have been given six months to isolate and destroy a woman who has been entrenched at your sire's side for the better part of two hundred years. When I accepted this commission, I accepted no time limitations, no constraints on the strategies I was permitted to use, and no third-party right of refusal or interference." She bit off each word precisely. "If you wished to renegotiate those terms, milord, you should have informed me of it long before now."

Geoffrey carefully eased his hand away from the knife. "You are... not entirely incorrect in that assessment, Lady Veronique. Very well. When you were commissioned, I had not yet decided on my course of action, and it seemed that a long-range political stratagem for weakening Saviarre over a longer period of time and separating her from power gradually was the wisest course of action, least likely to result in a vacuum great enough to destroy the stability of the entire Grand Court. That is no longer the case. Queen Salianna has failed, for her part, to quell the rebellion of Esclarmonde the Black, who should have been put down by now. The strategy you yourself employed to trump Saviarre's manipulations of the heretics and the refugee situation introduced a new variable in that situation, one outside of Queen Salianna's direct control. And Saviarre has proved herself to be more tenacious than even I thought she would be, and resourceful, as well."

"So, your answer to those facts is to provoke a confrontation before any of us are wholly prepared to support one?" Veronique demanded. "And let the victories fall where they may?"

"I had hoped," Geoffrey replied, softly, "that my sire would see the justice in my complaint and respond to it. This will no doubt sound foolish to you, Lady Veronique, hut I wanted to know what my sire had become. I wanted to see the truth with my own eyes, and determine if there was anything of the man that he once was that could be salvaged." His eyes closed momentarily, a ghost-trace of sorrow etched into his expression. "I no longer think that it is possible to resolve the situation in Paris diplomatically or politically. Even were Saviarre to vanish tomorrow, it would not make my sire the man he once was. He has changed, Lady Veronique, too much to recover—but I tell you now, if that were not so, if there were the slightest chance he would ever be the man or the prince he once was, I would never take this action against him. And I take it now with a heavy heart, for the sake of my city and my people, not for the love of power, or even the desire for it."

"You're right. It does sound foolish to me," Veronique replied coldly. "Milord Geoffrey, I seriously doubt that your sire has ever been the sort of man, or the sort of ruler, who would gladly submit to the judgment of another within his own domain. Your vision of him is clouded by your own desire that he be more than he ever was—your plan was destined to bring us to this point, whether we wanted to come here or not."

Geoffrey was silent for a long moment, and the struggle to master his own temper was clear to Veronique's trained eyes. Finally, he admitted, "I had hoped to manipulate this situation in such a way as to give us a concrete timetable for action, Lady Veronique. If my sire accepts Queen Salianna's demand, that tells us how much time we have to complete our groundwork, for the Court will be convened at a time of our choosing, and the added distraction of the preparations for the Court of Love would serve to disguise our activities. If my sire rejects Queen Salianna's demand, we need only wait until our forces are adequately built and emplaced to isolate both Countess Saviarre and my sire, and then we may act immediately. We will simply have to contrive another distraction in the meantime—which, given the political fallout that will result from any refusal of the Courts of Love, may be a less than onerous task."

"I see you've thought this through." Veronique watched his face closely. "Have you received any official notice of your sire's response as of yet?"

"No." He was not, apparently, lying, but Veronique didn't credit that with much weight.

"And the state of your forces?" she pressed, inquiring with a questioning eyebrow.

"Improving. We'll achieve adequate fighting strength, if not overwhelming superiority, very shortly." He was eying her reactions minutely, as well. "And the state of your endeavors, Lady Veronique?"

"The Latin Quarter is as insulated against Saviarre's mortal minions as I can make it, milord," Veronique replied evenly, "thanks very much to the men you kindly lent me. The regent has successfully managed to bar your haven and my own against shadow-spies, though those wardings may not be as effective against other sorts of shadows. He will," she added, "be attempting to capture a shadow-spy for interrogation, or at least that's his intent."

"Very good." He rose and stepped out from behind his desk. "Will you be staying the day, Lady Veronique? It is, unfortunately, a bit too long of a ride to make it back to Paris yet tonight, I fear...."

"I would be happy to accept your hospitality, milord." Veronique smiled through gritted teeth, and accepted the arm that he offered her. Sandrin preceded them to the door, unlocking it and exiting ahead of them to check the corridor outside. "I could not help but notice, milord, that many of the men you have here aren't from lie de France... Aragonese, unless I miss my guess."

"You have," Geoffrey murmured, "a very sharp eye, Lady Veronique."

The room was dark for but the steady flames of four candles and the circles of light they cast across the scrupulously clean floor and walls. Each candle stood at the point of a diamond, precisely oriented north, south, east, and west, the boundaries of that figure delineated in lines of salt extracted from seawater beneath the light of a full moon. They glowed, faintly, with a lingering radiance all their own. Spreading out from that central diamond were concentric layers of defenses, made visible to the human eye by lines etched first in chalk and then reinforced by a mixture of powdered salt, bone, and crystallized Cainite vitae. If one looked closely, one could see the glyphs of the wards themselves shimmering in the air, flickering in and out of visibility, walls of will and the word, fueled by blood, defending their makers. Between them, four dark-robed mortal apprentices sat, quietly murmuring the sounds that maintained the protective structure, while their master, standing at the apex of their five-pointed structure, wove a second thread through the warp and weft of the spell.

The trap was laid, and laboriously baited with what appeared to be a pinprick flaw in the sorcerous defenses around Geoffrey's house. Goratrix knew that it was only a matter of time before something took that bait. The wards had been tried at least once each night since their emplacement, forcefully at first, and then with gradually increasing subtlety as his opponent acknowledged that brute force would not be sufficient to undo those protections. He even admitted to himself, somewhat rue-fully, that given sufficient time in which to examine the ward structure, that opponent might very well be able to contrive some means to circumvent it. He was not, for a change, dealing with some superstitious Tzimisce hedge-witch but a foe of will, guile, and some amount of training in the shadow-weaving arts, a branch of sorcery all the more fascinating for the rarity of its true practitioners. That practitioner was not, Goratrix instinc-tively felt, Prince Alexander, for reasons wholly related to the man's well-known detestation of the Lasombra and everything about them. That left a strictly limited number of suspects as to the identity of the shadow-sorcerer and was one of the most burning questions currently inflaming the regent's mind.

The flames of the candles all flickered simultaneously, as though a sudden breeze caught them, and their light dimmed slightly. Something had bitten at the bait, and was even now considering whether or not to take it. Goratrix altered the tone of his own incantation, the words taking on the flavor of seduc-tion, invitation, a lure. The salt lines linking candle to candle shimmered faintly, taking on a phosphorescent hue.

A pinpoint of darkness began to form in the center of the diamond, drawing itself through the flaw in the defenses like a thread through the eye of a needle. It felt about blindly, a fila-ment of darkness so absolute it drew light into its unreflective substance, and Goratrix continued calling to it, a song of invi-tation, a song of hidden things and secrets just begging to be uncovered.

The shadow pulled itself completely through the pin-prick, and Goratrix closed the aperture behind it with a single harsh syllable. The lines of salt joining the candles rearranged themselves into their true form, a binding circle of wardings burning a cold blue-white, occasionally resolving themselves into marks that spelled the nature of their magic. The shadow froze, the slender filament collapsing in on itself to form an amorphous blob of darkness, welling up into a bubble as it realized its exit had vanished from beneath it. It was extremely disturbing to watch as it oozed around the confines of the circle, testing the integrity of the magics binding it with tiny jabs that shot equally tiny blue-white sparks from the wards.

The apprentices, to their credit, didn't flag or falter once in their incanting, and Goratrix was extremely pleased with them. One of their number would, if he had his druthers, earn the Embrace at the end of this affair, a reward for competence and constancy. He raised his own voice and demanded, in a language that hadn't been spoken in the living memory of most of mankind, "Creature of shadow, do you comprehend the words I speak?"

For an instant, there was no response. Then the shadow reared up like a striking snake, seeming to gather substance as it expanded, or else spreading what substance it had in an effort to look larger. Its head flattened into a rough oval on the long stalk of its neck, and it swayed agitatedly back and forth, clearly not wishing to respond.

Goratrix altered his tone slightly, adding layers to his words that demanded compliance. "Creature of shadow, I know that you understand my words. You will obey my commands and reveal yourself to me."

It shuddered as the weight of the sorcery settled on it—and flung itself at the edge of the boundaries holding it, ricocheted off one edge and recoiled, slammed into another, seeking a weakness, a flaw, some means of escape. Goratrix sensed, through those glancing contacts, a depthless malice utterly devoid of human reason, an uncontrollable and relentless compulsion to destroy and devour, a pure hate of all things of light or physical substance. The blood froze in his veins as he realized how much of his strength it was taking merely to contain the thing, and he knew, in the instant, that this was no spy, no creature made for skulking espionage, but an assassin, a killing thing called from somewhere beyond the bounds of purely physical space.

He extended a hand and let the twenty-eight syllables of the diamond's most hidden function fall off his tongue, just as the shadow-killer lunged directly at him, trying to bore through the wards by sheer force. The salt comprising the diamond lit up with a blaze of radiance that washed the entire room in white light, the candles consuming their entire sorcerously enhanced substance in a matter of seconds. The shadow screamed, a sound heard not so much audibly as in the mind and soul and blood, and writhed trying to escape, as its substance shredded, boiling away like wisps of smoke in a high wind.

For an instant after the light and that terrible soundless scream died, even Goratrix lacked the ambition to do anything more than hold his ground, swaying slightly, all the exposed skin on his body feeling tight and burnt, as though he'd stood too close to a fire. The apprentices had ceased their incanting with cries of surprise as the inner defenses exploded, but gathered themselves together with admirable aplomb. The eldest waited until his eyes adjusted to the darkness and then fetched an entirely mundane tallow candle; in its wavering light, he and his three fellows, all looking deeply shaken, turned to Goratrix for instruction.

Goratrix worked enough moisture into his mouth to speak. "Cleanse the room. Be careful of the diamond." There was a scorch-mark in the very center of their ritual space, perfectly diamond-shaped and still smoking slightly. "Something of the shadow's substance may be lingering there. Do not disturb the salt lines around it. Clean up the rest. I will be in my study."

So saying, he opened his own exit through the wards and stepped through it, deeply disturbed, and went to write both Lady Veronique and Lord Geoffrey with the results of the experiment. And then to find his own sustenance, for he had rarely felt himself so utterly drained.

There was a faint scratching at the door of Bishop de Navarre's office, hardly louder than the scratching of his pen across parchment, but enough to attract his attention. He looked up from the letter at which he labored and murmured, just loudly enough to be heard through the door, "Enter."

One of his apprentices came in, eyes on the floor, fell to his knees and bowed in full prostration as soon as he reached the desk. "I bear tidings from the circle, milord."

De Navarre laid his pen aside and folded his hands together. "What has passed, my child?"

"We have lost a piece of the killing darkness, milord." The apprentice, not given leave to rise, addressed his remarks to the floor. "And the shadow-watcher observing its progress."

A hiss through clenched fangs. "How did this happen?"

"Milord," the apprentice squeaked, and then paused to regain control of his voice. "Milord, the killing darkness was investigating the ward structure around Geoffrey le Croisé's house on Ile de la Cité, as you had instructed, seeking a weakness in the wards to be exploited. It found one. It extended itself within. It was not a true weakness, but a trap—when it entered, it was caught, and destroyed." He swallowed hard. "Francois was killed, as well. His heart burst."

"So," de Navarre murmured softly, in response, "the sorcerer is employed by Geoffrey and not Veronique d'Orleans." The knowledge was not quite sufficient to make up for the loss of a skilled shadow-handier, but it was enough, for now. "Go, tend to Francois's body. Make certain it isn't found by anyone who might recognize the signs of how he perished."

Bishop de Navarre laid aside the parchment he had been working on and began another, which was sent later that night to Countess Saviarre.

Jean-Battiste de Montrond was not having a very good summer, despite the steadily increasing flow of silver into his coffers from his usual clientele, or the fringe benefits that came of finally associating himself with the real power behind Paris's throne. He discovered, early on, that Saviarre was willing to entertain modest expense claims from him, provided he didn't try to bill her for anything completely outrageous. Apparently the woman actually read the expense reports her agents submitted, and responded accordingly. He'd managed to minimize his personal outlay on the whole project quite nicely and while the enterprise itself wasn't working out all that smoothly, his bottom line was shaping up well. If the entire thing went bad overnight, he had more than sufficient funds to vanish on, and keep running until either Saviarre or Veronique or both got tired of chasing him. He sat at his desk, going over his account books, and trying to let the sight of the filthy lucre accruing to him soothe away all his difficulties. It wasn't working.

No, money was not the problem. The problem was that he really hated—hated at a visceral, soul-deep level—to see a beautiful woman cry and know that he'd been the cause of it. Alainne had cried on his shoulder more than once over the last several weeks, and there was no way for him to weasel out of his personal responsibility for her sorrow, no matter how he tried to justify it to himself. Alainne wept for poor little Thierry and did so regularly; he'd been almost a brother to her, she said more than once. The sight of her tears and tear-reddened eyes pricked his conscience—his conscience, the last lingering bit of which he thought he'd neatly excised at least a decade before. Nothing he'd done in the name of his own personal survival had troubled him one damn bit in almost as many years as Alainne had been alive, and yet...

And yet her tears stung him, like salt on a raw wound. He hated it, even as he couldn't find a way to hate her, and was as miserably unhappy as he'd ever been since his sire condemned him with a kiss.

Serpent.

Jean-Battiste nearly leapt out of his skin like the snake he was, and looked around wildly for the source of that voice. He was alone in his bedchamber, which doubled as his study, unattended, his bed empty for a change.

Serpent.

The flame in his lamp flickered, and the shadow he cast against the wall lengthened and thickened, grew taller, took on the distinct outline of a man he knew entirely too well. The local air temperature dropped sharply enough that he could feel the cold through his clothes. Jean-Battiste touched his tongue to his lips and replied, as steadily as he could, "You called, Your Grace?"

Yes. I require your assistance on a matter of some importance. De Navarre's voice sounded as though it were coming
from the bottom of a well, hollow and slightly echoing. There is
a sorcerer dwelling on Ile de la Cité.

This was, at least to Jean-Battiste, not an overwhelming surprise. "I was not unaware of that, Your Grace. You yourself—"

Another sorcerer, beyond the one whose existence we
already suspected. De Navarre's voice took on an edge of irritation. Dwelling in the house of Geoffrey le Croisé. I require your
assistance in determining this sorcerer's identity and determining if he has had any contact with Veronique d'Orleans. I will
investigate matters here on the isle. I will require you to investigate in the Latin Quarter.

"As you wish, Your Grace—but I doubt that I'll learn anything useful. I haven't been much in Veronique's confidence,
of late—I doubt she'll blurt out that she's been consorting with
Lord Geoffrey's pet sorcerer." Jean-Battiste thought he did an
admirable job of keeping the sarcasm out of his voice.

De Navarre, evidently, did not agree. I do not care how
you accomplish it, serpent, so long as you obtain results. I will
require a report on this issue from you before minor court next
week. The shadows reverted to their normal shapes, and the
usual sticky summer heat reasserted itself.

Jean-Battiste shook his head and muttered aloud, "Why in
the name of God did I put myself in the middle of all this?"

The ride back from La Forêt gave Veronique a good length of
time to think, and none of her thoughts were soothing. The situation in Paris was moving in directions she had neither anticipated nor was entirely prepared to deal with; she wished she
dared to write to Portia or, better yet, Aimeric, and beg their
advice. Unfortunately, there was a good chance that any correspondence she sent to them would end up doing no good,
because by the time it arrived, the crisis she was hoping to avert
would already have been and gone.

"Milady, you're talking to yourself again." Sandrin pointed
out, in the closest he ever came to a genuinely wry tone, a little
smile trying to hide at the corners of his mouth.

"So I am," Veronique admitted, and did her best to think in silence. Unfortunately, her thoughts kept chasing themselves in the same entirely unsatisfying circles. A quarter-hour passed thus before Veronique spoke again. "I need advice."

They rode for another length of road without any further speech passing between them. Finally, Veronique edged her mount closer to his own and demanded, "Well?"

Sandrin blinked at her in surprise. "My advice, lady?"

"I'm aware that I rarely actually need to solicit any since everyone is so good about offering it whether I want it or not, but yes, I need your advice." Veronique hoped that didn't sound as tart as it tasted coming out. "You might not be a general but that doesn't mean you're not a tactician. You know the situation. What would you do?"

Another lengthy stretch of silence passed. Finally, he said evenly, "You've common cause with a weapon you haven't yet put to its fullest use, lady. I'd consider pressing them—and you know of whom I speak—to take a more active hand in events. Minimize the possible damage to your own. Send the girls who can be spared away with Girauda or Alainne—ask Lord Geoffrey to offer them sanctuary on one of his properties, if you must, somewhere outside the city."

"Something's going to happen soon. You can feel it, too, can't you?" Veronique reined up.

"Yes, lady, I can." He looked full at her, his expression grave. "Lord Geoffrey may be a good leader in the field, but I don't think this was a field he was ready to take."

"Delicate political adjustments don't appear to be his forte, no, but he does understand the mechanisms of how to provoke a reaction," Veronique replied sourly. "Not that it would take much just now, I admit. And, unfortunately, he's not as subtle as he thinks." She kneed her horse back into motion. "When we get back home, I want you and Girauda to put your heads together and decide who should leave and who should stay, in the event that we need to evacuate large numbers of the staff on short notice. And, yes, I want Alainne to be one of those who goes, no matter what." Her mouth thinned into a grim line. "And, as you say, I must have a discussion with our silent partner."

Veronique arrived home close to dawn, and barely had time to glance at the letters that had arrived during her brief time away before daylight lethargy was tugging at her limbs. She fell into her cupboard bed still clothed in her chemise and woke the next night feeling utterly grubby, in dire need of both a hath and a secretary. The bath she naturally obtained without difficulty, but the secretary she hadn't managed to replace since Thierry was lost. It aggravated her that there was no one else on staff lettered enough to take dictation while she tried to read all her correspondence, of which there were several important pieces.

Lady Rosamund had finally written a detailed letter in which she outlined her perception of Queen Salianna's strategy, the delivery of the ultimatum to Prince Alexander and, to Veronique's complete lack of surprise, Alexander's refusal to play Salianna's game. Veronique suspected that Alexander's response was already en route to Salianna and that Geoffrey would know of it before the week was out. That, of course, meant that Geoffrey would have no further reason to delay his own plans beyond the demands of common sense and the necessity of building sufficient forces to deploy against his sire's own and to secure Alexander's haven and those of his partisans. Veronique privately wondered how Geoffrey expected to handle Alexander himself. The prince was, despite his many flaws, both ancient and potent, and she strongly suspected that overcoming those hurdles was part of the duties being shouldered by the Tremere.

Goratrix himself had written, a polite little note that told her absolutely nothing, inquiring after her well-being and requesting a meeting. She laid that piece of correspondence aside for a response, and shuffled through the rest of the stack, which included the regular assortment of summer garden parties and boat outings and a note from Sir Olivier, likewise inquiring after her well-being. A little pang went through her when she saw his seal. She hadn't wanted to like him when she came to Paris, had strenuously resisted the idea that there was a decent person hiding under all the layers of noble breeding and the deliberately constructed brainless lap-dog facade, but there had been a man she could genuinely call a friend there. She hadn't wanted to like Lady Rosamund and her brother Sir Josselin either, but the combined power of their charm had no doubt conquered harder hearts than Veronique's over the years.

It took everything in her not to pen a series of anonymous warnings to be slipped under their doors, in the hope that they would take the danger seriously and flee before it found them.

"Sandrin, Girauda, I'll need that list as soon as you can have it ready." Veronique reached up and rubbed her eyes.

Too soft, Vero—did you really think you were going to manage an entirely bloodless coup? That everyone you said you weren't going to care about but came to love anyway would come through without a scratch? That there would be no price to pay for what you planned?

It was too late for regrets.

Veronique's messengers came and went, carrying letters and orders all over the Latin Quarter and Ile de la Cité. She was completely satisfied that, in the Latin Quarter at least, Saviarre's eyes had been entirely gouged out and that the countess was operating blindly. That was more or less the case. Saviarre's attempts to reintroduce mortal agents into the slums and stewhouses and students' residences of the Latin Quarter were a dismal failure fueled by the perpetual vigilance of Veronique's own network of operatives and the professional brutality of Geoffrey's men-on-loan. Even the effectiveness of Bishop de Navarre's shadow-spies was tremendously impaired by the fact that they never managed to see anything interesting, much less incriminating, barred as they were from accessing Veronique's house directly. In the Quarter, Veronique's agents still delivered their messages surreptitiously, because caution had been ground into them by repetition and the death of one of their own, but even so they felt themselves mostly safe from unfriendly observation. Only those couriers specifically tasked with the effort of contacting the minions of the Nosferatu warren made the effort to be completely invisible.

On the isle, invisibility was the norm, for the odds of being spotted by hostile eyes were much higher and the risks greater.

Lord Goratrix and Lady Rosamund both received letters from Veronique indicating her receipt of their notes. To Lady Rosamund, Veronique wrote that she would do what she could to support the position of the Courts of Love, come what may, and begged Rosamund's pardon for being so distant of late, having been much engaged in the minutiae of assisting Brother Anatole's departure. To Goratrix, she wrote advising him to dispose of any potentially incriminating correspondence in his possession and warning him that Geoffrey might very well choose to move as soon as he knew that Queen Salianna's efforts had failed.

At no point did Veronique, or any of her people, realize that nearly every move they made was under surveillance by Jean-Battiste de Montrond's own collection of guttersnipes, cutthroats, and Latin Quarter whores. Nor did they know that he had been watching closely since the night Goratrix's messenger had come from the isle, and caught the eye of the serpent as he sat in Veronique's own house, engaged in his weekly flirt-and-gossip session with Alainne.

Chapter Seventeen

"**M**ilord?"

Josselin looked up from the length of leather cord he was absently braiding, startled out of his peaceful inner rambling, the rare chance to simply sit and relax. Fabien stood in the door, a troubled look on his face, and Josselin gestured him in. "What is it, cher?"

"There's a woman here. Dressed as a man. She claims to be a diplomat of the city." Fabien sounded frankly dubious of that lofty claim. "She also claims her errand is extremely urgent."

Josselin laid his project aside and rose from his bench. "Did she give a name?"

"Lady Veronique d'Orleans. And she says that she's here to see you, not Lady Rosamund. She was very specific about that."

Josselin opened his mouth to respond to that, found a laugh lurking in the back of his throat, and only barely restrained it. It took him a moment to discipline himself enough to speak. "Very well, Fabien. Show her to the solar, I'll be there in a moment."

He took a few minutes to change into a more appropriate tunic, wash his hands, have a good laugh at the mental image of Veronique d'Orleans coming to him, dressed as a man, as Rosamund had so feared, and then put himself back to order. When he arrived in the solar, he found that Fabien had, in no way, been joking—Lady Veronique d'Orleans, her frost-blonde hair hacked off short, was indeed there and was doing a very credible imitation of masculinity, clad in hosen and high riding boots and a long green cotte. A straw hat, the wide brim of which she must have used to help disguise her features, and a sealed letter sat on the table before her. Beside both burned the last nub of a sigil-etched candle. The same quietly competent man-at-arms who had attended her at the temporary embassy stood behind her chair now, physically at rest and continuously watchful.

She rose to greet him, as was proper, and offered an abbreviated bow. Josselin duplicated it, bemused beyond the capacity for irony. "Lady Veronique. You cannot imagine how delighted I am to see you."

"Sir Josselin." Something about the way her lips twitched suggested she knew exactly what he was thinking and didn't particularly mind. "I'm grateful you were willing to see me at such short notice."

"As Milady Rosamund could no doubt tell you, I am always willing to attend the desires of a beautiful woman." Josselin seated himself opposite her. "Even if she happens to be pretending to be a beautiful man."

Lady Veronique smiled wryly. "I wish we had all night to sit and banter, Sir Josselin, but I fear that we do not. I have a question to ask of you, and a request to make of you."

"Of me, milady?" He asked lightly, uncertain where the conversation was going, and already not sure he liked the possibilities.

"Of you. It is my understanding that you are passably well acquainted with Sir Aimeric de Cabaret, presently the diplomatic envoy of Queen Esclarmonde the Black to Béziers?" Her blue eyes caught his and held them intently.

Josselin's mouth went a little dry as he considered how best to answer that question. Particularly to this woman, who had manipulated her own diplomatic connections in the south so capably and might already know more than she chose to reveal. After a moment, he admitted, "I am acquainted with him, yes. We met while I was in serving Queen Isouda's interests at the Court of Love in Toulouse."

"Sir Aimeric has asked me to pass on his fond greetings and felicitations, and his hope that you will meet again sometime soon in Toulouse, Sir Josselin." Lady Veronique pushed the letter across the table to him. It was sealed with ribbon and a wax medallion stamped with her own arms.

Josselin's heart quivered a bit in his chest at that. "Well, milady, you've asked your question of me. Now what is your request?"

"The request, I fear, requires a bit of explanation." Lady Veronique leaned back in her chair, and folded her hands in her lap. "As you know, my services were retained by the Courts of Love, and the specific task I was given was to facilitate Lady Rosamund's entrance into the Grand Court, and to undermine the ability of Countess Saviarre to interfere with Lady Rosamund's efforts." Josselin nodded. "What I told you and your sister with regards to my mission was not entirely fictional—but it was not the entire truth, either. My true mission—and Lady Rosamund's, as well—was to prepare the way for a coup, the overthrow of Prince Alexander and the installation of his childe, Lord Geoffrey le Croisé, in his place."

For a long moment after she spoke those words, Josselin could think of nothing intelligent to say in response. He could not, in fact, encapsulate the full depth of his shock and horror in words alone. Finally, he whispered, "Are you mad? This is impossible, Lady Veronique! The Courts of Love desire reunion with the Grand Court—"

"No, Sir Josselin, I fear that they do not. Some years ago, prior to Queen Esclarmonde's rebellion, a secret Court was convened that tried and condemned Prince Alexander in absentia for crimes against Love and, more importantly, against the ambitions of Queen Salianna. It was decided, at that time, that Prince Alexander had, by his actions, rendered himself unfit to rule and that he should be replaced by a monarch more sympathetic to the ultimate goals of the Courts of Love." Veronique's tone was brisk, businesslike. "I was commissioned shortly thereafter to assist this endeavor on behalf of my sire, Lady Portia, and with the tacit agreement of my patron, Prince Julia Antasia."

Josselin stared at her, unable to formulate an entirely coherent response to that statement, but neither entirely disbelieving it, either. No one in lie de France doubted the ambitions of Queen Salianna, or how frustrated those ambitions had been when another woman—Countess Saviarre—took the place at Prince Alexander's side that she felt rightfully belonged to her.

"My mission has always been to destroy Countess Saviarre." Again in that damnably calm, unruffled tone of hers. "But when I took that mission, it was with the understanding that there would be no limitations on the time I would have to accomplish that task, and equally no limitations on the tools I could use to do so. Those specifications have recently fallen by the wayside in a manner that may very well endanger us all."

"You said..." Josselin was somewhat surprised to hear his own words come out so steadily, "that Milady Rosamund shared your mission."

"She does—though if I have my way, she'll never realize it. I never told her the full scope of the mission and I never intended to do so." It took all of Josselin's self-control not to reach across the table and shake her until her head flew off. "Lady Rosamund's mission, to seek rapprochement between the Grand Court and the Courts of Love, was a distraction from the start, a means of focusing Prince Alexander's attention elsewhere while I dismembered Saviarre's grip on power. Queen Salianna did not tell her the truth of that matter and left it to my discretion."

"And you thought it was a good idea to deceive my sister—to let her sully herself with your... your duplicities and intrigues and never tell her the truth of why she had been called to service?" Josselin demanded, heatedly. "How dare you—"

"Sir Josselin." The steel in her voice surprised him and pulled him up short. "I never told her, and never intended to tell her, for her own protection. Think. You're not a fool. Were Lady Rosamund to know the truth, Alexander could pluck it from her thoughts the way you or I would pick a flower—the knowledge he could claw from her own mind would be used to destroy her, and any who could conceivably share guilt by association. You. Me. Queen Isouda. Ignorance is not the best of shields but, in this case, it was the only shield I could give her." She caught his eye again. "She can deny knowledge of anything that might come and do so truthfully. She is in less danger than you or I, now."

That sank through several layers of righteous outrage and threw a bucket of cold realization all over his temper. "Why are you telling me this?"

"Events have been put into motion over which I have little ultimate control. Lord Geoffrey returned, I suspect precipitately and against Queen Salianna's advice, to confront Prince Alexander before I had finished with Countess Saviarre, and before Lady Rosamund had managed to win Alexander completely to her side. It was," she hit off each word clearly, "a mistake of the first order. Lord Geoffrey may be a brilliant tactician but as a politician he lacks subtlety. And as a claimant to his sire's throne, he has chosen the most dangerous of possible courses to achieve it, also very much against the guidance of his advisors. There is a very real possibility that nearly everyone involved in this scheme will be exposed in some way and, if and when that happens, the consequences will, as always, roll downhill. Lady Rosamund is as ignorant—and as innocent—as I can make her. But—"

"There are others who aren't so protected." Josselin completed grimly. "And Aimeric is one of them, correct?"

"The Prince of Béziers, Eon de l'Etoile, Brother Anatole, and numerous others are all in extremely exposed positions. And I doubt that Lord Geoffrey cares one way or another about the fate of the Bitterois court—if he wins through and seizes Paris, it may take considerable efforts on my part to convince him to honor his sire's diplomatic agreements in that direction." Veronique glanced pointedly at the letter. "Aimeric was not in conspiracy with me. Believe that. He is, as you no doubt know, simply extremely skilled at dancing no matter what the tune—his strength has always been his flexibility in shifting situations."

Josselin licked his lips and replied, dryly, "You could say that, yes. What do you want of me, Lady Veronique?"

"I do not ask this lightly, Sir Josselin." Her expression was grave. "I ask that you carry this letter south to Sir Aimeric. It is a warning, for him and for Prince Eon, to prepare for what may very well be coming. I feel that I owe them at least that much for assisting me unawares. And because, as with you, Aimeric has been my friend for a very long time, and I look forward to many more years of sarcastic diplomatic correspondence from him."

Josselin closed his eyes. After a moment, he murmured, "If

I accept this deranged request—and I am not saying that I do—I would ask a favor of you in return, Lady Veronique."

"Ask it."

"In my absence, I would ask that you protect my sister as fiercely as you protect friends you've not seen in at least half a century." Josselin opened his eyes and glared at her.

"You have my word." She didn't even look embarrassed to say it. "Do I have yours?"

"Yes, damn you." He picked up the letter and raised his voice. "Fabien!" His squire's carroty head poked in the door. "Fetch Peter for me, I've a message to give him. Then go make certain our traveling gear is in order, and saddle Sorel and Whitefoot. We're leaving as soon as we can."

Fabien gawked a moment. "Milord, what—"

"I'll explain on the road, lad. Please hurry." Without further ado, Fabien scurried off to do his bidding. Josselin rose and offered Veronique a hand up. "Do the Courts of Love know? The queens? What you just told me?"

"I suspect that Queen Salianna has more ready access to Lord Geoffrey than I do, Sir Josselin. I doubt that any of this will take them by surprise," she assured him, dryly.

"Somehow that doesn't entirely surprise me." Lady Veronique's man fell in behind them as he escorted her to the door. "Do you need an escort home?"

"No, but I thank you for the offer." She let her companion precede her outside, set her hat on her head, and turned back towards him before she departed. "Ride quickly, Sir Josselin, and go safely. I hope to see you again."

"With all due respect, Lady Veronique, let us hope you do not. I understand why you did what you have done," Josselin smiled coldly, "but that does not mean I choose to forgive you for it. I suggest you not allow your path to cross mine again. Go with God, lady, and may He have mercy on you."

"Go with God, Sir Josselin, and may He watch over you in your toils."

He shut the door in her face. It was one of the more satisfying political acts he'd ever performed. Then he spun away, shouting for Peter.

Veronique departed the Toreador embassy with a heavier heart than she thought she'd suffer. She did, she supposed, have to consider that a victory in the loosest conceivable sense of the term. Sir Josselin had, after all, agreed to carry the letter, and that put him out of immediate danger and would serve to warn Aimeric, two fairly significant goods. The letter contained a warning, as she had told Josselin, and a second, coded message detailing her own observations regarding Lord Geoffrey le Croisé's fondness for Aragonese mercenaries, a fact that Queen Esclarmonde would no doubt find both amusing and food for thought.

After a laborious moment of trying to regard the goblet as half-full, Veronique admitted to herself that the situation could not possibly have gone well no matter how much effort she had put into it. There was simply no good way to tell someone that you'd been ruthlessly abusing the faith and trust of the sister he loves. There were nights when the price for playing the game was not at all worth the benefits.

They rode briskly toward the bridge linking Ile de la Cité to the Left Bank, Sandrin pacing slightly behind and to one side, vigilant as always. Even so, he wasn't quite vigilant enough to notice the small, indistinct figure lurking in the mouth of an alley they passed, whose quiet word stopped their horses in midstride. A second such word caused the beasts to rear suddenly, violently, as though they'd scented wolves in the midst of the city, pitching their riders off onto the cobbles and galloping off with high-pitched sounds of fear still ringing off the walls. For an instant, Veronique lay flat on her back where she'd fallen, momentarily dazed, listening to Sandrin make some fairly piquant comments about intractable horseflesh. Then she rolled to her feet, gripped his arm tightly, and silenced him with a shake.

The tiny figure—no larger than a young child—stepped from the shadows, swathed to the brows in cloak and scarves despite the wretched summer heat. It spoke in a voice barely above a hoarse whisper. "Lady Veronique d'Orleans."

It was not a question. Veronique nodded. "I am she."

"Milady commands that you come with me. Your man as well. The upper city is no longer safe for you." It delivered that pronouncement in an expressionless monotone that filled Veronique with dread, even as she followed, and gestured for Sandrin to accompany her.

"What's happened?" Veronique demanded, staying as close as she dared come without treading on the little emissary's trailing lengths of woolen clothing.

"I do not know. Milady commands that you come, and I am bringing you. You will learn more below." It neither turned around to see if they were following nor addressed either of them again as it led them through a series of narrow alleys and even narrower breezeways, the river-ward segments of town-house gardens, and finally to a heavy wrought-iron grate. This it hefted without noticeable effort, and held while Veronique and Sandrin ducked inside. A narrow, low-ceilinged tunnel plunged away before them, its walls unfinished stone, its floor damp with a shallow stream of drainage.

Every nerve in Veronique's body rebelled against going another inch farther, knowing as she did the dangers that could be lurking in the absolute darkness a few inches away. She pressed herself against the wall just inside the entrance to the tunnel, and gestured for Sandrin to do likewise. A square of cool blue moonlight fell through the grate, but otherwise there was no light; there had been virtually none for the entire walk. If they progressed any further, they would he utterly blind, a circumstance she didn't relish at all.

Their escort stepped inside, dropped the grate, and secured it with a series of hidden bolts only barely visible even from the inside. "Come."

A low fire had been burning in Veronique's sitting room all day and into the night. As a result, the temperature downstairs was utterly sweltering, even though Girauda and Philippe were taking the task of burning all of Veronique's letters in shifts. Philippe worked by day, sorting and stacking, peeling away ribbons and wax medallions to be broken up and melted down separate from the parchments themselves; Girauda worked by night, cutting parchments into strips with Alainne's scissors and feeding them strip by strip into the fireplace and a handful of braziers. Alainne and Nicolette organized the girls, determined who should stay and who should go, and were even now moving the youngest of the bathhouse's employees to what they hoped would be safety.

As it happened, they were both downstairs when a handful of ghoul knights, led by a Cainite functionary weasel trying to curry favor with the sheriff of Paris, kicked down the doors and began rousting out the few local customers who insisted on patronizing their favorite establishment despite the warnings of their favorite girls. Girauda shredded the remaining three letters that Veronique most wanted destroyed and fed them, with shaking hands, into the fire, watched them slowly blacken and curl. Philippe snatched up the rest, wrenched open the drain set in the middle of the floor, and began stuffing the remainder piece by piece down the ancient lead piping that emptied into Paris's sewers. From above, screams and cries of pain echoed down to them as they worked feverishly to complete their tasks. Girauda tossed the bundle of ribbons into one of the braziers, and disposed of the broken seal pieces by the expedient of pouring them into her sewing basket and stuffing the unfinished darning down over top of them.

Philippe had almost finished dropping the tightly rolled bits of parchment down the pipes when the door to Veronique's sitting room shuddered under the force of a tremendous blow, and simply fell inward, off its hinges. Girauda froze, halfway to Philippe's side, as the armored figure in the doorway drew his sword and advanced on them.

Alainne and Nicolette were hurrying back to the bathhouse, having spent a considerable amount of feminine wile convincing the commander of Geoffrey's force in the Latin Quarter to take in the youngest girls, for their own protection. Initially, the worthy Sir Charles was quite reluctant to allow it, making vaguely pious noises about the temptations of the flesh and the distractions pertaining thereto, but Christian charity ultimately carried the night, once Nicolette shed a few tears and the girls all pled their case very prettily. There was now a house in the Quarter containing a number of handsome youngish men sharing living space with a number of buxom and uninhibited young women, aged fifteen to seventeen, which was not technically a whorehouse. That amused Alainne to no end.

They hurried along the back alleys, trying to avoid the main thoroughfares and making special effort not to be seen by anyone who wasn't too drunk to tell either of them from the Virgin Mary. Before they even came within sight of the bathhouse, they smelled the smoke, and heard the shouts of alarm. As they rounded the last corner, Nicolette let out a little scream of horror and dismay.

The bathhouse was burning, and the fire was already well advanced, despite the efforts of the neighbors and no small number of the regulars to douse the flames. A bucket line had developed to fling water on the swiftly expanding inferno, and on the walls and roofs of the surrounding houses. Nicolette started forward to try to help; Alainne caught her by the arm and dragged her back into the alley. "Nico, there's nothing more we can do here. It's lost."

"How can you say that?!" Nicolette wailed, distraught. "Girauda and Philippe might still—"

"If Girauda and Philippe were inside when it went up, they're beyond our help," Alainne replied, fiercely. "Think! Go back to the safe house. Tell Sir Charles what happened. Look after the girls."

Nicolette stole another horrified look at the rapidly collapsing bathhouse. "...You're right... you're right... I'll go. What are you going to do?"

"I'm going to find Veronique." Alainne shoved Nicolette back in the direction they had come, not ungently. "Hurry, you. God knows what's going on now."

Nicolette nodded and scurried off, not quite at a run. Alainne watched until she could no longer see even a flicker of Nicolette's fire-red hair in the shadows, and then sped off in the opposite direction, heading toward the river and the bridges that linked the Quarter to the isle. Unlike some of the girls who had sought employment with Veronique, Alainne was not a country girl come to seek a better life than she might have found tilling the family fields and birthing sons for her husband. She had been born and bred in the city, she knew its streets like she knew the pattern of lines on her own palm, and she had caution bred into her bones, for no woman alone was safe on the streets after dark. Even so, she was so focused on her goal—the bridge to the high city—that she failed to realize she was being followed and was taken almost completely by surprise when her pursuers lunged out of a side alley and ambushed her.

She managed to get in a good bout of kicking and struggling, and one good scream before a strong hand clamped over her mouth, cutting off her voice and air both, and another twisted her arm behind her back, wrenching it so hard she saw stars of pain to go with the breathless black dots. She kicked one of her assailants in the chest as he went for her legs, and received a savage blow to the belly that took care of any lingering traces of air that might have been hiding in her lungs. In short order, she was being lugged deeper into the maze of alleyways, being allowed brief gasps of air, just enough to keep her conscious, as they went. It seemed much longer than it actually was and soon enough she found herself being dumped unceremoniously onto the cold cobbles of an alley close enough to the bathhouse for her to smell the smoke of its burning.

Alainne spent a moment just dragging breath into her lungs and blinking her watering eyes, trying to get her bearings. Near-silent footsteps approached where she sat, and she sprang to her feet, looking for a wall against which she could put her back and something to use as a weapon.

"Really, Alainne, is that any way to greet an old friend?" Jean-Battiste de Montrond asked her, standing a few feet away and sounding deeply, personally aggrieved.

Alainne's knees went weak with relief. "Jean-Battiste!" She flung herself into his not-at-all-protesting arms and hugged him for all she was worth, sobbing breathlessly in shock.

He patted her back comfortingly. "Now, now, my lovely, don't cry. It's going to be all right. Good God, did Jean and Albert handle you roughly? I'll have an ear each."

"The house—" Alainne choked out, pulling back a bit to

see his face. "Someone burned the house. Veronique was afraid something might happen—but I didn't think she believed it would be this soon—or this... this..."

"I know. I saw." Jean-Battiste reached out and brushed the tears off her cheek. "It just relieves me that you weren't inside, sweet Alainne, when the fire began." He ran his fingertips over her trembling lips. "Where is Veronique, my dove?"

"Not in the house." Alainne leaned gratefully on his arm. "She went out early as she dared, to the isle."

"The isle? Dare I ask what business took her there?" There was a suppressed urgency in his question, despite the effort he took to keep his tone light.

Alainne's eyes narrowed a fraction. "I don't know.... She didn't tell me before she left. She dressed to ride and took Sandrin with her."

Jean-Battiste ran a hand through her hair and murmured, "That's all right, my dear. You've done well, anyway, to tell me where she went."

His hand knotted tight in her hair and jerked her head back in one smooth motion; before she could even think of struggling, he had her slammed against the alley wall, his knee forcing her thighs apart, and one hand cupping her breast. She drew breath to scream and released it in a ragged moan of pleasure as he took her, his fangs piercing her throat at the juncture of neck and shoulder, his body undulating against hers in a pantomime of sensual intimacy. Had anyone glanced down the alley, that was precisely what they would have seen—a young couple engaged in the timeless art of pleasing themselves at any time, in any place, afire with passion and, no doubt, too much wine. For Alainne, it seemed to go on forever; for Jean-Battiste, it didn't last nearly long enough, before her heart began slowing, her breathing growing shallower, and he withdrew, lapping the wounds closed. Alainne swayed against him, her legs too weak to hold her, and he kissed her hard and fiercely on the mouth.

"That was wonderful, my lovely.... Better than ever I imagined it." He breathed against her lips, and let her drop to the cobbles at the feet of his bodyguards. "I'll cherish the memory of you forever." He flicked a glance at his men. "Do what you like with her, but when you're finished, make certain it looks like a crime of the streets." The look he bestowed on Alainne was much longer, and edged in something almost like sorrow. "I don't usually practice regret, Alainne, but for you? I'll make the exception. If you don't fight, it probably won't hurt as much."

He turned and walked away.

Goratrix, Regent of Rouen, Tremere Councilor to the whole of France, possessed finely honed instincts of self-preservation and rarely ignored them. When Veronique d'Orleans's note arrived, informing him of what she'd learned during her sojourn outside the city and warning him that disaster might very well be impending, it confirmed his own instinctual discomfort, and so he took the advice she gave without complaint. There was less to incriminate him in any sort of devilish conspiracy here in Paris, and so the destruction of sensitive documents took his apprentices comparatively little time.

The real problem was, of course, that neither he nor any of his kind were supposed to be in Paris at all, by order of His Most Gracious and Insane Highness, Alexander, Princeps Lutetius, and there was simply no good way to gloss over that fact. By day, he had the household servants scurrying among market stalls and shops to acquire a few bits and pieces his workings and researches required, and to give the general impression that life at Lord Geoffrey's household continued as normal, even in his absence. By night, he had his apprentices packing the most vital, irreplaceable, and useful pieces of thaumaturgic apparatus they had brought with them or breaking down and destroying or thoroughly concealing what couldn't be easily carried. To their credit, his apprentices also neither wept nor moaned nor complained when he told them to pack only their most essential belongings, nothing more than they personally could carry, and be prepared to move at a moment's notice. Goratrix himself spent those short summer nights deciding which of his belongings he would like most to carry away in haste, and making certain the emergency evacuation arrangements with Geoffrey's boatman were soundly entrenched in the man's mind.

The moment's notice did not, as Goratrix feared quite

deeply, come by day, but shortly after sunset, and it did not come from one of the spies in Alexander's household who worked for Geoffrey. It came from a Nosferatu envoy, who approached the doors as a poor old man begging alms of the household, who was admitted after he made the signs drilled into them by Geoffrey before his departure. He gave his name to Goratrix as Guillaume, suggested that even their lightest packing was too heavy for the paths they were going to travel, and advising them to lighten the load, for Alexander's men were likely already on the way.

The result was not exactly gibbering panic, but a good deal of rushing around did take place as bags and boxes were hurriedly opened, vital items removed and repacked, and the remains hidden as best they could in the storage rooms below Geoffrey's solar. As Alexander's ghouls, and the sheriff of Paris himself, were cutting their way past the door-guards and battering down the front door, Goratrix, four frightened apprentices, and Guillaume were escaping out the back, lugging a significantly lightened load of ritual gear and personal belongings. They made their way through the garden, and down the narrow staircase to the rear, leading down to the river front. To Goratrix's surprise, they turned away from the docks.

"Where are we going?" he demanded, in a whisper. "The evacuation route—"

"Not being evacuated." Guillaume rasped back, adding, belatedly, "Maestro. The Lady wants to see you."

"And the fight's not over. Yet."

The fighting was all but over at La Forêt, only the most stubborn of Geoffrey's defenders holding out against the force that assailed them. They were mostly holed up at the top of the manor's single, squat defensive tower, isolated and incapable of doing any real harm. There weren't, Sir Olivier's lieutenants assured him, more than a handful of them. They lacked food, water, a way to rearm themselves, and the force necessary to break out without outside assistance. Sir Olivier found that explanation satisfactory, offered generous surrender terms, and went off to have a talk with his older brother.

Geoffrey was not a fool. Once he had obtained a full picture of the force arrayed against him, he had ordered his men
to stand down, unwilling to spend their lives in a futile battle.
Only at a few places had that order been ignored, and most of
those men had been cut down without mercy. Aragonese mercenaries, Olivier couldn't help but notice, and wondered about
it absently as he made his way through the halls of La Forêt,
which were solidly in the control of his own knights, ghoul and
Cainite. Geoffrey had allowed himself to be taken and isolated,
locked in a windowless room to await what would come.

Sir Olivier was not looking forward to this at all. He had,
in fact, almost asked his sire to assign someone else to this particularly onerous duty but changed his mind when he saw how
Countess Saviarre was watching his response to the "honor."
Saviarre, he knew, would simply perish of glee if both of
Alexander's childer gave her an excuse to destroy them, and Sir
Olivier did not intend to let her have that satisfaction of him.
There was nothing he could do to save Geoffrey now, but he
could at least make certain that his brother didn't experience a
fatal accident during the siege of his house, or on the trip back
to Paris. He simply regretted that that was all he could ensure.

A pair of Cainite knights, young Toreador from one of the
innumerable family lines unattached to the Courts of Love,
stood guarding the door of Geoffrey's prison. They straightened
up quickly as he approached. "Has he been behaving himself?"

"Yes, milord." Young Sir Renier replied, reaching out to
touch the handle of the door. "Would you like to see him now,
milord?"

"For no other reason would I have dragged myself away
from the feast in the hall," Olivier assured him, sarcasm sailing
over his head with a foot to spare. "Open it. And, this time? Bar
it behind me. He's not personally helpless."

They did so, chagrined, as the door closed at his back.

Geoffrey didn't have a window to stare dramatically out of,
his back turned to the door, so he'd settled for a chair and one
of the smaller books from the shelf above his desk. He'd been
stripped of his arms and armor and battered in the process;
there was blood drying in his hair and the rust-stained padded

tunic he'd worn beneath his chain was torn at the shoulder. He also chose not to look up when his brother-cum-captor entered, and Olivier sighed heavily in response, reaching up to unstrap his helmet and set it aside, brushing the chainmail coif he wore beneath it down around his neck and shoulders. He crossed the room and set his helmet down with a solid thump on the smaller table at Geoffrey's elbow, a move which at last elicited a response. Geoffrey looked up, glanced irritably at the helmet, and then transferred the full force of his annoyance to his younger sibling-in-blood. "I'll ask you not to scratch the finish on that. It's from Lebanon."

Olivier sighed, closed his eyes, and massaged their lids. Without opening them, he remarked, "You realize you've made a complete hash of this, don't you?"

"Of what?" Geoffrey asked, closing his book and laying it next to Olivier's helmet. "Of trying to make our sire see reason? Of trying to convince him that if even I cannot trust or believe in him, there must be something wrong with—"

"For the love of God, Sir Geoffrey! Do you think you're the only one who sees it? Unlike you, I've been here for the last part of a century—I know that he's not the man he was. I know that he's changed, and not for the better, since that empty-headed little cow Lorraine and that witch Saviarre have had their way with him." Olivier spun away, agitated. "That's not the damned point, and you know it."

Geoffrey was silent as Olivier paced off the first rush of his irritation, crossing the room and then returning, standing an arm's length away. "He loves you, you know. You've been his pride and joy for longer than I've been alive. Even when you quarreled, he never ceased to have faith in you. He just didn't always like you."

"And I haven't always liked him," Geoffrey replied, quietly. "And, as you say, Sir Olivier, that's hardly the point. If I believed for one moment that he was still fit to rule, I would never turn on him. I would be content to marshal his forces when he wished it and dwell here in La Forêt and grow grapes and forge soldiers until the Last Trump. But he's not fit, Olivier, and we both know it. I'm just willing to do something about it."

"You swore bonds of loyalty and duty to him, Geoffrey.

Have-you forgotten those vows? Or were they conditional—so long as the man you swore them to remains worthy in your eyes, you'll serve, but the moment he falters, you'll fall on him like a carrion-eater?" Olivier asked hotly, stung.

"I've not forgotten them." Geoffrey's voice was cold as he struggled to rein in his own temper. "But I also gave a vow to serve and protect the realm and the people within it, and it's them that need me now. Our sire is unfit to rule—and to continue abusing his dominion and his people at the whims of his advisor. He misused and abandoned his own. If anything, Olivier, he's broken faith with me."

Olivier shook his head. "I can't argue it. But there must have been a better way to address it than armed rebellion, Geoffrey. There must have."

"Must there?" Geoffrey reached up and unlaced the neck of his tunic, holding it open. "You're here in an official capacity, Olivier. Perform it, and let's get this over with."

"You're not going to give an inch, are you?" Olivier asked softly. At Geoffrey's silence, he sighed heavily and drew the long wooden knife hanging at his hip, his tone taking on the cadence of a formal court pronouncement as he spoke. "Sir Geoffrey le Croisé, Lord of La Forêt, childe of Alexander, Princeps Lutetius, you are accused of treason against your sire and the Grand Court, of inciting His Highness Alexander's loyal subjects to rebellion, and conspiring with enemies of the Grand Court to compromise the security of that domain and the rule of its rightful master. You will be returned to Paris to stand trial for these crimes, and to face the judgment of the justicar summoned to hear this case. Until such time as judgment is levied against you, your men will be held at La Forêt, unharmed but hostages against your cooperation. Do you submit to these terms?"

"I do."

Olivier struck, smoothly, and Geoffrey slumped into his arms. Olivier caught him, eased him to the floor, and closed his eyes, holding the lids down until he was certain they would stay in place. There was, in Olivier's experience, nothing more maddening than spending an indefinite period staked and helpless with your eyes frozen open. It was the least he could do.

Chapter Eighteen

Veronique awoke, all at once, and sat up quickly enough to wake Sandrin as well. They sat together yet in the room they were brought to when they arrived in the warren proper, a small, perfectly square chamber, furnished only with a pallet on the floor and a candle set in a niche in the middle of one wall. They were told to wait, that the Lady would call for them shortly, and daylight had come before a messenger from Dame Mnemach. Veronique remembered falling asleep with her head on Sandrin's lap and his hand resting on her hair.

Sometime during the day, the room grew a small table on which sat a plate of bread and cheese and a pitcher of watered wine, as well as a bucket for Sandrin to relieve himself in. While he made use of the amenities, Veronique paced the opposite side of the room and thought furiously. She had expected that something would break loose soon, but she hadn't expected it to come so quickly on the heels of her visit to Geoffrey. Given that she was now in hiding with the most personally detached ally she possessed, she doubted the move in question was Geoffrey's own. Something had gone seriously wrong, somewhere; the only remaining question was how severe the compromise had been, and how many resources they had remaining at their disposal. Or, rather, those were the only questions she could consider without a cold fury rising in her, a rage that threatened to wake the Beast—she wanted, more than anything, to know what had become of her people, but didn't dare think too deeply on them.

Sandrin put himself in order quickly, sheathed the sword he had drawn the night before and laid out in easy reach, and regarded her uneasily. She offered him all the comfort she could. "She'll come for us soon. It's been—"

Someone scratched at their cell door, and it opened without waiting for acknowledgement. Guillaume slipped in and grimaced at them by way of greeting. "Come along. The Lady will want you soon."

"Guillaume, what's happened?" Veronique begged to know, as soon as they were out in the hall—wider, higher-ceilinged, and drier underfoot than the one they had come in by.

"Lots. You'll find out soon." He flicked a look over his narrow shoulder at her. "Don't dawdle."

He led them by the most direct route she'd ever traveled through the warren, which meant there were a third fewer turns and switchbacks, to a large open chamber less than half the size of the enormous underground meeting hall, but bigger than Mnemach's private quarters. A number of candles sat in niches on walls, which were also pierced at a number of places by irregularly shaped alcoves, most of them too deep to see into clearly. To her surprise, Goratrix was already there, looking thoroughly peevish and damp from the knees down, still reeking of the tunnels he'd waded through, along with an equally disheveled young mortal man. They sat on a bench occupying one side of a sunken firepit, in which a low blaze burned, chasing away a bit of the perpetual cool damp and allowing them to dry themselves. Lord Geoffrey's scar-faced standard-bearer, whom Veronique learned was named Sir Nicolas, occupied a smaller bench; he rose and bowed politely when she entered, and she returned the gesture sharply. Guillaume gestured for her to make herself comfortable, and departed again on some other errand. Veronique selected the bench directly across from the Tremere's and asked, "Do either of you two know what happened? Or where our hostess might be?"

"Lord Geoffrey's house on Ile de la Cité was raided last night," Goratrix informed her icily, his foul temper clear in every word, "by knights apparently in service to Prince Alexander. Dame Mnemach's envoy came to collect me and mine. We escaped just ahead of their blades. Otherwise? No. And I have not yet seen the lady herself."

Veronique found her hands clenching into fists on her thighs, and forced them to relax. "I was ambushed by a messenger from Mnemach returning from an errand on the isle." She flicked a glance at the silent ghoul. "And you?"

"I never left the city, milady. Milord Geoffrey left me here to coordinate between the men in the Latin Quarter and the men we had on the isle, at his house." Sir Nicolas glanced into the flames at their feet. "The men on the isle are lost, and I've not had contact with our forces in the Latin Quarter for more than a day."

Veronique slumped a bit in her seat, massaging her forehead with the heel of her hand. "So, in other words, our situation could only be worse in one or two ways."

"*More or less.*" *Goratrix eyed her sourly.* "*Did they ever make you walk through a midden tunnel that hadn't been cleaned since Caesar ruled Rome?*"

She decided to err on the side of perceived solidarity. "Yes."

"Well. At least they do it to everyone." The Tremere drew a dramatic breath and heaved a sigh.

A soft footstep sounded in the hall outside the chamber and, an instant later, Dame Mnemach herself swept in, still clad in the shapeless dark robes and mask she wore while above ground. Veronique and Goratrix both rose and offered courtesies, Sandrin and Sir Nicolas bowed to the floor, and Mnemach waved them all up, seating herself on the empty bench in a flurry of layered garments. "Sit. We have much to discuss."

She removed her mask, and laid it aside, her expression entirely grave for the first time since Veronique had first met her. Out of the corner of her eye, she caught Goratrix staring, his expression momentarily unguarded, constructed of equal parts surprise, revulsion and desire. Veronique was privately glad, for a flash of an instant, that she wasn't the only person Mnemach had that effect on. Mnemach noticed it too and smiled serenely in response.

"It is good to finally meet you, Maestro. I've heard a great deal about you." Mnemach's voice was, for just a moment, a husky purr. "It is my hope that we will have the opportunity to become better acquainted, later. For now," her eyes caught the

Tremere's, and she bared her fangs slightly, "let's concentrate on business, shall we?"

"Of course, Milady Mnemach." Goratrix bowed from the neck, looking a little dazed around the edges.

"Good." Mnemach gathered up Veronique and Sir Nicolas with a glance. "You, Lady Veronique d'Orleans, and you, Lord Regent Goratrix, have been declared anathema—enemies of the Grand Court and of Prince Alexander. Veronique, acknowledgement of your diplomatic credentials has been revoked, and a formal hunt has been declared against you both."

It took Veronique a moment to fully process that, and think the implications through. "He knows, then. Somehow Alexander learned of the ties between myself and Geoffrey—and somehow learned that the maestro was on the isle, and in Geoffrey's employ."

"Yes." Mnemach nodded slightly. "Moreover, I suspect he has either learned of the ties between yourself and the Courts of Love, or else his fear is truly ruling all of his actions. An emergency gathering of the Grand Court was called tonight. Sentence was presented against you both." She paused. "Both Lady Rosamund d'Islington and Lord Valerian were publicly called forth and put to the question in order to establish their innocence in the matter of a potential rebellion being fomented by Lord Geoffrey le Croisé. Lord Geoffrey himself is under arrest, and on his way to Paris in bondage as we speak."

"What!?" Sir Nicolas cried, appalled enough to forget his place. "La Forêt is—"

"La Forêt is fallen." Mnemach replied evenly. "Whatever forces you possessed there are now hostages against the good behavior of Lord Geoffrey, and likely that of any other partisans he might yet possess."

"And those were the one or two ways in which things could be worse," Veronique muttered under her breath, and looked down into the fire, trying to suppress her dread. "Have you received any word of my people, Lady?"

Mnemach was silent for a long moment. In that silence, in the place where Veronique could still feel her being joined to the matriarch of the Nosferatu, she felt something take hold of her, spreading soothing warmth through the whole of her being. "Your house burned to the ground last night, Veronique. I can only assume that any who might have been within it are dead now."

Veronique's field of vision washed red and it was only Mnemach's grip on the innermost parts of her will that kept her from frenzying on the spot. As it was, she surged to her feet with such violence that Sandrin leapt aside, recognizing the wild look on her face, and both the Tremere and Geoffrey's ghoul scrambled out of immediate reach. Only Mnemach remained where she was, unafraid. Veronique wanted to scream. She wanted to tear her clothing and her hair and beat something to powder with her bare fists, and even that wouldn't be wholly enough to release the rage thrumming inside her like a living thing. The Beast howled inside her and she choked out a growl of her own around the force of will Mnemach exerted on her. There was, in the end, no real struggle between them. Mnemach simply held her, unspeaking and unable to act, until the hate and fury sank back down to levels where she could control it herself. Veronique wavered on her feet, and sat down hard, breathing quickly and unnecessarily as the others crept back cautiously.

"I… thank you, Dame Mnemach, for that news." Veronique finally managed a semi-normal voice. "And I apologize for my behavior."

"Do not apologize to me for your grief, and your anger. I would think less of you if you did not feel so deeply." Mnemach turned outward to face the room again. "We are not entirely devoid of advantages." She smiled coldly. "Countess Saviarre did not dare suggest that I might be part of this conspiracy without proof, and she has none. She knows that to accuse me would start a war that she might not be able to win, whether or not Alexander favors her. And the resources at my disposal are not insubstantial. Moreover, my children in the Latin Quarter know the location of a pocket of Geoffrey's men emplaced there for the purpose of assisting Lady Veronique in her endeavors. They will be brought here tonight."

"Thank God." Sir Nicolas looked and sounded immensely relieved. "I should be there to greet them and explain the situation, Lady."

"Yes, you should." Mnemach raised a hand, and Guillaume came from an alcove where he'd been lurking unseen. "Guillaume, please show Sir Nicolas to the cells where his men will be staying, and explain the customs of the warren."

Guillaume sketched a courtesy. "Of course, Lady.

Sandrin," Veronique interjected. "Please accompany them, and assist in any way that you can. If Milady Mnemach does not object?"

"Not at all."

Sir Nicolas, an uncomfortable Sandrin, and Guillaume departed, conferring quietly together as they went. Mnemach turned back to Veronique and Goratrix, and continued. "Since neither of you has been caught in the city, there are those who suspect that you were forewarned of the danger and may have fled ahead of it. Sir Josselin de Poitiers certainly made a hasty departure from the city last night—and actually cut down one or two of the knights being sent to arrest him. One suspects that he is riding with a great deal of haste for Chartres." Mnemach smiled blandly at Veronique. "The assumption is that you, my dear, may have fled for Orleans or Frankfurt, where you might legitimately seek refuge with a ruler sympathetic to you, and that you, Maestro, are on the way to Rouen. There is a reward for your capture, but very few are searching for you here in the city. This is also to our advantage, I think."

"With all due respect, Lady Mnemach, that isn't much to build on," the Tremere said.

"Greater things have come from less, Maestro." Veronique coughed to ease the rasp out of her voice.

"Lady Veronique is correct." Dame Mnemach turned the full force of her considerable personality on Goratrix for the first time. "Or do you endorse your own abilities so timidly, Maestro?"

The Tremere's back stiffened and his face froze in a mask of icy offense. "Lady Mnemach, I hardly think my abilities are at question here, but rather the sanity of pursuing any further attempt at this time."

"Are you going to crawl back to the Prince of Rouen and beg his protection with Alexander's hounds on your tail, Maestro?"

Mnemach asked coolly. "I guarantee that even if you succeed in reaching Rouen, the little weasel who rules it will have you staked, bound and sold back down the river for some concession from the Grand Court before you can utter a plea for mercy. You have chosen, Regent of the Tremere, to leap on the back of the wolf, and the ride isn't done yet."

Goratrix was silent, the struggle to control his pride and his offense naked on his face. Finally he admitted, "You are very likely correct, Lady Mnemach."

"I know." Mnemach smiled gently. "I also know that you are a man of some cunning and wile, and no small degree of personal power. You have been curious, since before you returned to Paris, who the sorcerer was in Prince Alexander's court—since you successfully deduced that it was not him. I am that sorcerer, Lord Goratrix—and I know also that we will do great things together in these troubled nights and the nights to come."

Goratrix, for his part, didn't seem as utterly astonished by this information as Veronique thought he might. "I admit, Milady Mnemach, I suspected you were Prince Alexander's court sorcerer since I first learned of your existence, and of those marvelous candles you manufacture."

Mnemach inclined her head slightly. "Bishop de Navarre is the shadow-spinner responsible for most of our recent difficulties. It behooves me to defend my children from him, since Prince Alexander declined to discipline him as he deserves."

"Bishop de Navarre appears to be a man of many talents," Goratrix replied thoughtfully. "Though not as clever or as skilled as he thinks he is."

"Lasombra never are," Veronique added wryly. "He'll have to be dealt with before we can strike at Saviarre and Alexander, or else we'd best arrange for every house on the isle to be burning your candles if we want to be safe."

"He will be dealt with." Mnemach smiled at Goratrix, her eyes heavy-lidded with anticipated pleasure. "I believe the maestro and I shall be able to arrange something suitable for him. Your equipment and the rest of your apprentices await your attention, Maestro, should you wish to consider your preparations?"

Goratrix rose, his still-damp robes clinging to his legs. "Indeed, I would." He paused. "I would also not say no to a bath."

"I believe that can be arranged." The matriarch of the Nosferatu lifted her hand again and another of her servants scurried out of an alcove, this one a young girl, pale of skin, hair and eyes, clad in a simple grayish smock. She curtseyed politely to the maestro and his silent apprentice. "Floret, please guide the Maestro to the chamber set aside for his use, and then arrange for a bath to be prepared. Thank you, my flower."

The Tremere offered a deep bow, as did his apprentice, and both departed in the wake of the bone-pale child. Veronique sat and watched them go, feeling suddenly very small and alone and entirely outside any bounds within which she dared play. She also dared not meet Dame Mnemach's eyes, having failed so completely to justify her faith.

The matriarch of the Nosferatu rose in a rustle of cloth. "Come with me."

Some of those alcoves were actually recessed doorways, well-hidden by the gloom. The one Mnemach selected joined a second tunnel, which connected with a third that, to Veronique's surprise, led them to Mnemach's private quarters, where a low fire smoldered in the pit and a number of candles burned in nooks, the same as Veronique's first visit and looking as though she had never left. Mnemach placed her mask in a heavy wooden chest lined in lamb's wool, adding it to the several others already inside, and stripped off the outer layers of her costume, piling them on top of the chest. She turned to face Veronique clad in a floor-length tunic of black linen, glimpses of translucent flesh coming and going as she moved, settling into her nest of cushions and gesturing for Veronique to join her.

"Tell me your thoughts." It was a command, but a gentle one, as Veronique took her seat, resting her elbows on her knees and her head in her hands.

"I failed," Veronique admitted with some difficulty.

"Yes, you did," Mnemach replied not at all comfortingly. "The question is, what did you learn from that failure?"

"I learned," Veronique enunciated clearly, "that I should have *listened to my instincts, beaten Geoffrey le Croisé into torpor when I first met him, and continued doing things my way."*

Mnemach laughed, out loud and unaffected. "Well. I do suppose that constitutes a lesson. Crusaders should leave the politics to the politicians, after all. I simply hope that Geoffrey learned that lesson, as well."

"We can only hope," Veronique muttered. "What are we going to do?"

"For now? Nothing. We shall wait until all of Geoffrey's remaining men are here in the warren. And we shall wait until my eyes and ears have given me a better picture of what goes on in the world above. And, I think, I shall have a conversation with my old friend, Lord Valerian." She reached out and cupped Veronique's chin. "They will not act until the justicar arrives, and that will not be anytime soon—Alexander sent messengers to Lebach and Toulouse, but not to Frankfurt, for he knows that Julia Antasia will not believe you treacherous until proof is placed in her hands."

Veronique nodded slightly and closed her eyes, unaccountably soothed by the matriarch's touch. Tears prickled the insides of her eyes the instant she did so, and the grief that underlay her earlier rage welled inexorably toward the surface. She swallowed hard to stifle a rising sob.

"Tonight, we shall regroup, and mourn." Mnemach's tone gentled again. "It is all right for you to cry."

The tears escaped then, and the sob. Veronique's grief rose up and overwhelmed her as quickly as the fury had and she howled in anguish, burying her face in her hands. Mnemach's arms closed around her and gathered her close against a cold breast, stroking her hair and murmuring soothing nothings in her native tongue. Veronique wept until she had no more blood left to spare for it and sobbed hard for a time after, lying in the arms of the Nosferatu woman like a child. Eventually, even the sobs slowed, leaving her weary, empty and exhausted, unable to move and lacking even the will to try to do so, her head resting on Mnemach's breast, the matriarch's arms arranged comfortably around her. A cool hand cupped her chin, and turned her face up. Mnemach bent, and kissed the tears from her cheeks.

Chapter Nineteen

Countess Saviarre was extremely pleased with the state of her existence, the city, and the world in general. Everything had fallen together so nicely it privately amazed even her. Being a learned student of human and Cainite nature, she firmly expected something to go catastrophically wrong. While the entire plan had not unfolded completely without hitches—the escapes of Veronique d'Orleans and the Tremere hadn't pleased her—the majority of objectives were completed successfully.

Geoffrey was captured and defanged, staked and imprisoned under heavy guard, his men isolated at La Forêt, and all were awaiting execution once the justicar arrived. Lady Rosamund d'Islington was thoroughly cowed, rendered all but powerless despite the proof of her innocence, under heavy guard for her own protection, as her brother-in-blood Sir Josselin remained uncaught. Veronique d'Orleans's house in the Latin Quarter was ashes, her ghouls dead, most of her intelligence-gathering apparatus dismembered, and the woman herself a hunted fugitive. Let her run back to Frankfurt and hide behind the skirts of Julia Antasia—she would never set foot in lie de France again if she wanted to keep her head. "Lord" Regent Goratrix would he hunted down like a dog no matter where he ran or where he hid. Prince Alexander had already obtained a promise of cooperation from the Prince of Rouen in capturing the wayward Tremere in exchange for concessions to be named at a later time. The reward for both of them was, even in her estimation, outrageous, and it was only a matter of time before someone either captured them or betrayed them for the profit that could be reaped for doing so.

Sir Olivier was subdued on his return from La Forêt, but not sullen, and had personally overseen the imprisonment of his brother, hand-selecting the ghoul and Cainite knights who stood guard over him. Prince Alexander had approved all of Sir Olivier's selections and had declined to visit his imprisoned eldest. The prince himself was half-mad with rage and grief, and would see no one but Saviarre herself for counsel or comfort.

Soon. It was now just a matter of time, of exercising the patience she had spent centuries refining to a weapon in its own right. Soon, she would have either Veronique d'Orleans or Goratrix to interrogate, and she did not doubt that they would deliver the last of her objectives to her: Mnemach, who had been her enemy since Ile de la Cité was called Lutetius, and who had evaded her all this time. One way or another, that long struggle would soon be over, also.

Yes, Saviarre was very, very pleased.

Lady Rosamund d'Islington was doing what she had done for much of the week since the situation in Paris had swung from delicate to excessively unpleasant. She was methodically pacing every inch of her embassy, beside herself with a mixture of emotions so tangled she wasn't sure she could name them all.

There was, of course, fear in significant measure, for herself, for her queen and all her kin, for Veronique, and for Josselin. She had never, in all her existence, been so afraid that she would never see her brother again. He had ridden out the night she herself was being questioned on her knowledge of Lord Geoffrey's plot against his sire, in haste great enough that he had not taken the time to leave a note and, more damningly, had killed two ghoul knights sent to bring him to Prince Alexander. Rosamund lacked the imagination necessary to picture Josselin as a devious and cunning spy and provocateur in conspiracy with the rebellious childe of the Prince of Paris. Peter's message—that Josselin had been recalled to Chartres with some urgency—did not however assuage all her fears. She had, even in her own pain and fear that terrible night, pled for Josselin's survival, that he not be added to the bill of hunted fugitives, and begged for the chance to investigate the matter more fully herself. That boon was granted, and she had written to Queen Isouda in a state of high panic. Thus far, no reply had come.

The evidence presented against Veronique d'Orleans and the Tremere regent, whom Rosamund had never met, was irrefutable and thoroughly damning. On that score, Rosamund was not entirely stunned. She was, however, horrified by the strong implication that the Courts of Love had, tacitly at least, backed Lord Geoffrey's activities and that, by extension, Veronique was far more their agent than Rosamund herself. If that was true, then her entire mission had been a ruse, a smokescreen, a distraction from the start, and that realization filled her with a hollow pain and an icy fury. Her own sire had not trusted her enough to tell her the true nature of the task she was to perform. She'd shed a few tears over that possibility in the last several nights, and couldn't shake the thought away no matter how hard she tried.

Overlying all else was acute and painful humiliation—she was spared the indignity of the stake but was brought bound in iron fetters, blindfolded and gagged before Prince Alexander and Countess Saviarre and half the Cainites in Paris, and publicly questioned, ungently, regarding her knowledge of the plot. She was confused, frightened and outraged, all emotions it was apparently not her place to feel that night. It took what felt like hours—hours in which Alexander and Saviarre both questioned her without mercy, battering her with the combined force of their wills—before she finally, marginally, convinced them of her innocence. It gave her no peace when she saw from her place kneeling near the dais on which the prince's throne sat, too weak and disoriented to stand, venerable Lord Valerian receiving the same treatment.

The world felt as though it were tilting at a sharp angle beneath her feet, and any intemperate motion of her own would pitch her off into an abyss too deep to see bottom. She was not permitted to go anywhere, nor to see anyone. She was not technically suspected of being anything worse than a dupe for Cainites more vicious and treacherous and cunning than she herself. For all practical intents and purposes, she was under house arrest, her doors and gates guarded by men loyal to

Prince Alexander. She wanted very much to sit down outside in the garden and have a good cry, but she knew word of that would get back to Saviarre, and she refused to let the bitch have the satisfaction.

"Milady Rose."

Rosamund nearly jumped out of her skin. The raspy voice was coming almost from her elbow, but there was no one there. Rosamund sprang away, looking wildly around the solar for something she could use as a weapon.

The air in front of her shimmered slightly, and a figure began sketching itself into view, becoming solid and filling with colors, dark grays and browns, a penitentially skinny old man wrapped in wool, a wide-brimmed hat on his head. Rosamund gasped in surprise—it was the Nosferatu envoy who had so surprised her earlier in the year with his politeness and good sense. "Master Guillaume? How did you get in here?"

"Easy to evade when they can't see you, Milady Rose." Master Guillaume removed his hat and bowed as best he could with his rheumatic joints. "The Lady sent me. To watch over you."

"To watch over me? Please... please sit." She gestured towards a chair and sank onto a bench herself, her knees a bit unsteady beneath her. "Why did she send you to watch over me, Master Guillaume?"

The Nosferatu envoy seated himself, and withdrew a candle from somewhere inside his wrappings, carefully tied up inside parchment paper. He set and lit it before answering. "It's not safe tonight, Milady Rose. Much is happening. Quickly. There'll be a new prince by dawn."

"What!" Rosamund cried, appalled, leaping back to her feet.

"Sit. I'm to tell you some things." After a moment, he added, "Please."

After another moment, Rosamund did as he asked. And listened.

"Milord, there is something troubling the shadows."

Bishop de Navarre raised his pen from the parchment he was writing on, and lifted his gaze to the eldest of his apprentices, who had come to his study and entered without any of the formalities. The young man was pale, his forehead beaded with sweat, and his eyes wide in his white face; his breath was coming too quickly, and his heart was beating too rapidly. He practically stank of fear.

"What," Bishop de Navarre asked softly, "do you mean by 'troubling'?"

The boy licked his lips nervously. "Something is disrupting contact between the shards of the killing darkness and their observers. Almost none of the circle can reach their shadows now."

De Navarre rose from behind his desk. "Why was I not informed of this before now?"

"Milord, it only happened now. The killing darkness was probing several weak points in the underground wards." He took a ragged breath. "They began losing contact, one by one. When I left, only two retained contact with their—"

Bishop de Navarre brushed passed him and hurried down the hall, his senses suddenly sharpened by fear. Before he had made it halfway to the ritual chamber in which his circle of apprentices conducted their devotions, a scream rang out, followed closely by another. Soon, shrieks and howls of mortal agony were ringing off the walls, clear and piercing as though there were nothing to muffle the sound. Even sooner, filaments of shadow began leaching from beneath the door and oozing down the walls from above.

The killing darkness took a longer time with de Navarre than it had with his apprentices—it hated him more and had for far longer.

"We probably shouldn't let him enjoy himself that much, you know." Veronique murmured to Mnemach, as they stood watching the last of the night's preparations unfold.

"I know. But it was worth it just to hear him laugh once." The matriarch of the Nosferatu set her mask over her smiling face, an expressionless plate of featureless blackened bone, undecorated and stark.

Lord Regent Goratrix and Dame Mnemach had used their

time wisely. Veronique wasn't quite certain of the protocols involved, but they seemed to have reached an agreement, a sorcerers' truce of some kind, to focus their energies on the greater enemy. Goratrix had taken on the responsibility of rendering Bishop de Navarre incapable of assisting his mistress, the Countess Saviarre, on this of all nights. And he had done so in a way that could accurately be described as unpleasant though not, in Veronique's opinion, excessive. He had found a means of adapting the shadow-trap candles to capture, free, and return the things to their sender. Veronique couldn't imagine that turning out well for the bishop, and did not waste any particular tears on him, either.

Mnemach herself had spent much of the week in which they'd schemed their counterstroke in preparation for her own part in the evening's slate of events. Veronique was not herself any kind of sorcerer and had no real desire to learn anything of those arts, but she found it interesting to watch the degree of preparation that went into the smallest workings. She'd also learned how to keep quiet and hold still while acting as the object of sorcery. Mnemach had taken a positive delight in stripping her naked and laying her out on a flat stone altar, painting sigils from forehead to instep that would render her safe against the forces Saviarre could bring to bear, and against the magics that Mnemach herself would unleash. The men had received a similar, though less extensive, treatment, as well. Under pressure, Mnemach admitted that it would likely take all of her effort and concentration to keep Alexander contained—the task she chose for herself when they were dividing up areas of responsibility. The rest would have to lie on the shoulders of Veronique and, to her surprise, Lord Valerian, who pledged his support late and with a certain degree of noticeable personal acrimony against his ruler.

Veronique had personally prepared by acquiring a knee-length vest of light chain, a short, heavy-bladed sword, and a weighted wooden staff much like the one Portia had taught her to use many nights ago. Her part of the night's plans would be the most personally, physically dangerous, which suited her well. She was, she found, entirely weary of delicate political dances, feints, and maneuvers. The blood of her own cried out for a more visceral vengeance than the political dismemberment of an opponent. She chose the task of liberating Geoffrey and taking Saviarre, two goals that required the most careful tactical planning. The force at their disposal was not unlimited, and needed to be deployed carefully. She, Sir Nicolas and Sandrin pored over the intelligence at their disposal, and allocated forces using the detailed map of subterranean Paris possessed by the Nosferatu, and likewise exploited their knowledge of where the underworld touched the surface.

The first move belonged to Goratrix, and his strike succeeded brilliantly. The next lay in Mnemach's hands. Veronique finished the last of her preparations, and went to join her men, while the matriarch of the Nosferatu retired to her own ritual chamber, to bring the battle to Alexander's doorstep.

Alexander, *Princeps Lutetius*, was entirely and utterly alone. He sat in his own study, heart riven with grief and dry-eyed anguish, unable to comprehend how his existence had come to this. He was not a cruel or uncaring ruler, nor was he a brutal or unloving sire. He had done the best he could for his city and for his childer—he had sacrificed his own happiness on the altar of duty and torn away all the joy he might have known from existence to shoulder the responsibilities of rulership.

And how was he repaid, time and time again?

Betrayal. Betrayal by the woman he had dared to love, betrayal by the childe to whom he had given the gift of his blood and every advantage that could be asked.

He brooded on it, unable to banish the realization from his thoughts for more than a few minutes at a time. He was surrounded by traitors and lickspittles—even Valerian, whom he had loved as a brother, proved himself to be little more than a whining, cringing politician in the end. Only Saviarre, his sweet and gentle-hearted Saviarre, put his interests above her own, advised him truly and faithfully, and never demanded more from him than he was willing to give. (Under the layers of black depression and self-loathing, the rising waters of fear and hate, his mind tried to remind him of Olivier, his younger childe, whose faith had never wavered.) It was all he could do not to order the heads of the others brought to him. He had avoided visiting Geoffrey in his cell for precisely that reason. He did not trust himself enough not to order the summary execution of the faithless whelp, and he wanted the stamp of justicar-issued justice on that matter, that it not come back to haunt him, as Lorraine's death kept returning. (Olivier, his mind reminded him, had never condemned him for the death of Lorraine. He had understood what it was like to be wounded by the one you loved, devotion ignored and passion unacknowledged.) Even Rosamund was nothing more than a tool of her queen, but it was Rosamund he had some trace of pity for, knowing as he did how little choice she must have had, how used and betrayed she must feel.

He rose from his place by the cold fireplace and paced the length of the room twice, mind almost blank but for an endlessly twisting inner cycle of misery. Gradually, he became aware that he was no longer alone.

An image was sketching itself into the air before him, a woman, small and perfectly formed. Her eyes, and the cotte she wore to match them, were the perfect blue of a late autumn sky, her hair long and sunlight golden, unbound by braids or concealed beneath a veil, falling in a shimmering curtain to her waist. In her small white hands she held a single crimson rose, the same shade as her gently smiling lips.

Alexander felt something break inside him. "Lorraine?"

She did not speak, only shook her head, strands of golden hair falling across one slender shoulder, and smiled sadly. He fell to his knees at her feet, reached out to grasp her, but found her body as insubstantial as smoke, or dreams. A sob caught in his throat. "Lorraine, if this is you in truth and not some phantom come to torment me, I beg you, speak to me!"

Unnoticed, the walls around them writhed with sigils, drawn from magics etched into the bones of the isle before Lutetia of the Parisii, the city that had stood there first, burned to the ground. In a chamber almost directly beneath Alexander's feet, Mnemach of the Nosferatu, witch-priestess of the Parisii, smiled coldly behind her mask and wove the spells to bind her old friend and enemy.

Veronique was not at all surprised to discover that the Nosferatu had passageways connecting their labyrinth to the house of just about every major Cainite presence on the isle. Some of these entrances would, no doubt, be bricked up and relocated once all was said and done, for the Nosferatu were genuinely and understandably loath to lose the advantage those unknown portals created, and Veronique wasn't fool enough to think they trusted her as one of their own. That one of those hidden entrances opened in the garden of Sir Olivier and that he had remained in his haven that night, no doubt brooding on the situation, assisted her plans greatly. Sir Olivier was entirely too capable of playing spoiler if he were left to run around free. The unit she sent consisted of Sandrin (who could be as professionally free of conscience and chivalry as Veronique liked, which gave him a distinct advantage over Sir Olivier, she thought), a half-dozen battle-hardened ghoul knights provided by Lord Valerian, and two Nosferatu soldiers, who went to facilitate infiltration and escape. Their orders were to take Sir Olivier undead and immobilize him. Veronique was loath to have his blood on her hands.

Veronique, Sir Nicolas, the entire body of Geoffrey's remaining men in Paris, and a substantial number of Nosferatu ghouls made their way via the underground labyrinth to Prince Alexander's haven. Most of the entrances there lay in the lower levels of the haven, the rooms used for the storage of supplies for the house's mortal inhabitants, the ghouls who presented Prince Alexander's public, mortal face to the people of Ile de la Cité. It amused Veronique greatly to learn that he also used those rooms for the storage of prisoners awaiting trial or expulsion. Goratrix had confirmed that fact, also, having spent some time bound there, to his acute personal humiliation when first he came to lie de France. Unfortunately, one of those entrances did not, as Veronique had hoped, open immediately into Lord Geoffrey's prison chamber. Fortunately, the nearest such entrance was only a few dozen yards away, in the vaulted storage space beneath the private petitioners' hall.

One of the ghouls naturally went first, leading the way, unarmored but armed for what they hoped would be a quick and brutal struggle. The knights followed close behind, stripped to the minimum amount of protection, and still jingling despite it. Veronique brought up the rear, with the rest of the armed Nosferatu combatants, which was entirely fine with her. She intended to let the men trained and armed for battle do their duty as they saw fit, and keep her own head attached to her shoulders by so doing.

The tunnel they took slanted gradually upwards at a gentle but steady grade, narrowing as they neared the surface, terminating in a climb up a short flue lined in handholds. They knew already that the stone guarding the entranceway had nothing blocking it. The only real difficulty they had was making certain that a dozen armed men and a single armed woman didn't make a racket sufficient to rouse the dead climbing out. Sir Olivier's men were placed at regular intervals, watching all of the external entrances and exits to the underground storage areas. Each of the men in Veronique's party had been given the task of bringing down one of them, and each man knew which direction he was supposed to take once they broke cover. Even allowing for the possibility of human error and a propensity for personal heroics among the chivalrously inclined, Veronique thought little could go wrong at this stage, provided they acted quickly and prevented an alarm from being sounded. If that happened, their foes would easily have the strength of numbers necessary to crush them.

Ghoul knights paired with Nosferatu guardians and slipped two by two out of the storage room, rendered shadowy and indistinct by the efforts of their partners. Veronique waited behind, to guard the exit if necessary, and listened intently for the sounds of joined violence. There were, thankfully, very few—only two rapid clashes of metal on metal, too quick to draw attention, the gurgling sighs of throats being cut and Cainite hearts being pierced with sharp wooden daggers. In short order, dead ghouls and immobilized Cainites were being dragged into the storage chamber, and the scent of blood was sufficient to make Veronique's fangs lengthen involuntarily, despite the fact that she'd eaten well before starting on this little venture. She stepped out into the hall just as Sir Nicolas approached, bleeding lightly from a scratch on one arm, dragging a staked Cainite knight.

"Wait," Veronique whispered. "Bring that one. Geoffrey will need sustenance."

"Milord will not—" Sir Nicolas began stiffly, only to be cut off short.

"Your lord will eat whatever is put before him right now, human or Cainite, and we don't have knights to spare," Veronique hissed, low-voiced and fierce. "Now, bring him."

The entrance to Geoffrey's cell was held by three young ghoul knights of his own service, all of whom looked anxious—but not anxious enough to disobey her orders to leave the door closed until she came. As she approached, they lifted away the heavy oaken bar lying across it, and she shouldered the door open wide enough to let Sir Nicolas through with his burden. In the light from the torches outside, she could see that Lord Geoffrey lay on a carefully constructed pallet, covered to midchest by a woolen blanket, a wooden dagger through his heart, eyes closed.

She gestured to the floor at Geoffrey's feet. "Leave him there." She turned to the knights watching the door. "Be prepared to drop that bar again the instant I'm out of this room."

Reluctantly, Sir Nicolas dropped his burden on the milled stones at the foot of his master's pallet, and Veronique waved him out. She waited until she was certain the exit was clear, then leaned down and yanked the stake out of Geoffrey's chest without ceremony. His back arched, his eyes flew open, wild with hunger, and Veronique reached back and pounded him hard in the jaw, dazing him long enough for her to reach the door herself. She slammed it closed behind her and the two knights dropped the bar in place just as Geoffrey, frenzied and howling for blood, slammed into it, knocking them both sprawling with the force he applied to the opposite side. Veronique leaned her back hard against it and rubbed her knuckles, listening to him ravening on the other side, followed closely by the sounds of his feeding on the hapless Cainite prisoner. It didn't, she thought, go on as long as it could have.

Geoffrey knocked heavily on the opposite side of the door,

just to the left of her ear. "Lady Veronique."

"Yes, Milord Geoffrey?" she replied calmly.

A pause. "So." Another pause. "It is you. Would you be kind enough to release me?"

"Of course, milord." She lifted the bar with one hand and opened the door with the other, prepared to slam both back in place if Geoffrey were not yet fully capable of reason.

He made no such gestures, and she opened the door the rest of the way, letting him emerge, stiff and covered in at least part of his dinner's blood, but no ashes. He was immediately mobbed by his men, vastly relieved to see him still walking the night, and Veronique peered into the room behind him where his victim lay, not quite drained to ash, but in no wise capable of springing up and making trouble. She closed the door again and bolted it, just to be certain. Geoffrey looked up from comforting the stricken Sir Nicolas as she stepped away from the door.

"I owe you a great deal, Lady Veronique. I never would have guessed you would spend such effort on my behalf." Geoffrey tried to catch her eye, but she refused to meet it.

"Don't thank me yet, milord. We're not finished. Saviarre hasn't been taken yet. And while I believe that we hold your sire now, you must decide what you want done with him." She smiled grimly, checked her weapons, and nodded to the ghouls and Cainites she had selected for the next phase of her plan, to clear the way to Saviarre's haven. "Thank me when you're actually sitting on the throne."

Geoffrey took the time to put himself in order, stripping out of his torn and bloodied under-tunic, slipping on a short cotte that Nicolas had carried with him, scavenging a mail shirt and a serviceable sword from the bodies downstairs. Then he went to have a chat with his sire who was, Veronique d'Orleans indicated, trapped in his own study by the magics of the Nosferatu. Geoffrey couldn't help but shake his head and wonder at the surreality of it all—he, the scion of an ancient and powerful Ventrue line, a practitioner of the virtues of chivalry and rulership, rescued by a prodigal diplomat and two low-blooded sorcerers and set on the throne of his sire. He knew he hadn't yet begun to pay for those services rendered.

The halls were, fortunately, mostly clear of loiterers, and neither were there any overt signs of violence. Veronique had deployed her forces well, with an eye toward maximum efficiency, an approach that appeared to be working quite well. They were not, of course, facing the heaviest resistance that Prince Alexander could have mustered, but still, the accomplishment was a significant one, minimizing danger and loss. Tactics. He'd forgotten that politics, too, came down to short-term tactical maneuvering more often than not, and a skilled politician could play chess as well as a skilled soldier. He would not let himself underestimate her again.

The door to his sire's study was lit in its very center with a glittering ruby sigil the size of his fist. It did not prevent him from opening the door, but it hung in the empty air afterwards, and would not let him pass.

Inside, his sire knelt in the middle of the floor, his pale, youthful face washed with the dark streaks of tears, sobbing inconsolably in grief and anguish. Standing above him was a phantom, and she turned to face Geoffrey as he opened the door. His throat tightened as he beheld for the first time in two centuries the radiant beauty of Lorraine la Belle, as fair and as golden as she was the last time he had seen her. Even as he watched, the image flickered and faded, the colors washing away, until the air was empty of all hut the ghost of her fragrance.

Alexander bowed his head, his shoulders heaving with silent sobs, and Geoffrey's heart contracted with pity—sudden, absolute compassion for the grief of the man who had made him. After a moment, he spoke. "I should kill you. I know I should. If I do not, my allies will think me a fool and, perhaps, a weakling." He paused, and thought, seeking the right words to express himself to a man who had never understood compassion or honor, except as tools to manipulate others. "I pity you—"

"Save your pity for yourself," Alexander rasped, looking up, dark eyes fierce with rage and agony. "You worthless little monster—I should have twisted your head off as you lay helpless at my feet!"

"I pity you," Geoffrey went on, doggedly, "because you

have never once achieved anything you truly desired. You cannot love, only possess. You cannot rule, only dominate. I hope that you will one night find peace—I do not think you will, but I hope for it nonetheless. You are my sire, and you helped make me the man that I am this night—but the time I bent my knee to you as my better is over. You are no longer prince here."

Alexander roared in rage. Geoffrey waited for him to stop frothing before he went on. "The throne of Paris is mine, by right of blood and arms, and I will defend my claim before the justicar you have summoned to judge me. You are exiled, Alexander, formerly Princeps Lutetius, to whatever domain will take you, but if you return to lie de France while I still walk the night, I will see you destroyed. You may take with you those vassals and servants who choose to follow you and to share in your exile and the pain of death it encompasses. Farewell, my sire."

Geoffrey closed the door on a renewed flow of vituperation from the former Prince of Paris, squared his shoulders, and went to see what he could do to assist the consolidation of his own power.

Fighting broke out almost as soon as Veronique's men came in contact with Alexander's guards, which didn't surprise anyone. For a time, the struggle was fierce as they endeavored to force their way closer to the private chambers of the house's Cainite residents, a separate wing from its human inhabitants. That wing had already been sealed off by a second group of ghouls and a half-dozen of Lord Valerian's grandchilder who dwelt within riding distance of the city. Valerian, as it turned out, had a prodigious number of descendants outraged by Prince Alexander's behavior toward their esteemed (and exceedingly wealthy and well-connected), ancestor who were willing to leap to his defense and collect the debts of honor that resulted. Backed into a corner with nowhere to flee and no hope of reinforcement, Prince Alexander's men for the most part let themselves be talked into acknowledging the better part of valor. Those that didn't were made into a fairly graphic example.

Veronique was surprised to discover the halls surrounding

Countess Saviarre's haven to be completely devoid of guards or servants. Most of the rooms Veronique opened and peered into were empty—bare to the walls and devoid of even furnishings to give them the illusion of occupation. Mnemach's intelligence on the issue placed Saviarre's private haven in the rear of the building and on the second floor, at the top of a narrow stair, with only one entrance and exit. Veronique took three of the stoutest Nosferatu ghouls with her and stationed them at intervals leading up to that stair, with the last at the bottom, and went up alone.

Countess Saviarre was waiting for her, sitting calmly behind her desk, writing a letter, two lamps bracketed to the walls behind her. She did not deign to look up when Veronique opened the door to her sitting room, nor when that door closed at Veronique's back and she drew the sword hanging at her hip.

"Saviarre." Veronique fought to keep her voice level. "In case you haven't guessed it, this means you're coming with me, whole or in pieces. The decision is yours."

Saviarre laid her pen aside and looked up, her face utterly still and without expression. "Did my sister send you, Lady Veronique?"

"Your sister?" Veronique asked warily, keeping her distance, sword in one hand, the other clenched around the half of her staff. It was not a fighting stance any mortal soldier his salt would deign to use, but the sheer physical might that ran through Veronique's blood made it more than workable.

"Mnemach. My beloved elder sister. The bitch has been trying to engineer my destruction since before the Romans left Gaul." Saviarre rose and, for a moment at least, she seemed to tower above Veronique, exuding strength and perfect composure, clearly unafraid. "She never forgave me for contriving a way to make the horror of her flesh match the blackness of her soul. She is a vicious and conniving monstrosity, and always has been."

Veronique felt something pressing down on her, a force outside of her own mind and will, as though someone were grasping her head firmly between their hands and squeezing with all their might. For an instant, she saw Saviarre as she saw herself, beautiful, wise, without flaw, and yet consistently, unfairly denied, cursed to live forever in the shadow of a sister who despised her, her deepest wishes constantly thwarted by the malice of others. Paris was hers, hers by right, by the right of a Parisii chieftain's daughter, the hungrily sought-after second child, beautiful and sensual but denied the power her older sister sought and attained. Mnemach, the priestess. Mnemach, the speaker-for-the-gods. Mnemach, beloved first-born daughter. It battered at Veronique's mind with such violence that she wavered on her feet and her sword rang off the floor as she dropped it, unable to hold its weight and her balance at once.

Then, just as suddenly as it began, it ended, as though someone had caught those terrible pressing hands and yanked them away. Saviarre and Veronique both staggered back, momentarily too stunned to react. Veronique fell against the door with a resounding thump, her staff now little more than a cane. Saviarre reeled against the wall behind her desk, dark eyes narrowing to hate-filled slits.

"I see," Saviarre hissed, "that she has taken you under her wing, with her little pestilential little magics and her scheming against her betters." She lunged forward, snatched up the bowl of ink sitting on her desk, and hurled it at Veronique.

Veronique leapt to one side, just quickly enough to avoid being splashed as the bowl shattered against the door where her head had been a moment before. For an instant, the ink dripped down the wall as a liquid normally should—then it reared away, curling like vipers' bodies, and struck. Veronique scrambled to stay ahead of it, drawing on her own reserves of strength and speed. The world seemed to slow around her as her perceptions accelerated, drawing everything in shades of stark contrast. A whipping shadow tendril slashed her forearm, effortlessly slicing through layers of light chain and clothing. Ducking and dodging, she scrambled to stay out of the thing's reach. She hit the ground and rolled, barely avoiding another razor-edged stroke with a parry of her staff. The tendril cracked the weapon in half, leaving Veronique with only a broken length of treated wood and a split-second to dodge and roll once more. Coming up within an arm's length of Saviarre, she took the opportunity.

Veronique grabbed the soft fabric of Saviarre's cotte and, heaving the countess bodily over the bulk of the desk, hurled her at the center of the shadow-thing's mass. Saviarre shrieked as the thing caught her, black filaments digging into her pale flesh, one burrowing entirely through the joint of her shoulder and tearing off her right arm. She howled and frothed, but not, to Veronique's surprise, incoherently: The words she screamed had an effect on the shadow-thing. It withered and dwindled, dissolved into a fine black dust, leaving Saviarre battered, horribly wounded, and completely open to attack. Veronique took that opportunity, too.

Saviarre looked shocked as Veronique hit her, knocking her sprawling to the ground, and pounced, slamming what remained of her staff, broken shaft first, through the countess's heart with such force it struck the floor beneath her. After that, Veronique simply kept punching and kicking and pounding her opponent's recumbent body with smashed pieces of furniture until she was entirely certain that the bitch was torpid, stake or not, letting her rage spend itself against a worthwhile recipient. That lasted quite a bit longer than even Veronique thought appropriate, afterwards, shaking hard from the release of so much pent emotion and struggling with the urge to keep going until Saviarre crumbled to dust. She had given her word. She had made promises. And, as a diplomat and a woman of honor, her word was only as good as the actions that bound it. She took a ragged breath and stopped.

Veronique dragged Saviarre's battered body down the stairs by the bitch's remaining arm and gave it to the care of the ghoul waiting there for her. "Please deliver this to Dame Mnemach with my thanks and my compliments."

The ghoul bowed low in response, and Veronique sketched a courtesy in return, stepping out of the stairwell and limping down the hall. She hadn't noticed, during the fight itself, that the shadow-thing had managed to catch her on the leg and side, as well, but now that she didn't have the pleasure of pummeling Saviarre to distract her, she felt every ache and pain. If someone had appeared waving fresh-drawn blood under her nose, she wouldn't even have questioned the source.

From what she could see, the situation seemed to be very much under control, and there were more men about wearing some Tyrian purple token of Geoffrey's than there had been a half-hour before. One of them approached her. "Lady Veronique d'Orleans?"

Veronique felt the urge to ask if there were any other women stalking around the prince's house in armor that he knew of but quashed it. "Yes."

"Please come with me, milady. His Highness, Prince Geoffrey, craves your counsel." He bowed smartly and trotted off, with her at his heels.

Well, that was quick. Veronique was too tired to make an inner observation more sarcastic than that, and followed along obediently, hoping for a place to sit down. Geoffrey had taken over the main receiving hall as his command post and was barking orders, clearly in fine fettle, organizing matters to his liking. To her profound thanksgiving, one of the people he was trying to organize was her own man, who appeared disinclined to follow any orders not originating with her. "Sandrin!"

He turned to face her, looking a little beaten and more than a little weary, with a black eye and likely a broken nose, but the expression of perfect relief that spread across his face when he saw her was a wonderful thing to behold. "Vero—Lady Veronique."

Geoffrey caught sight of her then and gestured her forward. "Lady Veronique. Have you captured Countess Saviarre? She is the only target currently unaccounted for."

Which meant that the team sent to take Sir Olivier into custody had, indeed, succeeded at their task. And it was also time for Veronique to hope her powers of deceit were better than she thought. "We fought, milord. She had a shadow-creature at her disposal, probably given her by Bishop de Navarre." Sandrin hissed as he realized where the wounds she had sustained came from. "She flung it at me and while I was dealing with it, she managed to escape. The shadow-thing is destroyed, and I have some of the men combing the grounds between here and the river. She cannot get far—she was injured, as well."

Geoffrey tried to pin her to the floor with his gaze, but she avoided it by the expedient of slumping in quite genuine weariness. Sandrin wrapped a protective arm around her shoulders; she could practically feel him vibrating with outraged defensiveness. Finally, Geoffrey replied, "You've done well, but you should have waited until we had more men to support you. Sir Nicolas! Organize a group to comb the riverbank, as well. I want that witch's head on a pike before morning."

"By your leave, Lord—Prince Geoffrey," Veronique murmured, quietly. "I find that I'm quite weary tonight for some reason."

"I doubt it not at all." Geoffrey paused. "Have you some place to go? My second has briefed me—I'm aware that your haven was destroyed, and your chattels mostly slain. You will, of course, be compensated for the loss in due time, and your diplomatic status restored in my court. But for tonight...?"

"I have a place to shelter, Milord Prince, but I thank you for your consideration." Veronique looked up, and this time caught his eye. "We can discuss everything else tomorrow."

Epilogue

Josselin de Poitiers and his squire rode into the main market square of Béziers early in the evening for him, but late for everyone else. There were only a few loiterers spending the last of their coin at the wine shop that fronted on the square, and most of those were too bleary-eyed to appreciate the effect he was trying to achieve. That was probably fortunate, as there were very few Languedocien locals who looked kindly on the pretensions of northerners, even mounted and heavily armed northerners. He rode in on his destrier, clad in his full sky-blue and silver panoply, as was Fabien, the banner bearing his personal arms flying. He and his squire dismounted, set the pennon shaft in a gap in the cobblestone square, and waited to be noticed by someone other than a band of drunken mortals.

It didn't take long before he was.

Aimeric de Cabaret sat, lost in a rapture of his own making, his harp against his shoulder and his fingertips wandering across its strings. Had anyone been present to listen, they would have been awed and honored to hear a musician of such skill play, wringing a delicate melody from his instrument without thought or premeditation. He was playing for himself alone, however, taking the chance, after a long and exciting summer, to sit and relax and find his muse again. Tonight, it was working. Tonight, the memories of short summer nights in Toulouse and Carcassonne, of the autumn-clad mountains cradling Cabaret and long sleepy winters in Foix, were enough to move his fingers with inspiration. Rare, that.

It took him a moment to realize that someone was knocking

insistently on his sitting-room door, and a moment longer to disengage from the trance he'd put himself into with the music. As he lifted his hand away from the strings, his fingertips ached and stung, and around the irritation at being interrupted, he realized he ought to be grateful for it—he might have played his fingertips down to bare flesh if he'd gone on any longer, and not minded at all. He laid the harp on its bench next to his chair and rose, putting himself in order quickly, and opened the door, stepping aside quickly to avoid being knocked on himself.

The Mouse herself stood there, and he blinked in surprise. "Good evening, milady—I didn't think I was playing loudly enough to disturb you."

She took in the uncovered harp and the state of his hand in a single, sharp-eyed glance, her face that of a sweet young woman, cheeks and lips flushed apple-red tonight. "You didn't disturb me, Ambassador. We have a visitor—a French knight of the blood. He's asking to see you."

"Me?" Aimeric inclined a questioning brow. "That's amusing—my experiences with French knights of the blood have, in general, been something less than pleasant. Did he give a name?"

"Sir Josselin de Poitiers," the Mouse replied, watching him closely. "And he carries a letter that he will surrender only to you." She paused and scrutinized his reaction carefully. "Ambassador, are you quite all right?"

Prince Eon de l'Etoile was much more understanding than Josselin had thought he would be, and a great deal more humane than his reputation otherwise indicated. The prince, the sheriff, and the spymaster all questioned Josselin rather closely but did not mistreat him in any way—nor did they Fabien, who was dead on his feet but too proud to fall down in a heap. Josselin established his diplomatic credentials as a representative of his sire, Queen Isouda, indicated he had a message to deliver, and was granted the formal hospitality of the city for the requisite three days and three nights. He was escorted to one of the guest rooms Prince Eon kept for high-ranking visitors, a pleasant chamber separated into a sleeping space and a sitting space by the expedient of a wooden screen. Food was brought for Fabien, which Josselin insisted that he eat, and then he packed the boy off to his pallet at the foot of the bed in the next room. Food for Josselin arrived shortly thereafter in the form of a shapely and eager young woman who gave freely of her charms and took a brief nap herself to recover from the loss. Josselin hadn't fed in three nights, determined to make the last stretch to Béziers in as little time as possible. Warm water and towels came next, and he put himself in order, changing into a fresh tunic and washing the worst of the dust from his face and hair. He opened the shutters on the sitting room's arrow slit window to let in a bit of the warm evening breeze and sat to compose himself.

It had been a long time since he had last seen Aimeric de Cabaret. Half of him was afraid of what he would find, now that he was here. He had not, himself, taken part in the crusade against the heretics in the Languedoc, nor in the struggle against Queen Esclarmonde. He could not, in truth, bring himself to believe the charges against her, and he had no desire to take up arms against those who had, until a quirk of politics interfered, been his friends. He hoped that counted in Aimeric's estimation of him.

He almost leapt out of his skin at the knock on his door and it took him a moment to steady himself enough to speak. "Come in."

Aimeric de Cabaret slipped inside, closing the door quietly behind him and leaning his back against it. For a long moment, no words passed between them. Aimeric's pale brown eyes ran over him, his face professionally neutral, and Josselin silently drank in the sight of him as well—whole, safe, here. Finally, Aimeric smiled, a genuine smile, the expression showing itself in his eyes. "Bel companho, when I told Veronique that I wanted to see you again soon, I didn't think you'd ride all the way to Béziers to do my bidding."

It broke the tension completely and Josselin rose, laughing weakly, and stepped into Aimeric's brotherly embrace of greeting, and accepted a kiss on each cheek. "Good evening, my friend—it's good to see you at last."

"Let me look at you." Aimeric stood back, still holding him

by the shoulders, and shook his head. "Road-worn. Come, sit down. Tell me what's brought you all this way in such haste."

Aimeric led him to the padded bench below the window and sat him down, keeping possession of one hand as they did so. Josselin reached into his cotte with the other and drew out the letter he'd carried, safe in its own oilskin packet, and handed it over. "I wish I had better news, companho. And I had best not tell you the means Veronique d'Orleans used to coerce me into bringing this—I have yet to forgive her."

Aimeric blinked, deliberately, opened the packet and broke the seals on the letter. His face was carefully still as he read, quickly at first, then going back to the top to read through it again, more slowly. Then he looked up, his face still empty of expression, and refolded the letter.

"She's likely in great danger," Josselin admitted, somewhat grudgingly. "I heard, on my way through Chartres, that a Blood Hunt had been called on her in Paris, but not a word since then. I only barely escaped by the sword myself."

Aimeric lay the letter aside. "I fear I have some news that has outpaced you, companho—it came from my Lady Mouse's kin in Paris last week."

"What?" Fear clenched around Josselin's heart. "Aimeric, tell me, please—is my Lady Rosamund—" It had been his most terrible fear for the entire trip, weighing more heavily on him than the fear for his own person. "I did not want to leave her. I had no choice. Veronique gave me no choice."

"Your Lady Rosamund survives, the last I heard." Aimeric reached over and pressed Josselin's hand gently, smoothing it down from a clenched fist. "She is exiled from Ile de France in the company of Prince Alexander. Under pain of death, she is never to return so long as Prince Geoffrey le Croisé rules Paris."

"Exiled?" Josselin exploded to his feet, unable to keep still at that. "Exiled?! With Alexander? What the hell for?"

"Alexander was overthrown, evidently by Geoffrey with the aid of certain allies. Geoffrey chose to spare his sire final destruction and sent him into exile with those who were willing to follow him. Evidently Lady Rosamund was one of these." Aimeric paused slightly. "So was Alexander's younger childe,

Sir Olivier, and some small number of others."

"She was innocent! She knew nothing of these plots! How could Geoffrey—hell, how could Isouda. Josselin broke off, too agitated to speak calmly. "Willing to follow him? Willing? It's not right. She wouldn't..."

"I do not know, companho. We haven't received that much concrete information." Aimeric looked up at Josselin, his diplomat's mask firmly in place. "Queen Salianna rules at Geoffrey's side, as Queen of Love in Paris, and his closest advisor."

"Salianna." The venom in his tone made her name a curse. "This is her doing. I can smell it. She's been jealous of Rosamund since my Queen Isouda first sent her from Chartres on behalf of the Courts of Love."

"Yes. Salianna. It appears that she is going to enjoy the ill-gotten fruits of her endeavors despite Veronique's best efforts." Aimeric patted the seat next to him on the bench, and Josselin slumped into it, elbows on his knees, and his head in his hands.

"I never should have left her." Josselin addressed the floor, the anguish clear in every word. Aimeric's arm slid around his shoulder, comfortingly.

"Queen Salianna is playing a dangerous game," Aimeric murmured against his ear, "and I hope to be there when her plots strangle her in the end." A kiss was pressed to Josselin's shoulder. "I am sorry about your sister, companho, and I know that this is a terrible blow to you."

"I've failed her." Josselin whispered, and looked up, his eyes rimmed in red. "I should have stayed and taken my chances with her...."

"Had you stayed, Josselin, I fear you would be ashes now, and I would not forgive you that." Aimeric brushed a tear off his cheek and licked it from his fingers. "Your sister still lives, companho. While that is true, you have not failed her. She is even now traveling away from Paris—Julia Antasia refused them sanctuary, but the Prince of Lebach was of softer heart than she. They are moving north, into the lands of the Black Cross."

Josselin caught Aimeric's hand in his own and raised it to his lips. "I fear that I cannot linger long, then. I should go to

Chartres and speak to my Queen Isouda. There must be something I can do."

"I know." Aimeric smiled, a little sad, a little resigned. "Take your rest tonight, Josselin. Perhaps tomorrow I will have a song with which to see you off."

About the Author

Myranda Kalis's fiction has appeared in *Demon: Lucifer's Shadow*. She is also a contributor to many supplements in the Dark Ages game line, including *Dark Ages: Inquisitor*.

Curious about other Crossroad Press books?
Stop by our site:
http://store.crossroadpress.com
We offer quality writing
in digital, audio, and print formats.

www.ingramcontent.com/pod-product-compliance
Lightning Source LLC
Chambersburg PA
CBHW071129200626
46817CB00018B/2521